An English Impressionist

An English Impressionist

Brent Shore

Matador
9 Priory Business Park,
Wistow Road, Kibworth Beauchamp,
Leicestershire. LE8 0RX
Tel: 0116 279 2299
Email: books@troubador.co.uk
Web: www.troubador.co.uk/matador
Twitter: @matadorbooks

ISBN 978 1788034 661
British Library Cataloguing in Publication Data.
A catalogue record for this book is available from the British Library.

Printed and Bound in the UK by 4Edge Limited
Typeset in 11pt Minion Pro by Troubador Publishing Ltd, Leicester, UK

Matador is an imprint of Troubador Publishing Ltd

To the memory of Brian and Jean,
not to be confused in any way
with Mr and Mrs Penny

Provided a man is not mad, he can be cured of every folly but vanity. There is no cure for this but experience, if indeed there is any cure for it at all.

Jean-Jacques Rousseau, "Emile"

PART ONE

Jean-Yves

1999

From this distance it may look very much like a stick insect clinging to the battlements of a toy castle, a tiny trembling form silhouetted against an inky blue moonlit sky, but it is in fact a man, a middle-aged male. Hard to tell, but, yes, it *is* a man, breathing heavily, pausing then lifting himself out of the shadows on to the ledge of the pitted stone wall, one hundred metres above the glassy river, now edging along on his hands and knees, closer and closer to the very rim of the parapet.

Zoom in closer and you can see the torment in his eyes, the beads of sweat caught in the lines of his brow, the strain on the cotton of his shirt as he stretches to reach the next precarious handhold. He has ripped a small hole in his sleeve. Is that blood leaking from a graze at his elbow? Look harder and you may even see the hands on his watch, strapped to a quivering wrist, pointing to the dots which represent time, now at its most meaningless: it is a quarter to midnight.

It is a warm, windless night, it is early September, and the dark ephemeral shapes of soft, wispy clouds drift here and there, their fraying edges fringed in silver light which glints off the tortuous blade of the Dordogne as it cuts west through the silent, shadowy valley. Now the man is pulling himself up on to his knees as if to peer over the edge, to calculate his angles, and, quite suddenly, to realise his mistake.

Arriving at this point, at this fixed destination, has been the easy part. He has been here once before, of course, several weeks ago with the lighting crew, and he knows a little of the lie of the land. The castle walls, the higher ramparts, the towers and the turrets are all securely closed off, quite inaccessible, at this time of night. Somewhere on the far side are the residential apartments, still used but perhaps unoccupied tonight. Who knows? Their light has not reached the shadows of these lower confines. Save for a feeble streetlight and a dim curtained glow from the upper rooms of a pair of houses close to where he has abandoned his car, his short, deliberate walk has been in a grizzled darkness. He found his way along the narrow cobbled path beyond the castle entrance, down the hill, passing high defensive flanks of earth and castellated stone, reaching in no time the iron gate to the enclosures of the chapel. The air was faintly scented by a trace of jasmine. His eyes now accustomed to the gloom, and aided in fleeting moments by the moonlight, he arrived at a barrier of fixed wooden posts blocking access to the perimeter walls. As expected it was firmly shut and a familiar notice posted at eye level as a warning to trespassers: *CHANTIER INTERDIT AU PUBLIC*. Several weeks ago, when the workers renovating the walls were forced to accommodate on their patch a team of lighting technicians, he had watched as part of this heavy rustic fence was forced open without disturbing the padlock. The strength of an average man was enough to pull one of the loose end-pillars out of the ground and thus create a gap for a slim workman to fit through. And this is exactly what he did a minute or two ago, allowing him to squeeze through and on to the flat grassed expanse that is bound on three sides by the long rim of stone.

Look hard at his face. Is that a smile on his lips? A nervous, shallow smile of resignation? Now the man is rubbing his eyes as if he is waking from a deep sleep. Perhaps he's just wiping away the sweat with his knuckles.

It had been one of his final acts as a respected employee of the bank, that earlier visit to Beynac. The *Caisse d'Epargne du Périgord* was one of several companies in the area that had sponsored the lightshow and firework display as a contribution to the region's Bastille Day celebrations, and he had been invited to watch the creative director and his team at work for an afternoon. The bank: his saviour and his downfall. It had gone so well: a brilliant evening, a spectacular triumph, the flashes of blue, white and red flickering on and off in mesmerizing patterns over the ghostly surfaces of the castle, reflected in the watching faces of the hundreds gathered entranced in the valley. Then the crackles and cascades of the fireworks, fizzing explosions of light, dazzling crimsons and blues, glowing greens, blinding whites and sparks of gold dust had ripped into the night sky. A sky darker still than tonight's.

Once again the moon, almost full, peeps shyly from behind a bank of cloud and floods the valley with a shivery glow. Still kneeling, still shaking, he sees the outline of the wooded hills to the south, massed beyond the curve of the river, then its narrowing throat to the west, the flatter forested horizon to the east. But not a soul stirs in the moonlight, no voice can be heard, only the soft whine of a motorbike rolling invisibly along the strip of road far below. He is leaning forward, unsteadily, as if to see the rider, curious to locate the source of the fading sound. The pit of his stomach feels like it's falling to his feet as a wild fluttering fills his chest. The dizzying aspect of the drop confirms his mistake, as the moon slowly hides its face once more. Instinctively he shuffles back a little on his perch.

His plan, such as it is, is to put an end to his miserable, desperate days by striding off this wall to land, giddily free, some unimaginable moments later, on the iron-hard surface of the river. Had his memory played tricks on him? How had he misjudged the angle of descent? For at no point from the castle nor from this chapel enclosure could a person reach the water with a perpendicular drop. Directly below him, beyond rough outcrops of rock, is the faint outline of a pathway on a strip of land at the base of the cliff, which, only part way down, itself lies high above a level of tiny gardens, chimney tops, the roofs of houses tumbling a further distance to the hidden road, then finally to the riverbank. Even if he ran and threw himself off this wall he would land on the raw, unforgiving earth, broken and wretched, to be found, *the horror*, by some poor villager in the morning out walking his dog.

But these thoughts, and the guilt, the anger, the horror, all come and go in an instant, flitting and fading, jostling for space in a tortured, bewildered mind. Whether or not the cloak of the river is attainable, he knows he is prevaricating, and forces himself to refocus. To refocus on his purpose. He tells himself there is no going back.

Colour has drained from the unlit sky, and with its blackness returns the bitterness and the pain of the open wound in his soul. He is contemptible, a figure of hate, and like a cancer the revulsion will only grow; he knows this, there is no escape from it, and he knows too that he is to blame. Entirely. No-one else. Not his mean-spirited employers, not his vicious mother, not even Stéphane Garrigue. No-one else. No-one else has done what he did, no-one made him stoop so low, no-one forced him to become a criminal, took away the last shreds of his dignity, stole from him any last hope of redemption.

Look now: he is trying to get to his feet. He is clumsy, he wobbles, he steadies himself. From somewhere he has found a small bottle; he is unscrewing the lid, putting the neck to his mouth, tossing his head back to drink in a full, long gulp.

He tells himself this was meant to be. He is not a superstitious man but on his way here, as he drove his car hard along the dark country roads, he played a game with himself, he gave himself an escape. He would wait for an intervention of fate – that's what he told himself – a mystical alignment, a message, a sign from God, something like that. If he were to see the letters of his name, Jean-Yves, he told himself – all the letters, E twice, no particular order – in the licence plates of the other cars he came across before he reached Beynac, then he would abandon his plan. The roads were quiet, it was late, and in almost thirty kilometres he spotted only a J, an E and a V. But had he really been paying attention?

Look again: he is breathing deeply, stretching his arms high above his head, now out beyond his face as if he is about to dive into a swimming pool. The air that surrounds him is warm, sweet, comforting. His heart is pounding so hard in his ribs he thinks he can hear its beat. His mind is a blur but he thinks to give himself one last chance. A chance he knows he doesn't deserve. No-one will miss him. No-one will mourn his death. Not even his wife; no, not even Noisette. They will all still despise him whether he is dead or alive.

One more roll of the dice. There's a heavy cloud covering the moon, but if it reappears, he tells himself, if that frigid disk of white shows itself again before he can count to ten – not too fast, not too slowly, just a steady, unhurried count – then perhaps he will climb down off this rampart after all.

He feels very weary. He is gazing up at the scuffed blackness of the sky. *One.* He is facing out towards the indistinguishable horizon of distant treetops, silently groaning with their burden of dying leaves. *Two.* He lowers his eyes to find the snaking line of the river. *Three.* He takes another deep breath, and suddenly feeling a sense of clarity, of lightness, he steps off the wall into the liberating embrace of gravity, and falls forward into the void like a tired old puppet whose strings have been cut.

PART TWO

Books

1

I don't give much thought to my brother's life any more. After all, it wasn't very long, it ended almost twenty years ago, people prayed for his soul, grieved for him a little and then moved on. I moved on too, quite painlessly in fact. As adults we weren't especially close even though the accepted thinking is that twin siblings always are, or at least ought to be; that they are somehow spiritually bound together, that their ties of kinship are somehow mystically fixed simply because they came into the world from the same womb on the same rainy afternoon.

We were born twenty minutes apart in the autumn of 1950, a pair of twins, boy and girl, and by no means identical. We shared the thick black hair of our mother and the soft grey eyes of our father but as we grew up, the physical differences – Jean-Yves taller and leaner, myself shorter and more rounded – became more pronounced. We rubbed along well enough as children, living in this very same house where I now sit with my pen and paper scribbling these words. Sometimes we played together in our tiny shared bedroom at the top of the creaky staircase until the patience of one or the other grew thin and the squabbles would begin over a broken toy, a ripped page, an accusation of cheating. We ran around the garden when the sun shone, which in my memory was often. We called it a garden but you might think of it rather as a field: a large flat field, close to one hectare I would say, which rises and tapers over a crest at the far end, a field planted to this day with neat lines of walnut trees, more than one hundred, enchanting to us children, a vast open playground to explore or a space which offered quiet hidden corners for a moment of solitude.

The wide kitchen window gave on to this grove of nut trees, at the very front of which, a stone's throw from the house, lay our special circle of earth, ringed with bushes of thyme and sage and rosemary. It measured about ten of our father's long strides across its diameter: an area that could have been covered, more or less, by a children's fairground carousel. Which is exactly how I imagined it in my dreams – a private roundabout with a dozen leaping horses spinning around to the sound of an invisible accordion. My brother begged our father to buy him a trampoline and set it in the centre of the circle:

"Just for winter, *papa*, when nothing is growing. I can be an acrobat, like in the circus!"

But there was not a chance of him ever relenting, for nothing would be allowed to restrict, never mind replace, his sacred *potager*. It was his *cercle magique*, which our father, Jean Puybonieux, worked each springtime, pulling the winter weeds, feeding the soil, meticulously planting out his array of vegetables: onion sets, garlic, seeds for beans and squash and whatever else took his fancy. Jean-Yves loved to help, especially in the weeks of harvest.

"Come here, little man," our father might call out. "See where the bugs have been after our haricot leaves. You'll need to pick those beans today. Go and fetch your mother's basket."

And the boy would skip away and into the house, his heart swelling with the responsibility.

I was allowed to water the plants if our father was feeling too tired.

"Be generous, Amande! Those courgettes are as thirsty as a cyclist at the top of Ventoux."

I had little idea of what he meant but would obediently go and refill the can. He was rarely tired, it seemed. He was a tall, vigorous man. The grove provided only a meagre income and he worked in the town as a part-time labourer for a pair of brothers who ran a decorating business. He was never short of energy, he was always on his feet, and he never missed the chance to smile at his twins. Madeleine, as our mother was called, was the only part of his life that seemed to grind him down. Even as a little girl I had a sense that he would rather be outside in the rain with his spade and his wheelbarrow and his walnut trees than be shut up in the confines of the house listening to his wife. To me her voice from all those years ago still echoes around the walls of this old building:

"You spend all your days painting shelves for other women in the town, yet you'll do nothing for your own wife!"

"I'm at my wits' end, Jean," I can still hear her

complaining. "You expect me to provide a tasty meal for you and the children but you give me enough to buy only scraps of meat one or twice a week."

"Get out of the house with your muddy boots, you blind fool! Can't you see I've swept the floor?"

"You give more attention to those damn onions than you do to your family!"

Our father would sometimes wink at his son and let the insults wash over him. There was little doubt that Jean-Yves was his favourite. Often he would take him up to the top of the field, to the crest where they would sit together and look back over the ranks of trees, through the lines of space between them to the circle of earth and the house. There they would talk for hours, about plants and insects and animals, about the town and the antics of its folk, about the past and the present and the future. Our father would explain about the cultivation of the walnuts, the value of the crop and of the land his son would one day inherit. Sometimes I would follow them at a discreet distance with a picture book in my hand, eager to hear what they were discussing, what they were laughing about.

"Stop spying on us, Amande!" my brother would call.

"I'm not. I'm reading my book in the shade."

"You're a liar. Go away! Go and make us some bread and butter!"

My father assumed I would prefer to spend time with my mother, that I would naturally seek a feminine bond with her, and she with me. But there was no warmth in the woman; she was a brooding spirit, she tolerated rather than celebrated us children, a rebuke far more natural on her tongue than a word of kindness. She would often sit alone in the dark, deep in her thoughts, in a kind of trance, I thought, and she hated to be disturbed. Like a flower deprived of light I grew stilted; I was irritable, I became introverted, I squabbled at school.

Madeleine wore rough, unfussy clothes from day to day, saving her best – an embroidered blouse or a soft woollen coat in the winter with an inch of fake fur on the collar – for the church of St Lucien on a Sunday morning. Jean-Yves and I were obliged to accompany her, rain or shine, but our father only ever came with us on Christmas Eve.

"It's the least I can do once a year to say thank you to the baby Jesus," he said once with his familiar grin.

Our mother was known in the town, but only as a communicant or a customer, as an acquaintance or a neighbour; she had no friends to visit, and I don't ever remember anyone calling at our house to keep her company beyond her doctor or her priest.

My brother and I were twelve years old when our father left Frettignac and disappeared from our lives forever. Certainly as the days became weeks, then months without his warm voice, without his fidgety, energetic presence, I never expected to see him again. I gave up hope. From this distance I can understand him, I can even forgive him, but on the first day of that brutal emptiness I remember hating him for his betrayal with every fibre in my body. It was an execrable time and the pain still aches: we had started at a new school and were at our most vulnerable. Madeleine was distraught and blamed Jean-Yves for some imagined conspiracy: the boy was desolate, bereft of his father and the target for his mother's vitriol, but he was strong, stronger than me, and with the help of his friends and his teachers he steered a fairly steady path through his adolescence, troubled only by Madeleine's sniping and insults. As for me, I built up a shell around me, withdrew into the shadows, numbed my feelings and waited for something better to happen in my life.

There is a history behind our father's departure and now might be the time to relate it. I knew nothing of this as a schoolgirl, of course; it was revealed to me much later by an old woman in the town, a market trader named Pierrette, who took me under her wing. Like much of late 20th century France, events and the reactions to them were coloured by the war – which we all understand to mean the German occupation of our country. Some of her account is true, I know. Madeleine herself spoke to me about her time alone when our father was away. Some of it, however, I refused to believe: gossip turned into fact, as far as I was concerned, rumour retold as gospel.

For two years after 1940 Frettignac, like most of our region, was part of the territory under the theoretical control of the Vichy government. At that time my parents had been married for barely a year. The German involvement in so-called unoccupied France was generally at an arm's length but men were recruited from here to work at the strategically important port of Bordeaux, one hundred and fifty kilometres to the west in the occupied zone. When Vichy fell and the Nazis took full control, and as the Battle of the Atlantic intensified, more and more dockworkers were required; my father and half the men in the town were given no choice but to join up. He was there, I believe, from early 1943 until sometime after the city's liberation in August of the following year. Meanwhile Madeleine, a pretty young woman, vulnerable and alone, was a target for many a German soldier's roving eye. She was pursued, in spite of her protestations, by one particular officer, a handsome man of some authority, no doubt, who tried to convince her that he could make her life a little more comfortable. Eventually she gave in to his approaches and, secretly, they became lovers. She wasn't the first desperate French girl to fall for a German soldier and I offer no judgement on her. I cannot imagine how I would have behaved in those wretched times had I been in her shoes.

Sometime towards the end of 1943 – and here is where I believe that Pierrette had strayed into fantasy – to the horror of both of them she became pregnant, only realising her condition four or five months into her term. Her Kommandant had to use both his influence and his cunning to arrange, after some delay, to have her moved away from the town, and transported to an inconspicuous private clinic, in Grenoble, I was told, where the baby was prematurely induced and allowed to die. Nobody seems to know what happened to the German officer, but Madeleine never saw him again. She was given a railway ticket with her little bundle of possessions and made the long journey back to Périgord alone.

Jean returned a year later and their life together resumed. Happily or not, I am uncertain, but in 1950 Jean-Yves and I were born and a new family was created. The old market woman intimated to me that our father headed straight back to Bordeaux when he left us twelve years later; in spite of the conditions and the dangers, he had grown to enjoy working on the docks. He had been an adventurous, robust young man, he had made new friends, he had drunk the local wine, and he had slept, she guessed, with many pretty Bordelaises.

When I was thirteen I began to have visions. A little later the voices came: children's voices, clear and shrill, singing playground songs in a language I knew to be nonsense. The visions appeared mostly at twilight: I saw the walnut trees walking, marching in ranks like an army on parade, sometimes up away from the house, other times towards it, approaching in silence, a stealth attack. I would scream and shake with fear, and only a hard slap from my mother would bring me back to my senses. In my dreams I saw children hiding from the Nazis in caves: groups of them, in tattered clothing, running and crawling deeper into the darkness of the hillsides. The war had been over for almost twenty years. Of course there are caves, many of them, in our region, not so far from Frettignac, in fact, but at that age I had never seen them for myself. Only in the dreams.

Madeleine insisted that I speak to a doctor; she demanded that he prescribe some medicine to cure me. Months later he in turn recommended a psychiatrist in

Bergerac who visited me once, came to some kind of financial arrangement with my mother, and who then received me in his consultation room once a fortnight for about six months until he concluded that I was a troubling case, psychologically disturbed but generally harmless, and recommended confinement in a convent school. And so, a few weeks short of my fifteenth birthday I was admitted to the *Couvent des Soeurs de Supplication de la Sainte Thérèse* in Périgueux where I remained until I was released on a day of heavy snowfall over thirteen years later.

So, no, I don't give much thought to my brother's life any more. When I returned to Frettignac my mother had already turned into an old woman, and my brother was a man I hardly recognised and whose life I knew so little about. Jean-Yves Puybonieux had done well enough at school to secure an administrative job at the town's savings bank, with both training and prospects. He had grown in confidence despite the relentless tirades of Madeleine's sarcasm. She still undermined him, to his face and behind his back, comparing him with an old schoolfriend who had a better job and a beautiful wife, or to another who had moved to a large house in Le Bugue, or to another who was working for a firm in Paris.

"At your age your cousin Daniel was running a newspaper office in Poitiers," I can hear her saying. Jean-Yves would shrug his shoulders.

"You should be doing more with your life than stamping cheques in a poky little office in that bank."

"But I won't be doing that forever, *maman*."

"Oh, really?"

"I could be the manager's assistant this time next year. Old Labrousse is talking about retirement."

"We'll see," she would sneer.

When Labrousse offered his notice and my brother was duly given his promotion, I encouraged him to look for an apartment of his own down in the centre of town, which, to his credit and to our mother's dismay, he did.

I give even less thought to my brother's death. I have no reason to make it appear any more or less noble than it was. It was a suicide, of course, a mortal sin if you believe what the church teaches. My mother never forgave him, you can imagine. She had even more contempt for him in death than ever, managing to put aside her own part in his final act. I kept a few cuttings from the newspaper, headlines and then diminishing additions to the story, tittle-tattle. I rarely look at them at all but I have them here in front of me now to help me recall some of the details. When you have a fuller picture you may agree with me that Jean-Yves deserves a little of our sympathy.

By the middle years of the 1990s things had much changed. I had my own small apartment by the river in Les Saules – then a new complex for "modern Frettignac living" – on the other side of the town. My brother was now the manager of the *Caisse d'Epargne* and had recently married a sweet-natured girl, almost twenty years younger, called Yvette. She too was the child of a single mother, in her case a widow, and both were hairdressers, originally from Périgueux. Jean-Yves met her at a summer fair, was captivated by her long golden hair, her open smile, her bright hazel eyes, and was determined at once to marry her. For what seemed like the first time in his life, Madeleine gave him her approval, and as their wedding day approached she invited him to start his married life in the family home, at least for a while.

"Your apartment is too small, Jeannot," she said. "A girl like Yvette needs space. She likes it here, *non*?"

"She does, *maman*."

"Well then. I'll move into the little room. You can have my room, the two of you. We can be a family again. She can breathe the fresh air of our hills. You can work on the walnut trees. They've been neglected since your father left. Amande is no use; her head always in a book, a newspaper."

"I think it's perhaps a good idea, provided…"

"What?"

"Provided you give us space for ourselves. Properly, *maman*. You know, privacy, independence. Please don't interfere."

"Of course not, my boy."

"You promise?"

"I promise. I'll just be here to keep an eye on you. And help where I can."

"Perhaps I could revive the circle. It looks so sad as it is, covered in weeds and moss."

"That would be nice. I do miss your father's plantings."

"Then I'll start with some strawberries, that's what I'll do. Yvette's favourites."

With her amiable character and her pretty face, Yvette Puybonieux was quickly accepted in Frettignac, and before very long the banker's wife with the hazel eyes who lived in a walnut grove was given the nickname of Noisette. She was sociable, she loved to play her guitar in the park, to chat, to join in. She offered her services as a hairdresser, but finding no openings in the salons in the town, decided to advertise as a travelling stylist. She would take her box of tackle to the houses of clients and provide a home service instead.

It was inevitable that she drew the attention of the young men of the town, some even asking her to cut their hair even though she was only really available for ladies. Jean-Yves, overloaded at work and too trusting, failed to spot what was happening. Madeleine, however, did not.

"You'd better treat your wife this weekend," she would tell him, "or somebody else might."

"What do you mean, *maman*?"

"She's missing your attention."

"She hasn't said."

"She won't have. Women don't say these things to their husbands, Jeannot. Not directly. They expect you to notice for yourself."

Silence would descend on the pair for a moment.

"She has telephone calls."

"Telephone calls?"

"Yes. From men. I hear her gossiping and giggling on the telephone. When you're at the bank. When you are stamping your cheques and tapping on your stupid computer thing."

"Then I'll talk to her."

"You should. You must."

"I will."

"And take her out on Sunday. Somewhere nice."

"Yes, I will."

"And you should lose some weight too. All that sitting around in your office all day and your heavy lunches. You're getting a belly, you know. I expect she's told you."

"No."

"Well, now *I* have."

The wide hectares of land which border our walnut grove on its western side, sloping up and out of the valley, have been in the Garrigue family for as long as anyone can remember: gravelly, well-drained ground that in my lifetime has always been given to vines. There was a time when I was a small girl that I recall old man Garrigue asking our father to sell part of our field, the top corner that catches the afternoon sun, so that he might plant a new strain of vines on it. I remember it only for our father's reaction. He listened patiently to the outline of the neighbour's plans, then rejected the "fair" price as an insult.

"Then name your price, Jean, you old mule," persisted the other man.

"You're wasting your breath, Garrigue," stated our father before turning to walk away. "I wouldn't sell my grandfather's land, not a square metre of it, for a million francs!"

Just as my brother's grip on Noisette's attention was loosening, a similar request over land acquisition came to him from Stéphane Garrigue, now the owner of the vineyard since his old father's death. Stéphane was a bully of a man, huge and handsome, in his early thirties at that time. He was well educated, had studied business at a school in Paris and was determined to make the most of his rural inheritance.

"It's not for vines, Puybonieux," he told my brother one day. "I'm going to build a camping site up there on the top field. You know, the patch of scrub on the ridge. Added to your little triangle it could be ideal. The little spring still runs, doesn't it?"

"I'm sure you know very well that it does," said Jean-Yves.

"Plenty of fresh water, then. It's perfect. I'll fix up electricity, reshape the land a bit, maybe terrace it, set up a few buildings: office, sanitary block, maybe add a pool later. You can imagine it, up there in the sunshine, the tourists will love it. Those Dutch, those English. Such a quiet spot, lovely views over the valley. There's room for up to thirty pitches, I'd say, maybe forty. What do you think?"

Like our father but more politely, my brother refused to even consider the proposition, and, of a neighbour with whom relations until then had been distant but never cold, he made an immediate enemy.

Garrigue wasn't blind to the attractions of my brother's beautiful wife. He began visiting the house during the daytime hours when he knew, the often sleeping Madeleine aside, she would be alone. He brought her gifts: one day a box of fresh cherries, the next a bottle of his *réserve du propriétaire*, or a small piece of jewellery, expensive yet discreet, something she could keep hidden from her husband. He persuaded her to trim his hair, once even to shave him. If he couldn't have Jean-Yves' land, Garrigue would steal his wife instead.

"You're losing her, you fool," Madeleine would shout at her son. "Are you blind or stupid? You must woo her all over again. Take her away. Have a holiday together. Buy her some new clothes. Make her see how much you love her."

"I cannot afford to be extravagant, *maman*."

The old woman would sigh. Exasperated, she would take a different tack:

"Then there's another way."

"Another way?"

"You must make me a grandmother. Amande never will. It's up to you – don't you see, Jeannot? – to keep the family name alive."

A rueful smile from her son.

"We have tried."

"You have?"

"But so far without luck."

"Then you must try again, my boy, and keep trying."

And so this was how my brother's troubles began. He did as he was told, buying expensive new fashions for Noisette, flattering her with diamonds, taking her away on holidays to Paris, to Italy and twice to luxury beach resorts in the Caribbean. Of course none of this could

25

he afford. He lied about the holiday destinations – and made her promise to do the same, he secretly arranged irregular loans at the *Caisse d'Epargne* and as the months and years passed, and as his debts mounted up, bad credit upon bad credit, he began to set up false accounts which allowed him effectively to steal from his own bank. Could he have sold off a portion of our field? I don't believe the thought ever occurred to him, not that the land strictly even belonged to him.

Noisette meanwhile was enjoying a lifestyle she could only have dreamed of, no questions asked. Cosseted by both a kind, simple-minded husband and a passionate secret lover, she felt that all the stars had aligned in her favour for once, she was still young and for now motherhood could wait.

Madeleine was the catalyst for the eruption of the truth. Garrigue had become careless and one morning she caught the pair in the act of love, or *fornication*, as she called it, and having berated her daughter-in-law for her deceit, she reported the *crime* to Jean-Yves on his return later that day. I can only imagine the sorry scene: my brother's anger would quickly subside, he would take part of the blame, he would see his wife's point of view, and when she threatened to leave him for Stéphane he would beg her to stay. Our mother's harsh words for both of them would only fan the flames. And as darkness fell Noisette left the house, a small suitcase in her hand and tears in her eyes. She headed up the hill to the Garrigue estate, and she never returned.

Within a week the embezzlement scandal broke. Jean-

Yves had lost his wife, he was losing his grip on his affairs, and he had started to make mistakes. Investigations by agents of the bank, according to the newspaper reports, revealed the scale of the theft: over 250,000 francs had disappeared, all of it indirectly from the funds of what people still regarded as *la caisse locale*. In the great scheme of things it was not a huge sum, but the scorn of the local people – investors, borrowers, savers in what was still seen as *their* bank, as *the town's* bank – had more resonance than any I felt during more recent financial scandals which involved the loss of billions. Many people in Frettignac felt betrayed by a man they had believed in, years of trust and service swept away in an instant. It was the end for my brother, the pariah. And such a harsh, sudden end: he was dismissed, he was arrested, he was accused, then charged; he pleaded guilty and was due to be sentenced. He saved everybody's time, I suppose, by taking his own life, shattered on the cliffs below Beynac castle.

For all the drama of my brother's death, however, he is not the protagonist of this story. It does not revolve around him; he is merely a character who finds himself, literally, wandering like a silent ghost at the story's edge. And, for certain, it is not a story about me. I just happened to be a witness to parts of it. Besides, I am too modest, too self-effacing to believe that anyone would want to read about my unremarkable, uneventful life. If you know somebody who might push forward from the crowd for a moment in the spotlight, then you'll recognise me as the very opposite of that person. I'm the one stepping out of the way, deeper into the shadows, to let them elbow past.

And neither is this a story about moral cowardice. There is an echo of Jean-Yves' deceitfulness, I suppose, of his sense of injustice, even of his vanity. But far greater than his is the vanity of the real figure at the heart of this tale, the burnished vanity of a certain type of Englishman who for a while made his home in our town: an Englishman named Trevor John Penny. You will see how the story I tell has at its geographical centre our pretty cream-stone town, Frettignac-du-Périgord, sitting in its hidden, crinkled, wooded valley halfway between the city of Périgueux and the Dordogne river. We have our own river too, you should know: slow and meandering, reflecting on its southward course the lush greenery of its banks, the Vézère flows beneath the bleached stone bridge, *le Pont Napoléon*, which over its wide double arches connects Frettignac *nord* and *sud*. You will understand how the small savings bank, our library, the town hall just across our dusty square and many other points of local interest have linked the lives of Jean-Yves and Penny. To tell the tale in its fullest sense, however, I need to take you away briefly to the north-eastern corner of the United States of America, to visit a small university town in Canada and, less surprisingly, to lay out a deeply shaded backcloth which is England.

I have to admit at the outset that I knew Trevor John Penny only superficially. I observed him from a discreet distance, and on occasion I watched him from closer quarters; I engaged with him infrequently, exchanged pleasantries, talked a little business, patted back his flattery, quietly absorbed his jokes. I knew his girlfriend a great deal better, if girlfriend is the right term. A girl she certainly wasn't; she was already a woman turned thirty when she first came to France. She was his lover, I suppose, that goes without saying, his confidante, his co-pilot and his conscience. Confidante, most clearly, and she confided in me too. I think she found in me a lost spirit – she could sense that – with a gift for listening and a sympathetic soul. Where are you now, Columbine? I loved you more and more, and then you were gone.

It is a story in which I have gladly sacrificed my position of authority and have stepped off my first-person pedestal, dissolving from an *I* to a *she*. Forgive me, it seems more comfortable to be enveloped in the bosom of the narrative in that way. I apologise for any errors I might have made, mistranslations from English into French and then back again, insecurity with idioms in spite of a growing confidence in a feel I had for his turn of phrase, for his train of thought. And hers too. Much of the detail is direct from Columbine, recalled from our hours of hushed conversation, listening to her calm voice, laughing at her observations of the ironies in her life, hugging her close for consolation, wiping away the tears in our moments of sorrow. Parts are imagined, invented even: a snatch of dialogue here, a detail noticed there, but all are as true to the overarching spirit of the whole as my limitations as a storyteller will allow. Be certain that I know this story as well as that of my own long life, for it has carried me to heights of joy and to depths of sadness, the memories of which will stay with me until the day I leave this earth.

2

It was such a crisp, bright morning, the low November sun radiating the purest light, if little heat, that he had decided to leave his car in the *Place de la Résistance* and stride out for the address on foot. Angélique, the pretty estate agent he had taken a shine to, was tied up with some other business, but, *n'importe*, he had told her, much as he would have wished to spend another hour in her scented company. He was keen to see the place and, if she could arrange for the owners to be in to meet him and show him round, he could manage perfectly well on his own.

She had said he would find it about a kilometre's drive away, just five minutes from her office, across the bridge, up the hill along the *départementale* and out on to the edge of town past the first farmhouse on the right. She had underestimated the distance, he decided, as people who spend their lives in cars often do, having no sense of the inclines that an engine will manage effortlessly. He had been walking for over a quarter of an hour and the winding road was now bordered by trees on both sides. Had he missed the farm? He unfolded the printed page of notes she had given him and looked again at the photograph of the squat stone house with its discoloured red-tiled roof, its little windows and the faded blue paintwork. There was a telephone number. He adjusted his sunglasses, which had slipped down along the line of his nose. He lowered his hand and touched his trouser pocket to feel the outline of his mobile. He changed his mind and walked on. It wouldn't be much further, it was a glorious day, he was fit and healthy and, to be honest, he was enjoying the exercise.

And sure enough, around the next bend, there it was. The woodland opened up and a wide stony driveway of several metres presented the house, its blue door a darker shade than was suggested by the photograph. As the hillside grew steeper beyond it, his eye was drawn to the vast flank of wintering vines in their ordered rows, dark and skeletal, line after line of them rising and then disappearing at the horizon. By the side of the house, in the shade of a pair of low fir trees, someone had parked a car: a silver Clio, dusty and scratched at the bumper but fairly new. He strolled past it and approached the building. The front was as plain as could be: the shutters were bleached of colour, no patch of garden softened the advance of the stark driveway, no shrubs decorated the walls, no baskets of winter colour hung from the little porch. Nevertheless he had a warm feeling about the place; he had been determined to like it, for some reason, the moment Angélique had shown him the images on the website. He knocked three times on the door, commanding and authoritative, and, as he waited, he looked up and noticed above the frame a weathered wooden plaque whose varnish had long ago lost its sheen:

the name of the house, painted on the darkened strip in a stylised hand, read *Puis Bonheur*. He smiled, heartened by the words, as if they confirmed that living here would bring him good fortune. *Then Happiness.*

He heard footsteps scratching on a stone surface behind the door, the click of a lock and then standing there before him was the figure of a lady of late middle age, short and plump, in a shapeless faded orange jumper and loose denim jeans. Her fluffy grey hair covered her head like a little crown of curls. Her round face had a pale, flat colouring but lively eyes sparkled behind her frameless glasses, and fixing him with an inquisitive gaze she said in a gentle, vaguely musical voice:

"Bonjour, monsieur."

"Bonjour, madame," he replied, removing his sunglasses.

She looked blank, expecting more.

"Je suis John Penny," he went on, *"Pour voir la maison? Angélique vous a parlé, n'est-ce pas?"*

"Angélique? De l'agence? Oh, pardon. Je m'excuse, monsieur. Entrez, entrez. Vous êtes en avance, non? Elle m'a prévenue midi."

"Je reviens plus tard?"

"Mais non. Non, ce n'est pas grave. Mais vous êtes anglais, monsieur? Vous parlez parfaitement français."

And offering him a soft hand to shake, she added:

"Je m'appelle Amande."

Watching from the downstairs window, she had seen him arrive. She had already noted his confident gait, his healthy complexion, his neatly parted fair hair and his trimmed, stubbly beard which showed a touch of grey by his chin. He looked very foreign, she thought, and not just by his face. The cut of his jacket, the swish of his stripy varsity scarf and, now staring directly into hers, the pure blueness of his eyes suggested, moreover declared him to be an Englishman.

Penny was confident in his spoken French, and had been since shining in the Sixth Form, but it was always gratifying to be complimented by a native speaker. And so, buoyed by her words, this is how it was, an apology for arriving earlier than expected, then a conversation of fluency and some subtlety ambled along as the woman led him inside and took him around the unlit rooms of the house one by one. A couple of the windows were wide open, he noticed, in spite of the season, to dilute the fleeting smell, he assumed, of turpentine and bleach. At least it was a clean smell.

"The house *is* empty, isn't it?" he asked. "I mean, I could move in straight away?"

"Yes, of course, *monsieur*," she said, leading him back on to the narrow landing. "That is what I told the agency."

"It's just that it still looks lived in, if you know what I mean."

"It is true that I myself have spent some time here recently. I have my own place in Les Saules but I have had some workmen in and I like to keep an eye on how they are."

"The rooms are small but nicely done."

"The place needed a lot of work after my mother moved on."

"You inherited the house, *madame*?"

"No, no. Not yet at least!" she sang. "*Maman* is still alive. She's frail, she's losing her mind, poor woman, but no, she's living in an EHPAD in Le Bugue."

"A what?"

"An EHPAD. It's a state-run home. You would call it a nursing home."

"I see."

"Quite a good one."

"And is the work here finished?"

"More or less, yes. As you saw, the main bedroom is freshly painted. The other rooms upstairs need work but I would be able to get a man in at your convenience. This door is the small bedroom. That's where my brother and I slept as children. And this one," she said, pushing open the door to a room no larger than an oversized cupboard, a dark space that was filled with boxes and bits of furniture and rolls of carpet, "this was my room when we were too old to share. Can you imagine? No window and room for a little bed and nothing else!"

But Penny was not inclined to imagine. He had come to inspect the house, not to listen to a dull old woman chattering on about her past.

"Shall we see the kitchen?" he asked.

"Of course. It's a new kitchen," she said, following him down the creaky staircase. "New plumbing at last. The sink we had was here since Napoleon's time, I am certain!"

The view from the kitchen window offered Penny his first clear sight of the walnut grove.

"It's our land," said Amande. "All of it. You are free to wander around."

"All the way to the top of the field?"

"Yes, of course. These are our trees."

"Peach trees?"

"No, they're walnuts. It's hard to tell when they're bare, I confess."

"It's wonderful," he said, then seeing that the rickety back door was already ajar, added: "Shall we go outside?"

Penny was captivated by the sight before him: the dry, cropped field was the size of a football pitch, narrower but longer, rising gently to a ridge in the middle distance. Several rows of bare, spindly trees, neatly spaced up to ten metres apart, marched up to the crest like a stiff platoon of soldiers heading over the lip of the trenches at the Somme, their spiky upper branches disappearing over the near horizon. He wandered into the shadows of the nearest group and let the columns guide his eye line. There must be at least a hundred of them altogether, he guessed, one hundred and fifty, maybe even more, some looking withered, as old as the house itself perhaps, but most looked healthy. Beneath them on the tramped earth and the patches of short, tufty grass lay rotting leaves that had been missed a few weeks earlier when the grove had been cleared for the winter.

"We pay men from the *coopérative* to collect the nuts these days," she said, as if reading his mind, anticipating his questions. Penny noticed she had removed her glasses;

without them, he thought, she had the look of a tawny owl.

"They harvest, they rake over the leaves," she was explaining. "Of course they pay me back for what they collect. It makes a little money still, our grove."

"They press them for oil, don't they?"

"Generally, yes. It has a fine, delicate taste, as you know, perhaps. Or they are crushed for cakes and pastes. But with the better crops, they can sell the nuts themselves, the whole fruit. Our nuts are often the best ones. They are a small quantity but they are respected."

"And all those vines?" he said, waving an arm in the direction of the neighbouring hillside.

"No, they're not ours," she answered. "They belong to somebody else, to our neighbour. Just the walnut trees."

"And what's this?" he asked, turning back towards the house and indicating a circular patch of unprepossessing earth, fringed here and there by desiccated, spindly lavender. "This circle of garden?"

"That's my old father's circle. He grew his vegetables there when we were children. As you can see, it's been neglected. My brother used to live here some years ago with his wife. He tried to plant it out just like *papa* but nothing would grow for him. He tried everything. Different varieties, different feeds, but it was as if the land had lost its magic."

A cold breeze began to blow across the field, the sun had dipped behind the roof of the building and they were standing in its shadow. Penny tied his scarf into a loose knot just below his throat and rubbed his hands together.

"Shall we go back inside, *monsieur*?" the woman suggested. "It is chilly, no? Such a beautiful day but you can forget we're in November already!"

Curiosity beckoned him around the corner of the house, however, where he saw a most unusual garage, a long structure attached to the main building whose walls of less than a metre in height were fitted at intervals with thick wooden poles, which supported a kind of roof of wire mesh overrun with a dense canopy of vines.

Amande had followed him.

"You can keep a car there," she said. "Out of the sun. Two, in fact. You can see how long it is."

"I've never seen a garage like it!"

"No, I can imagine. You can see it is what we made from a half-built frame. My brother started it for an extension to the house. Over twenty years ago. His wife wanted a bigger kitchen. It's normal. An extra bedroom too, and the rest."

"He ran out of money, did he?"

"No," she replied curtly. "He ran out of time."

Had he been impertinent? Had he offended the woman? It didn't really matter. He was about to press her but she had already disappeared.

"Come inside and I will prepare a pot of coffee," he heard her call.

"I imagine this place will suit me perfectly, you know. At least for a short while."

Penny was standing in the main downstairs room, a

modest sitting room with a low ceiling, a parlour it might have once been called, furnished with two large armchairs, an empty woodstove in the hearth, an old sideboard, a bare bookcase and a folded wooden table, chipped at the edges. In front of the window was an ironing board stacked with folded plain blue fabric. Amande followed him into the room and switched on a central light which struggled to brighten the gloom.

"The initial lease is for six months, as you know," she said, readjusting her glasses.

"Yes, I know."

"I'm sorry about the ironing," she laughed. "You caught me starting on the curtains. They'll be hanging when you come again. *If* you come, that is. Upstairs in the bedrooms you have to close the shutters for darkness."

Penny had nothing more to say to her. He had declined her offer of coffee and seemed in a hurry to leave, or else he had simply seen enough and was running out of patience. Nevertheless, a small framed photograph, screwed to the wall by the fireplace, caught his eye and he stepped past one of the armchairs for a closer look. It was a wedding photo whose colour had faded to browns and dull oranges: a smiling middle-aged groom, dark hair ruffled in a gust of wind, wearing a suit that looked one size too small, was posing hand in hand with his bride. She was rather beautiful, Penny decided, and rather too young for the husband. She wore a white dress with a fussily embroidered bodice, her blonde hair was tied up in an arrangement of lace and flowers, and her eyes were not quite looking into the camera.

"That's my brother on his wedding day," said Amande.

"I see. He looks like he's just won the lottery."

The woman sighed softly before resuming:

"Well, it *was* a lucky day for him, I suppose."

"But…"

"But his luck did run out. You are perceptive, *monsieur*."

"So, they are no longer married?"

"No. No, they are not."

"I don't mean to pry."

"No, no need to apologise. They were very happy together for a time."

As he moved back into the centre of the room she added:

"One thing I would ask you to respect, *monsieur*. You know, if you do rent the house. You must leave the photographs where they are. They are fixed to the walls, as you can see."

"Yes, of course."

"For my mother's sake."

"You said photographs. There are more? I didn't notice…"

"Just one other. It's at the top of the stairs. Just a small one of my parents together. A small black and white. It's a favourite of mine."

"None of you?"

"Oh, no. I don't take a good photo myself. Never did."

"Oh well."

She noticed that he didn't offer even a pretence of polite dismay.

"And what about you, Monsieur Penny?" she asked

suddenly. "What brings an Englishman to Frettignac, and moreover, to live here, not just to visit like the tourists?"

"I'm at the university," he replied, resolving to keep his story as abbreviated as possible. He had been here long enough, listening to her rambling on about her family. He liked the house, he had already decided it would suit him, but it was time to be bidding the old woman goodbye.

"Which university?"

"I beg your pardon?"

"Which university, *monsieur*? Are you a student or a teacher?"

"I'm at the AULA. In Périgueux. I give lectures there. But I must say, the accommodation there doesn't agree with me. I don't have to be there every day by any means and here is not too far to commute."

"Forty-five minutes."

"Well, exactly."

"A little winding but a pretty route through the countryside."

"And then there's the Steeples connection." He couldn't resist displaying his knowledge.

"Of course. The great English writer. So you are a literary academic, Monsieur Penny?"

He was surprised that the name had registered at all with the woman.

"Yes. Yes, I am. English literature. And Steeples was a great attraction for me here."

"Well, we are proud of his links with our town. A few of us, anyway. I must say that most people here have no idea who he was."

"That's a pity."

"It is. I think so, too. There is a small display in the library."

"Yes, I have seen it. You are well informed, *madame*."

She laughed, following him out into the dark vestibule.

"I worked at the library for many years, *monsieur*. Until they retired me. I still volunteer from time to time."

"Then I may very well see you there some day."

"I dare say."

"But for the moment, I think it's time I left you in peace."

"You have seen everything you need to? Have you any more questions?"

"I don't think so. Angélique can talk to me about the details. Thank you. I do like the house, *madame*. I am sure I will be happy here."

They were already standing on the threshold.

"I was thinking that the moment I arrived," he went on. "The moment I saw the house name. Such an uplifting choice."

Amande was about to offer her hand to be shaken once more.

"Uplifting?" she wondered.

"*Puis Bonheur*," he said, stepping outside and pointing above his head to the plaque.

"Where? No, no," she said, smiling at his mistake. "You are misreading the word, *monsieur*. I can see it is hard to decipher these days. It says Puybonieux, our family name."

"Does it? So it does, I suppose. So that's a letter y, is it? And an x. I can see it now. How stupid of me."

"Not at all! I agree it could be misread. You *were* wearing dark glasses, I believe. And *Puis Bonheur*, well, it is an unusual name for a house, but a pretty one!"

Penny smiled through his embarrassment, shook her hand in farewell with exaggerated functionality, then tightened his scarf and turned to walk away towards the road.

She watched him reach the corner and disappear, glanced up again for a moment at the ancient nameplate, and then stooped back into the recesses of the house to resume her ironing.

3

In the middle years of the 1960s, in the same way as in much of the so-called developed world, the fabric of English life was changing from black and white to a new palette of colour. While London was leading and indeed embracing this transformation, it took a little longer, however, for the stubborn, industrialized, smoke-and-cinders greyness to clear in certain parts of the north of England. It was into this world of slowly opening doors and hints of brighter horizons, in a Pennine town sitting in the wider orbit of Manchester, itself a city just starting to rub the provincial, Victorian grime out of its eyes, that David and Michelle and Trevor John Penny were born. Their parents, children during the war years, were products of the grey days of rationing and limitations, of low expectations and narrow minds, a generation for whom the shadows of the recent past would never quite disappear. Working, earning just enough to pay the rent on a terraced council house in earshot of the factory hooter and afford a little bit of inexpensive fun at the weekend – sport, pub, cinema, eventually a television set – this was their world, this is what their three children discovered to be the backdrop to their lives when they were old enough to recognise it. David and Michelle were unexpectedly twins, a most difficult labour and an expensive consequence. Trevor, born two years later, was unexpected in quite another way, being unplanned, a clumsy bedtime accident.

He was an inquisitive child, a reader, a listener, an observer, and to some extent an outsider. He had inherited a sense of humour from somewhere – nobody seemed to know where – and he was always on the lookout for something or someone, fondly or wickedly, to laugh at. His siblings were an entity to themselves, rarely apart, quietly absorbed in each other, in their shared, bonded world. If for some reason his sister were left on her own, he would sometimes find her hovering around him, curious, as if she were spying on a foreign intruder.

His father, a thoughtful, introverted man, flitted in and out of his life according to the schedule of his long shifts at the factory. His mother, meanwhile, lacking in energy at the best of times, seemed so worn out caring for the twins that Trevor was left to look after himself. He wondered if his parents really loved each other; he was too young to understand what it was to be an adult, married with responsibilities, drained and careworn, but he had the impression from somewhere that his mother and father were simply going through the motions. He had no doubt that they loved *him* if not each other, but he was never hugged, never given a warm, affectionate embrace; dutifully loved but never allowed to feel *cherished*.

His escape from this house that smelt constantly of

chip fat and cigarettes, moreover his rescue from it, came at school. At the age of eleven he joined his brother and sister at a large new comprehensive, an uneasy amalgam in its early days of sets of teachers from the old grammar and secondary modern schools, both recently closed as selective education was abolished. Unlike David and Michelle, Trevor found himself excelling in subjects taught by the fussy but likeable old school masters from the grammar, such as Latin and foreign languages, and it made sense to follow that direction towards his O Levels and beyond.

When he was thirteen a letter from the headmaster reached his parents, advising pupils like him to *embark upon an academically defined pathway.* His mother, who was reading the letter aloud at tea-time, was stopped in her tracks.

"What's that when it's at 'ome?" asked his father, suddenly looking up from the puddle of ketchup on his plate.

"It means our Trevor is the brainy one in the family," said Michelle.

"Well, he thinks he is," muttered David.

Trevor said nothing, carried on chewing his fish fingers, grinning to himself inside.

He had seen his father read, or pretend to read, but at the time nobody had diagnosed his condition as extreme dyslexia. Trevor had a soft spot for his old man because he was so forgiving. If the boy had been caught stealing his brother's sweets, or more seriously, drinking from his mother's gin bottle, his father would be tasked with reprimanding him. Out of his wife's earshot he would take his son aside and pull his head close. He was an untidy shaver; he regularly missed the bits under his jawbone by his creased, leathery earlobes.

"Take your pleasures where you find 'em, mi lad," he would tell him. "Life's too short to be pickin' an' choosin'. Dunna pay so much 'eed o' your mother, Trevor. She means well, but she sees narrer. She don't see as wide as you an' me."

Was that the moment that the boy knew that his father was close to death? Then came the smile and the man winked at his son, as he often did. He never winked at the twins, at least not as far as Trevor had noticed.

A school leaver at fifteen like his wife, he had spent the next twenty-five years working in a paint factory. Breathing oil fumes, dust from astringent dyes and other assorted carcinogens during his labours, and inhaling the filthy tars of forty cigarettes a day gave the man's lungs no chance of reaching middle age in anything more than decrepit condition. He had a happy enough life, Trevor supposed, trying not to be too patronising: he'd married a dull but tidy woman who was eager to please him, and he'd sired three healthy children that he admitted to – *wink!* He enjoyed his smokes and his pint at the pub and his factory mates and his darts and his steak pie and chips – hot and ready for him at the table – and his *Daily Mirror* and his regular holidays in Blackpool or Rhyl. And his football on the telly and his harmless little racist jokes and sitting in his deckchair on the tiny square of lawn in the back garden, taking in the sun with a small whisky and ice on a nice summer's day.

"Come an' sit down 'ere wi' me, our Trevor," he might say in his croaky, dried-up voice, "an' tell me your life story."

And when he suffered the stroke that killed him, Trevor remembered that he still had most of his teeth, stained like rusty nails, a decent suntan and a full head of dark grey hair.

Trevor was fourteen years old, David and Michelle sixteen: more of an age than he was, he decided, to comfort their grieving mother. He was angry and confused, found reasons to come home late from school, he refused to go to the funeral, then sulkily relented at the last minute. His sister was ratty with him for days. In the weeks and months that followed he put more distance between himself and his family, and got on with his life as far as he could on his own terms.

His irritation with his mother, diluted while she was one of two parents, suddenly hardened. Uncooperative teenager he might have been, but even at his most magnanimous he found it hard to forgive her inertia. And this exasperation lasted for years, for she was never going to change, until in his adulthood, living away from her, it finally congealed into a dry, crusty contempt. She wasn't a lazy woman, but she had no energy, no ambition, no sparkle. She had never learned to drive, she had never been abroad, she had never even been into Manchester for a posh birthday meal, and it wasn't always for want of money. She had been a fan of the cinema in her younger days but the new stuff didn't suit her, she said. She was something of a regular at the bingo and even went with a neighbour until they had a falling out and she stopped going altogether. The centre of her life was her home, modest and unpretentious, and at the very heart of it was her living room. She loved her furniture, her curtains, her wallpaper, her little gas fire and her collection of ornamental china dogs. She loved her weekly celebrity magazines and her soft slippers and her colour television. In the years shortly after his father's death, Trevor remembered her filling the hole in her life with affection for Mrs Thatcher, Diana and Charles and the principal characters from *Dallas*. He noticed the pleasure she took in laughing at the foreigners being ridiculed in television comedies like *Mind Your Language* and *'Allo 'Allo!*, he sensed an undertow of racism in throwaway comments at mealtimes, and of prejudice against the likes of Elton John and other *daft pansy boys* like him.

One day she declared that she wanted a dog and David was given the money to buy one for her. He returned with the ugliest brute Trevor could imagine, a small yet overweight bulldog which his sister could only laugh at but which his mother fell in love with at once. After a long look at its flabby, dusky brown coat, its stunted, stocky legs, its shrivelled-up, smudgy snout – all suggestive of an amusing name – she decided to call it Rover, as unimaginative as it could possibly get.

"I think our Rover is a replacement for Dad," said Michelle quietly one evening, observing our mother cuddling the animal as they sat together on the little settee watching something inane on the television. Trevor remembered laughing to himself at the remark, whether his sister was trying to be funny or not. The dog was snarly and whingy, clumsy and malodorous but harmless and fairly obedient. Whatever, Rover gave him yet another reason to spend more time alone in his bedroom.

It was around this time that he decided to take on a newspaper round to earn some money. He was given an early morning round which took him nearly an hour each day before school but he didn't mind. In fact the cold air woke him up, he was used to the rain in any case and, when winter arrived, casting the first footprints on to virgin overnight snow was a special thrill. Most mornings he could afford to dawdle, he could stop on a quiet corner and in the yellow glow of a streetlight have a quick read of the headlines, a look at the TV listings, give himself a nice hard-on gazing at the tits on page 3. He generally gave the sport pages a miss; he had a passing interest in football as it was simply impossible to ignore, not just in the house where David was an obsessive, but in their street, on their buses, in conversations everywhere in fact in their corner of England. What did interest him was how different newspapers reported, or more accurately, interpreted the same story in different ways. Political and social bias began to fascinate him, as did the power of words. He saw how the battle between *The Mirror* and *The Sun* was no different from Coke v Pepsi or United v City. It also occurred to him at the time that the world was divided into three categories: those people who create the news, those who report it and, the vast majority, those who consume it. At that moment he was a consumer, he told himself, but he was already shaping an ambition to be a creator one day. One day, he promised himself, they'll all be reading about me.

He rarely arrived at school late. More and more it was his refuge from the banality of his home. Both David and Michelle had left at sixteen. His brother had always been a reluctant schoolboy and was desperate to leave and earn some real money. He found a job as a plumber's mate and was encouraged to attend college twice a week to study for his City & Guilds. Michelle also had little love for school and left at the earliest opportunity with just two O Levels to go to the same college and start a Combined Arts course. Trevor never lost his sense of superiority towards his brother but he would admit much later that Michelle was a late bloomer.

He loved the stimulation in the Sixth Form, not only in the classroom but also in the company of bright, talented young people just like himself. With a small group of friends he set up a subversive news-sheet entitled *Mischief*, declaring himself editor-in-chief, which became more and more scurrilous in its comments about the school and its staff until the headmaster's tolerance was finally exhausted and he banned it. Trevor discovered he had a gift for mimicking the voices of teachers and he would have his friends in stitches whenever he got the accent or the speech impediment or the catchphrase just right. He made a point of listening to celebrities on television or, better still, on the radio and practised their voices, their patterns of speech and their intonations, the pitch and the timbre and the vocal mannerisms they used. His impressions of certain comedians or presenters, politicians or sportsmen, mainly northerners, became his party piece. His brother shared his talent to a lesser extent and they played a game they called *Impersonation Challenge* for a while until David decided Trevor was too competitive and the whole thing was trivial and immature. Trevor struggled with Scots and Irish but developed a repertoire of southern accents and could do convincing women too. But the north-west of England's urban nuances were his speciality: if only rugby league had a higher profile, he told himself, he might have become quite famous.

His favourite teacher, and one of whom he could produce a near faultless vocal impression, was Mr Archer from Bradford, who taught him A Level French. Everyone guessed he was gay, but Trevor sensed that he would be too petrified at the thought of being caught to try anything on with his students. He wouldn't have minded if he had, actually. He wasn't very old, he always had minty breath and had clean, smooth skin. And he was a brilliant teacher, funny but never sarcastic; every lesson of his, it seemed, was an invitation to expand your mind.

Despite something of a crush on Mr Archer, Trevor found himself instinctively drawn to girls, and, to his delight, discovered that some of them at least were drawn to him. He was turning into an attractive young man: fresh-faced with long fair hair and piercing blue eyes, lithe in a non-athletic way, and always capable of making the most of the relaxed dress code. He was talkative and witty, generous with flattery and could make any girl laugh with a daft impression of someone they knew. Music and books, and even art if he was in the groove, these were the subjects, he discovered, you could talk to girls about: sexual things like suggestive lyrics, the erotic movement of a dance step, literary characters of charisma and daring. And talking to girls, engaging with them, getting close enough to sense the virginal softness of their arms, their shoulders, to glimpse a smooth, perfect knee, the delicate petal of an ear – this was really the only way you were ever going to end up having sex with them. Nothing highbrow, of course. He was only eighteen or thereabouts, and although he had his own laddish tastes in music, he knew what girls liked. He could talk about Sting and George Michael, about Michael Jackson and Madonna, and go all the way back to Cat Stevens and Bolan and Bowie if they wanted him to. And of course they were all reading the same set texts, the same recommended add-ons, even the same non-recommended surreptitious extras: *Lolita, A Clockwork Orange, Viz* magazine. What an aphrodisiac comedy was, by the way! A little joke to encourage a girl to break open her smile into a laugh and reveal the white of her teeth and the pink of her tongue. Comedy and cleverness: what a combination. Winning, whispered, wicked words: the best way ever to get inside a girl's pants. And a boy's too, if he felt like straying *off piste* once in a while.

The day that Trevor Penny's A Level results confirmed that he would be heading next for Oxford, Mr Archer took him to one side, gave him an audacious hug and then looked him in the eye.

"We're all delighted for you, Trevor," he said, a parent's pride in his broad smile. "All of us. You're the first student from this new school to win a place at Oxford. We're so very proud of you, young man. But a word of advice," and here the smile narrowed. "We all know you can do impressions of everybody around here, but can you do one of a man of refinement, an eloquent, educated man?"

"What do you mean, sir?" asked the boy.

"To paraphrase Hamlet," he said, raising an eyebrow, "*to be or to seem to be, that is the question*."

"Not quite with you, sir."

"You'll stand out a mile down there, Trevor. Most of them will be public school types, speaking the Queen's English. You know, RP. You'll sound like you've wandered in from a day at t' mill with bits of cotton still in your hair. They'll make fun of you, they will. And I dare say you'll take it, make fun of them too and get on with it. You're a strong character, we all know that. And you've got the brains. But just a tip: if you want to survive down there, if you really want to get on, you'll have to adapt. Smooth off a few of those rough edges. You might have to play a little subterfuge, have to become someone else, at least now and again."

4

Instead of working for the whole of that summer, earning some money in one of the town's mills, Penny was given the opportunity to spend two weeks of it abroad. The unlikely source was his mother, to whom he was speaking less and less. She mentioned one day, quite out of the blue, that she had been in touch by letter with a distant cousin who had emigrated to Canada in the late 1960s. Knowing that the country was bilingual, she thought that Trevor would appreciate the chance to spend some time there speaking French before he went off to university.

"It might give you an 'ead start," she said, hopefully.

"I suppose it might."

It took him a moment to realise that his mother was being thoughtful for once in her life.

"What's he like?"

"I don't 'onestly know. I've not seen 'im since he were a lad. 'E ended up marryin' a Canadian and they 'ave a family: three daughters, I think, grown up now."

He decided that he had nothing to lose, the factory packing department wouldn't miss him for a fortnight, and he told his mother that he would leave it all to her to arrange.

The thought of flying abroad on his own excited him. He had spotted the town of Victoria on a map of Quebec and was looking forward to an adventure even though there was a chance that any relative of his mother might turn out to be as uninspiring as her. When the airline tickets arrived, printed with the Pacific coastal destination of Vancouver, however, it slowly dawned on him that, like a badly labelled parcel, he was being sent to the wrong address: Victoria, British Columbia, to spend fifteen days in the company of a family he didn't know in a part of the country where French was officially recognised but was effectively shunned like an uninvited party guest. It took him a long time to forgive his mother for what in his eyes was her meddling stupidity.

Victoria was as English a city as any in England: attractive enough but not the reason why he had boarded a plane for the first time in his life and travelled five thousand miles. He spoke not a word of French, met a lot of people his mother's age, and the only silver lining was a friendship he quickly established with the family's youngest daughter, Molly, a recently divorced lingerie model with a very healthy sexual appetite.

After less than a week of his time at Oxford, Penny realised that the words of Mr Archer constituted sound advice. He found that first short, intense term a brutal one. He watched the leaves wither and drop and felt that his heart was falling too. On top of all the sharp-elbowed social jockeying as an undergraduate hierarchy established itself were the demands of his studies: a merciless workload of reading and written assignments, with extra reading as a compulsory option. He was not exactly ostracised by his peers, all of whom seemed cleverer and more at ease in the new environment, but he felt he was accepted not as an equal, rather as a curiosity, a novelty. He chugged along until December, dodging arrows, saved by his own wits, his thick skin and an ability to turn the other cheek. Nevertheless, during the Christmas holidays he resolved to reinvent himself; having got the measure of the place, it wasn't too late, he told himself, to begin again.

He would stop being known as Trevor, for a start. It was a name he had never liked, a name he knew had been chosen for him by his mother. Fortunately he had another: his middle name John, taken from his paternal grandfather, which, although prosaic, had a literary pedigree that appealed. He would buy some quirky clothes, work on his elocution and reappear in January as John Penny, a worthy acolyte of all the other Johns he admired: Milton, Donne and Swift, Keats, Ruskin and Steeples, Steinbeck, Betjeman and Lennon. Not to mention the French contingent: Genet, Anouilh, Cocteau.

He would make an effort to undo eighteen years of being hemmed in by the blinkered expectations of others, notably his family: eighteen years of short reins and grubby limitations, of being told that this or that wasn't *for the likes of us*, of being allowed to do things *weather permittin'*, one of his mother's favourite caveats, of being warned about having *ideas above your station.* Some of his teachers had been just as keen to keep him in his box. He had been considered *too big for his boots*, and after yet another less than respectful impression of the Headmaster, the Deputy Head had told him, at the start of an hour's detention, he needed *taking down a peg or two. Who do you think you are, Penny?* he had asked, *Mike bloody Yarwood?*

Well, now was the time to go up a peg or two. It wasn't too late to insist to the likes of Angus Barrington-Smith and Jasper Couttes that his parents also belonged to the middle classes, that he had close family in Canada, ranch-owners and investors in oil exploration. He also lied about his school. The further away he moved from the truth, in some ways from his own family, the more accepted he became in his new circles. He found it easier to be believed than he expected: it frightened him that he could lie so convincingly, and he quickly understood that people, on the whole, accept what they are told because they simply do not expect to be deceived. He was invited to spend a weekend at the Couttes' family estate in Berkshire and didn't put a foot wrong: he produced perfect table manners and sophisticated conversation, he charmed the boy's mother and made the father howl with impressions of the more colourful members of Mrs Thatcher's cabinet. He played a polite hand of cards with the grandfather and even managed to trot around a paddock on horseback without making a fool of himself. In his moment of triumph he couldn't help thinking how inept and embarrassingly uncouth David would have been in his shoes. His brother, his sister, his mother – he was leaving them all behind, culturally, socially, physically, but it was inevitable, he decided, it was normal; indeed it was desirable.

He developed a certain popularity around the college, or at least with his fellow students if not all of his teachers, as the work was hard and at times simply beyond him. He had put pressure on himself by choosing to read both French and English and the reading lists overwhelmed him. Sometimes there just weren't enough hours in the day.

It was a relief to spend his third university year abroad. Studying for six months in Rennes was less intense and he loved simply being a citizen of another country. Speaking in another language than his own, surrounded by people who didn't yet know him, he felt liberated and able to inhabit yet another personality: John Penny, at 21 years old, the open-minded, educated, relaxed, sophisticated European.

Making friends in Brittany offered him options to stay beyond Easter, working in this bar or that marina, but he took the more interesting choice, suggested late in the day by one of his tutors, who had contacts in Quebec. The large town of Trois Rivières, halfway along the St Lawrence River between Quebec City and Montreal, became his temporary home, and strangely, as these things often happen, he was offered a part-time job in a bicycle rental shop less than an hour's bus-ride away in Victoriaville, *that* Victoria. By the end of August, leaving his new *chums* behind, he didn't quite return to Europe with a *québecois* twang to his French, but he did have a plan for the next stage in his life.

The academic world had taken a hold on his imagination. Even if he didn't quite yet understand its workings, he believed that he would quickly do so. Moving into the postgraduate environment, still one year away, would require insight into a more rarefied area of study, however, and Penny was uncertain if he was up to it. While he was living in Trois Rivières, he was granted access to the facilities of the Université du Québec and it was while he was there that he formulated a strategy. It was 1986 and the internet was young; at that point very little academic documentation had been digitized. What began as an innocent hunt for ideas, for inspiration, turned into a deliberate *adaptation* of somebody else's research, becoming a disguised, borrowed dissertation, a long plagiarised document that he could reuse undetected in England.

Penny spent many hours in the university library, then the archive, reading scripts, ordering more, and finally starting to rewrite a piece of work in which he was genuinely interested: a 1969 thesis of one hundred pages written in French by a Marcel Lapointe. It was a comparative study of French and English authors of the nineteenth and early twentieth centuries. *Depuis Flaubert jusqu'à Pagnol, une tradition réaliste et sa déviation anglaise* reflected Lapointe's analysis in literature of fatalism, of a godless universe, of the weight and limitations of man's surroundings. Zola and Maupassant were covered in depth, and he referenced passages from Dickens, Hardy of course, and Steeples. It was high summer and the campus was open but practically deserted. A small number of students were working as relief staff in administration and Penny took an interest in a slim-hipped young man regularly on duty in the library, whose authority was signalled by a set of keys in a loose ring that dangled from the belt of his tight leather trousers. One quiet afternoon, in a dark musty alcove pierced by a strip of sunlight, Penny offered him a moist sexual favour in exchange for half an hour's unauthorised access to the photocopier.

A year later the bulk of the text became the template for his own PhD. By then he had translated it into English and renamed the piece *From Flaubert to Pagnol, the light of French realism refracted through an English prism*, a title he was quite proud of. No longer in French and as such at one remove from the original, he convinced himself that his work in itself was a thoroughly worthy academic exercise and not really copying, not really stealing at all.

He would admit to stealing from his brother, however, during a break at home shortly after his finals. He had been invited to spend a week's holiday with a few Oxford friends in a villa in Majorca: sun, beaches, easy girls, cheap wine, a spot of post-exam hedonism in a place that wasn't Blackpool, it seemed like a very decent idea, but he needed some money to pay for it. His sister Michelle had already moved to London but David still lived at home, still had the same bedroom he had shared with Trevor, now John, since they were boys. Penny knew all his brother's hiding places, unchanged since those days: the razor cut in the underside of his mattress, the false bottom of the drawer where he had kept his cash, his illicit cigarettes, his men's magazines. It would be too obvious if money went missing from there, however; the list of suspects would stop at one. David, struggling to complete his qualifications, was still a trainee plumber paid weekly with a small envelope of cash. He took a sum of around £200 to the bank at the end of each month, where he deposited it in a savings account; he was planning on taking a programme of driving lessons with a second-hand car as a prize at the end of them.

Penny contacted a couple of lads he knew from a previous holiday job in a towel factory and met them in a pub.

"This is the bloke," he said, showing them a recent photograph of his brother. "Rough him up a bit, nothing serious, just shake him up. Scare him. You know what I mean. His wallet is the main thing. Just a spot of bloodless mugging. He always takes the short cut over the back fields. There's twenty each for you if you bring it to me here, same time, on Saturday morning."

David was duly ambushed the following day, pushed about, tripped, took a few kicks in the ribs, got the message, and handed over his wallet.

"How did they know I was carrying so much cash?" he asked his brother when he arrived home holding his sides, wincing.

"They *didn't*, did they, Davie?" said Penny. "It was just bad luck. Or their good luck. They probably expected to take a few quid off you at the most. Hadn't you better go to hospital, mate, if you're in so much pain?"

The letter he had been waiting for from Oxford was one of rejection. To his dismay they had not invited him on to the postgraduate course he had applied for, but a week later a second choice, the University of L, did reply with an offer of a place which he accepted and so grudgingly moved back north. He consoled himself with the thought that his Oxford degree would always figure on his CV. Cashing in his re-polished thesis, he won admirers and supporters among his new peers; he went on to teach English Literature alongside them for the next ten years.

Physically in his prime, attractive and authoritative, Penny took advantage at this time of several of the vulnerable, impressionable students he was entrusted to tutor.

"I confess that I used my position," he would say much later in a plea to the Vice Chancellor.

"I think the word is *abused*."

"Very well. I do apologise for that. But at no time did I force myself on a student. Sex was consensual. In every case. I stand by that. Any claims to the contrary are based on lies."

The university gave him the benefit of the doubt on many occasions until his reputation as a philanderer overtook his reputation as an academic. The discovery of substantial amounts of cannabis in a false-bottomed drawer in his study was the final straw; Penny was found a job elsewhere, then quietly dismissed.

Elsewhere was a former polytechnic on the south coast, now a new university, on a relaxed campus by the sea, where he was employed to teach English Literature and French conversation to undergraduate students. He had learned his lesson and became far more discreet in the matter of sexual dalliances. Meanwhile he felt a growing need to make a mark on the academic world. He knew that for all their claims and ambitions, his new employers were running a second division establishment, and if he were to rejoin an elite institution then he needed to be heard, seen and read as a scholar of note.

He travelled widely on research projects, he published papers on his hero Hardy's influence on his contemporaries then on later writers, he published articles on Shakespeare's songs, on the role of music in modern fiction, on the televisualisation of literature. He attended conferences, often as a lead speaker. But it seemed that anything innovative he came up with was either shot at by some pompous professor from Cambridge or Durham, or else was shown not even to be original, the theory having been developed in Massachusetts or Heidelberg or somewhere else a year earlier. He felt like a chef who, having produced a wonderfully inventive new recipe, is devastated to discover that the restaurant down the street has been serving something similar for months. He started to write a novel of his own, the story of a man trapped in his class who uses crime as a means of escape, but in spite of creating a startling beginning and a satisfying ending he was unhappy with what he saw as a soggy middle and it remained unfinished. None of these efforts caused much more than a small ripple on the surface of the large lake of academia and each rejection, each frustration saw him drowning his sorrows in promiscuity.

Many students, male and female, still found him fascinating, funny and physically alluring in spite of a growing age difference. By now in his forties, Penny, still searching for his grail, his key to fame as a mark of success, remained single, fancy-free and overconfident. Encounters with students were one thing, but the tide turned against him when it was discovered that he had started an affair with the wife of a young lecturer in his own department who proved to be less than careful with her mobile phone. The fallout was bitter, tearful and decisive.

"It may very well be a private matter, Dr Penny," sighed the Dean of Faculty from behind his oversized desk. "But your behaviour in this case undermines the morale of the whole of the teaching body. For all your good work here, your reputation is badly tarnished, your colleagues undeniably see you in a less than favourable light. I have to say that there are some who would be glad if I were to simply fire you here and now."

Penny, submissively playing the role of the penitent, took this to mean that a reprieve was on its way.

"I do feel personally let down," mumbled the older man.

Penny stared at the carpet, feeling like a fifteen-year-old smoker up in front of the headmaster.

"We're shipping you overseas," the Dean suddenly said, fiddling with his pen. "That is, if you're agreeable."

"Overseas, sir?"

He hadn't meant to call him *sir*, it had just come out that way.

"Yes. There's no place for you here. It's that or nothing. They'll have you in Bordeaux. We have a relationship with the department over there. On probation, that is. A one-year contract."

Penny swallowed, and gave himself a moment to respond.

"English or French?" he asked finally, his throat as dry as a biscuit.

"Teaching English, I believe."

"One year? That's all?"

"To be reviewed. Starting next September. Take it or leave it, Dr Penny, as I said. It's the best I can do. You've come to end of the road here, I'm afraid. Too much damage. Too much debris."

He coughed to clear his throat before mouthing a word Penny never imagined he would hear in that office:

"We can't sweep it all under the fucking carpet forever."

5

It was a bitterly cold afternoon in December, the sky above the valley was covered with bruised, snow-bearing clouds but the day had stayed mercifully dry, a consolation to everyone in the group as the doctor had made them walk much further than anyone had expected to. Wrapped in padded coats, scarves and gloves and woolly hats of all colours, they were standing on the wide stone road bridge, *le Pont Napoléon*, mindful of the traffic, huddled together, one or two stamping their feet on the pavement for warmth.

"La Vézère, ladies and gentlemen," announced John Penny, scratching his beard. "As you can see, lazily flowing through the heart of Frettignac, effectively cutting the town in two. The buildings on this side have changed a little since Steeples' time, but looking the other way," and here he theatrically waved an arm to his right, "the *hôtel de ville*, the very festive *Place de la Résistance* and its shops," – it was true that a pair of workmen in green overalls were erecting a large fir tree in the centre of the square – "the church tower rising behind those trees, the wooded side of the valley, all this would have been a very familiar view to him. Standing here with us, over one hundred and thirty years later, he would recognise it perfectly."

There were a dozen in his party today, mostly female, who had signed up for this end-of-term trip to see some of the literary sights of the area. They had spent the morning in Bordeaux for the Mauriac leg, had been driven rather too many kilometres for comfort in an overheated minibus to Bergerac – home to Rostand's *Cyrano* – to finally land in Frettignac, where their estimable guide had plans to talk about the famous 19th century English writer Jonathan Steeples.

"He spent four years in this part of France," he went on, raising his voice over the rumble of a tanker lorry passing at his back. "Four full years away from his wife who stayed in England. That's quite excessive if all she said to him one day was *I think we need to spend a little time apart*, no?"

He smiled broadly at his joke as if to encourage a little laughter. Just two or three of the students politely obliged, but Penny wasn't offended. Most of the group were not good English speakers and probably had not understood him anyway. He had been instructed to speak English throughout the day but had relented and given a brief French commentary from time to time to keep the group together. He noticed that the pretty American woman with the shoulder-length dark brown hair and the pale blue beret was no longer listening to him; she was in conversation with her friend, the blonde woman she had sat at the back of the bus with, looking down along the river bank, pointing at a pair of swans in the distance.

"So, if you would follow me," he said loudly, heading

back over the bridge, "I want to show you a little treasure, the penultimate stop of the day, in the library, *la bibliothèque municipale*, over there across the square."

Like a small flock of sheep the students obediently formed a raggedy queue behind him and abandoned their river view for the heart of the town.

"I say *penultimate*," Penny turned his head back to them, "as I'm sure you'd like a quarter of an hour in a café to warm up before we head back. Actually, I might join you."

Their final destination, ETA 18.00, was not Bordeaux but Périgueux, principal town of the Périgord region and *préfecture* of the *département* of Dordogne. It was a pleasant place, provincial and modest, however, and certainly not cosmopolitan, not a bustling, attention-seeking city, not Bordeaux. To his dismay Penny had discovered very quickly that the Université de Bordeaux would not be his place of work, the august old city-centre buildings would not provide him with an elegant office, nor would one of the renovated riverside warehouses, now chic apartments, accommodate him. The one-year probationary contract had in fact been offered by a far less prestigious institution, *l'Association Universitaire de l'Aquitaine*, or AULA as everybody called it, which, supported largely by regional public funds, served the whole of the south-west from four local hubs. To be sure, there was a centre in Bordeaux, another in Agen, and a third on the edge of the Pyrénées in Pau. The fourth, in the north of the region, was based in Périgueux. Penny had been deflated when he first cast eyes on the complex of tired, faceless buildings on the edge of the town, but he reminded himself that he had nobody else to blame for being there and he resolved to make the best of the clean slate he had been granted.

And as he acclimatised himself to new surroundings, new colleagues, new classes, he soon appreciated the soft warm air, the smells, the sensation of being properly in France, living here, weaving himself into its fabric: a feeling he hadn't experienced since his time in Brittany over twenty-five years earlier. Not only that; he was reminded by the *Chef de Faculté* that one of his favourite English writers, Jonathan Steeples, often considered the forgotten novelist, lost in the shadow of Hardy, had lived in the region for a spell in the middle of the 1880s. It had not taken Penny long to track down the house he had rented in Bergerac and then the small town of Frettignac, near to which he had set his short lyrical novel of 1886, *Lucie l'Eglantine.*

By the time they left the library with its tiny, dimly-lit exhibition of dusty artefacts, the temperature had dropped further and people's breath was visible in the fading daylight. Penny gave the group thirty minutes' free time before they needed to rejoin the minibus, and then made a point of attaching himself to a foursome which included the American. She was a mature student, probably in her early thirties, he guessed, and had striking, nut brown eyes and the prettiest, perfect little nose. He had seen her around the university buildings, in the canteen once, even in a couple of his lectures, high up near the back row, but, sadly, she was not in his tutor group. He had her name on his list and quickly reminded himself of it.

As they stood in the doorway of the café, waiting for a large enough table to clear, someone shouted to him to close the door, shut out the draught, *pour l'amour de Dieu!* There was the smell of roasted coffee, the rumble of conversation, the click-clack of table football. Shuffling into the space, he found himself standing directly behind her, close enough to smell the citrus notes of her shampoo, to see the little star design on her earrings.

"I hope you don't mind if I join you?" he said. "I need a hot drink too. It's Miss Snow, isn't it?"

The woman turned to face him, her surprise melting into an open smile.

"Oh, Mr Penny, sorry, *Doctor* Penny, it's you!"

"May I?"

"Of course! Come and join us. You can fill me in on those missing lines from *The Heron.*"

"I'll try."

"I'm Columbine, by the way. Columbine Snow."

"And I'm John. Call me John, please. I'm pretty much off duty now, I think."

"This is Elise," she added, putting her hand on the shoulder of her friend, a petite younger woman with wavy blonde hair and glasses with orange circular rims, who turned to offer him a shy smile.

"*Enchanté,*" said Penny, "*Vous êtes française, n'est-ce pas?*"

The woman nodded but Columbine spoke first:

"Elise is from Paris but we speak English together most of the time. Her English is far better than my French, you see."

"Look," said Elise, "There's a table free over there in the corner."

On a large television screen high in one corner of the room there was a football match showing with the sound turned off. Only the man behind the counter preparing drinks seemed to be watching in between orders. Penny recognised one of the teams as the navy-shirted FC Girondins, the local favourites from Bordeaux. Suddenly there were adverts. The match wasn't live, probably a programme of old highlights. The women at his table were commenting on the collection of vintage cinema posters, framed and lining one of the café's smoke-stained walls. As their conversation lulled, he spoke across the table to the American once more:

"I've seen you in my lectures, haven't I, Columbine? What courses are you following?"

He had found himself sitting closer to Elise, and the French woman had been talking at length about her course in film studies, an area in which AULA had developed a growing reputation.

"I'm here to improve my French," replied her friend. "At least that's the theory! I'm here just for one year. So, French language and culture as a major, and I have a bunch of English modules and History too, to fill up my schedule."

"Just for one year?" he repeated, draining the last of his café-crème from the chunky cup.

"I know. Short, isn't it? I already have a bachelor's in the States. I wanted to spend a year in Europe. I'd never been. Daddy thought a year in France would be beneficial. It's hard to find a place short-term but AULA was happy to take the fees and slide me straight into a programme."

Her voice was calm, there was a confident, smooth flow to her speech, flavoured with a light, educated accent which he guessed was New England.

"Where did you study?"

"In the States?"

"Yes."

"The University of Maine in Bangor. My home town. And I have to be back there by August of next year," she added, lifting her left hand off her knee to wave an engagement ring over the cups and saucers on the table.

"You're going home for a wedding, I imagine," said Penny with a smile.

"Sure am."

"Anyone I know?"

"I doubt it," she answered, playing along. "A guy by the name of Patrick. Patrick McVie. He's in the Marine Corps, serving in Afghanistan right now – his third tour, due to end next summer."

"I see. Have you known him long?"

"Since I was about five years old!"

"Well, congratulations. I hope it all goes well."

"So do I."

There was the slightest hint of unease in her voice at that moment which raised a flicker on Penny's radar. A sudden hoot of victory exploded from one of the *babyfoot* boys in the back room. Then he realised the woman was still speaking.

"...too many of us to see properly."

"I'm sorry, to see what?"

"The manuscript in the library. *The Heron*."

"Yes, I admit, it was a bit of a scrum. It's such a tight space."

"We studied it in ninth grade, you know."

"Really? It's in most of the British school anthologies too."

"*Longshore lord of lake and stream...*"

"Exactly."

"And the lines from the second verse. Our teacher loved them... *A lethal lunge of flashing feathered foil...*"

"*Cold splash of death*," added Penny, "*a thrashing carp's recoil*. The grace and awesome power of the kill."

"We were always taught to think of the heron as an ugly brute. A predator, a bully."

"There is that viewpoint. Was your teacher a woman, by any chance?"

"Yes. Yes, she was."

"Women often see the attack from the perspective of the fish, the vulnerability of the victim."

"But you don't?"

"Well, I can see it, but I think Steeples is more interested in the bird as a symbol of strength, of virility. Then there's the political undertow, of course: a representation of aggressive capitalism, imperialism. If you look at the language of the third verse especially."

Elise was buttoning up her coat and tying her scarf.

"I think we must go back to the bus," she said, standing up. "Don't you? The group leader will be angry if anyone is late, I think," she added, with an enigmatic look towards Penny.

"Oh, I think he'll give you five minutes' grace," he responded. "Here, let me pay."

"No, no, we can get ours," insisted Columbine.

"My treat. No arguments."

"That's very kind, thanks."

As they emerged into the frosty air, into the half-light of the early evening, Penny caught up with the American and briskly walked back to the car park in step with her.

"I could take you back to the library, if you wanted," he offered.

"Now? We haven't the time, surely."

"No, not now. No, some other time. Whenever you like. This weekend?"

"Won't it be closed?"

"Yes, of course. Of course it will." He wasn't thinking straight. He hadn't felt like this with a woman since he was sixteen. "Sometime next week then. I have Friday free."

"Friday? Yes, I'm free in the afternoon."

"Great. So you'd like me to give you a proper look at the exhibits? I can ask the librarian to open up the display case. She knows who I am. She'd do that for me, I'm sure."

"Great."

"And I could provide home-made coffee afterwards."

"Really?"

"Yes, absolutely. I have a place here in town. I live here most of the time now, in fact. I prefer it to the digs in Périgueux."

"Okay. Okay, then. Elise? Elise, would you like to come back here next Friday for a private viewing of the Steeples collection?"

Penny's heart sank a little. He had invited her, not the both of them.

"Next Friday? I don't think so," said the French woman. "I plan to go to Paris for the weekend and will take the afternoon train."

"But *you'll* still come?" asked Penny a little too urgently.

"Yes, why not?" she replied after a moment's hesitation. "It'll be fun, I guess."

6

Penny had no idea if his landlady would be volunteering in the library on the Friday and so was encouraged to see her silver Clio parked by the kerb as they approached the building. It was just two weeks before Christmas but the days had grown milder and the low winter sun, casting its bright but tepid rays through gaps in the puffy white clouds, briefly turned the town's stone walls the colour of crème caramel that he associated with the long days of late summer.

He had waited to meet Columbine Snow at the bus station by the Brico-Jacques store, and when he saw her stepping on to the pavement, dressed in tailored trousers and tan leather shoes – neither jeans nor trainers – with a grey three-quarter-length top coat and a little honey-coloured cashmere scarf, he was gratified that she had made an effort. As indeed had he, deciding to wear a new, white, collared shirt instead of his usual end-of-the-week over-washed long-sleeved tee-shirt. She had put on a little make-up too, he noticed: a touch of lipstick, a light brush of eyeliner, and he caught a hint of her perfume as they greeted each other with a soft handshake and a smile.

"I'm so pleased you agreed to come," he said, guiding

her across the street towards the centre of Frettignac. "I've been looking forward to it all morning."

"Me too," she agreed. "It feels like a private tutorial."

"Well, let's keep the erudition to a minimum, shall we, and just enjoy the afternoon?"

The library was busier than he had expected it to be, the air seemed stuffy, and the only librarian on duty, the dumpy old owl of a woman, Amande Puybonieux, was occupied by one fussy borrower after another. Penny and his student gravitated to the area of the Steeples collection, no more than a glass case of exhibits and above it a large wall panel with reproduced photographs and drawings and a few paragraphs of text in French.

"Can you understand all this, Columbine?"

"I can get the gist, I think."

"Would you like me to translate for you?"

"No, thanks. I'll manage fine. I have your outline here which kind of tells the tale."

And she slipped out of her bag a neatly folded copy of the sheet of notes Penny had provided a week earlier for the members of his group. He was pleased to see that not only had she kept it but it was evident, as she spread it out on the glass surface, that she had looked after it: it was neither creased nor crumpled, nor stained with coffee rings.

Jonathan STEEPLES, English novelist and poet, 1845-1896

1845 *Born Bristol*
1865 *Begins career as a wine trader*

"That's an early photo of Anne, his wife," said Penny, adjusting his glasses.

"She looks quite fierce, don't you think?"

"Perhaps that's the reason he left her to come and live in France for four years. Mind you, it explains here that it was a mutual decision. That one is the house he lived in in Bergerac, see, in 1886."

He let her read the captions, looked away and noticed that Amande Puybonieux was free. He wandered over to the reception desk where she was rearranging a stack of books.

"*Madame Puybonieux, comment allez-vous?*"

"*Ah, Monsieur Penny, bonjour. Oui, ça va, ça va. Je peux vous aider?*"

"*Pourriez-vous nous ouvrir la vitrine là-bas, s'il vous plaît?*"

"*Oui, monsieur, aucun problème. Un moment, j'arrive.*"

The woman rejoined the pair in the corridor a minute or two later holding a small key. Penny introduced Columbine as *une de mes étudiantes*, before correcting himself, unnecessarily, and referring to her as *une amie*. Amande loosely shook her by the hand, welcomed her to Frettignac and then carefully placed the key in the lock, turned it and lifted open the lid of the cabinet, resting it on its hinges rather precariously, Penny thought, against the wall panel.

"*Voilà. Servez-vous, monsieur-dame.*"

The case contained antique copies of most of Steeples' work and a few artefacts: pens, ink bottles long dried up, a few damaged photographs of the writer, a map of Aquitaine printed in 1870, a magnifying glass, but only two original pieces of writing. In the centre of the display sat a pair of pages of handwritten poetry, the second and third verses of *Lord of the Lake*, the poem commonly known as *The Heron*, with numerous pencilled annotations throughout.

"There's your couplet, see," remarked Penny, pointing to the first of the pages. "The handwriting is large enough to be quite clear."

"*A lethal lunge of flashing feathered foil,*" she read aloud. "*Cold splash of death, a thrashing carp's recoil.* It's all very phallic, isn't it?"

"There's a representation of a certain sexualised aggression, yes."

"*Masculine* sexualised aggression," she insisted, raising an eyebrow.

"Fair point," he nodded. "But Steeples isn't lauding the heron. In fact he's not really judging it at all. How could he? He's showing a natural predator doing what it instinctively does. And he was actually something of a feminist."

"That's hard to see."

"In this poem, I agree. But he was a modern, enlightened man. Napoléonne is a heroic, swashbuckling *female* pirate captain. He supported women's claims for suffrage for many years."

"Really?"

"Right up to his death. And look at Lucie. A wild, strong-willed woman, buffeted by the whims of the male-dominated society she finds herself in. Some see in her a forerunner of Hardy's Tess."

Columbine was reading a section of the biographical text on the panel.

"There's nothing here about any of that. It's a shame."

Casting her eyes down again to study the pencil notes in the margin of the poem, she asked:

"What do you make of these, John?"

"Well, they're obviously in French, and to me it's as if he has written out the original as a translation exercise. *Une botte mortelle de sa lame emplumée* is rather neat, and how about this one; *son bec de poignard* for *bladed beak*?"

"More phallic imagery!"

Penny smiled.

"I suppose so."

"Was a translation ever completed?"

"Yes, but not by Steeples. I don't think his French was quite up to it. Several years afterwards, as far as I know, as were all of his novels."

"And this poem featured in *Reflections on…*?"

"*On the Dordogne.*"

"I wonder what happened to the first verse."

"Well, I suppose it was lost or destroyed or, who knows?"

"That's a shame. It's the one everyone remembers, isn't it?"

They walked up the hill together, out of town along the winding D road, skirting the woods until they arrived at Penny's house just before the darkening clouds began to release a cold, drizzly shower of rain.

"Come on, before you get wet," he said, turning the key and ushering her through the door. He was already quite proud of his home; he had lived there for only a matter of weeks but he had added touches of his own, filling the bookcase with personal favourites, hooking a picture or two on the painted walls, and he had even bought himself a set of bright orange scatter cushions on a whim. The stove in the main room was all set, and his first job upon arrival was to light it and bring a little cosy cheer to the place.

"This is nice," Columbine remarked, looking around the space. "A really cute house."

"It's owned by the woman we met in the library."

"If I owned a dinky little place like this I think I'd want to live in it."

"She's got a flat somewhere else in town. You'd like a coffee?"

"Sure, why not?"

"And an éclair?"

"I'd love one, thanks. The cakes in France are impossible to resist."

"And the *pâtisserie* here in town is especially good."

Penny disappeared into the kitchen and set the coffee maker to task. While he was waiting for it to brew, with one eye on the clearing skies through the window, he failed to notice that Columbine had moved to place herself in the doorway and was watching him from behind.

"How long you lived here, John?" she asked suddenly, taking him by surprise. He actually jumped, the woman had him on edge, for Christ's sake. It was an innocent question, framed through her beautiful, inquisitive brown eyes.

"Only since November. I have a room on campus but it's not so nice. I share a flat with a couple of other teachers. I doubt you know them: a French guy called Robert, long black curly hair, teaches Economics, and my friend Henrik the Swede, who's a physicist."

"No, I only know the staff I have courses with."

"They're okay, especially Henrik, but the place is small, a bit soulless."

"Yeah, I know what you mean. I'm in a block with seven other women, well, girls, really. I feel like their mom oftentimes. I've not lived like this since I was at college in Bangor, aged nineteen. Still, it's only for a year."

"That's a pity."

"Why do you say that?"

"Well, you know, no sooner will you be getting used to the place, making new friends and everything, and it'll be time to pack up and leave. One term is already over, for a start."

"Yes, but I am going back for a reason!"

"To be married, yeah, you said."

He handed her a cup of coffee and a small plate laden with cake.

"Let's go back through, shall we?"

Seated on the armchairs less than three feet apart they ate in near silence, Columbine stifling laughter when she smudged a spot of cream on her chin.

"I've always been a messy eater!"

"How come you've ended up in Périgueux, by the way, if you don't mind me asking?"

"To improve my French. I think I already told you."

Had she? He needed to relax before he made a fool of himself.

"Well, that's the short answer."

"But why here?"

"I got accepted. It's just a kind of foundation course. Not many colleges will take foreign students like me, not for a single year, anyways. But AULA were happy to take my money. Well, my daddy's money, strictly speaking."

"Are your parents still living in Maine?"

"Daddy is. He wouldn't live any place else. His job is

tied to the area. He runs a lumber business. My mom died five years ago."

"I'm sorry."

"It's okay." She paused to drink. "It was a car accident. She skidded on ice and hit a tree. Nobody else was involved. It shook Daddy up real hard. I was working in kindergarten at the time, been teaching for a while, but already starting to get a little bored. About a year later Daddy asked me to come and work for him. I think he'd gotten lonely and wanted to spend more time with me. I'm his only child."

"I see."

"So, he does a little business with the Canadians across the border. He wants to expand those links eventually, selling specialised materials, machinery, equipment and such in Quebec province. He needs someone alongside him who can get by in French."

"I've been to Quebec myself," Penny interjected.

"Really?"

"Yeah. Trois Rivières, on the St Lawrence."

"I don't know it."

"But never to Maine."

"That's a shame. Have you visited the States at all?"

"Once. From the other side of Canada, in fact, the far west. Washington State. You'd hardly know the difference. You know what they say about Canada: USA-lite, so driving into Seattle the kilometres became miles and everything was a bit cheaper, but it felt the same. Apart from all the flags."

"The flags?"

"Your flag, the US flag. Not just on government buildings but on private houses, in gardens, businesses, everywhere."

"I suppose you're right. When you live there it just seems pretty normal."

"In Europe we're a bit more understated about patriotism."

"You know, thinking about it, I do miss seeing flagpoles everywhere."

"But anyway, I've been just that one time. The east coast, never. Not yet, anyway. I just think of rough seas and lobsters."

"Well, there are lobsters in our waters, that's a fact. Daddy says to visitors that if you want to know Maine you have to think of its three Fs: forestry, fishing and, excuse my language, fucking vacationers from New York City!"

Penny smiled, not so much at Columbine's father's little aphorism than at her coyness with his expletive.

"And Patrick, he's from Bangor too?" he asked quietly.

"Yes. You've remembered his name. Yes, his father was my daddy's partner for a while. Family friends, almost neighbours at one time. And Patrick's sister Pamela, well, she's just about my best friend in all the world."

"You're lucky."

"What do you mean?"

"To have a best friend in all the world. You're lucky to have that. Something I've never had."

"You give me the impression of someone who is totally self-contained. Perhaps you've never really needed people so much, John."

"Oh, I need people, believe me."

"Well, I have heard something along those lines."

"You have? What have you heard?"

"Oh, nothing."

"Go on," he insisted, puzzled.

"Well, just that you're a bit of a ladies' man."

"Really?"

"I don't know. It's just gossip, I guess."

Penny sighed, sat back in the armchair and smiled, as much in resignation to himself as to her.

"Well, once upon a time perhaps."

"But no longer? You're a reformed character?"

Was she actually teasing him?

"I've had my moments," he confessed with another smile, this time directed at her. "But that's all in the past."

"Well, I believe you, Dr Penny."

"You must, I suppose. You came here to my house with your engagement ring on your finger in spite of all the rumours."

"Yes, I did. But we're here for a coffee and a cake, aren't we? And a chat about books. And don't worry, I can look after myself."

"I'm sure you can," he said, laughing.

He pulled himself out of the chair and took her empty plate.

"Let's tidy this up and then I'll show you my field."

"Your field?"

"Yes, my spectacular field. It's stopped raining. Look, even the sun's back out."

He led her out towards the kitchen door.

"You might have a zillion trees in your forests in Maine,"

he said, "but I bet you haven't seen a grove of walnut trees as pretty as the one out there in my back garden."

They strolled through the shadowy lanes between the bare trees with their dripping branches all the way to the top of the field and over the ridge where they paused to take in the view of the woods to the left and, rising to the right, the long, wide slopes of the vines, bathed in the last watery rays of December sunlight. He felt strangely possessive of the land, as if he had farmed it, had planted the trees, had harvested the crop every autumn, as if he were the true lord of all walnuts. She sensed it and made a joke of it.

Presently, when they reached the warmth of the house, Columbine paused on her way over to the woodstove to get a closer look at the wedding photograph on the wall.

"These aren't any family of yours, are they, John?" she asked.

"No, that photo comes with the house."

"I thought they looked French somehow. Must be the clothes."

"The marriage didn't last, apparently."

"Really? They look so happy here, on their big day."

"I disagree."

"What do you mean?"

"Well, look at the body language."

"I guess you just never can tell if a marriage will work out. Kind of sad, though. I wonder why they keep the photo up on display."

"I think it was a happy day to them at least."

Penny was on the other side of the room. He pulled out a hardback volume from the bookcase and offered it to her.

"You said you hadn't read this one, didn't you?"

"*Forty Barrels More*," she intoned, reading the gilded words on the spine.

"It's regarded as Steeples' masterpiece, even though it was only his second novel."

"The one about the wine trade."

"Well, yes, ostensibly. It's set in Bordeaux where he was living at the time; there are multiple layers to it, including a satire of the slave masters still operating in Africa."

"Yes, I remember from your notes."

"Take it with you, please. It's a wonderful novel."

"Thank you."

She was absent-mindedly flicking open the first pages and spotted his handwritten name on the flysheet: *Penny, Manchester 1981*. He noticed her reading the inscription.

"I bought it when I was at school," he explained. "We read it for O Level and I wanted to have my own copy."

"Manchester? I thought you were from Oxford."

"I studied there. But I haven't been to Manchester for years. Filthy place."

"Is it?"

"Well, it was. The sky was always a shade of grey. In my memory at any rate. A grimy, ashen grey. Even the grass was grey, wintry grey. Well, not really, more a washed-out green, a green with the greenness whipped out of it by the wind." He allowed himself half a laugh. "I know I should but I just can't picture a single day up there with a blue sky. When I think of Oxford I think of cloudless summer skies and soft warm air, of fresh-cut lawns, properly green, of buildings whose stones were free of soot, of furniture free of dust and oak-panelled walls and polished floors smelling of beeswax."

She waited for him to say more, but he was toying with his beard, nothing to add.

"There's a Manchester in Maine, did you know? A cute little place, a real small town out in the wilds – lakes, forest trails and such. It's about an hour's drive from Bangor."

"And there's a Bangor in North Wales."

"Really? I only really know bits of London."

Penny had moved away and was straightening the other books on the shelves.

"He dedicated it to *Béa*," she said, reading from the title page.

"That's Béatrice Valéry," he said, "the daughter of a wine merchant. She was his lover for two years."

"So, not to his wife."

"None of his writing was dedicated to Anne. Which tells us something, I suppose. Anyway," he went on after a pause, "please borrow it."

"Yes, I will. Thanks."

"And perhaps we can discuss it over dinner one evening?"

"Can we?"

"If you'd like to."

"Well, yes."

"If you think you can trust me."

She put the book into her little leather satchel and looked up to him, wrinkling her nose.

"I think I can."

"So, then. Shall I book us a table somewhere?"

"Sure."

"Here, or in Périgueux?

"In Périgueux, I think, would be better."

"If that's what you'd prefer. Next weekend?"

"Next weekend? It's Christmas, John!" she exclaimed with a laugh.

"So?"

"I'm flying off to the States on Wednesday."

He felt like a lottery winner whose ticket had just been whisked away by a passing gust of wind.

"Really? You didn't say."

"Sorry. But no, I can't. I won't be around for a couple of weeks. Daddy bought the tickets almost as soon as I left. He's desperate for me to be home for the holiday."

"I see."

"Sometime in January would be great though."

"That seems a long time away."

"Not really. I'll be back here in no time."

"Sometime in January?"

"Yeah. And it'll give me a little more time to finish the book, won't it?"

"Promise you'll read it."

"Of course I'll read it. I promise."

7

The car's underpowered engine let out a thin whine of complaint as John Penny found a low gear for a modest climb before the looping descent through the woods into the village of Montignac-sur-Vézère. He felt as though he were forcing an old pit pony to pull a tub of coal over a steep mountain pass. He had bought the little grey Peugeot back in September for a bargain price from the teacher whose apartment in AULA he had also inherited, and so far, despite a few scares and plenty of black exhaust smoke, the 206 had not let him down.

Although the day was a mild one for January, Columbine had asked for the heater to be turned up high. They were listening to music as they drove along the winding forest roads, songs from English *indie* bands, so he had called them, a genre he had been introduced to by his students in the 1990s. She was struggling to appreciate the sounds, to differentiate one song from the next, unfamiliar as they were, but was prepared to admit that the engine noise, once in the background and now very much in the foreground, was not enhancing the experience at all.

Montignac was the nearest village to the famous

prehistoric caves of Lascaux where the most sublime animal art had been painted on the walls around seventeen thousand years ago, only to be discovered by accident in 1940. The caves were another in a series of visits on which Penny had invited her since she had returned, wearily it seemed to him, from her Christmas trip to Maine. She had not wanted to talk about it but had hinted that at some point she'd had a colossal argument with her father. Penny was gratified that she had seemed genuinely pleased to see him again, and when they met for the first time, by chance in a busy corridor at AULA, she had given him the embrace of a long lost sister.

He had offered to show her something of Périgord; she had no transport of her own and gratefully accepted. Already they had visited the attractions in the towns of Les Eyzies and Sarlat, they had gone hiking in the hills above Frettignac. They talked enthusiastically of things both weighty and trivial, from political currents to favourite television shows. Although neither knew the other's country more than superficially, they each poked fun at the culture and habits of the other and then, worn out with point-scoring, would agree on how fatuous stereotypes and generalisations actually were. She had reminded him that she was older than most of the other students on her course and told him how little in common she felt she had with twenty-year-olds any more. She also told him, with a shy smile and a screwing-up of her pretty nose, that she enjoyed his company. Penny was already puzzled about his own feelings: without really knowing her, he had missed her during the long Christmas break much more than he had expected to. She was an attractive, intelligent woman, a woman with a warm, gentle but spirited personality, a woman to be respected in a way he found unfamiliar. That was his problem, he confessed to himself: he had treated people badly in the past, flippantly, carelessly, selfishly. At close to fifty years old perhaps he was finally growing up. With Columbine Snow he resolved to be more careful, more patient, indeed to be a better man. He sought to bury at the very back of his mind the awareness that she was engaged to another man, an American military man fighting in a war in a hostile moonscape of mountains four and a half thousand miles away, a man she rarely mentioned. He knew that they skyped when operations allowed, but Patrick McVie – he remembered his name perfectly well – was a taboo subject between them. Even if she could not, Penny tried as hard as he could to forget the man existed.

"Look up there!" she whispered, nudging him playfully and pointing to the rough arch of rock a metre or two above their heads, on which the shape of a galloping horse had been painted in natural dyes of dirt brown, brick red and ochre yellow. It seemed appropriate to whisper in here, a kind of underground cathedral, as dark and cold as any church in winter, filled with mystical, half-explained artistic treasures from a distant age.

They had found themselves queueing with a dozen or so middle-aged tourists, mostly from Yorkshire it appeared, waiting for the tour in English. They were loud and excitable, friends grouped together on an adventure from Leeds or wherever, cracking in-jokes and laughing like overfed hyenas. Penny and Columbine hung back a little but inside the cave there was little room and it made sense to stay close enough to the guide to hear her commentary as she illuminated the depictions on the walls with the beam of her torchlight and pointed at their details with the red dot of a laser pen. They were both overwhelmed by the sophistication and skill of the artwork, the use of the contours of the cave as outlines of the belly of an aurochs or the flank of a horse, the use of multiple images to convey a sense of movement, the attempts at perspective in pairs of legs and horns, many thousands of years before the Italian Renaissance.

The tour lasted for a little over half an hour. As they emerged into the daylight Columbine shivered and invited him to hug her for warmth.

"You know I didn't realise this cave was a facsimile," she said, letting him take her hand as they climbed the steps.

"Neither did I, to be honest," he admitted. "I'd not thought about it."

"That they should have to close the original one years ago to stop the paintings degrading from all the visitors breathing on them."

"I love the idea that apart from the few scientists allowed inside these days, the only other person granted access is the President of France."

"I wonder if they ever take it up, their privilege?"

"Probably. I would."

"Well, a copy or not, it was a beautiful experience. It *is* a pity in a way, though."

"What do you mean?"

"Well, you know, not to have seen the original. We came fifty years too late."

"I suppose so," he smiled. "Now it makes sense why they call this place Lascaux II."

"Let's buy some postcards," she said, following the others with a spring in her step towards the souvenir shop.

"Copies of copies," Penny thought to himself, striding out to catch up with her.

The audio-visual displays at the entrance to Lascaux II planted the seed of an idea in Penny's mind. He had long believed that the so-called Steeples exhibition in the library in Frettignac was inadequate, unworthy of the man's achievements, and even if the locals were less than enthused by them, to him it was frankly an embarrassment. He had searched the internet for a substantial memorial to the writer but even in his native Bristol he appeared to be little more than a footnote in that city's history, relegated to a modest collection of scripts in a university archive. He discovered that a pair of circular blue plaques adorned buildings in Bristol and London with associations to his life. There was a private museum in a village in Somerset which housed a small collection of first editions and, apparently, an original manuscript of *Calico and Silk*, but the website was clumsily done. Penny became all the more determined to do justice to the writer's memory. There were thousands of visitors to the Dordogne each year, especially British, who would have heard of the man, and many who would have read at least *Forty Barrels More*. The novel had been famously televised in the 1980s for a start, and there had been a Hollywood version, admittedly a flop, of *Capitaine Napoléonne* about ten years ago. There was so much more that could be done to improve the display, to make it a real feature of not just the library but of the town itself. For what else did Frettignac have to attract the tourists apart from its market, its architecture and its position on the river? Its association with a world-famous novelist was, in Penny's view, being utterly underplayed.

He discussed it with Columbine and she agreed to help if she could. Did he have a plan? Well, yes and no. His first task, he decided, was to find the time to arrange a meeting with the librarian herself, a Madame Rousseau, and then probably members of the town council, including the mayor, Frédéric Besse, a short, stout man whose photograph appeared with regularity in the local press. In the course of the following weeks, whenever his teaching programme would allow, Penny spent many hours pursuing leads and following advice given to him along the way towards his ambition. Monsieur Besse was shamelessly unhelpful but Camille Rousseau, a devotee of poetry, was more supportive, showing him a small storeroom in the library building that she had been meaning to sort out for years. She was a small, thin-boned woman with short silver hair, in her mid-fifties, he guessed, and she wore an unflattering grey serge jacket and a matching skirt which hung below the knee. He had no reason to doubt that she was a person of substantial character but she looked as though a fair gust of wind would be enough to blow her across the street. If enough space could be found somewhere else, she said, for whatever was worth keeping, the room could be used for the Steeples exhibits. Very briefly he felt like kissing her on the lips. It would not be immediate, she warned him, and she would appreciate some extra hands.

Any enhanced exhibition would also need money for materials, furnishings, equipment and the like. Penny contacted the town council but drew a blank, then the regional arts directive in Bordeaux, the British Council in Paris – after all he was promoting an English author – and he even decided a letter to Brussels was worth the price of a stamp to see if the European Commission could provide funds from one of their cultural grants. None of the organisations replied straight away with offers of help, directing him instead to fill in lengthy and complex online application forms, but a pleasant young man from Bordeaux did visit the town and spent half an hour over a coffee explaining the application process, adding that he thought there was a good chance that his superiors would provide a small contribution to the project. In the meantime Penny came to the conclusion that if he wanted to go ahead without serious delay he would have to pay for everything, at least initially, from his own pocket.

"Do you really want to fund this yourself?" asked Columbine as they watched the man from Bordeaux drive away.

"It's what I'll have to do," he replied, "if I'm to get the

thing started. And I shall get the money eventually. I'll be reimbursed."

"I suppose."

"I will."

"Why is it so important to you, John? I know you're a big admirer of Steeples and all, but…"

"I think it's a worthwhile project."

"Yes, I know you do."

"And I just want to do it."

"I imagine it would raise your profile in the town, even beyond."

If Penny had a selfish reason to promote the exhibition, he had kept the thought private. It seemed that Columbine, however, had in the space of a few months come to know him better than anyone else ever had. He had said nothing so obvious but she knew that he craved attention, even at this insignificant local level, she sensed that somewhere he wanted to leave a mark greater than anything he could achieve at AULA.

"Well, maybe it would, up to a point. It's only Frettignac, Col, not Paris."

"Hey, you never know where it might lead. Small acorns and all that."

The library storeroom was cleared over a weekend in March. Camille Rousseau, her husband – a burly rugby player who could carry heavy cartons as though they were filled with sponges – Penny and Columbine spent a day and a half amongst dusty books and papers, cardboard boxes, defunct computers, slabs of old magazines in elastic bands, a slide projector from the 1970s, rolls of ancient posters and other assorted forgotten items of stationery. Once the area was empty and washed down, Penny repainted the walls, employed an electrician to install new spot lighting and additional plug sockets, and had the door removed so that the space – the size of a small single bedroom – was more obvious and easily accessible. He bought two large display boards and a table, moved in the old glass cabinet, and designed a plaque to be hung by the door frame reading *ESPACE JONATHAN STEEPLES*. Items from the old display were rearranged, photographs enlarged and the text rewritten, translated and reprinted so that French and English explanations sat side by side.

"One of these days we'll need to provide German, Japanese and Chinese translations," he claimed in a moment of optimism.

Columbine looked up from her computer screen.

"It's looking so much better already, John. Great, in fact. But I think what you need now is something active."

"Active?"

"Something moving. Something else to attract people to look in. Like those projections at Lascaux."

"They're very sophisticated. And expensive. I can't afford to pay a designer for something as grand as that. At least not yet."

"Well, then, something more modest, maybe. But something to catch the eye."

"Such as?"

"Such as … I know, what about a video of some kind?"

"A film?"

"A short movie. You know, about his life and his time in France."

"We could run it on a loop on to a screen."

"Just five or ten minutes long."

"A film of what exactly? I could come up with a few scenarios, I suppose, but we'll need help with direction and all that kind of technical stuff…"

"Then why don't I talk to Elise about it tomorrow?"

Elise Correia, third-year student of cinematography at AULA, rooming two doors down the corridor from Columbine Snow, agreed to work for free on a project she realised she could actually use as part of her coursework, but hiring the university's equipment, she added apologetically, would have to be paid for. *No problem*, enthused Penny when he heard that the girl was willing to cooperate. He spent a week at his flat up in Périgueux, close enough to meet both Elise and Columbine regularly to devise a script and scenarios for a series of short films. It was decided that he would feature, in period dress, as Steeples, presenting aspects of the local area and its inspiration to his writing, scenes to include the riverside near Frettignac, its bridge, town hall and library.

"Have you acted before?" asked Elise one afternoon as they broke for coffee.

Most of my life has been an act, he wanted to say, but stopped himself from sounding pretentious.

"No, never, I've never been on stage or anything. But I don't think it's such a leap for me to play Steeples. I can learn a script. Especially if it's one I've written myself. Nobody really knows what he sounded like, how he spoke. I can give him a slight Bristol burr."

"A what?" Columbine laughed.

"I'll do an accent for him. Just a light touch. To make it real."

"But it's not real, is it, in the end?" snapped Elise. "Cinema is not real at all. That's the whole point. It's an illusion of the truth. The truth reimagined. *C'est du trucage, non?* Trickery, fakery."

"Well, I'm sure I can bring Jonathan Steeples to life, real or not," he insisted. "Don't be so po-faced, Elise. This is supposed to be fun!"

Columbine offered to play the role of Béatrice Valéry. Costumes were hired, at an exorbitant price, from a theatre company in Périgueux, and eventually they set aside a Friday in April, at the start of the summer term, for a daybreak-to-dusk session of filming, including a scene or two in Bergerac also, if time allowed. When everything was more or less in place Penny suddenly decided to script one extra scene: Steeples and Béatrice could embrace on a riverside bench, ideally in the golden glow of a setting sun.

"We need to show the intensity of their relationship," he declared. "Their love inspired many of his best poems in the Garonne *Reflections.*"

"Is the sunset really necessary?" asked Elise irritably. "We can't guarantee a photogenic sunset. We might get a cloudy evening instead."

"We'll take the chance. I suppose any evening light will reflect how their time together was coming to an end."

Columbine read the scene and said nothing.

"You'll do it, won't you?" asked Elise when they were alone together later.

"If John thinks it's important."

"It's only a kiss. And it's not real. You're not betraying Patrick or anything like that."

"I know."

"And, well, he is a nice-looking man."

"I know."

They shared a smile.

"I know."

"So do it. It's simply a role-play. You're *acting* being in love."

"I get it. I get it, Elise. But I'm just not a very good actor, is all."

8

It was during the Easter holidays, as the days were lengthening, as the sun was strengthening and as the yellow-green catkins on the walnut trees began to emerge in abundant, dangly clusters, that Penny received a short email from his sister informing him that their mother had died.

His instinctive reaction was one of shock, then of sadness. The more he reflected, however, he concluded that it was news he didn't really want to know. His mother had been dead to him for years, never more than a Christmas card sent to the old address and that out of fossilised habit. He had given no meaningful thought beyond mild contempt to that house, to that dark street in that dreary town full of stunted, pasty-faced ghosts in cheap clothes, that rain-sodden nest of small minds and low aspirations and stale cigarette smoke.

Did he really feel sad that his mother had died? Did he feel emptiness, relief? Did he actually feel anything at all? At that moment he was simply annoyed that Michelle had upset the equilibrium of a lovely April morning in his precious corner of Périgord. He made himself a mug of tea and gave himself more time to think.

He went for a walk up to the top of the grove, and sat on the crest for a little while, breathing in the sweet air until the dampness in the earth seeped through to his trousers. He made himself something for lunch. He found a few students' essays he had been meaning to mark. He checked his emails again: still at the top of the inbox list was the message, blunt and unembroidered, from the sister in London he hadn't seen for over twenty-five years. He could email her back, he supposed, but she had included a telephone number. It would be too evasive, too cowardly, not to call her. He tidied the kitchen first, washing and drying a few dishes, a little cutlery, and carefully putting it all away in the drawers. Finally he fished out his mobile from a jacket pocket, put on his glasses, checked the battery strength and then slowly dialled her number.

"Michelle?" he asked, realising that his voice was dry and husky. He carried the phone into the kitchen.

"Trevor? Is that you?"

"Hello, Michelle," he said, sipping from a glass of water.

"Trevor?"

"I call myself John these days. Please don't call me Trevor."

"You got my email then?" said the sister, ignoring his self-indulgence. Her voice sounded different: Lancashire remained, of course, but the pitch was deeper, older. He hadn't expected to speak to the middle-aged woman she had become.

"I did. This morning. I'm sorry to hear the news about Mum."

"She died three days ago."

"At home?"

"In hospital. She's been in a care home for these past four years."

"I didn't know."

"I know you didn't."

Penny was uncertain how to respond.

"You've just about abandoned us, really," she went on, "haven't you?"

"I have my own life to live, Michelle."

"Listen, I'm not going to argue with you, Trevor, It's just that it would have been nice to have had a bit of support, especially this last year. We had to sell up and move her down to a home near me."

"You still in London?"

"Clapham, yeah."

"How's Davie?"

"He's okay," she sighed. "Bearing up. He took it pretty bad. Even though it wasn't a surprise. She's had heart problems for ages. On top of dementia."

"I'm sorry."

"Are you? Are you, really?"

"I'm sorry. What do you want me to say?"

Was she letting him hang deliberately or had the conversation reached a dead end?

"It took me ages to track you down," she said after a moment.

"I'm living in France now."

"So I gathered. I got your email address from the last place you worked at in England. Eventually. You were a bugger to find."

"Well, thanks for getting in touch."

"Anyway, the funeral's at the end of the month."

"Oh."

"You *will* be coming?"

"I'm not sure."

"What?"

"Are you really expecting me?"

"She *was* your mother, Trevor! It's your own mother's funeral, for pity's sake! Yes, we *are* expecting you!"

"I don't know. It would seem hypocritical."

"Listen, Trevor. Get down off your high horse and act like a son for once. A proper son. A son whose mother has suffered a pitiful old age and a painful death. Show some respect, for Christ's sake!"

"I'd feel awkward. Unwelcome, after all this time."

"I don't really care how you'd feel. It's not just about you."

"Well, as far as I'm concerned, it *is* about me."

"I can't believe I'm having this conversation."

"I'll think about it, Michelle. How's that? That's my best answer right now."

There was a long silence on the line, like a chasm expanding between them.

"Michelle?" he asked eventually. "You still there?"

He sensed he could hear her sobbing quietly but it could have been interference on the line.

"Michelle? When did you say the date was?"

"The date?"

There was still anger in her voice.

"For the funeral."

"The 26th. It's a Friday. It'll be at the crem near me in West Norwood."

"The 26th?"

He didn't need to think about the date; it was the day Elise had arranged for the filming.

"I can sort you out a hotel if you want me to."

"I can't come."

"What?"

"I can't come."

"You *can't*? What do you mean, you suddenly *can't*?"

"It's not that I don't want to. I can't. I've got something on here on that day, that Friday. Something important. Something I can't rearrange."

"Something you can't cancel for a funeral?"

"Sorry. I'm afraid not."

There was more silence as brother and sister stewed, the one invisible from the other, the atmosphere between them ever tauter.

"So, that's it, is it?" she asked. "You're decided? Our David will be devastated."

"I'm afraid you'll have to manage without me."

"Are you for real?"

"You heard what I said, Michelle."

"So you'll not be coming?"

"Very unlikely."

"Well, fuck you, Trevor, you bastard! You're a disgrace."

The phone went dead immediately.

Penny stared out through the window but only the face of his sister filled the space. He saw her as a teenager still, keeping a spiteful eye on him even now. Then her image faded and his pang of guilt lasted just a short moment longer.

9

The rehearsals for the filming went well. Penny, having written the scripts, found it easy to learn his lines and Columbine enthusiastically committed her much shorter part to memory.

"You must resist the urge to giggle on set," Elise reminded them both. "Real actors rise above all that. You'll have to focus properly or else it will look like an amateurish piece of rubbish."

"Yes, dear Elise," stuttered Columbine, looking at Penny and trying to disguise a smile. "Of course you are right. Absolutely."

The locations had been scouted and checked for lighting, sound quality, frequency of background traffic, and finally Elise and the friend she had bullied into helping as a sound engineer were both satisfied. They had tried to find a stretch of river where they might spot a heron, where they might film a take-off or a landing or, even better, a diving kill. So far there had been no sightings; perhaps it was the wrong time of the year, perhaps you just had to be incredibly lucky to see one.

Meanwhile it had crossed Penny's mind that, in

the interests of authenticity, Columbine would have to remove her engagement ring in her scenes as Béa. He was not surprised but nonetheless irritated when she refused.

"I don't imagine anyone will even notice," offered Elise in support of her friend.

But Penny was adamant.

"If we are going to do this at all, we are going to do it properly. And that means historical accuracy. Béatrice Valéry was not engaged at that time in her life. It would be misleading, it would be wrong. Actually sloppy."

"I'm not prepared to take off this ring," Columbine maintained. "Least not for a thirty-second video where my hands aren't even in close-up."

"I think you're being unreasonable."

"I think *you're* being unreasonable."

It was the first time they had had crossed words. Elise suggested that a pair of light silk gloves would be a solution, which indeed it was: a solution that both Penny and Columbine accepted and laughed about later.

The day before the filming Penny was asked to cover a seminar for an absent colleague and he could not refuse. When Columbine called into his apartment after breakfast he was flustered and short-tempered.

"He's in a terrible mood today, my dear," commented Henrik the Swede, raising his eyebrows as he passed her on the stairs.

"Listen, John," she suggested once she had made him a coffee and settled him down at the table. "You go into college, do what you have to. It's not a big deal. I can go into town and pick up the costumes on my own. I don't have anything on till after lunch. I'll manage just fine."

"I suppose," he admitted. "I've got so much on my plate today, it's not funny."

"Relax. I'll take your car, okay? That's okay, isn't it?"

"Yes, of course."

"Cool."

"The keys are in the hall."

"I may as well go right now. They'll be open by the time I get there. See you in the canteen for lunch? Around one?"

"I'll try," he said, picking up the coffee cups and rinsing them under the tap.

"Do you want me to mail this letter for you?" she called from the hallway.

"Letter?"

"It's under your car keys. Is it a card? Addressed to Michelle Penny, Clapham. Isn't that your sister's name?"

Columbine was not supposed to see that envelope. Penny had been meaning to post it for the past day or two but kept forgetting: a sympathy card, a token apology for missing the funeral.

"Leave it," he shouted. "I'll deal with it. Just go and pick up the costumes."

"Fine. See you later."

"Yeah," he grumbled.

Penny put his heart and soul into his seven-and-a-half-minute performance as the frock-coated Victorian writer

Jonathan Steeples, recalling incidents that had influenced his work, visiting notable places, quoting lines of verse, a sentence or two of significant prose in a stilted, faintly West Country accent. Sometimes he posed with a meaningful, soulful glance at the river, or the sky, or into the eyes of Béatrice Valéry who stood at his side holding a parasol in a dress that reached the floor and gloves that reached her elbows.

If Elise filmed him with the intense eye of a hawk, Columbine too watched him studiously, missing nothing. She witnessed a grace, an intelligence, an earnestness which she had come to expect. He wasn't in any way the insincere, sharp-tongued libertine she had heard rumours about back in September. She enjoyed his company, he was kind, funny and generous. And respectful. He had touched her hand, had kissed her cheek. She had felt his warmth, she knew his particular smell. But he had pushed her no further, made no uninvited advances, no coded suggestive remarks.

If she was so pleased with their friendship, so happy to help him with his project, what then was this curious feeling lurking in the background? Disappointment? Anticipation? Behind the beating of her heart could she hear the distant sound of gunfire rattling over the head of her fiancé as he cowered in a shattered village somewhere in Helmand Province? It was confusion that she felt, if anything. Confusion, and a little fear.

When it came to their filmed embrace, caught in the reflected orange glow dancing on the surface of the Vézère, as he gently pulled her head close to his own, she kissed him with a passion whose truth surprised him, excited him and left him wondering just how much of that brief moment had been an act.

The *Espace Jonathan Steeples* was ready for visitors. Freshly painted, exhibits crisply displayed, it now offered an audiovisual experience of a standard close to professional on a large brand new computer screen paid for, initially at least, by Penny himself. He was coming to terms with the only deficiency in Elise Correia's film: the missing heron, the one he had hoped to see at the edge of the river as he recited the first verse of *Lord of the Lake*. She had pasted in a twenty-second clip of a bird she had found on YouTube instead; it was better than nothing, he had agreed, but the flat, open wetlands in the background looked more like Norfolk than Périgord.

Monsieur Besse the Mayor had been invited to the library to officially open the room, but, regrettably as his office had said, he was unavailable. In his stead, Camille Rousseau bought herself a new hairstyle to cut the scarlet ribbon and was photographed doing so by Amande Puybonieux and a press photographer who had come along with a young reporter from *Dordogne Libre*. A small gathering had assembled in the library, including Columbine, Elise and Amande, to watch and listen, to chat and drink a small glass of *vin mousseux* as Penny too was photographed and interviewed and roundly congratulated.

"We can devote a page on the library website to today's

events," said Madame Rousseau, inspired to burst into English as she patted him maternally on the arm.

"I'll get AULA to do something on theirs too," he nodded. "It's reflected glory for them."

As the building gradually cleared and quietened, Penny and Columbine wandered outside for a breath of air and found an empty bench to sit on with a view of the bridge.

"Glory?" she teased.

"Did I say *glory*?"

"You sure did."

"Oh, well."

"It isn't much more than a spruced up old broom cupboard, Dr Penny."

"Hey, it's *my* broom cupboard!"

"I'm sorry. I'm joking."

"Yes, well. Please don't mock," he said, grinning through his self-importance.

They watched a pair of pigeons land close to their feet, peck around at the loose gravel for a moment and then fly off, the one a second or two before the other.

"But it does matter to you," she picked up, "doesn't it?"

"What?"

"A bit of reflected glory. Alright, *recognition*, is that a better word? You have a need to be noticed."

He smiled, firstly to himself and then to her.

"It's a modest thing, I know, but maybe the start of something. The start of a Steeples industry. Not industry, that's the wrong word, more an awareness, delivering a message. Head curator: Dr John Penny. Me."

114

Columbine smiled back. She had read him perfectly.

"Yes, you're right," he went on slowly. "I do need it, recognition. A bit of fame, something like that."

"I can understand that, John," she said. "I'm not like you but I can understand a person's need for acknowledgement."

"It's hard to find as an academic, if that's what I've become. In other fields it's easy to be famous, if you're any good: sport, entertainment, politics, or just if you're rich."

"You want to be loved."

He paused to take in the weight of those five words.

"Yes," he said. "Yes, you're dead right. I do."

"Weren't you loved as a child?"

He laughed ironically.

"Listen, I had an okay childhood. My parents weren't cruel or vicious or anything, but the whole experience, what I can now recall of it, was just, well, just neutral. Flat, somehow. Uninspiring. Forgettable."

"So you were loved or you weren't?"

"I wasn't *un*loved."

An open-topped sports car drove past almost noiselessly, with a woman at the wheel in a crimson headscarf: nobody he knew, but he watched her until she merged into the evening traffic and disappeared.

"You remember that song I played in the car the other day?" he asked presently.

"You played a whole bunch of songs."

"*I Wanna Be Adored.* The Stone Roses?"

"Vaguely."

"He sings it over and over: *I wanna be adored.* Guitar,

bass, drums, vocals. It's more than a cry for adoration, I think. It's a cry for help. A cry for warmth. I think that's about where I am right now. Where I've been for ages."

She took his hand in hers. He looked up to her, into her big, deep, brown eyes, and saw her smile.

"I think Camille already adores you, anyway," she said. "And you have another fan right here."

She squeezed his hand and stared back at him.

"That's the look Béa gives Steeples in the film," he said quietly.

"Is it?"

"We gave the costumes back, Col. You don't need to stay in character any longer."

"I'm not," she said. "This is me, John. Just me."

10

Quite how John Penny came to be sitting to the right hand of the owner of the Château du Beautrottoir, sharing his foie gras, sipping his chilled Pouilly Fuissé, one of five dinner guests on a warm evening in the middle of May, he could only guess. The woman to *his* right, early forties, her slim figure and small breasts covered by a flamingo-pink silk blouse, touched his arm softly and said:

"It's about time that somebody raised the profile of our town's literary heritage."

She put her napkin to her mouth and gave a quiet, short cough to clear her throat before adding mischievously:

"Pity it had to be an Englishman."

She laughed and waited for a reaction. Penny swallowed his wine.

"Steeples is, after all, one of ours, *madame*," he replied. "I'm glad you approve nevertheless."

Well, of course, he was here because of the *Espace* in the library. The brief wave of publicity Penny was riding was at its modest crest and he was suddenly a minor celebrity in a town patiently waiting for the tourist season to bring back some sparkle.

"Your husband was very supportive in giving us a quarter-page in his newspaper," he went on, aiming a glance towards the balding man in a patterned bow tie directly opposite him who was listening to a long story in French about solar panels related by the baron himself. Penny had been introduced to the features editor of *Dordogne Libre* less than half an hour earlier over champagne cocktails on the terrace.

The dining room had walls panelled in light oak and was illuminated by the soft glow of dozens of electric candles adorning two enormous gilt candelabras. He noticed that one of the little lightbulbs had gone out and needed replacing. Further down the table beyond the journalist's wife sat Columbine Snow in a loose-fitting mint-green designer tee-shirt. He hoped she wasn't too uncomfortable, trapped as she was in conversation with the baroness, a fragile, bony-faced woman with a shrill laugh, and an elderly man in a crimson corduroy jacket who seemed to be having difficulty, if not in breathing perhaps, then at least in swallowing his food, which had been cut up for him into bitesize pieces in the kitchen.

"As I was saying earlier," the baron was now addressing Penny, "I enjoy having interesting new people come to the château. And of course with foreigners such as yourself, Dr Penny, it is a pleasure to practise my English."

"It's perfectly fluent," replied Penny, "and please, call me John."

"Of course. You know, I seem to speak French less and less," he laughed. "We do get over to the United States quite regularly these days. The children, you see."

118

"Oh?"

"Our son is now a junior at Harvard, our daughter a sophomore at Stanford. East coast, west coast. An entire continent apart."

"I see."

"Excellent institutions, of course, the both of them."

"I believe so."

"I have no doubt my wife is quizzing your fiancée about the American education system right now. Quite a bonus to have an American on board."

"She's not actually my fiancée," stated Penny.

"Well, she behaves like it!" laughed the baron. It was true that Columbine had clung to him for support over drinks like a shy lover.

"She wears a ring, I think," he continued. "Third finger, left hand. Am I right?"

"Yes. Yes, she does," answered Penny, already weary of the subject. "She *is* engaged, as a matter of fact, but not to me."

"I see. I can sense it is something you are not so comfortable with. I apologise for mentioning it. A private matter, no doubt."

"Indeed."

"And where did *you* study, John?" he asked, moving on discreetly.

"Oxford."

The single word was enough, a passport to respect.

"Excellent. Such a reputation. But it's not a city I know, sadly. And now you teach at our university in Bordeaux, no?"

"Not exactly."

"No?"

He regretted his words immediately. Had he suddenly lost the ability to bluff? Whatever, it was already too late.

"I'm at AULA," he said, raising his tone optimistically.

"AULA? In Périgueux?"

Penny nodded.

"Oh dear." The baron wiped his lips with the corner of his napkin as if he were erasing a blasphemous remark. "Nothing but bad reports."

He smiled sympathetically before resuming:

"I suppose it's the clientele you get. A rather proletariat student body, am I right? Mind you, from what I've seen of some of the teaching staff too… leftists, militants, no? Not all of them, I'm sure. But some. A little more Fuissé, John?"

Nine days ago Penny had never heard of the Château du Beautrottoir. Originally a thirteenth-century manor house, extensively rebuilt in the nineteenth century, it stood in a large forested park about ten kilometres south of Frettignac, and the circular windows in its twin turrets gave a distant view of the wide, sweeping bend in the course of the Vézère. Once he had steered the Peugeot off the main road, he followed the curving driveway up into the woods, then along an avenue lined with mature beech trees and covered in beautifully arranged shiny-smooth cobblestones which glinted here and there in the ribbons of evening sunlight. The boulevard, perhaps five hundred metres in length, brought them directly to the main entrance of the cream stone château where a young man wearing a white shirt, black trousers and a rather feeble moustache had greeted them politely and led them inside to an airy reception room. Spirited piano music was playing at a subdued volume: Chopin, perhaps, but Penny was not certain.

The baron, a healthily tanned man of about the same age as Penny, had approached them with an open hand extended in welcome. He was tall, a little jowly with short, thick hair already greying and had a handsome face Penny had seen before in the pages of not only the local but also the national press. He was casually dressed in a pure white polo shirt, a mid-grey cashmere cardigan, buttoned, and chinos the colour of biscuit.

"*Enchanté de vous voir*, Dr Penny, Mademoiselle Snow. *Je suis Jean-Louis Sainte-Marie Lachêne du Beautrottoir.* My friends call me Ludo. Easier than the other, *non*?"

His smile was indulgently reciprocated.

"And let me present my wife," he continued, "*Madame la baronne.*"

The woman had held out a thin, loose hand which Penny gently shook. Was he expected to lift it to his lips? Probably not. Columbine followed his example nervously.

"*Enchantée*," said the baroness. "Please, you must call me Mirabelle."

"And our other guests," interrupted the baron, "are out on the terrace. It's too lovely to be inside. *Suivez-moi, s'il vous plaît.*"

By the time the main course had been cleared away,

Penny felt he had the measure of the baron. He was an ostentatious, opinionated snob, that was obvious – he spoke in admiration of what he perceived to be a rigorous class system flourishing in England – but he was no more intelligent, no wiser, no better than any of his guests. He had poked fun at Penny and Penny had absorbed it gamely. Now it was time to give him some back.

"Do you know Manchester, Ludo?" he asked, idly straightening his dessert spoon.

"The city? No, I've never been there. No reason to."

"I actually meant the man. The Earl of Manchester."

"The Earl?"

"Yes. Lovely chap. He does a lot of charity work these days. Thought you might know him. He's a relation of mine, in fact. Our mothers are half-cousins or some such. His mother was Lady Arabella of Moss Side."

"Really? Then you have a little aristocratic blood in your veins too, my friend."

"I suppose I do. Half a pint or so, maybe."

The baron laughed.

"He has a modest estate in Cheshire," Penny continued. "We visit every Christmas."

"Cheshire?"

"Like the cheese."

"And the cat in *Alice in Wonderland*?"

"Exactly, Ludo. You are well read, even if you haven't read any Steeples yet."

"I aim to start. You have whetted my appetite."

A maid appeared carrying a tray laden with glass bowls of what looked like raspberry meringue.

"Yes, every Christmas," Penny ploughed on. "Weather permitting we go hunting in the forests nearby. *La chasse*."

"*La chasse*, of course."

"My favourite is the royal forest of Salford. Perhaps you have heard of it?"

"Salford? No. The hunting is for game?"

"Actually, no. It's mostly for women. *La chasse aux femmes*. Chasing skirt, you understand."

The baron hesitated, then replied:

"You are making a fool of me, Monsieur John. Yes? And I thought you were such a polite chap."

Penny laughed, in the hope of encouraging the same from the baron, but his host suddenly removed his napkin from his lap, stood up, shook it vigorously in the direction of Penny, and began to walk down the table, behind the editor, behind his wife, towards the elderly man.

"I forgive you, *monsieur*, I do. I am in a forgiving mood. Now, Oncle Charlot," he shouted, raising a hand to touch the old man affectionately on the shoulder, "how did you find the guinea fowl? *Pas trop cuit, j'espère*."

The meal was delicious and drawn out but the evening did not turn into a long one. Great Uncle Charlie was already drowsy before his brandy and the baroness made unnecessary excuses for him and led him up to a guest room on the first floor. The editor insisted he had an early start the following day – an important meeting with the proprietors in Bordeaux at nine – and he left with his slightly squiffy wife shortly after coffee.

By this time they had moved into a drawing room, a large space with long, curtained windows which nevertheless felt cluttered with furniture. A shiny black grand piano guarded one corner and the walls were hung with ancient tapestries and heavy framed portraits of somebody's anaemic ancestors. The baroness was at the far end of the room showing Columbine a collection of vintage prints of views of the château. The baron had pulled Penny to one side.

"I like you, Monsieur John," he said, lowering his voice, "but do not treat me as a buffoon. I do not know what impression you are trying to create in our *commune*, but I trust your intentions are honourable."

Penny was unsure how he should react to the man's neutral stare.

"As for your impersonation of a man of nobility," the baron went on, "you have a little way to go. Your appearance is quite acceptable – we have no truck with formality at our little soirées here at Beautrottoir – your manners are almost impeccable, even making fun of your host is forgivable if it involves a certain charm, I would say. But do you know what gives you away, Monsieur John? What gives you away as a very *ordinary* man?"

Before Penny had a chance to even decide if he wanted to hear an answer, the baron spoke again, in almost a whisper:

"Your shoes, Penny. Simply your shoes. I can always tell what I would call a true gentleman, frankly, by the quality of his footwear."

His eyes met Penny's briefly, in a look as cold as winter. Then, with the flicker of a smile:

"Now, do you imagine your girlfriend who isn't actually your fiancée is ready for another cognac? I'm afraid Mirabelle is boring the knickers off her over there."

Not much after ten o'clock they were standing in the hallway, the four of them, waiting for the boy to fetch Columbine's coat.

"Before you go," said the baron, gently tugging at Penny's arm, "let me show you something interesting."

He led him into a side room, which was revealed, once he had switched on a trio of matching table lamps, to be a large study, covered on two sides by walnut bookshelves and at the centre of which stood an antique writing desk dominated by an oversized computer screen.

"Look here. What do you make of this, then?"

The baron was already standing by a wall cabinet and had opened a shallow drawer at waist height. Penny approached and fished out his glasses to study the contents of a plain beige card folder. Inside was a single sheet of paper, aged and torn across the bottom, on which was written, in a distinctive hand he immediately recognised, five lines of poetry under the capitalised title: *LORD OF THE LAKE.*

"Take it," said the baron. "Have a good look."

Longshore lord of lake and stream
With muscled arch of skysail wing
Lifts from the mudbanks with unbridled spring
To soar, the heron, then glide supreme

Highborn hunter from a prehistoric dream.

They were the lines Penny knew by heart, the first five lines, annotated, just like the examples at the library, in heavy pencil, with snippets of suggested French translations:

L'essor du héron, vol plané de gloire
Chasseur altier d'un rêve de préhistoire

"Why is it torn?" he asked presently. "The final three lines are missing."

"I don't know the answer to that," replied the baron. "But I do know that this is an original script. In Steeples' own hand. You recognise it, I imagine."

"Yes. Yes, it's his hand."

He passed it back carefully as if it were a holy relic.

"If you don't mind me asking, why isn't it in the exhibition with the other verses? Why is it here?"

"Well, because it belongs to my family, Monsieur John. Isn't that obvious?"

"Would you be prepared to *lend* it to the library? For the sake of completion, if nothing else?"

"Well, you are the first person to ask permission, so that is gratifying, but I'm afraid it's out of the question. It is an original artefact, you see. On the other hand, the verses in the library, in your *Espace*, have never been verified. And in any case, you don't have the security to guarantee its safety."

"We could upgrade the systems."

"*Non, monsieur.* It is going nowhere, as the Americans might say. It is staying here."

He placed the folder on the desk and guided Penny to the door.

"Now, I imagine your girlfriend is ready to go home." In the hallway the baroness was pointing to a pattern in the floor. The whole area was surfaced with small, smooth pebbles embedded in a kind of glazed cement.

"We call it *pisé*," she was explaining, "*très typique de la région*. And here, I was just showing Columbine, Dr Penny, the design made with the light-coloured stones, you see, in the shape of a heart? Yes? And inside the heart..."

Columbine and Penny moved closer to see, despite the dim lighting, the initials T and C.

"...Thibaut and Cathérine Fontenay d'Auluc," she continued, in the vein of a tour guide, "the owners of the château at the start of the nineteenth century who had so much of it rebuilt. A love affair and a marriage that lasted for fifty years."

"My wife is an unashamed romantic," interrupted the baron in mock apology.

"I have invited Columbine to use the pool, *chéri*," said the baroness, stepping over to take his hand. "You too, of course, Dr Penny, when the weather warms up. We will be absent for much of June and July."

"California," added her husband. "That's a nice idea. The house will be open. Ask for Zacharie when you arrive. He's our head gardener. He can let you through the gate to the pool. Yes, you are most welcome to use it."

"Thank you, Mirabelle," said Columbine. "I'm sure we'll drive up and have a swim, if you're sure you don't mind."

"Of course not."

"Provided that you don't bring along any of those undesirables from AULA," added the baron with a wink in Penny's direction.

"He's not a real baron, you know."

"What do you mean?"

"He's not, John. He's playing at it. He calls himself a baron but he's no more an aristocrat than you or me."

A week after their dinner at the Château du Beautrottoir, Columbine and Penny had met up for lunch in the canteen at AULA. He had a pile of examination scripts to mark but it was no sacrifice to make room in his day for an hour with her. In any case he expected that the marking wouldn't take him long; much of his students' work was superficial, trite even. So few of them seemed to actually enjoy reading, researching or putting together an energising, insightful analysis of anything at all.

He happened to meet her in the queue. They had both chosen the pasta and sat down at a table by one of the open windows.

"Of course he's a baron. All that history in the château…"

"*His* history only goes back one generation. His father bought the place in the 1950s."

"How do you know all this? You've got mayonnaise on your chin, by the way."

"Amande told me."

"Amande?"

"You know, Amande, the lady in the library."

"So, you're a friend of the old librarian now, are you?"

"Well, not exactly."

"She's just a volunteer, by the way."

"Yes, I know. She told me."

"Did she?"

"She's nice, isn't she?"

"I suppose."

"Nice and helpful."

"Do you speak in French to her, then?"

"A little of both. She speaks good English, you know."

"She speaks English? I never knew."

"People have hidden talents, I guess."

"She speaks English?" he said again, this time to himself, scratching his beard.

"Anyway," Columbine went on, "she told me the so-called baron's father made a fortune importing tobacco after the war. Bought the château, tidied the place up, renovated parts of it – it was crumbling, apparently. Quite neglected. His son has just continued the story. Maintained the illusion of the Lachênes as a family of nobility. It's all a charade."

"I would never have guessed."

"When you actually boil it down, Ludo's no more a baron than you are, John."

11

As the month of June slipped into July, as the green fruit on the walnut trees slowly swelled and ripened, the sight of ever more minibuses pulling trailers laden with canoes along the riverside roads prompted Penny to invite Columbine for a gentle paddle downstream one afternoon.

"I was all for suggesting it myself," she enthused.

"I picked up a few leaflets from the tourist office," he said. "They're all more or less the same. You just choose your exact route, how long you want to be on the river. I think we can just turn up. No need to book anything. By the way, I saw your friend Amande there."

"*My* friend? She's *your* landlady too."

"Yeah, but you're the one she likes chatting to."

"Don't exaggerate, John."

"It seems she volunteers at the tourist office as well as the library."

"Yes, I know."

"I thought you might."

"Two mornings a week."

"Really?"

"I think that's what she said."

"Well, then, I'm sure you're right."

"So, you said you've canoed before?" Penny asked the following day as they were driving northwards towards the base they had chosen to use.

"Lots of kayaking. Pretty much the same thing. Lots of lake kayaking back home."

"It sounds fun."

"Yeah, we had a lot of fun camping out in the wild. Mainly with my folks, you know, as a kid. On summer vacations."

"And Patrick?"

He regretted mentioning the man's name the moment it had passed his lips; he couldn't think why he had.

"Yeah, Patrick too. He's a strong kayaker. White water and all."

He turned up the volume on the radio.

"This is a great song," he stated, accelerating the flagging 206 to overtake a fluorescent posse of cyclists.

Once at the base they had to wait a while for a group to assemble before a driver would take them further north to start their river journey back southwards. They found some shade and sat with a few tourists, mostly English, clutching cumbersome life jackets as if they were about to abandon a sinking cruise ship. The manager of the operation, when he finally decided the time was right, sauntered up to them all in sweat-stained tee-shirt, shorts and flip-flops, grunted, pointed in the direction of a dusty old minibus and hitched up a trailer as the passengers embarked. Penny had not met a ruder man for a long time; he made Frédéric Besse the mayor seem quite charming.

It was a simply beautiful afternoon. The sun, gaining its early summer warmth, shone high above them and sparkled on the water, its rays filtering through the high trees in the narrows like a heavenly blessing. The gentlest of breezes caressed the tree tops and tickled the surface of the Vézère, and as their fellow travellers spaced out behind and ahead, Penny and Columbine found themselves paddling along in a relaxed rhythm, almost soundlessly, only the soft scooping of the water, the echo of distant voices and the warbling and cooing of the birds breaking the silence.

The slow-running current helped them along and the canoeing was easy, almost effortless. With Columbine sitting in the prow and Penny six feet or so behind her trying to follow her lead, they struck up a comfortable tempo and soon there was a harmony in their movement, even in their breathing, a symmetry to his strokes on the left, hers on the right, piloting the boat in a perfect line through the clear water. Penny was surprised that he suddenly felt blissfully happy. He could only see the bright yellow of the back of her life jacket and the soft flow of the breeze through her sun-kissed auburn hair. He could only imagine her bright eyes set on the river ahead or on the dark undergrowth beneath the trees or following a sparrowhawk emerging from the high branches. He could only guess at the set of her lips, the exact angle of her perfect nose, her expression. He couldn't see that she too was smiling, content, imagining him sitting behind her, dependably mirroring her strokes, smoothly doubling their momentum.

"You paddle pretty good," she shouted back to him,

teasing, "for a professor. Did you do much of this at school?"

He pretended not to hear. His parents had never even heard of a school with a rowing club, never mind having the gumption to send him to one.

They had chosen to navigate a two-hour route which took them downstream past tiny islands, through areas of dense woodland, skirting craggy limestone cliffs and catching glimpses of farmland and campsites and isolated cottages as they drifted by. After about an hour they pulled into the shore at one of the camping grounds which advertised a riverside *buffet*. Clambering out of the canoe was harder than clambering in. They steered hard on to the gravelly sandbank and Columbine was able to step out with ease. Penny stood up too early, however, and discovered the rear of the boat, still afloat, wobbling uncontrollably as he tried to step forward. Losing his balance, he almost fell sideways but managed to jump out into the shallows, splashing up the water as he tumbled into her arms.

"Sorry!" he spluttered. "Not the most elegant manoeuvre."

"It's fine," she laughed, still clinging on to him as he steadied himself on the uneven ground. "You haven't drowned."

The flicker of a thought occurred to both of them that they were holding each other a fraction longer than was necessary.

"These life jackets are real passion-killers," he joked, pulling away and turning back to the canoe to straighten up the oars.

"Let me buy you a beer," she offered, watching him.

"Sounds good. The colder the better."

Penny's feet were dry in no time. They found a bench in the sun in a quiet garden at the edge of the campsite; a few distant voices rang out but they were undisturbed. There was a smell of meat grilling on a barbecue, the chink of glasses over by the bar where a small group of teenagers were telling each other stories.

"So, how is your sister?" Columbine asked, quite out of the blue.

"My sister?"

"Yes. Michelle, isn't it? Didn't you send her a card or something a while ago? You two back in touch?"

"I sent her a card, that's all," Penny said dismissively. "Hardly back in touch."

"What does she do for a living?"

Penny sighed at the thought of making idle conversation about his sister.

"The last thing I knew was she was in advertising," he said. "Design, graphics, something like that."

"Did she ever marry?"

"I don't know. I got a Christmas card about ten years ago from her and a guy called Rob, but I have no idea who he is, who he was."

"You're very defensive talking about your family, John," she went on, looking up from her drink. "Why is that?"

"What *is* this?"

"Tell me, John. I don't feel I know the whole you. I

know bits and pieces. I want to know more. Why did you two drift apart?"

He took a sip of beer and fell silent, gazing through a gap in the trees towards the river. It was hard to talk to anyone about his family but even harder to deny this woman. He had never met anyone like her, anyone so sincere. If she wasn't worth opening up to a little, then who was? A problem shared, and all that. But then again, he had never thought of his secrets as problems. Secrets, even dark secrets, and problems were not the same thing, were they?

She was waiting for an answer, but she wouldn't wait forever.

"You won't like it," he said at last.

"Try me."

"I think I've become a different person these past few months, Col. What I was like before, and me and my sister go a long way back, was not so edifying."

"Try me."

"We were never close, for a start. She was closer to her brother."

"You said."

"Davie. They were twins. They *are* twins. There's a bond between them which kind of shut me out."

He looked up to the sky, scratched at the stubble on his chin, caught sight of a cloud that looked vaguely like the shape of Australia.

"Growing up, I just happened to live in the same house as her. As them. I've never spoken about this, really. Not to anyone."

"I'm sorry. I'm not forcing you to."

"It's okay. I feel like I can talk to you about anything."

He took a deep breath, gave himself a moment to collect his thoughts.

"What broke us apart was her wedding," he said finally. "Well, the wedding that didn't happen. Because of me."

"Of you?"

"Because I was a selfish, arrogant shit, I suppose."

"Hey, I won't judge you," said Columbine after a moment's silence. "Whatever you tell me."

Penny smiled a smile of resignation.

"Michelle was engaged to this lad, Mark," he took up with a sense of inevitability. "A soft lad, head in the clouds, pretty face, I don't know if she loved him, but I suppose she did. I don't remember if I was jealous of him, or even jealous of her. I think I thought I was doing her a favour, that he wasn't good enough for her. I think that's what I told myself. But it was spite, really. It was a nasty thing to do, breaking them up, I can see that, of course I can. And I did it just because I knew I could."

She let him pause, take a drink, then carry on.

"It was his stag do, stag night, I don't know what you would call it in America."

"I know what you mean. Like a bachelor party."

"Yeah, the weekend before the wedding. We'd been out in Manchester, me, him, a few of his mates from college. Pubs, clubs, singing in the streets, the usual drunken nonsense. No trouble, nobody got hurt or anything like that. We finished up in a hotel where we'd booked rooms.

I ended up sharing with Mark. It was all planned. He was drunker than me, we smoked some weed, and, anyway, the long and short of it, I seduced him. I knew exactly what I was doing. Man sex. Full on."

He looked at Columbine. Her expression was unflinching. *Go on*, her eyes were demanding.

"We woke up next morning, his mates banging on the door, going down for their full English, and there's Mark, half asleep, mortified. *What have we done?* he's asking me. *You gave into your real instincts, Marky*, I say. *Face it, you're gay and you've known it for ages. And you know what that means, don't you? You're no good for our Michelle. You can't marry her and live a lie.* The boy's in fits of tears. Blubbing and swearing and throwing up in the bathroom. And of course, he calls it off, just days to go, everything arranged, church, reception, honeymoon. Michelle's beside herself with anger. Her world is turned upside down. She'd been mad about him, met him at college, he was clever, funny, a budding artist. She saw him as her ticket out of town, I reckon, away to something better."

He looked to finish his beer but the glass was already empty.

"She found out about my part in it later," he resumed softly. "I think he told her when they were back on speaking terms, months after. I didn't see the point of denying anything. I was hating the lot of them by then. It was a very long time ago."

In his mind's eye he could see once again the guilt on the boy's face, and the agony in his sister's. Suddenly he realised that Columbine had placed an arm around his shoulders.

"Thank you," she whispered. "It was brave of you to tell me. I know you're not that person any more, John. I know what you are now."

"Perhaps."

"And I'm glad you're back in touch with Michelle. Families should stick together, if they can."

"Come on," he said, standing up. "It's time to go. Let's get back in the canoe. We've been here long enough."

12

When John Penny was introduced to Zacharie, *jardinier en chef au Château du Beautrottoir*, he was surprised to find himself shaking the large, firm hand of a black man. He had seen so few in this corner of France, even at AULA, which was regarded as a melting pot of nationalities. Zacharie looked down at Penny and Columbine Snow through heavy sunglasses from his position three rungs up a stepladder from where he had been picking cherries. The brief handshake was not enhanced with a smile. The man looked unimpressed. *Who were they? What were they? Tourists? Freeloaders?*

"*C'est pour la piscine, non?*" he grunted in what Penny discerned to be a Caribbean accent. "*Attendez là, je vais chercher la clef.*"

He stepped down from his harvesting and disappeared down the gravel path with the moustache boy back towards the house.

From this side of the building the full extent of its architectural beauty was apparent: its high round-roofed turrets, the elegant slim windows on two storeys, the butter-cream stone of its long, renovated walls. Beyond their view, hidden by high pruned hedges and lines of fruit trees, were sections of the original thirteenth-century walls and the small family chapel with its pink-glass rose window, described at some length to Columbine by the fake baroness on their previous visit.

The air was still, sweet with the smell of petals and freshly mown grass. They waited, slightly on edge, reminding themselves that they were not trespassers, they were guests. Penny's rucksack was irritating him and making his back sweat.

The gardener returned presently, limping a little, brandishing a set of keys in the air.

"*Suivez-moi*," he said, reaching the spot where they were standing, and then striding off towards an area bordered by a row of flowering oleander bushes and a six-foot screen of thick green netting.

They passed an ornamental pond in the centre of which a small fountain spurted water into the air through the mouth of a stone cherub. Captured in mid-spring at the top of a plinth it held in one hand a tiny lyre to its chest and in the other, between its two forefingers – and both Penny and Columbine caught sight of this at the same instant – protruded a six-inch carved cigar.

"You were right about the tobacco," he laughed.

"It was Amande who told me," she reminded him. "I think she's right about most things."

At the far corner was a high gate in the fence which Zacharie opened with the largest of the keys, pushing it open with a vacant smile.

"*Amusez-vous bien, monsieur-dame*," he said emptily, already turning to resume his work elsewhere.

"Zacharie is a charming man," said Penny with a grin.

"Let's not worry about him," said Columbine, pulling him towards the edge of a large sunlit swimming pool. "Look at this. It's gorgeous. I'm so hot already, I can't wait to get in the water."

It was a very warm afternoon, humid for early July, and it felt to Penny like the true start of summer. The university term was over, he had spoken to the *Chef de Faculté*, his contract had been renewed for a second year, and today he felt relieved and refreshed and relaxed. Yet behind this sense of wellbeing was the knowledge, not quite accepted, that with July, with the end of the term, inevitably came the end of his time with Columbine. She would leave him very soon, in a matter of days, she would fly back to a marriage, resuming a life in Bangor, Maine, an ocean away, and next term would start for him without her.

"Come on, John!" she was shouting, already stripped to her costume, dipping a toe into the water, about to plunge into the deep end.

They swam, they play-fought, he pushed her head underwater and she squealed with delight like a six-year-old. They pulled a pair of loungers together into the sunny side of the garden and dried off in the heat. They shared a bottle of cider he had brought in a cool-bag. She turned on to her front and asked him to rub a little sun cream on her shoulders. They chatted, talked nonsense, giggled and dozed. It was mid-afternoon and there wasn't a cloud in the sky. The only sound was that of a lawnmower clattering softly somewhere in the distance. The surface of the water in the pool was as smooth as polished glass.

Behind her shades Columbine had closed her eyes to shut out the day from her daydreams. This was her house after all, she owned the château, of course she did. She would live here forever, *la châtelaine du Beautrottoir*, here she would stay surrounded by her panelled rooms, her tapestries, her floors of *pisé* mosaics, her pink rose window. Zacharie would pick her fruit and bring the very best of it to her table in a basket, covered with a little gingham cloth. He would smile at her and delicately peel the skin from the ripest, sweetest peach, setting it before her on a plate of fine china. And she would live here in luxury and perfect happiness with – who? With her husband? With Patrick? The illusion shattered at the very thought of a heavily armed US marine in filthy combat boots invading such a heavenly, tranquil, secluded spot.

She was woken from her reverie by the deep splash of Penny diving into the pool again. She sat up and rubbed her eyes, took a gulp of the cider, already lukewarm. He hauled himself out at the far side of the pool to face her, stretching his arms up to take in deep breaths of air. She had to rub her eyes again to focus. And then again, a third time. He was no longer wearing his swim shorts, was he? Was he?

"Come on in again, Col!" he called. "Let's have a race!"

"Have you taken off your…"

"Don't be shy! There's no-one else around. Join me in a skinny-dip. It's so liberating!"

And he slipped back into the water, his body disguised in the eddies and ripples around him.

He hadn't expected her to follow his lead. He even thought she might scream, take fright, run a mile. But follow him she did; he watched her step into the shallows, submerge herself up to her neck and then, and only then, he saw how she unhooked the thin straps of her costume, peeled it down her slim body, down her legs and then kicked it away at the bottom of the pool with her foot. He swam away, paddling a few metres towards the deep end, for no other reason than to still his growing erection.

"This is fun, you're right!" she laughed. "I haven't done this since I was in a paddling pool aged two and a half!"

She swam across towards him, and they met in the centre of the pool where the water was of a depth they could stand up in. And there was something inevitable, primeval about their embrace, their kisses long and fierce, their hunger for each other's body, clasped and caressed and stroked through the water.

"I want you," he whispered in her ear.

"I've wanted you for weeks," she murmured, catching her breath.

"I want you right now."

"I wanted you half an hour ago."

"There's a pool house over there."

"Let's go."

"Follow me!"

"Lead the way!"

She chased him out of the water, splashing across the patio, grabbing towels, heading to the white wooden building that bordered one side of the pool. He was ahead of her, running, as naked as the day he'd been born.

"Shit. It's locked."

"What about over there?" she suggested.

On the other side of the pool, set back beyond several metres of lawn, was a larger glass structure, a conservatory of sorts.

He grabbed her by the hand.

"Come on!"

From the heady, honeyed scent that welcomed them, Penny decided they were entering an orangery. A paved walkway skirted four sides of a central rectangular bed which, along with narrower beds bordering the glass, was filled with lemon trees as well as oranges in fruit, huge banana plants, riotous vines, palmettos, sturdy cacti and species of exotic flowers neither had seen before. The centrepiece was a large grey-green cactus with fleshy arms and a scabby-skinned central stem that almost reached the glazed ceiling, with a set of rich crimson flowers bursting from its tip.

It was here, in the shade of these fruit trees and succulents, in the steamy, fragrant heat captured under the glass, on a pair of beach towels hastily set down in the middle of the paving stones, that Penny and Columbine made love for the first time. It was spontaneous, delicious, perfect, as natural and instinctive as the delicate orange fruit forming where there had once been blossom on the branches above them. They heard the soft buzzing of an insect, perhaps a wasp, trapped in the hothouse, tapping against the glass wall of its prison. The sound stopped as suddenly as it had begun. He told her he loved her, wanted her more than anything, words that made her smile and then cry. They made love a second time, slowly this time, less aggressively, and he too found he had tears on his cheeks. She felt a little dizzy, didn't notice him wipe them away with the corner of a towel. *Must be the chlorine in the pool*, he was about to say. *Or sweat dripping into my eyes.*

No need. She was facing the ceiling, still panting, beginning to smile to herself, a picture of satisfaction.

"I want you to stay," he said, recovering his own breath, leaning on his elbow, gazing into her bloodshot eyes.

She looked away.

"I want you to stay with me," he said again. "Don't go back."

"Don't, John," she whispered. "Don't speak now. Don't spoil the moment."

She kissed him on the lips again, then they lay back in silence, her head resting on his shoulder, eyes closed, then staring up at the glass ceiling, stained by patches of viscous leaf mould.

"It's so hot in here," she said softly.

"That's the idea, isn't it?" he laughed. "I left the door wide open."

"But the air is so still, so heavy."

"Let's leave, then, go back outside."

"No, let's stay a little longer. I want to remember this moment. I want to remember these smells. Look, there's a window in the ceiling up there."

"I can't reach to open that. It's far too high."

"Is there a ladder someplace?"

Penny stood up and looked around, scratching his beard.

"Or a pole?"

"Nothing I can see."

He wandered down the path, hoping to see something to stand on hidden behind the foliage. She sat up to watch him, smiling at the sight of his pale pink buttocks in all their tender vulnerability.

"I know," he was saying. "Do you think that cactus would take my weight?"

"I've no idea. They're quite tough, aren't they? It's like a tree, isn't it?"

"If I can just climb halfway up, I can stand on those arms and maybe reach the window catch."

"Try it. I'm baking. We need some air."

He stepped on to the shredded bark that covered the bed of earth.

"You should wrap a towel round you," she said, laughing. "You don't want to catch your soft bits on that rough skin."

"Good idea."

It was just as Penny reached his destination, part way up the trunk, that he began to feel the cactus wobble a fraction. Stretching up to the ceiling, he could just manage to unhook the latch and push the skylight open by a few inches. The plant lurched again at its base with his weight – only a little way, but the movement was violent enough to knock him off balance. Feeling himself falling, he flailed a desperate hand towards the top of the trunk for support, but only succeeded in delivering a glancing blow to the nest of flowers which broke off surprisingly easily and fell to the ground with a soft thud like a bundle of soggy red tissue paper.

"Shit!" he said, jumping to the floor. "I've broken the flowers off the bloody cactus!"

"Oh no! I think we'd better go," said Columbine, gathering up her towel. "What will the baron say?"

She was laughing aloud and soon Penny was too.

"The baron who isn't a baron?"

"What will he say about the flowering cactus that isn't flowering any more?"

They were giggling like naughty schoolchildren as they skipped past the pool, grabbed their bags and raced out through the gate.

"What will Zacharie say, more to the point?"

"Shit, we'd better get out before Zacharie sees the damage."

"Which way, John?"

"This way."

"Don't you think we should put our clothes back on first? A bit less conspicuous?"

"You're probably right. Put our clothes back on and just act naturally."

"I'm sorry about earlier," said Columbine.

They were sitting on a pair of old folding chairs at the back of Penny's house in Frettignac, on the edge of the *cercle magique*, facing the army of walnut trees, now in full fresh leaf and already heavy with bulbous green fruit.

"What do you mean?" asked Penny. "I have absolutely no regrets. Do you?"

"No. None. No, I don't mean that. I mean not wanting to talk about leaving. About the summer. The future."

"I don't think I really want to talk about it now either, to be honest."

He had opened a bottle of supermarket champagne. To mark the occasion. He topped up both their glasses.

"You know I can't stay here, don't you?" she was saying. "Deep down, you know, don't you?"

Finally it had arrived. The moment. Whatever he said now, nothing would ever be the same between them. He hesitated, drawing it out, longer and longer until it was ready to snap.

"I'm in love with you, Col. There, I've said it. That's all I know right now. That's all I'm sure about."

"Please don't say that. Don't make it impossible for me."

He edged his seat a little closer, took hold of her hand and looked into her eyes.

"Do you love him?" he asked. "Do you? Really?"

"I think I do," she answered, before pausing.

"It's been arranged for months, John," she went on, sliding her hand away. "For years even. I *do* love him. Patrick is my fiancé."

"You can call it off. It wouldn't bring the world to an end."

"It would break his heart."

"Would it break *yours*?"

"I can't do it."

"Would it?"

"And it would kill Daddy. He's expecting me back real soon. He's got a job waiting for me, I told you."

"And you'd leave what we have here, just to keep your father sweet? He can hire another secretary, can't he, for Christ's sake?"

"I love Patrick, John. Accept it. Please, accept it."

"What about me? Don't you love me too?"

Columbine looked away, up the field, through the trees to some indeterminate space where there might be a bird, a squirrel, nothing at all. She was fighting back the tears that were budding in her eyes.

"I think you do," insisted Penny. "I think you're in love with me. Just as much as I am with you."

"He's already back in Germany," she said abruptly. "Patrick. His section were moved out from the front line two days ago. We spoke for five minutes last night."

Now Penny lost himself in his thoughts: vicious, thrashing thoughts. He drained his glass and suddenly she was standing up in front of him.

"I have to go, John. You know I do. Listen, I don't want to spoil today. It's been a special day. A day I'll never forget."

"Doesn't what we have, what we did today, mean more? More than anything else?"

"It was lovely, John. I wanted it. We both did."

"You make it sound like a bowl of strawberries."

"I'm sorry. It *was* wonderful."

"But…"

"But it doesn't change anything. I'm sorry."

He stood up, collected her glass and moved towards the house.

"I'll keep in touch," she called after him.

"Sure."

He took a step before turning back to face her.

"Will I see you again?" he asked. "I mean, before you leave?"

"I don't think it's a great idea, John. I was hoping we'd leave each other on a high. As true friends. Today."

"What about next weekend?"

"I'm going up to Paris for four days. Elise has invited me up to stay with her family and do the sights."

"I see."

"It'll be fun. She's so sweet."

"When's your flight home?"

"Three days after I get back."

"Paris too?"

"Yes."

"So, what, you'll take the train up there again from Périgueux?"

"Yes. I have my ticket booked."

"So, I could drive you to the station?"

"I can call a cab. It's no bother."

"Come on, Columbine. Grant me that at least. I'll drive you to the station and play you a couple of my favourite tracks on the way and then wave you off and wish you well for a happy marriage and a great career in timber sales and a large, smiley family and a fulfilling retirement and, shit, I'm drowning here."

"Come here, John," she said, walking over to him and holding him to her. She could feel his fever, his trembling, his sobbing. "I'm sorry. I really am. I don't want to hurt you. It's just an impossible position, and you have to respect my decision."

"It's just very hard."

"Hey, don't cry. We'll keep in touch, I promise. Maybe I'll come over one day and visit the biggest museum of literature in Europe, right here in Frettignac. And you'll show me round. A personal guided tour."

He forced out a hollow laugh and wiped his cheeks with a knuckle.

"Maybe."

She took the glasses off him for fear he would drop them.

"Let's get these inside, and I'll be heading back."

She was already stepping into the kitchen.

"Come on," he heard her say.

"I thought you might stay here the night," he called after her.

She reappeared on the threshold, the empty glasses still dangling from her hand.

"I don't think so, John. Not after all that's been said."

"No. Fine. I understand."

"But I'll need a ride," she said with a smile, wrinkling up her nose. "Please?"

"All the way back to AULA?"

"It's up to you. I can catch a bus."

"I'll take you home."

"Thanks."

"I don't want to have any regrets, Col. Either of us."

"I'm trying."

"In the end they'll eat away right into your soul."

13

John Penny had decided some time ago that if his contract were extended he would give up the flat at AULA and live full-time in Frettignac. If he ever needed to stay overnight in Périgueux he knew enough people by now who would put him up on a spare mattress once in a while. Meanwhile he was saddened by the news that his friend Henrik the physicist was leaving at the end of the term, returning to his partner in Stockholm and a job at some nuclear research centre.

"But we can extend this friendship a little longer, John," he had said as they shared a plate of croissants one morning after the last of the students had packed up and left.

"What do you mean?"

"Come and spend a few weeks in Sweden. I can see that you need a change of scenery. Your heart is broken, is it not? She did that to you, your American? You need some Swedish air to clear away the pain, my friend. You would like that, yes?"

Penny was still thinking of what might have been. How he had envisaged them, him and his American, spending August together, hopping on to a train to Nice or challenging the old Peugeot to make it as far as the Var. Fatuous thoughts.

"And some fine Swedish beer, eh? And lovely Swedish women. Forget her, my friend."

And so Penny emptied his room, bought himself an airline ticket to Stockholm and spent a week with Henrik and Anna, then borrowed his friend's camping equipment, hired a Volvo and, on Henrik's recommendation, drove three hundred kilometres north-west to the town of Mora in the Dalarna region of rivers and vast lakes, endless forests and unassuming villages where he could lose himself first and then maybe find himself again a little later.

He zipped up the flap on his tent and collapsed into the camp chair by the smouldering fire he had built once the sun had set and the temperature dropped. This place was new but somehow familiar. It was not difficult, for example, if he closed his ears to the language, to imagine himself driving or walking or cycling through the wild landscape of Maine, in New England, on the far side of the Atlantic Ocean. It might be just a short drive through the pines to her home; he could fantasise that on the far side of the lake was a track leading directly to the Bangor expressway. The last thing he wanted to imagine was her wedding day, but he could so easily see her face in his mind's eye, he could conjure up at any time her sparkling nut brown eyes, her perfect nose, her generous smile. A part of him hoped she was smiling now. He hoped she would be happy in the end. But he could not bring himself to forgive her in full. Not with all his heart, he couldn't.

It would be early evening in Bangor. Was she preparing a barbecue for her new husband? Pouring him a beer into a favourite glass? Laughing with him at some intimate memory that they alone could find funny? Or was she sitting alone watching some awful television show? Or were they upstairs on the new marital bed making babies? He screwed up his eyes.

As he gave her one last hug on the station concourse, as he secretly slipped into her bag a paperback copy of *Lucie l'Eglantine*, signed *To darling* Béa, she had promised again that she would keep in touch: email, text, call, whatever. But so far, nothing. It was close to a month ago now since he had last smelt her hair, last touched her face. No word. And now here in the midnight wilderness where there was no sound beyond the crackle and hiss of his camp fire, he stared at his phone, its screen reflecting the light of a thousand stars blazing in the clear, cold sky over the lake. She would never call him, he knew. It was too late. The perfect little sandcastle they had built together had already been swept away by the inrushing tide. She was back home in the bosom of her friends and family, people she had known and loved long before he had come into her life. And his was a chapter that was now over. A year in France. An adventure in Périgord. A fling. Over.

He poured himself another glass of vodka, threw another couple of logs on the fire and gave it a kick. He would pick up his own life once more, of course he would. But he would not get so close to happiness ever again.

PART THREE

Paintings

1

In the two years that followed his lover's departure, Amande Puybonieux noticed, usually from a discreet distance, how her tenant's mood swung between the calm and the storm, between the smile and the frown, how his hair was allowed to grow long then to be severely cropped, how his little beard was shorn, whimsically grown back longer and then brutally shaved off once more. She saw how he favoured certain clothes for weeks at a time and then suddenly grew tired of them, how a much loved striped scarf, for example, worn almost daily over the whole of a winter, would be abruptly superseded for a week by one of a quite different *rayure*, then would reappear just as dramatically, restored to honour.

In John Penny she had found the perfect tenant: he was accommodating if a little distant if ever she were to visit, he was tidy, thoughtful, scrupulously clean and as respectful of the house as if it were his very own property. He showed no inclination to dabble in the garden but then nor would she have expected him to. Perhaps he might watch as the nuts were harvested, but he displayed little interest in becoming in any way involved in the laborious rituals.

Meanwhile his suggestions about little improvements to the interior were modest and considerate, the only damage was the result of acceptable wear and tear, and his monthly rental payments were never late.

Two years passed. Two contracts fulfilled. He explained to Amande once that he had tried to negotiate an arrangement of more than one year at a time but even though the administration were happy with his work and wanted to keep him on board, their hands were tied financially and a twelve-month deal with an option to renew was the best they could come up with. At least he felt valued, and to be perfectly honest, as he admitted, perhaps it was for the best. The students rarely offered him much of a challenge and he found most of his colleagues rather dull, self-absorbed, unimaginative. One of these days he might wake up and think to himself that, yes, he had been here long enough, it was time to move on, and thankfully he didn't have a longer contract to serve out.

Penny's interest in the little Steeples museum faded noticeably in the immediate aftermath of Columbine's return to the United States, as if the joy of the endeavour had been stolen away from him like some hidden item of luggage in the hold of her transatlantic jet. Although he had based himself permanently in the town, in the early weeks of the first autumn term he was notable in the library only by his absence, and Camille Rousseau was left to keep an eye on things alone. Not that there was much to do beyond tidying or polishing the glass cases and the computer screen; the tourist season was over, visitors were rare and the tiny exhibition, once established, ran itself.

It transpired that Penny was devoting more of his energies to his work at AULA, which was as it should be, no doubt: here, rather than the *bibiliothèque de Frettignac*, was the institution that was paying his salary after all. He had spent much of his summertime in the Swedish wilderness discovering, among other things, a little of the breadth of European literature and he had decided to devise a new module to be included in the courses he taught, substituting a handful of the English texts he had begun to tire of with some accessible eastern European works. His original plan had been to slide one or two American moderns into his teaching, perhaps a Hemingway or a Steinbeck, but that idea faded quickly. No, he would use English translations, naturally, but the introduction of Kafka and Dostoyevsky, Kundera and Mann would spice things up both for him and his new intake. Actually he had found the chapters of Kundera he had read to be almost unfathomable, so perhaps not Kundera. The *Chef de Faculté*, ever a man to treat his colleagues at arm's length, concurred without blinking an eye. And so he decided to drop Hardy, Lawrence and maybe even Orwell, although *Animal Farm* was always a favourite with its lively cartoon tie-in. For all his tinkering, however, he would remain loyal to Steeples, of course.

Of his new flock, young men and women almost all dressed self-consciously and with healthy tans, almost all earnest of spirit and mediocre of mind, the beautiful Florence Barrière-Hulse was exceptional. A twenty-year-old with skin the colour of Alpine chocolate and the radiant face of an angel, she joined his second-year tutorial directly from the Université de Bordeaux where, in spite of high grades and the admiration of her tutor, her first year had ended badly. Nobody seemed to know why and even when she told Penny the outline of a story, the mischievous smile she produced served only to sow a seed of doubt in his mind.

The girl was more than a cut above the rest of his students; while they struggled to finish the reading on time, she was already relating to his more ambitious musings on comparative literature or the subtleties of disguised imagery. Having an English-speaking Afro-Caribbean former glamour model as a mother gave her a certain advantage and Florence's own delicate sexual appeal completed a package that Penny could not resist unwrapping. It appeared that she had little interest in boys of her own age who, in her eyes, were either loud and boorish or gormless and as timid as kittens. When it came to older men, however, it became clear that she had a track record.

He had broached the subject of her dismissal from Bordeaux several weeks into the term, on the morning after she had shared his bed in the house in Frettignac for the first time. There was something inevitable about their coupling: a mutually aroused excitement, a bubbling of adrenalin, an animal urge in both, all desperate for a physical release.

"I was shagging a lecturer of economics," she announced nonchalantly before pulling the sheet over her knees and taking a large bite of one of the warm croissants

Penny had carried upstairs on a tray. She spoke a slightly stilted English with a faint French accent that Penny loved. Her father was the owner of a prestigious vineyard on the edge of Saint-Emilion, or so he was led to believe.

"He was a neo-Marxist," she added.

"It's not a crime," said Penny, pouring two large cups of coffee.

"Being a Marxist?"

"No, the other. Consenting adults and all. I should know. Look at us."

She sipped at the coffee and licked her lips.

"Of course, it may be frowned upon," he went on. "Do you know that expression? More so in some universities than others, I dare say. Discretion is everything, in my experience."

"Oh, we were very discreet. At least *I* was. His wife knew nothing about me at all. He kept me a secret even from his colleagues, from his best friends. Flattering, no? Men do like to boast, don't they? Especially if they have a lover twenty years younger!"

"I've never been one for boasting," said Penny, offering her sugar. As she shook her head, her braided hair swung around her face like strands of willow in a breeze. Then she was looking up at him with her big, bright eyes.

"I'm not the first then, am I?" she said with a grin.

"The first?"

"The first student you've had? 'Had' as in 'had in your bed'?"

"No. No, you're not," he laughed. "But you are the prettiest."

161

"My God! John, is that the best you can come up with?"

"I'm sorry. It's too early for creative compliments."

She pouted theatrically, drank some coffee and pulled away another chunk of croissant with her teeth. Penny opened the shutters. The sun was already bright. He hadn't checked the time. He sauntered back to the bed, plumped up his pillow, kissed her on the shoulder and slid back in next to her. It was only last night that he had noticed for the first time the initials GBH tattooed below a tiny heart on her upper arm. He had explained his surprise by enlightening her as to the violent significance of the three letters in the English justice system, only for her to illuminate him as to the more violent loss of her older brother Grégoire, less than a year earlier, notably his suicide by leaping from a bridge just as the Paris-Bordeaux TGV was hurtling underneath it.

"Anyway," she picked up. "It wasn't just the sex that got me kicked out. It was the drugs mostly."

"Really?"

"Once we were caught, you know, me and the prof, the fac was always going to side with him. You know, if it came to that. Much harder for them to replace a brilliant academic than a disposable student, no? He has written books, you know. He was an adviser to the local government. Anyway, it was my own fault. I should have seen it coming. They actually sent a woman inspector round to my room while I was in class one day and she found the coke."

"Cocaine?"

"Small amounts. Tiny amounts."

"They found their excuse to expel you."

"Exactly."

"That's a shame. And so you came to AULA."

"That's right. I did. And met you."

She laughed, loud and shrill.

"My father still has not forgiven me."

"Will he?"

"Eventually, of course."

"And your mother?"

"She's cool with it. Not that she cares too much. I haven't actually seen her since last Christmas. She spent the whole of the summer in South Africa."

"I see."

"Good coffee."

"Thanks," he said, taking a sip himself.

"Are you sure I can't have a cigarette?"

"Absolutely not. House rules."

"You are such a bully."

"You weren't complaining last night."

"You ever tried coke, John?"

"Actually, no."

"Come on!"

"No, it's the truth. Could never afford it for one thing."

"Oh well, there's always a first time."

"No, thanks."

He leaned over and kissed the nipple of her left breast.

"I have all the stimulation I need right here in front of me."

"So I can see."

Florence popped the last of her croissant into her

mouth, batted the crumbs off her fingertips before licking them clean. She slid a warm hand under the sheet and ran it gently over his thigh. Penny desperately looked for somewhere flat to place his coffee cup.

"I find that on the whole socialists are better lovers than conservatives," she said quite suddenly.

"You talk as though you have had plenty of experience," he said.

"Well, for a girl my age I think I have."

"I see. And why do you suppose that is, your theory, I mean?"

"I believe they are more inclined to share."

"Well, that can be an advantage."

"For sure. And what would you consider yourself to be, John? You know, politically. Of the left or of the right? Where does your vote land?"

"Me?" he said, clasping her hand in his. "I don't do party politics. If you really want a label I suppose I'd best describe myself, in the area of love-making at least, as something of an anarchist."

He had quite forgotten that the men from the *coopérative* were due that morning. The previous night had felt like a Saturday but was in fact a Wednesday. Neither Penny nor Florence needed to be in Périgueux on a Thursday but now he remembered: of course, this was the Thursday that Amande Puybonieux had warned him was the day the farmers would be at work in the grove, shaking the trees down and gathering the nuts. Maybe Friday too. Maybe even into the following week, depending on the weather and the size of the gang.

The morning was fine and dry, as had been the pattern for days. They had slept with the bedroom window wide open and now the throaty noise of at least one tractor chugging past the house and into the garden was as clear as if they had been riding in the back of the rusty trailer it was towing. Penny had no need to go down and speak to them. Amande had advised him to simply let them get on with the job. They came every autumn; they knew what they were doing. There was absolutely no compunction to offer them food or a drink, not even water; they would bring their own refreshments. And in any case, she had added, if you gave them a reason to stop work it could take them half an hour to get started again.

It was time to get up anyway, and when Florence wandered back into the room from the bathroom wrapped in a towel he slipped past her and took her place in the shower. By the time they came downstairs the men had already started the job. It looked like a team of four or five labourers dressed in tee-shirts and overalls had arrived in two vehicles, for besides the old tractor and trailer a large dust-covered pick-up truck was parked on the stony ground directly outside the kitchen window. Penny watched them as he rinsed the coffee pot and the breakfast dishes. On the earth around the nearest five trees a pair of men, neither in the first flush of youth, had already laid a pattern of dirty sheets on to which the walnuts would fall for collection. A third man, shouting orders in a heavy accent that Penny could barely decipher, was standing in the back of the truck passing out tools, poles, shovels and rakes to a fourth, a swarthy younger man who wore a scarlet bandana. Florence joined him at the kitchen window and he linked his arms around her slim waist, giving her an affectionate little squeeze. The work looked as rudimentary as it had ever been, a task whose methods had not changed in centuries. On such a small scale, Penny guessed, modern technology had scant place; surveying the scene it was almost as if industrialization had never happened – the Toyota aside, they could have been watching a pastoral scene from the time of Louis-Napoléon and the Second Empire.

Two of the men had begun to shake the lower branches of the trees and it took little effort for the green-podded nuts to drop loose along with leaves and the flimsiest twigs. For the higher branches they made use of long forked poles which they pulled and twisted and yanked with skill and force until the limbs were stripped and the fruit cascaded to the ground, bouncing off the cloth like loose stones at the edge of a rock fall. As they moved on to the next trees it was somebody else's job to draw the corners of the sheets together and lift the crop into the trailer. It was earthy, sweaty toil, and if the men were moving now in lithe, dynamic bursts, Penny could imagine that by the middle of the day, as the sun rose higher in the cloudless sky, as enthusiasm and energy flagged, how tiring, how utterly draining this lifting and stretching and pulling and prodding would become. Already a couple of the men had taken off their shirts and rolled the tops of their overalls down to their hips; their backs and arms glistened with the morning's first sweat. Somebody switched on the radio in the pick-up and turned the music up loud. One of the old men started singing along out of key and his mates laughed and scoffed. The boy in the bandana walked from one to the other with a large plastic bottle of water, offering each a drink which was readily accepted in long, greedy gulps.

"Shall we go?" asked Florence, pulling away from Penny's loose grip.

"Yes," he agreed. "I suppose we should. Do you still want to see the exhibition in town before we drive back?"

"Of course I do."

"I'll be bringing the whole group down here next month anyway."

"But I want my private tour. You promised."

"Hardly a tour. It's one room."

"Don't diminish it."

"You're right. And I'd be happy to talk you through the exhibits."

"I'm halfway through *Forty Barrels*."

"Only halfway?"

"I've got a lot of other stuff to catch up with."

"Don't worry. I'm only kidding. As long as you get your essay for me in on time."

"*Oui, monsieur*," she responded, grabbing his hand and dragging him to the door.

"What's the punishment for lateness, by the way?"

"Oh, I'll think of something appropriate."

"Something inappropriate might be more fun," she giggled.

"Come on, there's your bag. Let's go and meet Jonathan Steeples."

"I need a cigarette first," she insisted. "Can I smoke in your car, yes?"

"*May I?*, not *can I?*"

"*Je m'excuse, monsieur. May* I smoke?" she repeated, exaggerating his pedantry.

"You may," he smiled. "Just this once. As long as you wind the window right down and don't cough over the music."

2

When John Penny met Joyce Sweetacre for the first time he wondered why their paths had not crossed much earlier. In a brief but expressive email she had virtually begged him to meet her, at a date and time convenient to him, at the library in Frettignac, so that she could *drink at the fount of his expertise.*

Although somewhat flattered, Penny put her off for almost a fortnight. He had been suffering from a cold, for a start, and had no enthusiasm for socialising. Moreover, it was a busy time at the university and his choice of eastern European texts had been less than successful; it seemed that even his best students were reluctant to read English translations and found the subjects too challenging to get beyond the first ten pages of any given book. To compound his mood he was becoming increasingly convinced that Florence Barrière-Hulse was sleeping with one of the postgraduate agriculturalists. He should not have been surprised at the appeal of a wealthy, handsome twenty-six-year-old champion yachtsman but he was more than irked by her fickleness. As things stood he knew they were no more than friends, there was a generation between them, but her shallow excuses for missed rendezvous hardened his suspicions. He couldn't complain; it was never really a question of being in love with her, was it? Their liaison was too risky for them to have become an item, a relationship destined to be clandestine, sexualised and temporary. Penny knew all this, but still.

A scrap of good news arrived in a letter addressed to him at the library as *Monsieur le Conservateur de l'Espace Steeples*. Camille Rousseau telephoned him one day to announce that he had a piece of mail waiting for him in her office drawer. He was happy for her to open it there and then and read the contents out aloud to him: an under-commissioner on one of the cultural committees in Brussels was pleased to offer the *Espace* a grant of two thousand euros as a contribution to maintenance with the strong possibility of a larger sum to follow dependent on the next EU budget discussions. Two thousand euros: not a life-changing amount but substantial nevertheless, and the first tangible encouragement he had received. It had been explained to him several months earlier that the regional funds promised from the man from Bordeaux were still blocked in some bureaucratic pipeline.

On a bright spring day as his head cold finally cleared, Penny emailed back to Mrs Sweetacre and arranged to meet her, if she were free, at the library on the following Saturday morning.

He arrived early but the woman was already there, sitting by a magazine rack, doused in perfume, leafing through the glossy pages of *Dordogne Visiteur*. As he had suspected, she was as English as a Dorset cream tea, of which first impressions suggested she had eaten more than her fair share down the years. She recognised him the moment he came in, dropped the magazine as if it were contagious and, drawing scowls from the few library visitors, stood and approached him loudly:

"Doctor Penny! Joyce Sweetacre. Call me Joyce, please do! It's an absolute delight to meet you! I adore your scarf, by the way. Liberty's?"

"Actually, Monoprix," replied Penny. "It's nice to meet you, Joyce."

And catching the eye of Camille Rousseau, who was furtively watching the meeting from behind her counter, he added:

"Shall we talk around the corner, so as not to disturb the other library users?"

Joyce Sweetacre was a large woman whose girth was mitigated by her considerable height yet accentuated by a close-fitting embroidered tee-shirt and a pair of knee-length khaki shorts whose elasticated waistband was stretched to the point of cruelty. He guessed that she was a few years older than him. Nevertheless, her hair was expensively cut and bleached in a youthful bob on top of which was perched a pair of designer sunglasses, her face had the healthy glow of a privileged life, and she had a wide, lip-glossed smile which revealed excellent teeth. Her pale blue eyes twinkled with excitement as she spoke, her shrill voice revealing a back story of head girl, student social committee chair and latterly backbone of a Women's Institute branch in some market town in East Sussex.

Penny pulled a couple of chairs into the side room. Once they were settled, facing each other in somewhat cramped intimacy, he listened patiently as she explained how she had come to Steeples late in life and regarded the discovery of his work as a new chapter in her personal enlightenment.

"We've had a place in the Dordogne for nearly ten years, Hughie and I, and only now am I finding out about the treasures of Frettignac. Jonathan Steeples living here! Who knew?"

"The old display *was* below the tourist radar," Penny conceded.

"You've done an absolutely marvellous job here, John," she rolled on, looking around at the walls and touching his knee in a congratulatory pat.

"But it's still tiny."

"Yes, but you've made a start. And it's an absorbing display. That *is* you in the video, isn't it?"

The monitor was switched off but Penny knew what she meant.

"Yes. It was fun to shoot."

"Must have been a hoot. And what a natural you are! Good-looking and so talented!"

"Now you're embarrassing me," he protested in mock modesty.

"Nonsense," she stated, offering him her full smile. "And you are a university professor, I believe?"

"Yes."

"So, extremely busy, am I right? In demand from every direction?"

"Well, there are peaks and troughs."

"I only ask as I was hoping you might honour us with your presence one of these evenings."

"Us?"

"Sorry, yes, the English Ladies Reading Society in Sarlat. I was thinking of suggesting a Steeples for our next discussion group. Or the one after that. I've had my fill of chick lit, thank you very much. And I *am* Secretary this year. We'd love you to come along and give us a little professional insight. Such a coup! Perhaps you'd read a few well-chosen extracts?"

"Oh, I don't know."

"We'd pay you."

"It's not that. It's just…" Penny really didn't know what he wanted to say.

"Never mind, don't feel obliged at all. Sorry if I've been too pushy. Hughie says I railroad people into doing things that they don't want to do, so they nod and smile at me in the moment but hate me for it for months afterwards."

"No, not at all. Don't beat yourself up on my account."

"So, you'll do it?" The woman couldn't help herself.

"Let me think about it."

"So not next month?"

"Probably not."

"The one after that?"

"We'll see."

"Sorry! There I go again. Listen, let me buy you some tea or something. I remember there's an acceptable little café by the bridge, isn't there? But before we leave, I did have a question about the location of one of those photographs."

She stood up briskly and, leaning over him, pointed to a sepia image of Steeples posing with a thin man in a top hat and a dress coat who held in one hand a cane and in the other a square box which might have contained a cake.

"Do you think that photo was taken at Le Bugue, by any chance?"

The corporate banker Hugh Sweetacre and his wife Joyce had owned a large, tasteful home in Le Bugue with five bedrooms, a twin garage, an art studio, wide lawns and a heated swimming pool since before the financial crash.

"Poor Hughie was obliged to forgo his bonus for a year or two," Joyce told him over a pot of surprisingly decent Earl Grey and a substantial slice of *millefeuille*. "It was horrible, you can imagine, but we did manage. A directive from Head Office. *Can't be seen to be rewarding failure in the current climate.* Failure? Hughie is the most dedicated, conscientious, profit-searching, single-minded striver the bank ever had. The crisis was the Americans' fault, don't you agree, John? Anyway, thank the Lord, people's memories are short and he's back on the bonuses again. Nothing too extravagant, but he's worth every penny."

"Which bank does he work for?" asked Penny absent-mindedly.

"Giltmann-Rusard."

"Oh."

"It's a European subsidiary of Giltmann Brothers of New York."

"I think I've heard of it."

"You probably read the jokes after the crash. Guiltmann, you know, spelt with a *u*. Not Hughie, though, he's a scrupulous as a monk."

"And is he a reader?"

"Hughie? Heavens no! Unless he's reading about fast cars or helicopters or private jets. You can meet him in a minute, if you like." She was checking the time on her phone. "He dropped me off earlier, went for coffee at an estate agent friend's place and is picking me up here at midday. Lovely to have him back. I hadn't seen him for six weeks until yesterday. He works so hard. Spends all his life in the City, it seems."

"And you live here in France permanently?"

"*I'm* here most of the time. We kept the house in Uckfield. You never know what's around the corner, do you? It *can* get a little lonely here on my own. But I have plenty of time to paint. And we've made lots of friends. There are loads of Brits out here, aren't there?"

"So I gather."

"It makes things so much more comfortable. My French isn't up to much beyond grocery shopping and antiques."

Penny was sensing that this little conversational avenue was a dead end.

"So," he probed, "you're an artist?"

"I dabble," she smiled, pushing her plate into the centre of the table. "Watercolours, mainly. I studied History of Art at uni back in the day and worked in a gallery in Knightsbridge for a while. Renzo. You might know it. Sculpture on the ground floor, paintings up on the first. Quite pricey. Anyway, Hughie insisted that I stop. Said he was earning enough for the both of us and I should put my feet up. Said he never planned on marrying a working woman."

She opened her handbag, dug out a business card and passed it to him.

"If you're interested in taking a look at the things I paint I have a little website. Mainly landscapes, some abstracts. Living here is very conducive to creativity, John, don't you find?"

"That depends. I've been writing a novel for the last five years and haven't got much past chapter three."

"Keep at it, John! I'm sure you'll get it finished one of these days."

He gave her a smile of resignation.

"Anyway," she continued, "regarding Steeples, I'll tell Cilla and the others that you're bearing us in mind, shall I? I'll spread the word about the exhibition, of course. Do you use social media, by the way?

"Not much," he replied." Not as much as I ought."

"Leave it with me. I'll have your *Espace* on everybody's home-page before you can say *twitterati*. Look, there's Hughie!"

Joyce insisted on paying and within two minutes they were walking back over the bridge towards the library. Sitting in a parked open-topped, highly-polished snow white Bentley a sturdy-looking man of about sixty was straightening his thick grey hair in the rear-view mirror.

"Hughie, this is John Penny," announced Joyce when they reached the kerb. "He's the literary expert I was telling you about."

"Were you, darling?" asked Sweetacre, slowly stretching out a hand over the car door for Penny to shake. Clearly he wasn't planning on removing himself from the comfort of his pastel-blue leather upholstery.

"Yes, dear," insisted his wife. "I was. On the telephone last weekend."

"Whatever you say, darling," he intoned, and lifting his sunglasses to raise a conspiratorial eyebrow to Penny, "Nice to meet you, old sport."

Old sport? Penny was inclined to pull away his hand and walk away on the spot.

"How are you?" he asked fatuously instead, an enquiry which received no reply.

"Do please keep in touch!" shouted Joyce, settling into the spacious passenger seat beside her husband.

"Of course," said Penny. "Nice to have met you. You too, Mr Sweetacre."

Penny was embarrassed to realise that the white Bentley was parked directly in front of his dusty 206, the tired old car that looked as though it had recently emerged from a war zone. He wanted to let the Sweetacres glide away gracefully before it became obvious that the Peugeot belonged to him, but Hugh had not even started up the engine, Joyce was carefully tying a silk headscarf over her neat coiffure and it was already too late. He could have wandered into the library but it was now closed for the weekend and he was opening his own car door without even realising he had the key in his fingers. Why on earth should he be ashamed of his car, anyway?

He got in, shuffled himself comfortable and turned the key: the ignition gave a choked sigh and the engine failed to respond. This had happened before. He tried again. The motor coughed as an orator might clear his throat, but no oratory followed. He turned the key once more: there was a faint, aimless whirring, then silence. He counted to five and tried again: nothing. Before he tried for the fifth time, his door was pulled open and there, leaning into his face, was Hugh, followed by an invisible mist of expensive cologne.

"You got a problem, mate?" he bellowed.

Mate? Penny's contempt rose another notch.

"It sounds like it," he said quietly.

"Nice little motor, the Peugeot," said Sweetacre, casting an eye around the neglected interior. "Fairly reliable for two or three years, aren't they? But how old is this little monkey, eh?"

"About ten," answered Penny, before realising it had been a rhetorical question.

"I'd offer to have a quick butcher's under the bonnet for you, mate, but we have to be somewhere. There is a garage in town, I believe. Gaston's."

"Yes, I know."

He *did* know Gaston, of course he did. Gaston had serviced the car last summer and the one before that. He didn't need some stranger from Giltmann-Rusard, whose own luxury sports would only ever be handled by the kid-gloved technicians at the dealership's air-conditioned service centre, telling him about the opportunities for second hand car repair in his own town.

"You're lucky it's not much later," Sweetacre was offering. "Those sorts of places usually close up around lunchtime on a Saturday."

"Do they?"

"I'd help to push you over there, but…"

"You have to be somewhere."

"Indeed we do. You can walk there, though. It's not far."

"Yes, I know."

"Then he can tow you back."

"Yes, he can."

"Well, good luck, mate. Hope it's not too serious."

3

Two thousand euros, with the promise of more. Not payable to him personally, of course, but to the account he had established through the *comité des affaires culturelles* who met four times a year in a draughty office in one of the more austere government buildings in the centre of Périgueux. This was a body co-chaired by a geriatric former professor of history and a humourless, much younger female civil servant whose husband was apparently standing as a *député* in the nation's next general election. This was a committee, Penny had noticed, who had placed no obstacles in front of him as he set up the fund to expand and develop the *Espace Steeples* but who had no inclination whatsoever to contribute towards it. Meanwhile the British Council, to whom he addressed emails at regular intervals to remind them of his existence, replied with plenty of polite, warm words but no financial support. It seemed that operations were overstretched in the Baltic countries *for the foreseeable*, news which was of little interest to Penny and even less of a consolation.

Two thousand euros, paid with the blessing of some accountant in an office in Brussels. Not a huge amount, but a start. What was he to do with it? Spend it? On what? Or save it? Until when?

"I can give you a few ideas on how to spend that money," announced Florence Barrière-Hulse one evening, gripping his buttocks through the back pockets of his jeans and pulling him up close to her groin. "I hear it's lovely in Corsica at this time of the year."

Their relationship, based more than ever on expediency, was going through a phase of frictionless pleasure while the postgraduate agriculturalist was away on a five-day yachting regatta in Cannes.

Over the following months Penny toyed with the idea of moving the collection into larger premises. He could afford to pay rent on a room somewhere and made enquiries about the town hall. The collection was a municipal resource, after all, and surely somebody in authority could find a suitable public space and nod through a subsidy. The mayor, no longer the lugubrious Monsieur Besse but a man considerably less amenable, led him to a believe that there *was* a room in the *mairie* itself, unloved and neglected, quite possibly perfect for Penny's plans, but which was due to be rewired and replastered, and the start date was uncertain. *Better to look elsewhere, monsieur.* He asked Amande Puybonieux about using a corner of the tourist office, but it wasn't up to her and her bosses insisted they needed the space for the summer promotions.

Whenever he had a setback Penny turned to his novel, having been reminded of it by Joyce Sweetacre and still harbouring the ambition to make a name for himself beyond the Dordogne. He worked on what he considered to be an ingenious plot based around a stalker and opportunities for blackmail, framed in a clever structure of time-shifts and increasing dramatic impetus. Snatches of convincing dialogue came to him out of nowhere and he had moments, full days even, of excitement and positivity. But for all the vigour in their words and deeds, the characters remained as flat as cardboard, as soulless as zombies. Try as he might, he could not bring them to life.

His consolation was sex. It mattered not that Florence was available less often as he had already quietly opened his account with a thirty-year-old divorcee, Marie-Jo, who had been working for the past year in the marketing department of AULA. Their relationship had no future, he knew: she was flighty, selfish and punctuality was a concept she was unfamiliar with, but she had a very comfortable apartment, excellent taste in wine and the sex they shared was delightfully superficial.

. Meanwhile he had wondered about giving Joyce Sweetacre a helping hand. He had driven to Sarlat for an evening with her reading group and had been a triumph, or at least that is what Joyce and her gushing friend Cilla had insisted on calling him. The ladies would have him back in a jiffy, *in a heartbeat*, he was told as he left the gathering, breaking away from one perfumed embrace only to be ambushed by another. He had remembered how it felt to be appreciated for his insight, for his education, for his mind, even if the lady readers of Sarlat were not the most discerning of critics. Joyce was warm and genuine, if a little fulsome and loud. And her artwork, at least the pieces she presented on her *Tout de Suite* website, interested him. It was hard to gauge the quality of the brushwork from an image on a computer screen but the tones were more vivid than he had expected in watercolours and several of the subjects had captured his attention, notably a river scene in Bergerac and the view of a stone bridge in a spot that could be taken for Frettignac, with a bustling street scene in the background. To him both works had a relevance to Steeples and he knew exactly where there was a little wall space in the library in which to hang them. He had the money to buy them outright or he could simply borrow them and help promote her art next to the Steeples artefacts.

It transpired, however, that Camille Rousseau was not disposed to encouraging private commercial activity in the library. He was knocked off his stride and somewhat disappointed. What he needed was another night with Marie-Jo from Marketing to think the whole thing through post-coitally.

It was around this time that John Penny reached, without fanfare, the age of fifty. Two score and ten. After a good night's sleep, a cold shower, a cup of strong coffee and a fresh *pain aux raisins*, he often felt twenty years younger, and his cheerleaders, from Camille to Joyce and Cilla, would swear that he still had the appearance of a thirty-year-old, too. But there were times, increasingly frequent times, when he felt his true age, and, catching sight of himself naked in his bedroom mirror, he had to admit that he no longer had the body of a young man. He decided to shave off his beard for good. To the individual chest hairs that seemed to have turned grey overnight he took a pair of tweezers, and as to the other sight that deflated him, the soft sag of his buttocks, he vowed to start a regime of twice-weekly jogging, following a punishing circuit up beyond the Garrigue estate, through the forest to the telephone mast and back. In the past twelve months he had begun to smoke irregularly; he had rarely bought a packet of cigarettes in his youth and had come late to a habit which from time to time he enjoyed. But did it combine well with ambitions of athletic self-improvement? After the first run he collapsed at his back door with his lungs bouncing so hard off his ribcage that he thought he would certainly die the moment his chest finally exploded. A week later he was more circumspect, walking up the steeper slopes and returning to base feeling quite invigorated. He made up his mind to buy a new pair of trainers and some proper sports kit, and slowly but surely went from strength to strength. Several months into the exercise plan and he was feeling the rewards: a healthy tan, lighter on his toes, a little weight lost around the midriff, sleeping like a baby, a clearer head for work and greater stamina for love-making, but for all that, the sagging buttocks still sagged. Two score and ten.

He had misguidedly spent too much of the summer with Marie-Jo in a *mobil-home* on the Côte d'Azur and now saw her only if he bumped into her along the corridors of AULA. They had grated against each other daily and had a colossal row over the triviality of a choice of restaurant. In a rage which she later regretted, she left him that afternoon and returned alone to Périgueux by train.

The new intake of students provided slim pickings as most of them seemed to be perversely obsessed with partners of their own age. A pretty art student who called herself Sam caught Penny's eye and she allowed him to take her into town for coffee. He told her of his valuable contacts in the art world, dropping the name Sweetacre, the famous English colourist, as if he really meant Hockney. Sam looked impressed but couldn't place the name. On another occasion after a little too much *vin rosé* he offered to pose for her if she was in need of a male figure for her life drawing. She smiled at him and politely declined. The next time she saw him in the canteen she made a point of introducing him to her girlfriend, a dark-skinned girl with the build of a female wrestler who was holding a tennis racquet in one hand and a small bowl of salad in the other. Penny went home and spent the weekend having another unsatisfying bash at his novel.

Once again it was harvest time in the walnut grove. One sunny morning the sound of a tractor rumbling past the house reminded him that a year had passed since Florence had told him about her dead brother, her dalliance with the professor of economics and her occasional cocaine use. Although he now saw her less and less, he had his suspicions that she was becoming increasingly dependent on the drug.

Penny had classes today and the next day and would

stay in Périgueux in a friend's spare room. He was happy to be out of the way as the raw-boned labourers thrashed at the trees, as their vehicles kicked up the dust, as their radio blared out dubious popular music from halfway up the field. At a glance it looked as though the gang was composed of the same handful of men as in the previous year, including the bandana man, apart from a second younger man he did not recognise, a slim youth with a tattoo on the inside of his right forearm who was gibbering to his boss in what Penny guessed was unrefined Spanish.

The days were still long and dry, and so when he returned home the following evening he was surprised to find the trees only part-way cropped, the tractor and pick-up had disappeared and only the trailer remained, parked at an angle halfway up the field. Beneath the darkening sky, caught in the slanting rays of the setting sun, a solitary farmer was tidying the sheets and tipping handfuls of stray fruit on to the heap. It was the young man with the tattoo.

"*Hola!*" shouted Penny from outside the back door. The boy looked up, stopped working and wiped his hands on the sides of his shorts.

"*Hola, señor!*" he replied, striding towards the house.

"*Terminado?*" asked Penny.

"*Si, señor.*"

The boy was wearing a sweat-stained tee-shirt, football shorts and a pair of filthy working boots. He was coated in dust and grime from his day's labours in the field. He found his discarded overalls outside the kitchen window and picked them up off the ground. Penny had no confidence in his Spanish and asked in French why the young man was on his own and what had happened to the rest of the gang. The boy answered well enough in broken French for him to gather that the tractor had been needed for some emergency at another farm, and with it a crew of five. Penny was not to worry, he insisted; they would all be back tomorrow, no problem, *señor*. He had the brightest of chestnut eyes, the lashes of a girl and an innocent expression of apology.

"And you? What about you?" asked Penny, pointing at the boy's chest. "How will you get home tonight?"

"I go to town on foot. Paco, he meet me by the bridge."

"Someone will pick you up, yes?"

"*Si*. Paco, he pick me up. Seven o'clock."

Penny's watch told him it was five minutes to six.

"Well, if you've finished," he said, "you would like a drink, yes? A beer? *Cerveza? Si?*"

"*Gracias, señor.*"

"And a shower, while you wait? *Ducha?* I can drive you down into Frettignac. Five minutes. No problem."

"Okay."

While they drank a beer together the boy explained briefly that his name was Luis, he was twenty-one, a Catalan, one of hundreds of Spanish workers employed in the area at the time of the grape harvests. The man in the bandana was his older brother. Penny remarked on the boy's tattoo, now that he could read it: Barça, his football team. Their group was accommodated in caravans on the outskirts of Bergerac. And, no, the food was no good. *But, thank you, yes, the beer is good.*

Penny found his open, fresh face captivating, his

accent hypnotically alluring, but it was with the clearest of minds that he followed the boy upstairs, and with the most basic of intentions. He showed him the shower, handed him a towel, and waited on the landing, slowly unbuttoning his shirt, until Luis had finished washing. As he emerged with the towel loosely wrapped around his waist, his damp black hair standing on end from rubbing, his hairless chest gleaming in the lamplight, his slender legs slightly apart, Penny cupped a hand around the back of his head, and pulling his smooth face towards his own, kissed him on the lips. Luis tensed, recoiled an inch, then relaxed into a reciprocal embrace. Penny breathed in the scent of his shampoo on the boy's hair. He loosened the towel and, as it fell to the floor, he took his hand and led him naked through the open bedroom door.

In the past two years he had had nothing further to do with the baron, but Penny had not forgotten the full extent of the man's imaginative name. Jean-Louis Sainte-Marie Lachêne du Beautrottoir had dropped off his radar since the long-ago visit to his swimming pool. Nothing had come of the damaged cactus flowers but neither had any further invitation to the château been received. Penny had mentioned the page of handwritten poetry to Camille Rousseau, those first five lines of *Lord of the Lake* he had been shown that were so markedly missing from the display in the library. Perhaps now was the time, so many months later and with persuasive funds in the bank, to reopen negotiations with the baron.

He decided to bite the bullet with an early morning telephone call but was told by a private secretary that the baron and baroness were out of the country, away on a three-week family holiday on the islands of Bermuda. He declined the invitation to make an appointment and set to compose a polished email instead, which would reach the baron in mid-Atlantic should he choose eventually to open it. Not more than two hours later when his mobile rang, Penny was surprised to hear the Frenchman's voice as clear as a bell on the other end.

"Doctor Penny? Is that you? I've just been re-reading your email over breakfast. Yes, we're five hours behind you here, you know."

"Yes," replied Penny. "I was told you were in Bermuda."

"Paradise."

"I wouldn't know."

"Believe me."

"Well, anyway, thank you for calling me so promptly. You have obviously noted my request for the manuscript?"

"Indeed I did. I have been expecting you to contact me for many months."

"Well, now I have."

"Like an itch you finally had to scratch, no?"

"Something like that."

He waited for some witty follow-up remark but nothing came. He decided it was probably up to him to make the running:

"Now we have a little money, Ludo, I feel I am in a stronger position to appeal to you. We can buy some security cameras, for a start. I know that was an angle that concerned you."

"Of course."

"And I can pay a sum to borrow the page if you are adamant it's still not for sale."

There was a pause in the conversation. Just as Penny was wondering if the line had failed, the baron spoke up:

"Let me put you out of your misery, Monsieur John. And forgive me if I struggle to stop myself from laughing."

"Laughing? This is a serious request."

"I assure you I am laughing at the joke, Monsieur John, not at your offer, which I am certain is as honest as you are."

"The joke?"

"Yes, of course. The page I showed you is a total forgery, my friend."

"But…"

"I was playing a little game with you. I apologise. An expert would tell you in five seconds it's a fake."

Penny could hear a trace of hilarity in the man's voice and felt the heat of fresh blood rising at his cheeks.

"You should know," the baron was saying, "it's something my mother produced several years ago to entertain herself."

"To *entertain* herself?"

"A little *divertissement*."

"So, it's worthless?"

"Quite."

"And the original? The missing paper?"

"I have no idea about that."

"Can I believe you?"

"But of course."

Penny could think of nothing else to say. He wondered if the baron could hear the sound of his hopes deflating three and a half thousand miles away across the ocean.

"Please send my regards to Miss Snow," he suddenly heard him say. "Or perhaps she is your wife by now? Mrs Penny? I have lost touch, I am sorry."

Another short pause, then "Goodbye, *monsieur*," and, before Penny could reply, the line went dead.

John Penny knew that clarity could never be achieved by alcoholic means, that not even a fine Margaux from a year like 2009 could provide meaningful enlightenment. This did not prevent him from drinking, however, on rare occasions, more than necessary to achieve a glow of wellbeing. Drinking alone beyond his limits was self-indulgent, weak-minded and ultimately painful, but there were evenings at this time of his life when he had no better plan. And there were mornings when only a strong coffee and a brisk walk up through the walnut trees to the top of the field would begin to rebalance his system.

It was on one such morning, a bright day in early summer, when Penny came across a character he might have expected to meet many times before, many months earlier. Nevertheless, it was true that since her younger days of frivolity and games, she had become the most elusive and sombre of creatures.

He tramped up the sloping end of the grove, kicking up stones in the dust, head down, paying scant attention to exactly where he was going. As he had done tens of times before, he was vaguely heading towards the banking where he could sit and admire the view. His headache was slowly clearing, he was breathing heavily, and from between the forefingers of his right hand poked a freshly-lit cigarette. For over a century the border between the properties had been indistinct and yet undisputed: a little ditch here, a raised bank there, walnut trees and scrub on one side, the edge of the ascending rows of vines on the other.

There she sat, on the highest point of the crest, a woman of indeterminate age whose long, unruly hair was being tossed this way and that by a light wind. She did not appear to notice him at first, but moved her head to face him as the brittle shuffling of his feet on the dry leaves reached her ears. On her knees sat a little dog, a white-haired Scotch terrier, whose head also jerked up at the sound of his approach. The woman's instinct, briefly delayed, was to stand up and, if not to hide, then at least to move away surreptitiously down the hill and melt into the vegetation of the vines.

"*Ne quittez pas à cause de moi!*" Penny called out, lifting off his sunglasses and tossing his cigarette away. "Don't leave on my account!"

She looked hard into his face, trying to recognise him.

"I'm sorry to disturb you, *madame*," he went on, "I'll leave you in peace."

The woman did not immediately respond. He wondered if she were deaf or even to some extent deranged. Her face was pale, her hazel eyes failed to shine, and her thin body remained rigid. She wore no shoes, a tattered woollen shawl covered her shoulders, and a faded floral cotton dress fell over her bony knees.

"I'm sorry to disturb you," he said again, and the dog wandered away towards the edge of the vineyard.

"*Vous êtes l'Anglais?*" the woman suddenly asked. "You are the Englishman?" Her voice was delicate but clear.

"Yes. Yes, I am."

He leaned in a little closer to her and offered a hand which she ignored.

"My name is John. Are you the wife of Monsieur Garrigue?"

"My name is Noisette," she said with a stare, before looking away in the direction of her pet. "Rigolette! *Reste-là, bonbon!*"

"A pretty name," offered Penny.

The woman looked puzzled.

"Your name, *madame*. Noisette. It's a pretty name."

"Are you happy, Monsieur John?" she asked him with a sudden intensity.

"Happy?"

"Are you happy at the house? Living in that house?"

She looked past him, down the field towards the building that was his home.

"You are living there since a year at least, no?"

"Nearer three."

"Nearer three," she echoed, looking away again and letting the breeze blow her fair hair across her face.

Penny recognised in her expression the resignation on the face of the bride in the photograph that still hung in his sitting room – the woman whose husband had, according to his sister, *moved away*.

"You lived there once, didn't you?" he said, to no reply.

"Would you care to come down the grove with me and have some coffee? Have a look around the old place?"

It seemed that the very thought made her shiver but it could have been the wind on her neck.

"I am not well, Monsieur John," she said at length. "No woman can be who lives there. Who has lived there, in that place. *Ça apporte du malheur.* The place is cursed, and that's the truth."

Suddenly she stood up with an agile spring which surprised him, and her dress billowed softly between her legs, caught by a light gust.

"Rigolette!" she cried, looking about her and shielding her eyes from the sun. "*Viens ici!*"

"She went that way," said Penny, pointing.

"*Ça apporte du malheur.* Only walnuts grow there. Nothing else. Only walnuts. You have noticed, no doubt. Nearer three years."

She hesitated, focussing her gaze on a point in the middle distance.

"You see that circle of dead earth?"

Now she was pointing with a quivering, bony finger towards the house.

"That is cursed, Monsieur John. Nothing grows in it. *C'est un cercle maudit.*"

"I don't believe in curses," he said.

Again Noisette had no intent to reply.

"I must find my dog," she mumbled to herself presently, ambling along the bank, down the shallow ditch and into the ranks of vines.

"*Au revoir, madame!*" shouted Penny.

"I must find my dog," he heard her say again before she moved out of earshot.

He sat down on the bank, put on his sunglasses and watched her figure disappear. Rigolette is a pretty name too, he thought. A perfectly musical name for a spirited little Highland terrier. Rigolette. He rolled the name around in his mouth. For some perverse reason he thought of Rover, the smelly old dog his mother had petted and given the dullest of names. Fat, lazy, stupid Rover: avoiding that sickly beast was a lifetime ago.

All of a sudden he noticed a trail of smoke rising from a pile of dry leaves not far from his feet. He jumped up and stamped on it, but a flame had ignited and he had to kick the smouldering leaves apart and flatten them four or five times before the sparks died and the smoke finally dispersed on the wind. It was his cigarette, of course. The browned grass and the fallen brush were tinder-dry. It was lucky that the woman Noisette had not come down to the house with him after all. How close had he been to starting a bush fire on the hill, to causing a conflagration that might have brought disaster?

4

John Penny was never given an acceptable explanation as to why the confirmation of a fourth single-year contract was delayed until part-way through the summer holidays. As a matter of fact he was less worried about his employers' hesitation as he once might have been: he could face down any scurrilous rumours (actually, facts) about his relations with members of – one of his favourite expressions – *the student body*, and he was confident that his colleagues valued his teaching. In addition, should AULA choose not to renew his terms he would threaten litigation on the grounds that they had kept him in the dark way beyond the eleventh hour. And on top of that, if he did find himself in Périgord with no teaching work to occupy his time, he was sure he could find other fruitful means of filling it.

In the meantime there had been gossip among scaremongers in the press, both British and French, that employers in continental Europe were already nervous about taking on British staff on lengthy contracts in the face of projections about the referendum that he been offered by the Prime Minister for the following year. Out of curiosity Penny did a little homework and was reassured to glean that all of the commentators he respected, and even most of the ones he did not, were predicting a nasty, negative campaign with the strong likelihood of Britain *remaining* a member of the Union. He also contacted his Swedish friend Henrik, who he knew was interested in such matters.

"The British will have to vote with their heads and not their hearts," his old colleague warned him, "but you are a sensible, pragmatic people, I think. The Brits know which side their bread has butter. This is an expression, John, yes?"

"Which side their bread *is buttered*."

"Bread is buttered. Okay, I was close."

"You were very close."

"And you get it, right?"

"Yes, Henrik. I get it."

In the event Penny received an email from *la Section de Ressources Humaines* on the second day of his visit to Nice. He had treated himself to an elegant hotel on the *Promenade des Anglais* and once arrived was reminded of his wish two years earlier to bring the American woman there. Somebody in the *secrétariat* apologised on behalf of AULA for any inconvenience caused by the delay but was pleased to confirm that he had been granted a further twelve-month extension. He closed down the laptop and strolled out of the hotel into the bright sunshine to find a congenial sea-front bar in which to celebrate. Two full years since she left him behind, here he was, still standing, still smiling, on the cusp of his fourth year in the Dordogne.

"Feckless" Fiona was a pretty-faced, blue-eyed, blonde-haired English girl who looked all the more attractive when Penny first saw her: slim, curvy, lightly tanned, lying on a sunlounger in a baby blue bikini by the side of the oval shaped swimming pool in the Sweetacres' secluded garden.

"Here's Doctor Penny, Fi!" announced Joyce in high excitement. "I told you he'd be here on time. You should have moved off that lounger ten minutes ago to get yourself ready."

She rolled her eyes at Penny, the put-upon aunt with her wilful niece to deal with, and, holding his hand, pulled him gently out of the shade of the awning.

"This is Fiona, John. I'm sorry she's not dressed."

"That doesn't matter," smiled Penny, and addressing the girl who was by now sitting up and tidying her hair, "Call me John, please. It's not as if I'm your real teacher, is it?"

The girl smiled back demurely, stood up and offered him a limp and slightly damp hand to shake.

"Thank you for coming over," she said quietly.

"Go and put some clothes on, for Heaven's sake!" snapped Joyce. "John doesn't want to wait for you forever."

Fiona sighed and made a point of slowly picking up her sunglasses and a magazine lying on the tiles.

"Can I get you a drink, John, while Fiona gets herself sorted? I thought you'd be better inside, by the way. Cooler, obviously. The dining room okay? It's nice and airy. Big table to sit at."

"That'll be fine," replied Penny, watching the niece sashay out of view through the patio doors.

"And something to drink?"

"Sorry, Joyce?"

"Can I get you a glass of something? There's a Vouvray open in the fridge."

"Oh, no thanks. Maybe just a juice if you have it."

"Orange? Apple? Cranberry?" she smiled.

"Apple'd be nice. Thanks."

Penny had grown rather fond of Joyce Sweetacre in a platonic, pally kind of way. She was excitable, gregarious, extremely well-mannered and could take a gentle ribbing. As for him offering to display one of her watercolours in the *Espace*, the riverside in Bergerac, she had told him that she would be eternally grateful for his patronage and given him a tight, fragrant hug.

She had brought up the subject of her niece several weeks earlier. Fiona was a student at the University of Southampton, she said, coming into the second year of her degree course in English. The first year had proved to be a difficult one for both the girl and her parents, and there had been times, apparently, when she had been on the verge of packing it all in and joining the navy. In the end she had been persuaded to return for her second year and had chosen the nineteenth-century novel as one of her modules. Aunt Joyce had contributed to the process by offering her a fortnight's holiday in the Dordogne just before the start of term, along with a little extra help in the form of some private tuition from the dishiest professor she could ever imagine.

"Please, John, just a couple of sessions," she had begged. "Fi's a sweet girl, just a little mixed up. If she had a head start for Year Two I'm sure she'd sail through it. It's a confidence thing with her."

"I'm not sure I'll have the time, to be honest."

"Just a couple of hours, John. I'm pleading to your better nature. I know you have one," she added with a wink. "I'll pay you, I'll make it worth your while. You can use the pool, if you want. I'll make you some lunch, dinner, whatever. Please!"

"Oh, alright, you win!" He had caved in without a fight.

It was no hardship really. The AULA term tended to start slowly and he was already more than prepared for it. He had ditched Kafka and Dostoyevsky for another shot at Dickens. Le Bugue was not such a long drive, the money would be useful and, frankly, Joyce was too nice a person to refuse.

Penny sipped at his chilled apple juice and took in the clean lines of the Sweetacres' contemporary dining room: the white furniture, the vase of lilies in the centre of the oval, glass-topped table, the abstraction of the chandelier, the wide picture window with mint-green blinds giving a full view of the sloping lawns and cedars. He sat down on a chair positioned by Joyce, he assumed, as one of a pair at the end of the table where a student folder lay closed. Its front was covered in graffiti and the five individual letters of *Fiona* had been cut out from magazine headlines and glued together in a stylized anarchic fashion.

Joyce had retreated to her studio; she didn't want to be

in the way. Presently her niece reappeared with her hair tied back in a golden ponytail, and dressed in a sloppy plain grey tee-shirt – one of Uncle Hugh's? – that barely covered her shapely backside. She was carrying a couple of paperback books which she tossed on to the table. She smiled at Penny, sat down in the seat next to his and flicked open the folder as if it were a fashion magazine. She found a page of notes and slid it closer to give him a better view: it was clear that she had been reading Hardy. When pushed she tried to explain that she was interested in exploring the writer's female characters but she had already grown impatient with Tess' "girly" acceptance of her fate.

"But you have to see her as a victim," he countered soberly. "A victim of her time. Tess is an uneducated force of nature tamed by men. Bullying, manipulative men who at that time – you need a sense of all this being over a hundred years ago, Fiona – at that time not only had all the power but also society's blessing in keeping it. And she's very young at the start of the story, remember."

"I still think she's a bit of a loser," she grumbled, "but I can't, like, say that in an essay, can I?"

"You must give Tess a fair chance. There's more to her than meets the eye. Have you reached the end yet? The scenes at Sandbourne? At Stonehenge?"

"No."

"Well, that's your first job."

The girl offered no response. She seemed to be mentally counting the number of lilies in the vase.

"And have you read *Lucie l'Eglantine* by Steeples?" he tried. "A contemporary of Hardy."

"No."

"Give it a go. I bet Joyce has a copy. It's quite short. You have a heroine a little like Tess but more proactive, if you like."

Fiona had stopped listening. She had started to doodle on a blank page inside the folder.

"Or Bathsheba Everdene," he persevered. "Now there's a feistier Hardy heroine."

"Aunt Joyce fancies you, I reckon," Fiona said suddenly, looking up at him with mischief sparkling in her eyes.

"I'm sure she doesn't," laughed Penny. "We're friends. Just good friends."

"That's what they all say, isn't it?"

"Listen, your aunt is happily married."

"I wouldn't believe that if I were you."

There lay a path Penny really did not want to tread.

"Hugh's a bit of a dick, really," the girl insisted, turning her eyes back to her page of doodles. "Away in New York. Again."

"I don't know him," said Penny with a little cough to clear his throat. "Now, let's read a couple of key scenes, shall we? Tess and Alec in the fog in The Chase?"

"Well, I reckon Joyce has the hots for you, John."

"Honestly, she really isn't my type."

"But I reckon you are definitely *hers*." She looked up again and, catching his eye, added: "And I wouldn't blame her."

And it was at this point in the conversation that Fiona tossed her pen on to the table, edged her chair a little closer to Penny's, and slowly inched her tee-shirt up over her hips. His instinct to look down was rewarded with a view of the girl's milky white lap and confirmation that she was quite definitely a natural blonde. Rather than changing out of her bikini she had simply taken it off, bottom and top too, he imagined, and had come back downstairs wearing nothing more than a flimsy, oversized tee-shirt and a hiss of *Coco Mademoiselle*.

Before he realised she took hold of his left hand and pulled it between her thighs. Penny felt the soft warmth of her skin but jerked his hand away as though it had been scalded.

"What the hell are you playing at, Fiona?"

"Come on, John. Relax. Joyce won't disturb us. She's in her art room with her headphones on. Take That, at a guess."

She looked up at him with a twinkle in her clear blue eyes. Penny gasped to think that she had actually formed some misguided plan. She tried to grab his hand again but he pulled back and she missed.

"I don't care about that," he said. "That's not the point. How old are you, for Christ's sake?"

"Twenty-one," she announced defiantly.

"Your aunt told me you were nineteen."

"Okay. Nineteen. I'm twenty in a week's time. And that's the truth."

"You need a boyfriend of your own age."

"I have one."

"Perfect," said Penny, straightening up.

"He's in England, though, right now. So, basically, he's, like, no use to me here, is he?"

"Well, I'm kind of flattered, Fiona, but really, it would be a huge mistake. Deep down, you know it, don't you? Cover yourself up, move your chair away and let's get back to work, eh? Better still, go and put some pants on first."

"Screw you, professor!"

"Hey, don't be like that."

The girl was already on her feet. Almost knocking over her chair, she straightened the tee-shirt over her bottom and walked around the table, swearing under her breath, and stared out of the window in a sulk with her back to him.

Penny decided to ignore her and half-heartedly flicked through some of her notes, waiting for her to calm down. His own pulse rate returned somewhere close to normal. He swallowed the rest of his apple juice, no longer so chilled. Presently she walked back towards him, smiling.

"Well, it was worth a try," she said.

"I suppose it was."

He pretended to smile back. She plonked back down on her seat, flicked to a blank page in her folder and asked him quite serenely:

"So who the fuck is this Bathsheba Evergreen, then?"

It was a less than enlightening tutorial for either of them, but at least they reached the end of the full hour without further embarrassment. Fiona would struggle in her second year, Penny could tell quite quickly. She was a superficial reader with a short attention span; understanding a novel's plot was all she really wanted. Characterization, social context, imagery, classical references, these were all victims of her drive, first and last, simply to work out what had happened by the final chapter.

He declined to stay for lunch even though Joyce had bought a quiche from her favourite *charcuterie*. The spacious house, for all its open rooms and its large, rolling garden, felt strangely claustrophobic. It was partly for Joyce that he had refused to play Fiona's game. He had too much respect for the woman to take advantage of her nymphet niece while her back was turned. And it was partly for himself too, of course, for his own self-esteem. For in spite of his track record of profiting from the naiveté of adoring students, even in his rampant thirties and certainly now at this disquieting age, he had always drawn the line at sex with teenagers.

Several days later Penny was sitting in one of the classrooms at AULA, typing up a few notes for his second – and final – tutorial with Fiona, when a colleague wandered in carrying two cups of coffee. It was a new teacher Penny hardly knew, a Frenchman who, like several other younger members of the faculty, seemed to regard him, amusingly, as a father figure. Penny was unsure how he felt in this unsought role of mentor. A few of the staff who had known him longer began to refer to him jokingly as *le doyen*, with its connotations of elder statesman, which was harder for him to laugh off.

As they drank together he was peppered with questions, mostly banal, and he was eventually obliged to be brusque in signalling that he really wanted to be alone and given the chance to get on with his work. The interruption had broken his flow. Before resuming he took the opportunity to check his emails. There was nothing in his personal inbox, but waiting for him at the library address that Camille Rousseau had set up for him was a message that set his heart beating a little faster. He read it through and then read it again, the second time more slowly, looking for nuance, but it seemed to be a letter of pure practicality:

Dear Mr Penny,

I have been appointed by the company of Hatcher Cross, Solicitors of Bath, to act on behalf of their client Mr Gareth Overthrow.

Mr Overthrow, a landowner in North Somerset, has recently discovered on his property a collection of paintings which, ostensibly, were produced by a local artist named Thomas Steeples at the end of the nineteenth century. Currently the paintings have not been authenticated, and neither has their discovery been publicised to any degree.

Our client has done a little research, however, and is keen to give a chance to independent curators of seeing the works before the major museums become involved, as they inevitably will. As you may know, Thomas Steeples is not an artist of any great repute, but the new works represent an exciting development in how he may come to be viewed in the future. There is a small number of interested parties whom I have also been charged with contacting, mainly collectors who own a Steeples already, but our client asked me to write to you also as he has some knowledge of the museum you curate devoted to the artist's brother Jonathan. In addition he is considering the factor that all of the newly discovered paintings represent French subjects; indeed there is a likelihood that they were painted in the Dordogne region of France.

If you are interested in discussing this matter further, by all means email me by return or telephone my office on the number below.

Forgive me for emphasizing that respect for confidentiality is paramount.

Yours sincerely,

Stephanie Chimes
Head of Private Client

5

As the massive tyres bumped to the ground with a rolling squeal, as the braking systems flexed their mechanical muscle, as the Airbus decelerated along the damp, grey, endless runway, and as the anxious passengers waited impatiently for the seat-belt lights to fade, John Penny was considering the notion that this was to be the first time he had set foot on British soil, the first time he had breathed English air, even the first time he would eschew the euro to hold instead a handful of the Queen's pounds and pennies, for over three full years.

The captain had a honeyed conceit in his voice that reminded him of Hugh Sweetacre and, much further back, of Angus Barrington-Smith and Jasper Couttes and many others of that particular English ilk who had populated his time at Oxford and provided much of the strangled soundtrack to those distant days. The plane had slowed to a heavy crawl and was turning cautiously towards the boxy limb of an arrivals gate. It had been raining in Bristol and the late morning sky was the puffy, pale grey of factory smoke. It was likely that they had descended through the same vast flank of thick Atlantic cloud as the one they had climbed through on leaving Bordeaux, where although the temperature was a few degrees higher, the sky had been of the same drab, stagnant froth.

Penny had booked a single night's stay in an airport hotel and a twenty-four-hour hire car. The university had granted him two days' leave, initially unpaid as he had given such short notice. He had convinced the *Chef de Faculté* that so early in the term it was acceptable to set his students reading assignments, and had gone on to remind him of the reflected kudos the institution was earning by association with the project in Frettignac. This could be a great opportunity to expand it, to take it to another level, to create something not just of local but of national interest. He could hear himself saying these words in his polished French, he could see the other man's faintly paternal smile, he could hear again his concession: *Très bien, Docteur Penny. Naturally we won't deduct the two days' pay after all. Even in this climate that would be a petty way to behave, non? On your absence form write down "research purposes" and I'll countersign it.*

At the rental desk a young Asian man with a circular name badge the size and colour of a tangerine displaying the word *Kamal* provided him with a newish Polo which had a rip in the passenger seat. He decided to haggle and to his surprise was offered a slight discount. As long as it got him reliably to the Mendips and back, not much more than twenty miles, he wasn't seriously concerned about the seat fabric. The hotel was clean, functional and promised a full English breakfast. He had time for a sandwich but regretted it: gluey coronation chicken on the type of

209

square white bread that he hadn't tasted since he lived on the south coast. *Tasted* perhaps being the wrong word.

Two thirty, she had suggested. He had a meeting with Stephanie Chimes at half past two in a village café just about ten minutes, she had mentioned, from the farm. *Head towards Cheddar. I think it wise that I speak to you before you meet Mr Overthrow,* she had said. *And it'll be much easier for you to find his place if you follow my car.*

The prospect of meeting him, and indeed her too, for her voice held a sultry tone that already smouldered in his mind, had excited him for days. His thoughts had raced out of control like a wild horse galloping full pelt, careering along a wide, flat beach towards the glittering waters of a shoreline. This could be the oxygen that the spark of his ambition needed to ignite. He already imagined a new Steeples museum, a proper gallery of paintings and books and sketches and manuscripts, a museum devoted to both brothers, to Jonathan and to Thomas, a magnet for lovers of literature *and* art, in strikingly modern, twenty-first century premises in Frettignac or Bergerac or both. He visualized an adjoining conference and study centre, accreditation not from AULA but from the University of Oxford, a spacious, elegantly furnished first-floor office for him as Curator-in-Chief, managing a team of scholars and researchers, specialists too in marketing and experts in multimedia promotions. He could foresee a touring exhibition, visits to galleries in Bordeaux, in Paris, in London. He could hear only accolades and congratulations on his vision, his acumen, his drive, his leadership skills, his intellectual prowess.

He had to put a noose around the neck of that wild horse and rein him in. Firstly he had to make some checks. He must proceed with caution. There was so little on the internet about the very modest Thomas Steeples. Penny was well aware that the author had a younger brother but his life was utterly unremarkable as far as he could tell. While Jonathan was the creative spirit, the genius, his brother had remained deliberately and deservedly in the shadows. The man's art was quite mediocre, it seemed, and he had ended his days as a humble cleric with the mildly interesting footnote that he died on the fourth day of August 1914, just as Britain declared war on Germany.

Penny also used search engines to investigate Gareth Overthrow and Stephanie Chimes. The man was indeed a Somerset landowner, a dairy farmer on a large undulating site known as High Reach Farm, a supplier to the cheese industry with a secondary income from extensive apple orchards. Meanwhile the woman, whose website photograph failed to tally with the appeal of her voice, had the look of a thirty-something maternal type, round-faced with heavily-rimmed glasses, mid-length light brown hair and a businesslike, unreadable smile. He noticed that like himself she was an Oxford graduate. He guessed that she was married with at least two children, hired a nanny unless she worked on a part-time basis – unlikely – and had a husband who also worked in Bath, a businessman of some kind (still guessing) whose hobbies involved rugby – playing still but mainly watching these days – and, perhaps with Stephanie, a shared interest in horses. Hers was one of several portrait photographs on the solid but rather dull Hatcher Cross website. It was a firm of solicitors like many others, whose residential, commercial and agricultural affairs were dealt with by partners, associates, solicitors, consultants, trainees and the rest. The home page showed freshly painted premises in an imposing sandstone Georgian edifice on Queen Square. He was dealing with a firm of standing.

If John Penny had half-forgotten England, the Copper Kettle tea rooms brought impressions of a certain warm and comforting Englishness flooding back to him in abundance. He found it, as described, set back a little from the road on a corner of Church Lane, among a cluster of houses – some brick, most rendered – and next to a small B & B, whose hostess had posted a notice on her ground-floor window advertising Nora's dog walking service. On a painted wooden ledge directly above the door of the café sat an actual copper kettle, badly tarnished by the weather, and the window was edged with pleated floral curtains. Instinctively ducking, he pushed open the door, a little bell tinkled and he felt at once that his entry was being judged by the watching eyes of everybody inside. The room was not large, having space for half a dozen small circular tables, and he counted only five people, three of whom quickly lost interest in him or considered it rude to stare: a retired couple with a black Labrador and, behind the counter, a stumpy middle-aged woman in a white apron who was arranging fruit in a large porcelain bowl. Floating invisibly in the air was the faintest aroma of mushroom soup.

"Good afternoon, sir," she said, without taking her eyes off an unsteady bunch of black grapes.

"Good afternoon," Penny replied, his gaze already drawn to the far side of the room where, sitting facing him behind a china teapot and a vase of posies, he recognised the features of Mrs Chimes. She was already on the point of standing up to welcome him. He was surprised to find a thin-faced man at her side with a cup to his lips.

"Two thirty on the dot, Mr Penny! Perfect timing. How are you? Welcome to Somerset."

He approached the table, shook her firm hand and sat down. She was older-looking than her photograph had suggested after all, and had applied a touch of make-up which accentuated the deep green of her eyes, her cheekbones, the soft curve of her lips. She wore a plain white blouse and a navy blue trouser suit with a badge on her lapel.

"Let me introduce Mr Broadfoot," she continued once Penny had settled and taken in his surroundings. Her neighbour rose slightly out of his seat and offered his hand over the tablecloth. He had sandy, receding hair and was exceptionally tall, his long limbs appearing trapped behind the furniture.

"Simon Broadfoot. A pleasure to meet you, Mr Penny. I represent Earles of Bristol. I dare say you've heard of us. No? Auctioneers, valuers of fine art and collectibles."

"How do you do?" said Penny, taking in a slight, slowly-spoken West Country accent: educated, but rather more *du terroir* than Stephanie Chimes' breathy, neutral delivery. The man wore a light cotton suit and an open-neck shirt of broad check.

"Mr Broadfoot is on board at the request of Mr Overthrow, whom you will meet in due course. Shall we order you a drink? A bite to eat, or is it too early?"

Penny looked over to the counter. The waitress had disappeared. A range of teas and coffees was advertised, and a soup of the day. In a display-case he saw fresh rolls labelled as cheddar and pickle, ham and cream cheese, and chopped egg and cress. Beside the display were three cake stands, each disguised by a gauze cover but neatly annotated: chocolate fudge, rich Dundee, Victoria sponge. Finally he spotted a wicker basket which held a collection of home-made scones. In a briefly reassuring, unexpectedly nostalgic way, he felt a very long way from France. He recalled his half-eaten hotel sandwich and ordered a slice of fruitcake with his tea.

"You can imagine how excited Mr Overthrow is by this discovery," Mrs Chimes was saying, flicking her hair behind her ears. "It is potentially huge. Life-changing."

"Potentially," advised Broadfoot, draining his cup and sitting back in his seat. He seemed impatient to leave.

"Well, of course," continued the solicitor. "But if the paintings *do* turn out to be validated, then, well, an aspect of British art, namely the contribution of *English* Impressionists, will have to be totally re-evaluated."

"I don't think we're quite there yet," said the man from Earles, sniffing.

"And do you believe," asked Penny, "that I, or the museum I represent, can play a part in promoting the collection?"

"Who knows what Mr Overthrow will decide?" she

answered. "But I can say that you are one of only four individuals he wanted to see before he engaged the media."

At this point she opened a briefcase and pulled out several sheets of glossy paper.

"I dare say you will be shown the originals later," she said, "but these are the works we are talking about."

She flicked loose strands of hair behind her ears again. They fell forward over her cheek almost immediately and Penny wondered if the woman regretted having had her hair cut in that particular style. She passed the pages over the table. He had seen the images before in email attachments, but these reproductions were considerably more revealing. He wiped his hands on a paper napkin and fingered through them hungrily one by one. There were five paintings, each one catching his breath more than the last.

He surveyed a view across a river to a port, recognisably the Dordogne at Bergerac, busy with water traffic, the light of a wide, orange sky smouldering over the roofs of the town in the background. Then there was a street scene on a market day: classically impressionistic, bold dabs of colour creating a sense of movement, of jostle, the sway of clothes, the play of light; Penny felt he could hear the voices, the shrill claims of the traders, the clucking of the women, he could smell the fruits, feel the rough skin of the vegetables – and this was merely a photographed reduction. There was a stylized view of a sunlit, honey-coloured castle high above a river in a steep-sided verdant valley: was this so-called post-impressionism? Something reminded him of Cézanne's paintings of villages and mountains in Provence. Next he took in a rendition of a familiar view: the twin-arched bridge over the Vézère at sunrise, if not in Frettignac, then somewhere very like it. It was a masterpiece of misty, silvery blues and dissolving violets and shape-changing greens: pure Monet. And finally the human form in close-up: a man and a woman in a country setting, lying on a blanket as if at a picnic, simply tasting fruit.

"Perhaps I shouldn't be telling you this, Mr Penny," said Mrs Chimes as the valuer shifted uncomfortably on his seat. "But it's really no secret that, regarding one of the local galleries, Mr Overthrow doesn't get on terribly well with the curator."

"Really?"

"I think a personal connection with him would go a long way. And also in your favour, you will discover that he is quite the Francophile."

Penny smiled and handed back the prints.

"And there are these," she went on, passing him a second sheaf of photocopies. He was holding the sketches she had mentioned, drawings he had not seen before. He took in a pair of complementary views of a shoreline and rock formations which recalled the limestone arch he had seen photographed in Dorset. So, not all of the works were done in France. Next there were several sketches, again from various angles and of different sizes, of a fortress on a hill, perhaps the same location as the finished painting. The lines were confident, clear, controlled. Finally there were outlines of faceless figures eating, crouching, sitting; some unfinished, again possibly studies for the portrait of the fruit tasters.

"They are wonderful," he said.

"They are delightful," agreed Broadfoot, sniffing again, "but there's a great deal to be done before anyone can say for sure that *a*, they are genuinely nineteenth-century works and *b*, they are genuine Steeples."

Penny swallowed the last of his cake.

"Shall we go?" suggested Mrs Chimes, fastening her briefcase.

"Indeed," said Broadfoot, already out of his seat and buttoning up his jacket.

"Lead on," said Penny, who had been so absorbed by the art that he had not witnessed the solicitor paying for the refreshments. "Thank you for the tea."

"I wasn't actually sure you'd have had the time to buy some pounds, Mr Penny. Anyway, my pleasure. It's not far to High Reach. Follow my car. I'm the little white Audi."

Penny had never been to a dairy farm before, had never before caught in his throat the acrid yet strangely sweet smell of the herd, had never listened to the clatter of cattle on concrete as they wearily crossed the yard to the milking sheds, had never heard the tinkle and thrum of the machinery, the cries of the herdsmen in their wellingtons and waterproof aprons, sleeves rolled up to their shoulders, the faint swoosh of their hosepipes, the lowing of cows in mild distress.

Today he caught a glimpse of this world, slowly following the Audi and Broadfoot's mud-splattered company Vauxhall past the gates, through puddles, up the cracked lane with his window wound down. On they drove, first and second gear, passing outhouses and barns, stables and sheds, farm buildings of every type he could imagine, then out along the open windswept fields, under the wide, dirt grey sky, following a line of hedges to an assembly of whitewashed stone buildings, the largest of which was the family home. In a paddock he saw at least three horses. He heard the clucking of hens. The air smelt different here and not just because of the animals. The breeze had an English accent, moreover an English *scent*: it was the grass and the moss, tree bark and nettles and dampness. The air in Frettignac was different: herby, perhaps, more fragrant.

Gareth Overthrow was a large red-faced man with tufty greying hair and a slight stoop to his gait. He looked to be in his fifties. He wore corduroy trousers and a chunky cable-knitted jumper in beige, from the sleeves of which protruded two huge hands. He offered his right to his three guests in turn and invited them to join him at the long pine kitchen table. There was no sign of Mrs Overthrow beyond a pair of pink rubber gloves by the sink. The offer of drinks was politely declined.

"I'm glad you could come over, Mr Penny," the farmer was saying, pulling up his sleeves to reveal thick, hairy lower arms. "And at such short notice."

"Well, of course, Mrs Chimes' emails have piqued my curiosity."

"You are an academic, am I right?"

"I work at the university, yes. Teaching English."

"So the museum you run is a kind of hobby?" said

Overthrow, raising an eyebrow and glancing towards Mrs Chimes. She and Mr Broadfoot were sitting next to each other across the table like a pair of detained schoolchildren unsure of interrupting their teacher.

"In a way, I suppose," answered Penny, "but it is one I take very seriously. As I have done for over two years now."

"I did visit your website, of course. You have what looks like a very small space."

"The photos are a little misleading. It is much larger in reality. Plus, I have plans to extend it."

"And the emphasis is obviously on books; that is on the *other* Steeples. On Jonathan, the writer."

"Indeed."

"And so your interest in paintin's would be peripheral, would it be fair to say?"

Overthrow had a stronger accent than Broadfoot, a soft burr that even thirteen years of private education had not polished away.

"Combining the brothers' output would be an exciting, even pioneering development, Mr Overthrow."

"Call me Gareth, for Heaven's sake."

"And John, please. Such an exciting development. I do know something of art, of course, and the French provenance of the works you have found is something that I feel my museum has a distinct advantage in exploiting."

"Hmm. You may be right."

"Provenance that is still to be confirmed," interjected Broadfoot, who had finally found a handkerchief and was about to blow his nose.

Overthrow ignored the remark and continued to talk directly to Penny.

"I do love France, John. Big fan of Brittany. We have a little place near Quimper."

"Very nice."

"And my mother-in-law, she actually spends more time over there than she does in London these days. Down near you."

"Really?"

"She actually knows your museum. Can you believe that? It's in a library, isn't it?"

"For the time being, yes. The library is more of an annexe to the museum."

"Yes, the old girl has visited. I had her on the phone last week. She's a big fan of Steeples. *Your* Steeples, the writer. She loves her books. Lives in a village called Eymet. You know it, John?"

"I've heard of it."

"South of Bergerac. Sounds nice. We've never been. Well, the wife has, I tell a lie. *I've* never been. One of these days, eh?"

"You'd be very welcome in Frettignac, I'm sure."

"I've been doin' my homework, see, since all this kicked off. Plenty on the web about *your* Steeples. Famous author and all. So very little about *my* Steeples. Poor little Thomas. Quite the shrinkin' violet. Younger brother in the shade, eh? Well, at least until now. And that's where Mr Broadfoot comes in, eh, Simon?"

"Exactly," said the valuer, "but, as we know, it's early days."

"Can we safely say whether Thomas actually ever went to France?" asked Mrs Chimes.

"I think we can," said Broadfoot, selecting a page of typed notes from a plastic wallet. "Yes, I know we can. Let me update you all. My enquiries have centred so far on a chap called Sainty. An elderly chap, lives in sheltered housing in Wells. Anyway, he taught art at the Bishop's School near Bath for many years, a real Steeples aficionado. *Your* Steeples, that is, Gareth. In fact, he's probably the only one who knows close to the full story. Steeples himself worked at the school in the early twentieth century, as a chaplain. He was still painting a bit: there are two oils of the abbey in the Bishop's grounds. I've been up there and seen them, in fact. The current headmaster has them hanging in his study. They are very accomplished, I must say, and in the style of Monet's studies of the cathedral in Rouen – the series he did in differing light, in a variety of tones. Quite a departure from Thomas' other known works, which are mainly watercolour landscapes, all English subjects, plus a series of random portraits commissioned over many years by local worthies. All of little value, in my judgement. No, the abbey oils are the other side of the coin. And they are absolutely genuine. A third was painted, believed to be in a private collection somewhere in Bath. I'll track it down."

"You're guessing Thomas had seen the Monets in France?" asked Mrs Chimes.

"It's uncertain. Doubtful, in fact. They were painted around 1892. Jonathan was no longer in France, for a start. Thomas probably saw photographs, read about them."

"But he was in France at some point? While Jonathan was living there?"

"Quite definitely. Sainty has two letters written in France by Jonathan to his brother, in one of which he asks questions about his time in Paris. It is dated 1886. In the second, dated a year later, Jonathan invites him back to Bergerac. Categorically *back* to Bergerac, as though Thomas has already been at least once. That said, we don't know for certain if he did visit his brother once, twice or never."

"What does Mr Sainty believe?" asked Penny.

"He is convinced that Thomas spent time in the Dordogne as well as in Paris."

Broadfoot paused while the others digested this flurry of information.

"Also in his collection," he picked up after a moment, "Sainty has a pamphlet dated 1886 for the Eighth Impressionist Exhibition in Paris. It was the final one, as you may know. Sainty is certain this proves Thomas visited the exhibition. Gauguin, Seurat, Degas were all showing. And it seems that Thomas was something of an autograph hunter. On the back of the pamphlet he has Degas, Pissarro, the writer Zola, and, most treasured no doubt, Claude Monet himself."

"That would make a very interesting addition to the collection," said Penny.

"It's not for sale," cut back Broadfoot. "I asked myself. Sainty was adamant: not at any price."

"Just a thought."

"Mind you, things change. He *is* a frail old man."

"What else do we know about Thomas?" asked Mrs Chimes.

"Well, he was never a professional artist," said Broadfoot. "He worked as a journalist for many years. Bristol, then London. Some of his writing survives. He wrote about politics, religion and such. Like his brother, it seems he was something of a social radical. A reformist, a latter-day liberal. He took to painting as a hobby."

"Kept his light hidden under a bushel," added the farmer.

"Never married," continued the valuer, "and no heirs. When his brother died he turned to the service of Christ. Attended theological college in his fifties and was ordained but never served as a vicar. He preferred to work as a chaplain in boys' education."

"This is how he met Matthew, we believe," said Overthrow, "don't we, Simon?"

"Matthew?" said Penny.

"Matthew was the only son of the family who had the farm here way back, before my great grandfather. We think the trunk we found the paintings in belonged to Matthew. Had the initials MMW on the front. It was up in an enclosed attic space in one of the barns – one of the old ones that's toppling over, one we're having demolished for new stables. The trunk must have been up there for, well, for a hundred years. Hard to believe, eh? Never touched. Never opened."

"Why would the paintings belong to Matthew?" wondered Penny.

Broadfoot took over:

"Matthew was a trainee priest at the same time as Thomas. Same college. Both local to this area, they must have been friends, even though Thomas was twice his age. Very close friends, we're guessing. It wouldn't be out of character for Thomas to give Matthew his art when he knew that he was dying. Sadly Matthew did not live much longer himself. He survived the trenches but died in the twenties in Southern Africa. He was working there as a missionary."

"Thomas had no other family?"

"None. His only brother had died childless. No nieces, nephews."

"You've been busy, Mr Broadfoot."

"That's what I do," he said with a self-satisfied air.

"Rather like detective work, I imagine."

"There are similarities in our investigations, yes."

"But you're not tracking down quite so many criminals."

"You'd be surprised, Mr Penny."

"Let's have another look at the treasure!" suggested Overthrow, lightening the mood. "Are you sure no-one wants a drink? Glass of cider? No?"

He disappeared into a back room, re-emerging a moment or two later with an armful of loosely rolled canvases which he spread haphazardly across the kitchen table.

"If we can just find a bit of room for these?"

He had separated one from the next with what looked like folded squares cut from cotton bedsheets. The enhanced effect of seeing the prints in the tea room after the subdued versions on a computer screen was magnified a hundred-fold when Penny first took in the splendour of the actual paintings themselves, uncurled in all their glory on the pine surface under the bright kitchen spotlights. For a start they were much larger than he had imagined, mostly at least a metre by just under, about the size of the top of a card table, with the sketches rather smaller. Then the smell reached his nostrils, a mix of oily mustiness and dry mould. Now he could examine the exquisite brushwork, the delicate gradations of colour, their depth and range. Standing back a little he saw the dazzling effect of true art, scenes of vibrancy, awash with patterns of sunlight, scenes of noise and chatter, of melancholy and serenity, scenes of calm reflection and intimate conversation.

"They are very fine," said Overthrow with pride, showing off one ahead of the next as Penny looked on.

"They have no titles that we know of," said Broadfoot. "They have never been catalogued as far as I can tell so far."

"We call this one *Market Day* or *Jour du Marché*," remarked the farmer with an exaggerated accent. "And then this one," edging forward the quayside scene, "*Les Gabares*. My mother-in-law explained that that's what they call those shallow-bottom sailin' barges that ferried up and down the river carryin' barrels of wine."

"This is perhaps the finest of them all," noted the valuer. "It is the work of a truly accomplished artist. Stand back a bit further. Consider the translucent quality of the evening sunlight."

Penny couldn't help but think of the depiction by Joyce

Sweetacre of a very similar scene across the Dordogne, the one he had hung on the crowded wall of the *Espace*. He had thought her painting extremely worthy but here in front of the Steeples, he was looking at something from another world. Another idea came to mind:

"Looking at these little figures on the quay, I'm also reminded of Jonathan's poem *Doctor Tombo*." He looked at the three faces but none was nodding in agreement. "It's a comic poem, about a quack doctor travelling on a river boat selling exotic medicines from West Africa. He claims cures for sunstroke, morning sickness, even hangovers. Of course, he is a swindler, a trickster. *Herbs and roots of doubtful worth / And ripped them loose from France's earth…*"

"That's not one I know," said Overthrow after a moment.

"Shall we move on?" proposed Broadfoot.

The farmer lifted the view of the hilltop castle into sight.

"Shades of Cézanne?" suggested Penny cautiously.

"Well," hesitated Broadfoot, wiping his nose again and leaning forward to flatten the canvas a little more with his long, bony hands. "A bold use of colour, definition to the line, yes. There *are* murmurings here of a more modern, geometric approach, I grant you. I imagine this one was the last of the set to have been finished."

"Has anyone recognised the castle?"

"It's almost certainly at Beynac. The curve of the river, the height of the cliff, the shape of the tower, the adjacent building which has the look of a chapel, they all point to

Beynac. We've compared it with photos of such fortresses all around France."

"And the bridge?" said Penny, moving over to the moody study of shifting light through the mist, the stone form hanging like the spine of a dinosaur reflected in the shimmering water.

"No idea yet."

"I think it's *le Pont Napoléon* in Frettignac."

"Perhaps. Perhaps not."

"Well, John might be right, Simon," said the farmer. "Don't underestimate him. After all, he does live there, he knows the terrain."

"It's a possibility," conceded the valuer.

"If it's any use," offered Penny, "for a geographical context, Thomas could easily have known the places, if we think they are Bergerac, Beynac, Frettignac, from recommendations from his brother. Jonathan certainly knew them all, they might well have visited them together."

"Your observations are valid," said Broadfoot, "in a sense."

"And therefore useful? Helpful?"

"Useful, yes. In a sense. This is delightful too," he skipped on. "*The Fruit Tasters*. Look at the joy in their faces. It's in the eyes, you see? And how he dapples a moment's light on the clothes, on the basket, the polish on the cherries. It's very Renoir. We'll need to check the historical accuracy of the fashions, of course."

"The signatures are interesting, aren't they?" said Penny, carefully pulling a corner of the market scene canvas towards him. "On the bottom left."

"We must assume that Steeples was left-handed. Far easier to sign on that side, of course; less chance of smudging. And all of his other signed works were completed in this way."

"Could a signature have been added later?"

"It's possible but the paint in all cases is consistent with the colour palette used in the paintings. At least to the naked eye. And you see, sometimes he signs 'Steeples', the full word, and sometimes, like here, it's just 'St' and a squiggle with a down stroke for the 'p' and then a upward flick and the 'l'. As if he's in a rush. But this habit is also commonly seen in his known works, especially his portraits."

Stephanie Chimes had moved to the far side of the table and was holding one of the sketches up to the window.

"This is Durdle Door, isn't it?" she said. "An English subject."

"I'd say so," agreed Broadfoot. "The influence is Monet. He painted versions of a very similar scene at Etretat in Normandy. Coastal rock formations, open arches, seascapes."

"So there is no doubting the quality?" asked Penny, sitting down.

"No. Not at all. The doubt is whether Steeples painted them."

"And if not?"

"Well, I suppose, then who did?"

"I'm goin' to give Simon a bit more time," said Overthrow, also taking a seat. "Time to dig around a bit more. I've shown these to several other interested parties, so far under conditions of confidentiality. But we will have to involve the big museums eventually, if only to use their expertise."

"And the press," added Mrs Chimes.

"Well, of course. I imagine they'll cause quite a stir."

"Would you be prepared to sell any of them?" Penny asked. Overthrow looked at him quizzically. "I imagine the price could be high," he went on, "if they are authenticated. Beyond what we could afford, for sure. I just wondered."

"I think not," answered the farmer at length. "Certainly not in the near future. In fact I have grown very fond of them already. So's the wife. She's out with the dogs, by the way. Wasn't sure if a couple of yelpin' great mutts would be up your street, Mr Penny. I know Stephanie isn't keen."

The solicitor dutifully nodded.

"And we don't want them slaverin' over the artwork in any case, do we?"

"So you'd perhaps consider *loaning* them for exhibition?" resumed Penny.

"That is something for discussion, John," interrupted Mrs Chimes, flicking her hair up over her ears. "In terms of promotion, exposure, validation, then exhibiting the works makes good sense, whether in a private gallery, a public museum, England, France, short term, long term, but we aren't there yet."

"But you would be interested, John?" said Overthrow.

"Absolutely."

"Well, I thank you for your interest."

"No, absolutely."

"It would be quite an undertakin' for you."

"We could manage. I have a motivated team."

"Transport, storage, security, insurance…" intoned Mrs Chimes.

"We could manage, I assure you."

Broadfoot was busily reassembling the canvases and linen strips into a neat curly-edged pile. Overthrow stood up suddenly and held out a hand to Penny. It appeared that the viewing was over.

"Well, we'll be in touch. It was nice to meet you, John. At least you now have a clear idea of what I have, even if," he laughed, "I still have no idea what to do with them!"

"It was a pleasure."

"And you'll deal with Stephanie from now on." The solicitor nodded to them both. "She is lookin' after my interests in this business."

"Fine."

"It will be in a week or two, probably" she said, "but if we are going to involve Frettignac, then of course I'll be in touch again before too long."

The meeting ended quite abruptly. Mrs Chimes and Broadfoot were evidently staying behind at the farm a little longer, but it was clear to Penny that his presence there was no longer expected. The light was fading and he had the evening ahead of him. At one stage he had considered asking the solicitor to dine with him but the opportunity had not arisen. As he left them, Broadfoot had recommended an Italian restaurant in Bristol's Old City and had even offered to ring and make a booking for him there and then.

And so, a couple of hours later Penny found himself sitting on a banquette in a dimly-lit *ristorante* in front of a glass of house Sangiovese waiting to be served one of the locally famous charcoal-baked pizzas. He didn't mind eating alone; he was quite used to it. And apart from a copy of the city's evening newspaper to keep him company, he had his warm, private thoughts: his mind was fizzing with ideas for a brand new gallery, *Steeples & Steeples*, where pen on page met brush on canvas, visions of a glorious future of public appearances, statements to the fawning media, keynote speeches in university halls, high-profile meetings in European capitals, all to the accompaniment of a steadily rising wave of unfettered applause.

6

He really should have been marking essays, in the case of his new students their very first one, the one he would always read most closely and comment on most assiduously to set a marker for his expectations of their work ahead. The small pile of pages was sitting by his laptop on the table at his home, some bound by staples or a coloured paperclip, *un trombone*, some sheathed in clear plastic envelopes. He had cast his eyes over the first two or three efforts: they were worthy if predictable. Nineteenth-century literature: *Compare and contrast a French novel with an English one of the same period.* It was his standard opening challenge to the Year Ones. *Any two books, any two books at all from that most fertile of times, what can you tell me about them?* One of these days he would get a Balzac and an Eliot or a Flaubert paired with a Brontë but he was expecting the usual Zola versus Dickens or, for those who enjoyed reading less, a short story from each of Maupassant and Hardy. Yes, there were plenty of students for whom reading was less of a joy than you might imagine.

But, incidentally, wasn't he too becoming a little predictable?

John Penny stretched his arms to the ceiling, yawned, took off his glasses, stood up and wandered into the kitchen. As he waited for his coffee to percolate, he stared out at the walnut trees, their branches sagging with fruit and foliage, swaying lightly in the warm breath of the wind. He would find his shorts and trainers and go running in the hills later. He opened a window to let in the dry, scented air.

Presently he returned to the laptop whose screen had been enticing him away from his students' work for most of the morning. He swallowed a mouthful of coffee, clicking from one page to the next, from one image to another: Stephanie Chimes' attachments, *Jour du Marché*, *Les Gabares de Bergerac*, the couple tasting fruit. It was Jonathan and Béatrice, wasn't it, eating cherries and peaches on a summer's day by the river, June or July, 1886 or '87, the fleeting happiness of two lovers caught in paint on canvas by the man's younger brother? Well, perhaps. The man lacked the full beard that photographs of Jonathan always showed but the shape of the face was right, as was the man's wild, long hair and the sense of mischief in the eyes. And the woman? It was not an exact resemblance but Thomas had captured elements of her, elements he had chosen to highlight: Béa's childlike smile, her wide brow, the fair curls reflecting the sunlight, falling loose from her bonnet, the delicate pale slimness of her wrists.

Penny's thoughts were interrupted by a sudden knocking at the door. He hadn't heard a car approach, nor was he expecting a visitor. He got up and walked through to the vestibule.

"*Désolée de vous déranger, Monsieur Penny.* I am sorry to bother you."

It was Amande Puybonieux, somewhat out of breath, standing on the threshold of her mother's house. Penny invited her inside.

"*Votre voiture, madame?* Where is your car?"

"I decided to walk, *monsieur*," she replied, slowly rolling her eyes as if to suggest a mistake. "I need to take more exercise, you see. But it's a hot day, and the hill is a pull for someone my age."

"What can I do for you? Come through."

The woman waddled into the room, unbuttoned her cardigan, smoothed down her wispy hair and sat down in an armchair as invited. Penny remained on his feet with his back to the empty hearth.

"I came to tell you about the painter," she said at length, wiping the lenses of her glasses with a small handkerchief.

The painter? How on earth did she know?

"The painter?"

"Yes. I could have telephoned, of course. I felt like stretching my legs."

"Which painter?"

"A man in town I use. Didier. I booked him to come up and paint the shutters. Front and back."

"Oh, I see."

"He said he would do them next week, but now it's going to be tomorrow. *A court délai, je m'excuse.* Short notice for you too, Monsieur Penny. I hope you will not be disturbed."

"Tomorrow is fine, *madame*. The forecast is good, I

234

believe. Didier will be able to finish the job and I will be in Périgueux all day in any case."

"That is a relief."

"It's not a problem, *madame*."

"May I have a glass of water, *s'il vous plaît?*"

"Of course. Or a coffee?"

"Water is perfect. I have such a thirst."

Whether it was out of a sense of guilt that Penny had placed himself in front of the wall from which he had, against her express request, removed the wedding photograph of her brother and Noisette, he was acutely aware that, the moment he stepped towards the kitchen, Amande's eyes were sure to be drawn to the space he had been concealing. He half-filled a glass at the tap and returned, setting it into her open hands.

"*Voilà, madame*"

"*Merci, monsieur*."

He hovered by the fireplace waiting for her reproach.

"Are you very busy?" she asked instead, turning her head towards the table and the computer that sat on it.

"Not really."

"That's a pretty picture."

Through her frameless glasses the woman was contemplating Thomas' lovers and their basket of fruit, slightly askance, filling the screen.

"It's a Steeples," he said automatically.

"Really?"

"Not Jonathan. Thomas Steeples, his brother."

"His brother was an artist?"

"Yes, he was. A very gifted artist."

"Well, I can believe it."

"As a matter of fact, *madame*, I have only recently found out anything about him."

Amande Puybonieux was a curious, inquisitive soul, a natural gatherer of information, a collector of knowledge. There was no reason to keep the story from her. Stephanie Chimes' code of confidentiality would not apply to this harmless Miss Tiggywinkle of a woman. Penny brought the laptop over to her seat and within five minutes had unburdened himself of his secret and felt all the better for doing so: the solicitor's email, his flight to Bristol, his meeting with Overthrow, the sight of the canvases, their discussion of a prospective loan, the ongoing investigations of Mr Broadfoot of Earles.

"You must not speak to anyone else about this, *madame. S'il vous plaît. C'est important.*"

"Of course, Monsieur Penny. I understand."

"Perhaps I should not have told you."

"*Je suis la discrétion même, monsieur.*"

"For the moment it is a secret."

"And it will stay a secret, *monsieur.*"

She stood up and handed him her empty glass.

"*Merci.* It is time I left you. Don't forget about Didier. He will start early so maybe you will see him before you leave the house."

"*Madame?*"

Didier was far from his mind. Penny was ordering different thoughts, framing a different question:

"Can you recommend a lawyer?"

"A lawyer? You are in some trouble, *monsieur?*"

"No, not at all. I'm just thinking ahead. If, and it is a big if, I, we, go ahead with a loan of some or all of the Steeples artwork, I believe I will need some representation in dealing with legal matters, contracts and the like on my behalf. Wouldn't you agree?"

"Yes. Yes, it is always wise to have things formalised, I would say."

"So. Is there a man in Frettignac?"

"There is a woman, I would say. Very good, very *efficace*. She is a member of the *conseil municipal*, also, the town council. Marie-Françoise Perrier."

"Perrier? Like the water?"

"*Oui, exactement.*"

"*Merci, madame.*"

Penny was already typing her name into his search engine.

"And one other thing. I'm sorry, my head is swimming with random ideas. The *Espace* won't do it, will it? The library is too small. We'll need bigger premises, obviously. A proper exhibition space. Somewhere we can turn into a gallery."

"In Frettignac?"

"Ideally."

"That is not easy."

"Yes, I realise. But can you give it some thought?"

"I could ask Camille."

"No. Please keep it to yourself for the moment. She'll want to know the whole story. You know the town just as well as her. As well as anyone."

"I will think for you, *monsieur*."

"You're very kind."

"It was kind of you to share your secret with me."

"I think I needed to. It's too big a secret for one person to keep to himself."

Before he double-knotted the laces of his running shoes and filled his plastic bottle with chilled water from the fridge, Penny checked his emails again. Nothing new. Still nothing at all from Stephanie Chimes. And once again he quickly searched *Thomas Steeples paintings discovered*: there were no revelations, there was no breaking news, the story remained buried, contained within a couple of office buildings in Bristol and Bath and a windswept dairy farm in the Mendips.

He ran cautiously through the grove, avoiding first-fallen fruit, reached the crest of the field where he always now instinctively looked out for the woman Noisette and her dog – always in vain – and headed up along the edge of the vineyard, into the woods, breathing hard, picking up speed as the shaded track began to level off. Garrigue was a mystery: the owner of the vines and, it was said, another vineyard across the valley, he was a man who was rarely seen. The word was that he spent most of his time in Paris these days and left the grapes to a team of managers, and there was talk of a mistress on the Ile Saint-Louis and possibly a second in Saint-Cloud. Noisette had borne him a son, now in his middle teens, who had been sent away to a boarding school near Versailles several years ago. The woman, in Penny's mind at least, had been virtually abandoned to live as a recluse in the rambling family home, without a family and with only her gentle Rigolette to love. He may have been jumping to conclusions, it was actually none of his business; nevertheless he could not help but feel sorry for her, the hesitant bride in the photograph which he had unscrewed from the wall the very day he had met her on the mound. Her happiness with her husband was short-lived and with Garrigue perhaps had become even more fragile. The woman's melancholy had overwhelmed him, filling the room; he had carefully carried the old frame upstairs and placed it inside a cupboard on the landing between a pair of stale blankets which he never used.

The run energised him. His muscles ached but he felt healthy, his face and limbs were tanned, his mind was clear. He drank a pint of cold water, showered and sat outside for half an hour with some bread and cheese and a couple of ripe tomatoes, listening to the birdsong.

He was surprised to find that Stephanie Chimes had been in touch while he was out, and a long email had been left waiting at his address. He opened it and read it voraciously:

Dear Mr Penny,

Hoping this finds you well. You will be interested to learn of developments at this end in relation to the artwork discovered on the premises of my client, Mr Gareth Overthrow of High Reach Farm.

I have been instructed to inform you that Earles of Bristol have advanced their investigations into the authenticity of the paintings and Mr Simon Broadfoot has confirmed that the signs (what he calls "the mood music") are positive. Apparently experts from the Victoria in Bath and the Bristol Museum believe the works to be genuine nineteenth-century pieces, and representatives from the University of Bristol Department of Fine Arts and Tate Britain in London are helping with research into the career of Thomas Steeples.

The work is not completed and so far has been done behind closed doors but my client feels the time is ripe to publicise the find and so you can expect to read the story in the British press (no doubt online in your case) very soon. Your name and potential involvement will, of course, remain undisclosed. As I am sure you know, the taste for exaggeration to the point of inaccuracy is one that much of our media is prone to, so please do not be alarmed if you read anything that contradicts the content of the conversations we had last month.

The situation remains that you are among a small number of interested parties with whom my client is of a mind to do business in terms of exhibiting the works. Selling, as you know, is not an option for him, but his consideration in loaning some or all of them to a reputable independent gallery is ongoing. In that regard, and with the caveat that nothing is yet finalised, you may be advised to make preliminary preparations at your end in terms of securing premises, legal representation, promotional material, indeed all the logistical arrangements with which I am sure you are already familiar.

*As the picture becomes clearer be assured that I will
be in touch regularly, and in the meantime please do not
hesitate to contact me if you have any questions about
the process.*
  Yours sincerely,
    Stephanie Chimes

He smiled at the woman's formality, the unquestioning
adherence to professional standards. He pictured her in
her heavy-rimmed glasses and business suit tapping out
the words on the silent keyboard in her smart, oatmeal-
carpeted office, a vase of flowers on her wide desk,
perhaps, a black and white photo of her family, for sure,
framed in a narrow rectangle of bleached oak. He read her
message again. His heart was beating a little faster; the ball
was rolling, and, he was convinced, was rolling straight in
his direction.

After several hours reading manuscripts, digesting the
printed word, studying text and images on a computer
screen, it was indeed the case that Penny's eyes grew tired.
In spite of his glasses, regularly strengthened to reflect the
weakening of his natural vision, there were times when
he had to pull himself away, stop his reading, close his
eyes, rub them and simply give them a rest. Years ago,
when it became clear that he would need magnification
to enable him to read comfortably, he had baulked at the
idea of wearing a pair of framed lenses over his face. It
was an affront, like having to walk with a cane. His first

spectacles, bought in a fit of pique, were wire-framed, cheap and unflattering. Gradually he became convinced by a persuasive optician that spending more on designer frames to suit his face would be a way of optimising his reliance on glasses. He experimented with styles and colours, quickly finding that a largish, rounded design complemented his look and, moreover, attracted favourable remarks.

His current pair, exclusively and expensively styled in navy with pale blue temples, were closed, sitting snugly in the top pocket of his linen jacket as he strode along the busy corridor from the staffroom at AULA on his way to pick up a coffee before his final tutorial of the morning. He had a fullish day and would ask a colleague to put him up for the night; give Didier a free run at the shutters and anything else he felt the urge to give a fresh coat of paint. He wandered into the canteen and could comfortably see, from twenty metres, that the day's lunch special was chalked up as *les spaghettis à la bolognèse*; his long-distance vision was absolutely fine. There was no queue ahead of him. He ordered a *grand crème* and waited at the counter. It was eleven thirty and the canteen was mostly empty. Out of the corner of his eye he could see someone discreetly waving at him: over by the wall he spotted Sam, the art student, giving him the thumbs-up. He hadn't seen her since before the summer. What a pretty girl she was. If only. He would have loved to go over and enthuse to her about what he had witnessed at Overthrow's farm. Sitting next to her, with a sweatband stretched around her head, texting someone on her mobile, was her lover, the dark girl who looked as strapping and as thick-set as ever.

He paid for his coffee and made to leave, sweeping the rest of the room with a vague interest. It was then that Penny really did become anxious about his vision. He blinked his eyes and tried again to focus. In the far corner of that large room, flooded with morning sunlight, sat a group of four students: three women and a young man in a bright red tee-shirt with long thin hair brushed into ponytail. It was not the man who attracted Penny's attention, however. It appeared that the group was engaged in a lively conversation. Two of the women were becoming quite heated, gesticulating, puffing out air, arguing in an intense yet amicable way. Very French.

He took a step closer to their table. He couldn't quite believe what he saw. Who he saw. Who he was looking at. She was sitting with her back to him, and it was only when she turned her head, or lifted it to laugh, that he caught the profile of a face he would never forget. She was trying to follow the discussion, two or three steps behind the flow. The woman's hair was shorter than he remembered, she wore a shirt he didn't recognise, but he knew, the instant she suddenly turned his way, that he was staring, rigidly, at the enchanting face of Columbine Snow.

7

"You've shaved off your beard."

"About a year ago."

"It suits you without. You look younger."

"Thanks."

"You *do*. It's taken ten years off of you."

"If you say so."

"I do."

"You've had your hair cut."

"Why yes, I did."

"Quite drastically."

"I've gotten used to it."

Penny had offered her a cigarette even though he knew she didn't smoke. His own was lit and he took another long drag.

"I didn't mean that in a bad way."

"No?"

"No, I like it. It's neat. Brings out your cheekbones."

"I have to hide the grey these days."

"As you can see, I don't even bother trying."

His smile of resignation brought out a smile from her too.

"It's good to see you again, John. What's it been? Two years?"

"You know exactly how long it's been."

"Yes. You're right. I know exactly. To the day."

She had stepped outside, leaving her friends to their sparky conversation, beckoning him to follow. In a dusty courtyard, under a line of plane trees, they had found a shaded bench by a classroom block and there they sat in a stumbling dialogue, words without rhythm, a half-remembered melody played hopelessly out of tune. John Penny, scratching his chin, sipping his coffee, and Columbine Snow, tightly clasping her bag to her chest, sitting a foot or two apart but with the whole of the Atlantic Ocean still between them.

"What are you doing back here?"

"I'm studying."

"But I thought…"

"My marriage is over. Things broke down a year ago."

"I'd no idea."

"Of course you didn't."

"Do you want to talk about it?"

"No. Not here. Not right now."

He drew on his cigarette again; he had almost finished it already.

"So. You're back in France."

"For a year at least."

"AULA took you back."

"Yes, they did."

"What are you studying?"

"I'm majoring in French. I want to get competent. Maybe even fluent. Like you."

"Good for you."

"And IT. Programming. Web design."

"Sounds good. When did you start?"

From across the courtyard someone called his name. He recognised one of his students in a group heading to class and exchanged a wave.

"*J'arrive!*" he shouted.

Columbine watched them disappear through a glass door.

"Sorry," he said to her. "When did…"

"I arrived a couple of weeks ago."

"I've not noticed you around."

"I haven't noticed you either."

"I don't come in every day."

"You still in Frettignac?"

"More than ever."

"Still in the house with the walnuts out back?"

"Still there."

"How's the *Espace*?"

"Same as."

A robin flew on to the arm of the bench nearest the woman and, with its little head twitching nervously, stayed there for a moment as if to eavesdrop. Columbine watched it with a smile until it finally hopped away and took to the air. Penny was rubbing his cigarette end into the dust with the heel of his shoe.

"I'm living in town," she said, following the little bird with her gaze. "An apartment."

"How's that?"

"It's fine. Homely. It's near to that place where we hired those costumes that time. You remember?"

"Of course."

"I have a view of the cathedral. It's better than where the students live here, for sure. And I've bought myself a Vespa."

"A scooter? So then, you're quite independent."

"That's the idea. The buses aren't so bad here, but you know, evenings a little hit and miss."

He nodded, allowing a pause, giving her a space to fill with more words, more talk, if she wanted to.

"And I can't really afford a car."

"No?"

"You still drive the old Peugeot?"

"Just about. It's even older now."

She offered a hollow smile.

"Well, it's good to see you, Columbine. I hope the year works out for you. I should say welcome back, I suppose."

He stood up as if to leave.

"Thanks. You have to be some place?"

He tossed the coffee cup into a bin.

"Yes, I do. I have a class to teach. I'm already late."

"Well, I may see you around."

"Bound to. Take care."

He offered her a brief wave, turned on his heels and strode off to his tutorial.

"So long," she said, but he was already out of earshot.

Penny didn't know what to think. His emotions were

in limbo, static, as though someone had taken out the batteries. He was neither pleased to see her nor was he angry that she had come back. She had a tale to tell and there was no doubt that he would get to hear it whether he wanted to or not. His class was a mess. Already ten minutes late, he rushed his introduction and complicated his instructions; the students were baffled and he was short with some of them. A sullen atmosphere descended and his attempts to lighten the mood were tolerated rather than embraced. The class dispersed muttering like conspirators. He needed another cigarette to calm his nerves but at the end of it he was no closer to seeing a clear picture. All he saw was a fog, all he felt was confusion.

As for Columbine, the meeting was inevitable from the moment she had signed off her re-application to AULA and shortly afterwards booked her airline ticket to Paris. After everything that had happened she knew she needed to be in his orbit once again. And there he was, two years later, sitting close enough to hold her hand but far enough apart to be a stranger. He'd been pleasant enough, neither rude nor enthusiastic: neutrally polite. As was to be expected, of course. She would see him again whether by accident or by design, but where it would lead she was too superstitious to consider, and too unsure of herself to even know what it really was that she held in her heart.

8

When Hatcher Cross whispered the secret to the media – local, national and social – the flow of reports and commentaries and informed opinions was more of a steady trickle than a foaming torrent. The national press quickly superseded the regional operations, who were granted no special favours. Internet chatter remained, as usual, the blunt instrument of the strident amateur.

Stephanie Chimes posted a short email to Penny to warn him that the dam had burst and to remind him that as long as he was circumspect at his end, then his identity would not be revealed by her firm until any deal was brokered and signed off. She added that all the paintings and sketches had been moved from the farm and were now in the safe hands of Earles of Bristol.

One of the broadsheets was first out of the blocks with their story, drenched in suspicion, about a mystery cache of supposed Impressionist masterpieces. Overthrow was not mentioned by name, neither was his farm, a spokesman – more likely a spokeswoman, Penny thought – preferring to talk of a barn in an unspecified West Country location. So the dairy farmer had opted for the anonymity chosen by certain lottery winners; it was something of a surprise to Penny but a decision he could understand. The newspaper questioned why a trunk full of so-called treasure had lain undisturbed in a draughty outbuilding for over a hundred years. Although a photograph of *Les Gabares de Bergerac* was printed, there was little discussion of the artistic value of the works and the journalist showed no scholarly interest.

A second paper took more of an academic approach and was prepared to judge the paintings on their merits, the reporter conceding at the outset, however, that the chances of them being authentic were slight. She granted that not only the style of painting but also the subject matter leant itself to the Impressionist period. As a reaction against the classical, against religious iconography, the French Impressionists had chosen to paint subjects of sheer mundanity, capturing them quickly as if to hold a fleeting moment in time, the passage of light on aspects of life the viewer might recognise as his or her own: bathers, dancers, men playing cards, women ironing, people taking lunch, strolling in parks, scenes of local interest – meadows, floods, beach umbrellas, busy streets and railway stations. In this context, she argued, Steeples' market, the port, the bridge, the castle, the fruit tasters, all outdoor scenes, painted fashionably *en plein-air*, they all made sense. *Have we discovered an English Impressionist worthy of the name?* she asked. *Very probably not*, she concluded self-righteously.

One or two of the tabloids latched on to her epithet. *Lost works of the English Impressionist*, ran one headline to an article which had little to say but filled an entire page thanks to photographs of all five of the Steeples paintings; smudgy black and white did them absolutely no justice. Another had plenty to say about the artist and, to his credit, the journalist had done his homework. He accurately covered the main points of Thomas' life but was less convincing in a paragraph devoted to Jonathan, failing to mention his time in France and misnaming his masterpiece *Forty More Barrels*. One of the Sunday supplements displayed three of the paintings in glorious colour and included a failed piece of detective work to discover their Somerset provenance.

Eventually the magazines dedicated to the art world, expressly the British art world, had their say. Not all had online editions but Penny garnered a flavour. Those he read were, if anything, a little less dismissive, treating the works and the validation process with much more respect. One writer was so enthused as to chance his arm – and his reputation – there and then to wager the paintings to be genuine. *There is always reason to doubt that sudden finds of this nature could be genuine,* he wrote. *So very often the skill is to be applauded but it is the skill of the modern forger. In this case, however,* he went on, *Steeples' works strike me as so fine, the period so vividly reflected, it seems as though Claude Monet himself might have breathed on them. We should doubt not that these paintings are real but that they could ever be produced by mere fakery.*

Penny's heart soared, only to swoop again on reading, a day or two later, a short article in another august journal which stated that although the works were of exceptional quality and the subject material very much of the time, this was no proof of anything: these subjects had been painted in infinite variations throughout the twentieth century. And Steeples' other known works were drawn into the argument: the critic dismissed the man as third-rate, an amateur, a hobbyist. *The English Impressionist remains a myth*, she wrote. She drew attention to the renewed interest in early twentieth century works by Wynford Dewhurst, referred to in some quarters as the *Manchester Monet*, which were derivative, authentic and yet barely influential. *The closest we had was Sisley but he was born in Paris and lived almost all of his life in France. The American Whistler had his acolytes in London but none were quite so gifted. The notion that Thomas Steeples has eclipsed them all is laughable.*

Stephanie Chimes was in touch again. A specialist from the Musée d'Orsay in Paris had been invited to consider the paintings and the next stage in verification would be a scientific analysis to date the components. If he were interested she suggested he research terms such as infrared reflectography, Wood's light, spectroscopy and stereoscopic microscopy.

Three days later came a further email: a BBC reporter had discovered the involvement of the retired art teacher Alec Sainty, whom Broadfoot had mentioned in their meeting. A fifteen-minute item on *Newsnight* had featured an interview with the old man, clearly struggling with his memory, blinking at the camera, gripping the sides of his armchair for reassurance. He was quizzed aggressively on his personal research and notably on his conviction that Steeples was capable of such fine art. The solicitor expressed her admiration that under such pressure the eighty-year-old had fought his corner. *It will be on the web no doubt if you wish to see it.*

In this day and age did anyone ever write notes any more, secreted slips of paper inked with intimate messages suggesting times and places for furtive trysts? Wasn't a text message more the way of things in the digital age? Perhaps Columbine Snow was deliberately tipping a nod to the device so favoured by those nineteenth-century storytellers. Perhaps she wanted to add a touch of romance to a banal request. When Penny unlocked the door to his study the following Monday morning he found a small, folded piece of paper at his feet. He opened it on the spot, recognised the American's handwriting and quickly digested her simple proposal:

> *John*
> *I'd love to come to Frettignac and see the Steeples exhibit again. Would you meet me there on Saturday?*

And beneath a long sequence of numbers:

> *Please call me. Col*

9

If it was a little unnerving for John Penny to spend time with Columbine Snow, it was no less so for her to be in his company once again. The only difference between them was that it was she who had instigated the meeting. For his part he had tried to give little thought to his memories of her; he had dealt well with her long and, he believed, indefinite absence from his life, and he had nothing but doubts about wanting to see her again. After he had rung her mobile number and blithely arranged to see her at the *Café des Sports* at ten thirty he had felt palpitations, a cold sweat began to form on his brow and he was convinced that he had made a bad mistake.

She seemed to be in excellent spirits, arriving on her blood-red scooter, lifting off her helmet as she came into the café, shaking out her shiny, short-cut hair and smiling at him across the room at the novelty of her transport arrangements. He had bought her a *grand crème* and a croissant. He couldn't help himself warming to her as she spoke for at least a couple of minutes about one of her eccentric new tutors with a small flake of pastry stuck to her chin.

Old habits prompted him to take her hand as they crossed the street and headed towards the library, but something stopped him at the last moment. They spent just ten minutes inside the building like a brother and sister. He let her review the exhibits, little changed since she had last seen them, while he chatted inconsequentially to Camille Rousseau, who was already eager to close up for the weekend.

"This is new," she called out to him. She was studying the watercolour of the riverside scene in Bergerac.

"What do you think?" he asked, joining her.

"Not bad. Who's J Sweetacre?"

"She's a friend. Joyce. A local artist. I put it up as a favour, but she has talent, don't you think?"

"It's not bad."

"Ties in with Steeples' world."

"I guess. So, who's Joyce?"

"A friend. I said."

"A girlfriend?"

"No. Not a girlfriend. She's a friend. A supporter of the *Espace*."

"English?"

"Very."

The little landscape had its merit but once again Penny silently compared it with the similar scene painted with infinitely more skill and energy by Thomas Steeples, a painting now sitting swathed in cloth at optimum temperature and humidity in a strongroom somewhere on the premises of auctioneers in Bristol. Apart from his loose words to his landlady he had kept all of this to himself for weeks, but he already knew that if he spent the afternoon with Columbine he would end up sharing with her the whole story of High Reach Farm. As they emerged into the sunlight and she suggested they take a stroll, he had already decided that not only did he have to tell her, he actually wanted to tell her.

And here they were, almost an hour later, walking downriver together along the shaded footpath which skirted the Vézère, chewing over the implications of a Steeples art exhibition mounted somewhere in or close to the town of Frettignac. Columbine was excited, enthusiastic and practical, as he knew she would be. She asked him about the monetary value of the art, the transportation from England, the search for larger local premises, the need for extra help. They were questions he had asked himself, of course, questions to which he had so far no proper answers. He told her she was jumping the gun, nothing had been validated and certainly no contracts had been signed.

"Even if they're not originals, I'd still have them here if I could get them," he admitted.

"They'd still cost you."

"I know."

"And you'd still need more space."

"I know."

"I'd be willing to help."

"Let's talk about something else. You know as much as I do. For now it's a waiting game. I don't want to jinx it."

They had already wandered over two kilometres out of the town. The path, scattered here and there with eddies of fallen leaves, was hard to navigate in places, overhung by fading, straggly summer growth, but Penny remembered that just a little further on was the edge of a village where, until the winter months set in, a tiny bar-bistro was in the business of serving hot snacks. As the track finally veered away from the river they skirted a field of browning, uncut sunflowers and followed a gravel lane to a group of cottages, at the end of which stood the shabby café.

There was nobody else around but the place was open. A bored-looking young man, not much older than a teenager, served them, eventually, with *hot-dogs de merguez*, a plate of *frites* and glasses of beer. They sat at a table outside in the watery sun with a view of a line of horse chestnut trees whose flame-yellow leaves flickered in the light, and beyond them the shadowy, pale green strip of an empty sports field.

They smiled, they chewed, they drank, swallowed and smiled again. Penny mentioned that he had been here once before, failing to add that he had shared a huge *pêche melba* on that occasion with the divorcée Marie-Jo from Marketing. The service had been slow that day too, he remarked.

More than the rickety, wrought-iron table between them, there was still a gulf the size of the State of Maine. When the question came, she seemed relieved, eager to answer it.

"So how's Patrick?" said Penny, wiping his mouth with a paper tissue, keeping his eyes on the last few chips, already cold.

"I've no idea. I haven't seen him for almost a year. He's some place in New York City, I think. At least he was."

"What do you mean?" he asked, looking up at her. She was facing the lane, her stare fixed at some point between the cottages. "He left you?"

"Exactly that. He left me. I filed for divorce months ago. Just waiting on it now."

"I'm sorry. Really, I am. You know, that it didn't work out."

"Don't be sorry. I'm not."

Penny emptied his beer glass. Suddenly voices could be heard from behind the trees, the muffled shouts and harsh bursts of laughter of young men who were kicking a ball around. Some wore red football shirts, a few walking around in little groups beyond them wore pale blue. A match would surely be starting before too long.

They were both distracted. She still had half a glass of beer in front of her.

"Are you warm enough?" he asked. "Shall we move inside?"

"No, I'm fine."

If she wanted to tell him more she would. There was no need for him to push.

"The wedding was great," she went on presently, elbows leaning on the table now, talking quietly to the hands that were clasped in front of her face. "Exactly what I had always wanted. Not a big deal, but nice, you know? A small gathering. Family, a few friends. It was a lovely day. High summer. Cloudless skies."

She turned to face him, offering an ironic smile.

"And that was as good as it got."

"I'm sorry."

"Well, not quite. We had a few good weeks. Patrick was already showing signs that he was not the man I thought I knew. Not the man he had been. I think the war changed him. Easy to say, I know, but I think there's a grain of truth in that. He was quick to anger, short on patience."

She sighed and stood up.

"Have you paid already? Shall we walk? Head on back?"

They rejoined the path and it was a few minutes before Columbine picked up her thread.

"Almost as soon as we were married I got pregnant," she said in little more than a whisper. "It was what we both wanted. We were both delighted. Then after three months I miscarried."

Penny didn't know what to say. Not wanting to sound glib or banal or unsympathetic, he chose to say nothing at all. Eloquent silence.

"You can imagine the emptiness, the devastation, the pain. I don't mean the physical pain, I mean emotional pain. We both suffered."

Rather than walking they were merely drifting forwards, slowly, side by side. He gave her time to order her thoughts.

"The doctors found fibroids." Her hand moved to touch her belly. "Right here in my womb. I had an explanation of sorts, I suppose. I had something to blame. Patrick simply blamed me."

Penny held back stray bramble canes that had grown across the footpath and helped her through the gap. A moment or two later she resumed:

"He wanted to try again, almost straight away. I wasn't ready at all. I needed more time. He felt I was pushing him away, which I suppose I was, in a way. We fought all the time. About other stuff too, trivial stuff, but at the heart of it was the lost child and what it had done to me. To us. The relationship was scarred. It never healed. Just got worse."

"I'm really sad for you, Col," he said finally. "You had support, I hope?"

"Well, my daddy was kind of in two minds. Course he was sympathetic but he's always been a fan of Patrick's and he saw his side of things just as much as mine, his own daughter. It was hard to swallow. Pammy was great, though."

"Pammy?"

"Patrick's sister, Pamela."

"Yes, I do remember you spoke of her."

"She's been a rock. She's a nurse, she's trained to understand. She always figured deep down that her brother was a jerk. Now she actually hates him. Even more than I do."

They were approaching a bend in the river, where two young teenage boys were sitting on folding stools dangling cheap fishing rods into the dark water. They were waiting, chattering, bickering like Vladimir and Estragon over the thin sound of music from an old transistor radio. Neither looked away from their bobbing floats as Penny and Columbine passed their spot one after the other.

"I stayed another year," she said as the tune died away in the distance, "working for Daddy's business, but my heart wasn't in it. I needed to get right away. It was a big decision, I guess, but I just needed to get free from that place."

"You have friends here."

"I know I do. I'm lucky."

"You'll get over him."

"I'm already over him, believe me."

"But not the baby."

"That'll be harder."

"Of course."

After a short period of silence she stopped to face him. She wiped a tear away from her cheek.

"And I'm sorry too," she said.

"What do you mean?"

"I'm sorry for how I left you. How I left you here."

"I worked it out. I understood."

"I think it was the wrong decision."

"Easy to say now."

"I guess."

"You were engaged. I did, I understood."

"I know I hurt you, John."

"It's in the past."

"And I'm truly sorry."

"Forget it. We've both moved on."

At the next narrow point in the path he stopped to let her walk ahead, found a cigarette and lit it. She smelt the smoke and turned around.

"You started smoking, didn't you?"

"Just occasionally."

"Since when?"

"A while."

She wrinkled her nose, that pretty nose that stayed pretty even when she screwed it up.

"You should quit."

"Should I? Says who?"

"I do. Patrick started smoking. In the army, I guess. Stank out the house. I tried to get him to quit, but he wouldn't. Got him to smoke on the stoop, out in the yard, but he wouldn't quit for real. Smoked all the more in fact."

Penny finished the cigarette but the taste had already been tainted by her words.

Gradually they were coming up to the houses on the edge of Frettignac, the little development known as Les Saules. The sun had already sunk below the line of the hillside and the warmth in the air was dissipating as quickly as the pale, empty sky was leaching its wash of blue. Slowly coming into view, in one of the gardens whose hedges bordered the river walk, was a familiar figure holding a long-handled brush; her head disappeared and reappeared as she bobbed up and down at her task. Firstly Columbine and then Penny recognised Amande Puybonieux. As they came closer they could see that she was sweeping up cuttings that had collected on the garden path.

"*Monsieur Penny, bonjour!*" she called as she spotted their approach. "*Et Columbine! Ça va, vous deux? Beau temps, non?*"

They stood for a moment, exchanging pleasantries,

congratulating the old woman on the neatness of her plot and the fecundity of late fruit hanging on her pear tree, relating the geographical details of their walk, the bite of lunch they had had downstream, commenting on the nip in the autumn air.

As they left Les Saules behind it struck Penny that the sight of the American, absent from the area for more than two years, had elicited no surprise in the gardener.

"I've seen her a couple of times already," explained Columbine.

"Really?"

"I've been over here on the Vespa. Just last week, in fact. She cooked me supper."

"I'd forgotten she was something of a friend of yours."

"Still is."

"An unlikely friend, if I may say so."

"Not really."

"But she's so much older than you, for a start."

"She's actually not *that* much older than you, John!" she laughed.

"She's a different generation!"

"Well then, in that case, so am I."

"Okay," he groaned. "Touché."

"Anyway, I like her. We talk about all sorts."

"Were you in touch during, you know, from the States?"

"To my shame, no. I thought I had to make a clean break when I left. Thought that's what I wanted. I was wrong."

It was still too early for the streetlights but the

shadows were deepening as they walked on towards the town. The light was fading but it still held a chill, ghostly glow which reflected off both the rippling water and the clouds of mist that had begun to rise from the river's surface. In the distance the bridge appeared, its stonework cloaked in a veil of shimmering, silvery vapour. Penny instantly recognised the view: he was looking from the same point, from the same angle, in the same half-light as Thomas Steeples when he painted the same bridge in his Impressionist masterpiece. He remembered that the Steeples was of a bridge at sunrise but it didn't really matter and it was already too late: his heart had begun to beat more quickly the moment the thought formed in his brain, the moment the matrices matched up. There could be no argument: Steeples' subject was the twin-arched *Pont Napoléon*.

Columbine had already wandered ahead. He would tell her later, another day. This day was over.

"Thanks for coming," he said to her as they reached the top of the steps and headed to the square. "I enjoyed myself."

He saw the flicker of disappointment on her face but he had decided that he had had enough of her for one day. What more did she want? He didn't want to think about it. He didn't want to know.

"Well, thank you for looking after me, John."

"I think it's better we take things slowly, don't you?" he said, regretting that he'd even tried to explain anything.

"I guess."

"If we are to be friends, I mean."

"Yes. You're right. I'm sure you are."

"Okay, then."

"Okay."

"Let me walk you over to your bike."

"Sure."

It was only when he had arrived back at the house, switched on the lamps, poured himself a glass of red wine, pulled off his shoes and sat down in his favourite of the two large armchairs that he concluded he had made the right decision. On leaving her their brief embrace was not one of any great warmth. And he had waited until she had put on her helmet so that a kiss, any kiss, even the chastest of kisses was out of the question.

She had admitted that she had hurt him. Of course she had. More than she could imagine. And now that she'd come back to France, uninvited, into his part of France, back into his life, he was going to make sure that she never had the chance to hurt him so badly ever again.

10

Around lunchtime on a cloudy day towards the middle of October, Stephanie Chimes chose to speak to John Penny over the phone rather than tell him the good news in a rambling email.

"Two reasons to be cheerful, Mr Penny," she said, her crisp voice relayed from Queen Square, Bath, to his mobile as clearly as if she had been standing outside his kitchen window. He listened to her words, his smile broadening, his heart thumping, his breath shortening with her every sentence.

"According to Simon Broadfoot, it's conclusive. No doubts at all. They're all originals, all authenticated nineteenth-century pieces, all contemporary of the great French Impressionists, and all painted by Thomas Steeples!"

"That's wonderful news!"

"It had to go way beyond Broadfoot's own judgement, expert though he is. Earles' top table were involved, plus all the academics you can think of."

"And the science?"

"The lab tests came back positive. As for the Steeples

angle, the keys seemed to be one, his time in Paris and two, the subject matter: his subjects tally with those of the lesser works already attributed to him – his watercolour landscapes of meadows and streams, of villages and churchyards, and of course he painted many portraits."

"Overthrow must be delighted."

"You'll be interested to know, by the way, that the characters in the fruit-tasting portraits have been identified as his brother Jonathan and a French woman he apparently had a long affair with, a Béatrice Valéry."

Penny felt a glow of pride. Of course they were.

"Broadfoot thinks it should be retitled *Forbidden Fruit.*"

"He's wrong, of course."

"Really?"

"*The Fruit Tasters* is an objective title. In my opinion it's up to the viewer to make his or her own moral judgement."

"I will let him know what you said."

"Please do."

"The only place they haven't identified," she continued, "is the bridge. The bridge in the mist."

"It's Frettignac."

"That's what you said before, isn't it?"

"I'll send you a photo, Mrs Chimes. Tell Broadfoot. I know exactly the point by the river where Steeples set up his easel. I'll send you a photo tomorrow, and when it gets really misty again I'll send you another, an even better one."

"Fine. It looks as though the mysteries have all been solved."

"So, then. What's next?"

"Well, what I've just told you has been known *in house* as it were for a day or two already. We'll be announcing it to the press tomorrow. In the meantime Mr Overthrow has been taking advice from several quarters."

"I see."

"And that's the second reason to be cheerful, Mr Penny. He has decided to offer you first refusal on an extended loan of the paintings – between twelve and eighteen months is what he has in mind – subject to various conditions, of course."

Penny had to sit down. His hands were trembling with such excitement he almost dropped his phone.

"I don't know what to say. You must thank him for me, of course."

"Absolutely. In the meantime you must continue to deal through our offices here, if you don't mind. Do you have a lawyer over there who can represent you, Mr Penny?"

"Yes. Yes, I do. It's all in hand."

"So can you text me his details?"

"It's a she, in fact. I'll get on to it."

"There are quite a few hurdles to jump, as you can imagine, decisions to make and so on, but if you can convince my client that you are running a competent operation, that you can give certain guarantees, and of course, that you can provide the financial resources, then I should say that those marvellous paintings could well be hanging in your gallery within six months. I will outline everything to your lawyer – does she speak English, by the way?"

"Yes, she does. That won't be a problem."

"She will receive details of the arrangements, she can talk things through with you and then if everything is clear and acceptable, a contract will be sent across for signatures and so on."

"Perfect."

"So, on behalf of Hatcher Cross, I should say congratulations, Mr Penny! I hope it all works out splendidly for you."

Did Marie-Françoise Perrier understand English? He had not even met the woman yet. Everything was so provisional and yet now the future had become the present. He would contact her later that day, maybe even call in at her offices in town. He had written the address down somewhere.

Six months? He would need to find premises in a hurry, some half-neglected shelter in Frettignac, waiting to be discovered. He didn't want to take the exhibit to Bergerac or Sarlat or anywhere else even further afield, and in any case the *municipalité* would not allow the Jonathan Steeples collection to leave the town.

He needed help, he needed to organise a team; it was obvious that he could not do all of this on his own. And what he needed more than anything, if his dream was to become a reality, was money. What had she said, *guaranteed financial resources*? Well, exactly. Now more than ever he would need funds from those cultural committees, from those educational grants, from those government subsidies for the arts, from those generous benefactors – all those pots of gold that had been so slow to appear so far. He allowed himself a smile, the adrenalin finally abating. An English Impressionist, a lost genius, brother to another genius, would surely provide his aces in the poker game to come.

11

It was a wild evening across the entire region, the weather reports confirmed, with violent gusts of wind and localised downpours causing traffic disruption and damage to trees and rooftops from the Atlantic coast to the A20 motorway. One meteorologist suggested it was remnants of the same storm system that had ravaged several small Caribbean islands as a Category 3 hurricane four or five days earlier.

John Penny had left AULA as planned but a detour near Sainte-Marie-de-Chignac had added twenty minutes to his journey home. For his first "council of war" in the library in Frettignac he arrived embarrassingly late. And although he had convened the meeting, had the entire agenda in his head and was its unofficial chairman, they had started somewhat aimlessly without him. Sitting under harsh strip lights, on three sides of a long rectangular table, were Camille Rousseau, looking tired and as wiry as ever, the shaggy-haired Nicolas Duchemin, assistant director of the Tourist Information Office, and, still wearing her raincoat, Amande Puybonieux. Penny had contacted them all within hours of Stephanie Chimes' telephone call. Madame Puybonieux aside, they knew little or nothing of Thomas Steeples and in spite of misgivings about how realistic it might be to successfully exhibit his paintings in the town, they were both prepared to be swept along by the force of Penny's ambition.

He apologised for being late and handed out to each a blank sheet of paper. There was plenty to talk about: from publicity material to funding, from security issues to legal representation, from timeframes to manpower, but nothing was more urgent than finding new premises – an appealing, generous local space to house the exhibits relating to both the brothers.

"There really is nowhere I can suggest in the centre of Frettignac," admitted Madame Rousseau. "We have considered school buildings, empty shops, *la Salle des Fêtes,* vacant rooms in the town hall. If, as you say, you are aiming for a display that could last for twelve months, even longer, then none of those would work."

Penny scratched his chin.

"However," she continued, "Nicolas has come up with an idea, a possible site on the edge of town."

"The old Protestant temple," the young man cut in enthusiastically.

Penny had come across him only once or twice before but he already decided he liked him. He wore his hair unfashionably long with a shabby beard that gave him the look of a rock guitarist from some American band from the 1970s.

"Do you know it, Monsieur Penny?"

"I don't think so."

"On the road towards Les Eyzies, just about a kilometre

out of town. Past the old ironworks, on the left. There is a chapel, an old Protestant chapel, disused – in fact it hasn't been used for fifty years, my grandmother says. It's empty. Totally neglected. Set back a little, off the main road, a dark stone building, not pretty."

"I must have driven past it but I can't picture it."

"Nicolas was thinking of the annexe," said Madame Rousseau, "weren't you?"

"*Exactement.* There is a brick building attached. Self-contained, I think; it was a kind of vestry or storage space."

"Would it be big enough?"

"I think so, yes. You would need to take a look, obviously. And it goes without saying that it would need plenty of work – cleaning it up, renovation, certainly new electrical provision."

"Who owns it?"

"I looked into this for you, Monsieur Penny. Both the temple and then much later the annexe were built on land leased by the *municipalité*. The chapel was built in the early eighteenth century by the local Protestant community, and they paid a small nominal price to rent the land. As it has been long abandoned, I imagine that the ownership of the property has fallen into the hands of the town, to the local council."

"We can check with Madame Perrier," Penny said. "I spoke to her earlier in the week and she has agreed to act as my lawyer. She strikes me as an impressive woman and I will invite her to all future meetings." He noticed that Amande Puybonieux was quietly nodding as he spoke.

Penny had indeed spent almost an hour in the offices

of Marie-Françoise Perrier, an intense, tightly-sprung woman of about forty with straight, honey-coloured hair scraped back into a short ponytail and such a ghostly complexion that he had wondered if she ever saw the sun. He had outlined the situation, explained what she would be required to do, baulked at the amount she proposed to charge him, was reassured that he would be a priority client, and, for want of so convenient an alternative, he shook her warm, tight hand and followed her signature with his own, scratched across the bottom of a pale grey form of agreement.

He looked across at the three faces in turn.

"The bottom line in all of this" – he hated the expression and was annoyed with himself for using it – "is money. I believe in the project so much that I am prepared to pay up front for whatever is necessary, but I believe the money is out there to support a venture like this if we look hard enough."

"We've been here before, haven't we?" Madame Rousseau reminded them.

"We have, but perhaps I just didn't push hard enough."

Between them they listed the familiar agencies and committees, and Duchemin suggested contacting local companies for sponsorship.

"Not just local ones," Penny thought aloud. "Big ones too. In France and in Britain. It's English creativity we are celebrating here, after all."

The rain was still battering against the windowpanes. Just at this moment the front door was forced open and a woman covered from head to toe in a dripping set of bright orange waterproofs was virtually blown across the threshold.

"Sorry I'm late! The roads are real scary," she shouted in English, pulling back her hood. It was Columbine Snow. Only Penny seemed shocked to see her.

"Hi, everyone!" she went on a little breathlessly, shaking the water from her rain suit, and catching the look of surprise on his face. "Amande invited me, John. I hope you don't mind. I'm here to help. The more the merrier, I guessed."

"Sit down, dear," said Camille Rousseau with a motherly smile. "We were talking about how to pay for Monsieur Penny's outrageously ambitious plans."

He knew she was joking, but funding was a serious issue. It didn't help matters that at this stage he had no real idea of how much the whole venture would cost. The American found a seat next to the librarian and Penny passed her a sheet of paper. She looked puzzled that it was blank but he didn't explain; he was already moving on to the next point on his mental agenda.

There was a premature discussion about ticket prices – it was decided to investigate the charges of similar galleries – and a vague, optimistic timetable was drawn up. Penny was convinced that if all the stars aligned they could have customers queuing up by the May Day holiday. Ideas were floated for ways of expanding the Jonathan Steeples exhibit, given that a larger space was in the offing: Columbine suggested panels of photos and text relating to influential contemporaries of the brothers in the realms of both art and literature. Penny made a note to speak to a colleague in the *Section Arts et Dessin* at AULA. Duchemin, who understood marketing and publicity better than anyone else in the room, offered to see how social media could be exploited and was keen to set up a new website, inadvertently treading on Columbine's toes, Penny thought.

If he had been the kind of chairman who insisted in drawing up detailed minutes of meetings, he would have made a note that, with thanks to the participants for their attendance, the session was brought to a close at 19.40. He was more than satisfied with what had been achieved; a simmering excitement ran through him as it had for the past few days. There was so much to do yet he was convinced that it was all perfectly possible. He had a team of willing supporters, he would find more in the coming weeks, but above all he himself was committed and confident and determined to drive the project forward. Penny himself was the difference between failure and success.

The wind had dropped, the rain had abated but the night sky had darkened to pitch. Camille Rousseau studiously locked up the library doors behind them and to the sound of their footsteps fading Penny watched as the group dispersed this way and that. The town suddenly seemed very quiet, drops of rainwater falling silently from blackened branches into great puddles in the pavements which reflected the soft glow of the streetlamps. His mind abuzz with thoughts, he was approaching his car when he heard Columbine's voice a little way behind him.

"John, wait up!" she called, striding out to catch him up. "Hey, will you help me celebrate?"

"Celebrate? What are you celebrating?"

"Today's my birthday."

"Is it? I'd no idea. Twenty-nine again?"

She laughed, her eyes sparkling in the flickering yellow light. For the first time he noticed she was wearing the earrings with the star design.

"Mid-thirties again!"

There was a moment's hesitation on both their parts.

"So, what, you want to go for a drink?" he asked finally. "I don't think there's much open in town tonight."

"No, I've got some food. Brought it with me, in my little trunk on the scooter. A quiche we can warm up, *tarte tatin* from that place near AULA, a bottle of champagne…"

"You mean, take it up to my place?"

"Could we? Do you mind?"

"No. Yeah."

"You're sure?"

"Well, yeah."

"Really sure?"

"Yeah, we could do that."

He was taken aback for a moment, unused to being shanghaied. He couldn't refuse but decided there was no reason to. After the meeting they had plenty to talk about, and he had no other plans. And he was hungry; her food sounded appetising.

"Listen," he said, "go and pick up your bags and we'll take my car. Leave your bike here. You don't want to have to get all that waterproof stuff on again and drive up in the dark. We can collect it later."

"If you're sure?"

"Of course. Great idea. Happy birthday!"

"You've taken down the old photo," she had remarked the moment they set foot in the room.

"It depressed me," he had said. "I don't think it was a happy scene. It spoke to me of disappointment, of unfulfilled promise."

"So what happened to them?"

"She lives on the Garrigue estate. Literally up the hill. He moved away. That's all anyone says."

"You should put something on the wall there in its place. One of your Joyce's paintings."

"She's not *my* Joyce."

"I know. You said."

"It's better just left as a blank wall."

"Whatever. The kitchen looks very familiar," she had said, stepping through with her shopping bags.

The void of two years suddenly seemed meaningless. With a half-finished glass of wine in his hand and his cheeks reddening, he stood in the warm kitchen of his own house and watched her take control. She had remembered where everything was kept, even the baking tray and the salt and pepper and the clean tea towels. She knew how the oven worked, where to find a tablecloth and a pair of candles, which lamps should remain switched off to create the best ambiance, and she would have lit the fire for him if he hadn't insisted on doing it himself. It was entirely effortless, as though she had never been away. He smiled, and carried on smiling as, stooping by the open fridge, she looked up at him.

"You're out of cream," she said.

"So we'll have it without."

And for that moment she seemed to him, once again, after so long, to be the very reason why there were two armchairs in the sitting room.

They ate a meal of delicious simplicity, exhausted the champagne and laughed about his oft-aborted novel, whose shifting plotlines he tried to explain but which had stalled again after a summer of near inertia. He put on an exaggerated American accent to infuriate her and pressed her to talk a little about Bangor but it was clear that she was reluctant. He detected in her, in her embrace of France, a sense of escape from America, from Americans, from part of her life that had caused her so much misery and regret. And he was right; Bangor was in her past and her eyes were fixed on the future.

He found a dusty bottle of Saint-Julien, a 2005 that he had been saving.

"Here's to your ambition," she toasted, clinking her glass against his.

"My ambition?"

"To be loved, to be adored. You remember telling me?"

He smiled.

"You said you wanted to be acknowledged, to be recognised."

"Of course I remember."

"You're closer to it than ever, I'd say. This Steeples project, you could fly to the moon on the back of it!"

"We'll see."

"And I told you you already had your admirers, didn't I? Back then. You had a room full of them this evening. Hanging on your every word."

He sipped his wine and let her carry on.

"Including me, of course."

His eyes held hers, nut brown and warm. She hadn't changed, he thought, in spite of everything. She was as adorable as ever.

"I adored you too," she said in a whisper. "I loved you, John."

"But you loved someone else."

She sighed, took a long breath.

"I loved you both. I think, somehow, I did. I found a way to box you up, I guess, to keep you apart. In different ways I loved you both."

"And now you love neither."

She looked down at her glass and lifted it to her lips. He watched and waited.

"I could love you again, John," she said, "if you'd let me. Do you really think I came back just to learn French?"

One of the candles was burning out. The fire was losing its light and the room was filled with flickering shadows.

"You broke my heart, Col," he replied after a moment. "You realise that, don't you?"

"I know I did."

"It's taken this long to get over you, and now here you are again. I don't want it to happen again."

"Perhaps I'm the only one who can really put your heart back together."

He sighed and looked away, down at his empty plate, at the label on the wine bottle, anywhere.

"Will you let me try, John? Please?"

She offered her hands across the table.

"Please. I loved you once. It'll take just one little word to let me love you again."

He looked up, took in the plea in her eyes, the sincerity he had never truly doubted.

"You remember that time we were talking about flags," she said, "the US flag in everyone's front yard and I said I just took it for granted? I said how you only notice something when it's not there any more? I felt the same about you, John. How much I noticed you not being around, how much I realised I hadn't appreciated what we had until it had gone. Let me love you again, John. Just you this time."

Slowly he took her hands and nodded almost imperceptibly. She noticed a single tear trickling down his cheek and came to him, pulled his head to her belly as she stood over him, and felt the gentle pulse of his short sobs.

"My John," she whispered. "I'm so sorry for what I did to you."

The following morning they were both woken by the twittering of the birds, louder and more excitable than ever as though they had been released by the sunlight and the cool, calm air, after sheltering in fear like helpless prisoners of the storm.

He kissed her on the cheek and her eyes slowly opened.

"I should be at work this morning," he said with a sleepy smile.

"Me too."

"But I don't expect I'll make it."

"Me too."

Once again, after so long, it struck him that she was the very reason why there was room in his bed for two.

She pulled the covers loosely off her shoulders and he felt her warmth, smelt her body, touched her hair, brushed her soft neck with his fingertips.

"Last night was wonderful."

"I thought so too."

"I missed you."

"I missed you too."

"I'm glad you came back."

"I'm glad you think so."

"I'm so glad it was your birthday."

"I'm so glad you said yes."

"I'm so glad you asked."

She brought an end to the nonsense by rolling over, pinning him down with her arms and planting a kiss firmly on his lips.

"I want to take you to Paris," she said breathlessly, kneeling up on the bed, her hands on his knees, looking down at him like some prey she had ensnared.

"*You* want to take *me* to Paris?"

"For sure. At Christmas. Visit some museums. Check out the competition for the tourist dollar. What do you say?"

"But…"

"Don't worry, John. I'll give you some say in what we do when we get there. It'll be on me. As a thank-you."

He still felt half-asleep, yet she had woken as bright-eyed as a sparrow.

"I'll call Elise," she ran on. "I still have her number. We could even stay with her, I bet."

"With Elise?"

"Elise Correia. You remember her?"

"Yeah, I remember her. Of course I do."

"So?"

"I'd rather a hotel, I think."

"Whatever."

"Gives us some independence."

"I'll want to see her."

"See her, fine. But not be beholden to her."

"You have some old-fashioned ideas, Mr Penny."

She skipped off the bed and disappeared out on to the landing.

"I'm taking a shower," she called.

"Come back to bed."

"Will it be worth my while?"

"That depends."

There was no answer.

"And if you insist on taking me to Paris," he persevered, "I'm going to take you to Nice."

Her head appeared around the doorframe.

"To Nice?"

"I always said I'd show you the Riviera. Remember, in our other life?"

"Our other life?"

"We'll go in the summer. Once the show is up and running. I'll hire a manager, we'll escape to Nice. How about July?"

"July, sure."

"We could be there for the Fourteenth."

"Bastille Day?"

"Why not?"

"Sounds great. Let's do it."

12

C'est ici la porte de l'Eternel.
Les justes y entreront. Ps118 v20

Staring at the weathered inscription carved into the sandstone block above the darkened double-door, *the gate of the Lord*, locked to the sinners of the world for as long as anyone could remember, John Penny wondered if he were worthy to cross the threshold of the old Protestant temple on the Route des Eyzies. It was a sturdy, simple structure whose design and dark stone, stained by years of smoke and fumes from passing traffic, reminded him, on a smaller scale, of the mills and factory buildings he used to pass every day under grey skies on his walk from his mother's house to secondary school.

"It says only the righteous shall enter," he explained to Columbine, trying to keep a straight face. She was standing close to him, linking his arm, mainly for warmth. With November had arrived cold, short days and angry clouds from the east.

"I don't believe that applies to atheists," she said, meeting his eyes with a sideways glance. "Are you sure about the annexe? I think it's kinda cute."

"No, it'd be hopeless."

His mind was made up. With its crumbling brickwork, its broken windows, its spongy roof, the outbuilding was in a poor state; to his unprofessional eye it was beyond repair. The space inside was smaller than he had expected: well-lit, he granted, but the large windows precluded sufficient wall space. The air was damp, smelt of sewage and the very fabric of the place seemed to be half rotten away.

"This is no good," he had said to Madame Perrier who, breathing into a perfumed handkerchief, had nodded wordlessly in agreement.

Now the lawyer was buttoning up her overcoat, preparing to leave them for the warmth of her office.

"Do you have a key for the chapel also, *madame*?" he called.

The doors were stiff but gave way to a hefty push. They stepped inside.

Space. Cold, grainy light. Unambiguous lines framing great flat shapes of chalky plaster. Space, and more space. It was perfect. Penny strode into the hollow, echoey centre of the building, followed more hesitantly by Columbine and Madame Perrier. There was the same smell of decay, the same damp, stale taste in the air, but this place was different. It was large, substantial, solid. It could have held up to one hundred worshippers in its day, maybe more. All traces of religion had been removed, from the wall decoration to the furniture to the last iron crucifix. Here was his blank canvas. He looked up to the roof, the geometric lines of the black wooden beams and the steep pitch of the ceiling above them. He saw the rows of high rectangular windows, three on each side, clear of Christian imagery but darkened by a hundred years of grime. Below them mildewed, limewashed walls, scarred here and there with mud-brown traces of damp, offered space enough to hang a dozen paintings at the very least; with a central screen dividing the room, double the number. The paved floor was cold and bare but for patterns of draught-blown dust, the pitted, dried excrement of pigeons and mice, and strangely, in one corner, by a redundant coil of black electrical cable, the desiccated carcass of a raven.

"This is perfect!" he shouted, his voice resounding off the walls.

At the back of the hall was a second door, unlocked, which, lifting a rusted latch, he passed through. He found himself in a narrow room with a small rear window: as empty as the other and just as featureless save for a pattern of grey mould below the window ledge and a bolted wooden door which allowed access to the annexe. This must have once been an office or a cloakroom perhaps. It smelt of wild mushrooms.

When he came back into the main space the two women were still hovering in silence by the large doors.

"Come on, John," called Columbine. "It's cold. Let's get back in the car."

"This will do, Madame Perrier," he shouted.

"Really?"

"It's empty, isn't it? Obviously unused. Can you find out for me what the mayor's office would be asking to lease it to me for the next eighteen months?"

*

"Have you seen this article about Lascaux?"

Columbine held up a copy of *Dordogne Libre* as he walked over to her table with a paper cup in each hand. It was a time of day when gaps in their timetables coincided, when they had arranged to meet for a *pause-café* in the canteen, when they could link fingers and giggle like teenagers, when he really should have been in his study marking essays.

"If I've got this right," she said, reading out bits of the text she recognised, "next year they're opening a super-modern, multimedia, visitor centre in Montignac."

"Yeah, I heard something about that."

"*Lascaux IV: A detailed facsimile of the entire... 'réseau'?*"

"Network."

"*Of the entire cave network, with wall paintings*, obviously, and much more besides. I can't translate all this, it's a whole bunch of technical stuff. What did we see? Lascaux II?"

"That's right."

"That'll stay open too, right?"

"I suppose so. They must reckon there's enough demand for two venues. It does sound as though there'll be some duplication."

"The new one will offer *a twenty-first century perspective*, it says."

"Fair enough."

She folded the newspaper and put it to one side.

"I thought Lascaux II was awesome."

"There's your coffee."

"Being up there in the woods, so close to the real cave and all."

"So you wouldn't fancy going to Lascaux IV when it opens?"

"Not really. It can't be so much better, can it?"

"Is there a Lascaux III?"

"It mentioned something in the article. I think it's like a travelling exhibition."

"Prehistoric paintings on tour."

"I guess."

"Maybe I should go and have a word with them about logistics."

"You haven't even got Steeples II up and running yet!"

"Don't remind me."

"Hey, I asked for it black!"

"Did you? Sorry, Col, I wasn't listening."

She took a sip anyway. She was in a forgiving mood.

"You know what I *would* like to do again?"

"What's that?"

"Canoeing."

"Yeah?"

"It was a lot of fun. We had a lovely day, didn't we? Maybe on the Dordogne this time."

"Well, there would be more to see. They do trips on the river from near La Roque Gageac."

"Shall we do it? This weekend, say? Or next?"

"I don't think they'll be open for business in November, out of the tourist season."

"Yeah, of course. I wasn't thinking."

"It would be pretty cold out there on the river this time of the year."

Disappointment clouded her face; she looked like a child deprived of Christmas.

"I'll have a word with Nicolas," he said. "He'll know some of the operators. Maybe he can sort something out for us."

Penny expected to receive contract details directly from Stephanie Chimes but he found himself reading through the legal technicalities, through the lists of assets, through the dates and costs and percentages, through waivers and conditions and sub-paragraphs of indemnities in the office of Marie-Françoise Perrier.

"I can follow most of the English," she was saying to him across her desk, partly hidden behind a large flat-screen computer monitor. The light from it made her face glow silvery white like the moon and, save for the loose ponytail, her hair appeared to be applied to her skull like a coat of metallic paint. "I have taken the liberty, however, of having everything translated." She was waving a second sheaf of papers at him to illustrate the point. "I understand that the owner…"

"Mr Overthrow."

"Yes, Mr Overthrow," she repeated, horribly mispronouncing the farmer's family name, "I understand that he had to have the paintings valued before the contract was drawn up. Therefore the delay."

"Indeed."

"And the value is rather high, don't you agree, Monsieur Penny?"

"I imagine it was a fair estimate. They have never been sold, of course. Never been on the market before."

"It's a matter of the value not to a purchaser but to an insurer, *monsieur*."

"Of course."

"And you can see the figures for yourself. A single payment to borrow, or, more strictly, to rent the paintings for a period of fifteen months, which seems quite reasonable. *Très raisonnable*."

"I suppose it is."

"Plus a rather more elevated fee for insuring them while they are under your supervision in France. That's the figure at the top of page two."

"Yes, I can see it."

"I understand the five paintings were originally valued at around £100,000 each, actually one or two a little more. For the purposes of insurance, however, it seems the value has been raised markedly. Additionally we are dealing with some valuable sketches, am I right?"

He nodded.

"Storage in Bristol and shipping also to be arranged in the United Kingdom," she continued, skipping to a new clause. "Payable before the assets leave the country. Also an elevated figure to my mind, but I admit I've no real experience in these matters – transportation of goods and so on. You've read all of this section, *monsieur*?"

"*Oui, madame*."

"There's also a sum for framing. Is that correct? The paintings are not already framed?"

"No, they are simply loose canvases. I must say that framing had not crossed my mind."

"It looks like a large sum."

"It does."

"We are looking at several pieces in total, however. A dozen, was it?"

Penny nodded again.

"And there, on page three, stipulations about *sécurité*, storage and so on in France, stabilization of *température* and *humidité*, guarantees of the condition of the assets upon return, and so on."

"Mm."

"And the option to extend the loan if both parties are in accord, in agreement?"

"Yes, that makes sense."

"The total payable is there, in that long paragraph. In sterling, as you can see," she added through her thin, bloodless lips that barely seemed to part.

The figure was dancing in front of his eyes, taunting him, teasing him, daring him to stand up, hand back the documents and call off the whole business. He took off his glasses, helped himself to a tissue from a floral box on the lawyer's desk and gave the lenses a wipe.

"With the pound being rather strong at the moment, sadly, I have calculated that you are due to pay Mr Overthrow just over €24,000. I have written the figure for you here. We can transfer the funds in pounds for you if you provide us with that amount."

"Where's your figure?"

"There, *monsieur*. In the margin."

"Oh, yes. I see it."

"Take your time, *monsieur*. Don't let me hurry you."

Penny skimmed over the documents again, one page at a time.

"Did you bring your passport, by the way?" asked the lawyer.

"I have it here somewhere."

"It's just that, well, as I'm sure you can understand, I have to confirm that you're not pretending to be someone you're not."

Within ten minutes he had signed in multiple places and the die was cast. He had also discovered that the woman's own services were priced at a level he considered rather elevated. Declining a glass of celebratory *pineau*, he left her to her paperwork, wandered past the potted palm in the foyer and out of the building, numbers cartwheeling around his head and a nauseous feeling in his stomach as he realised he had just signed away close to £22,000. It was a huge portion of his savings, and that was only the beginning. He wandered across the square, through the busy market, trying to remember where exactly he had parked his car. He would get the money back in the long run, he told himself. Grants, subsidies, sponsorship, profits: this is how all successful men and women started, by investing, by speculating, by going out on a limb, by taking risks. *Short-term pain for long-term gain*, as somebody once very flippantly remarked.

*

The clouds were no more than a white gauze, shredded here and there by sunlit strips of the palest blue, a winter's blue – sky that promised no rain but cold air and, at the level of the river, even keener breaths of wind which were already rippling the dark, chill waters.

They had already paddled for more than half an hour and had gradually settled into a steady, wordless rhythm. The slow-running river was deserted of traffic, blackbirds circled overhead searching for nesting sites, and the liquid sound of paddles dipping and pulling, dipping and pulling was exaggerated by the echoey walls of rock then muffled by banks thick with tumbling vegetation.

"Cut the water, John!" she called from the front of the canoe, face forward, hair buried under a thick woolly hat. "Slice it, don't tear at it."

"I *am* doing! There's no splashing back here."

"Your breathing is good."

"Is it?"

"Can't hear you panting."

"I'm not."

"Must be you quitting smoking."

She turned back to toss him a brief grin.

"I've quit, have I?"

"I think so."

"You think so?"

"Well, there are no cigarettes at your place."

"What? You checked? In my drawers, in my things?"

"I might have. Keep paddling, Scout!"

After a difference of opinion earlier in the morning, harmony had been restored. Favouring a shorter trip on a bitter day, Penny had planned the seven-kilometre stretch from Vézac back to Port d'Enveaux, a one-hour taster, as it were, perfectly long enough with plenty of time to find a spot for lunch and warm up afterwards. Columbine on the other hand would only be satisfied if she also saw La Roque Gageac and the fortress at Castelnaud, worthy sites needless to say but requiring a fourteen-kilometre paddle instead. The man in the beachside office, reluctantly opened as a personal favour to Duchemin, was already short of patience.

"*Alors, monsieur?*"

"*Bien, quatorze, je suppose.*"

Columbine had won. She had squeezed him from behind as he searched his wallet for the right cash. He had wriggled away from her in an undisguised sulk.

But he could not be angry with her for too long. She was so enthusiastic, she had that charming naivety of certain Americans who love to delve into a treasure chest of history far deeper than their own, scooping out fascinating fragments of the past like a child at a tombola stall. She had done her reading on the rival castles set high on their promontories overlooking the Dordogne: Castelnaud and Beynac, at the centre of hostilities between the Plantagenet English and the Valois French, defiant bastions of the Hundred Years' War. And the way in which they had slipped into an easy, synchronised oarsmanship took his mind back to the smooth, almost effortless progress along the Vézère now three warm summers ago, and the happiness he had felt on that day.

"There it is, John, on the left. Coming into view!"

The Château de Castelnaud loomed ahead, partly hidden by the trees clinging to the hillside, its pale stone ramparts catching the sun, rising into the sky. As they drifted beneath the central arch of a wide, cream-stone bridge, Penny found himself paddling alone; his passenger was transfixed by the fleeting view of the castle and the restored limbs of its trebuchets – dominant, terrifying, master of the slopes. She took several photographs on her mobile and seemed very pleased with herself.

They paddled on under darkening skies.

Within ten minutes the nemesis of Beynac came into view, a second seat of power in local stone, defensively set to face the river's approach, a marker to the enemy offering a supreme challenge to the reckless English, perched unfeasibly high and on the very edge of the sheerest of cliffs. In miniature at first like a distant film set, then gradually becoming more real, more solid, more awesome, the castle hung in the air like a muscular, brooding beast, king of the valley. Their view from the south, Penny noted, was not quite the one Steeples had in his painting: the artist must have planted his easel over in the valley at a south-eastern aspect.

As the sun disappeared they followed the river's course as it curved left and westwards, skirting the cliffs, the road, the fragments of the village that had spilled down the hillside to the water's edge. A little way beyond was a stony beach where they could take a rest, a sip of water, a photo of the château and its spectacular seat.

"Come on," said Columbine after a minute or two. "Let's go. It's too cold to stop and admire the view forever."

They paddled along, ferried by the languid current, buffeted by chill draughts, on past great banks of trees and ferns and creepers where, far from the road, they entered a silent, watery landscape of darkest green, of lichen-covered trunks and twisted roots, of broken branches and tangles of ivy dribbling into the shallows, of shadows cast by overhanging boughs, of muddy islets whose thick tufts of weeds and wild grasses seemed to be floating in the middle of the flow. As the river curved again, as a sandy strip of shoreline came into view, even at a distance he spotted it at once.

"Col!" he whispered. "Look, it's a heron!"

With her ears covered, he had to raise his voice.

"On your left! A heron!"

They were still a good thirty metres from the bird but had already disturbed it. Penny gently placed his paddle down at his feet, pulled off his gloves and tried to remember which pocket his phone was in.

"Stop paddling. Keep still. Let the current carry us past. I have to film this!"

The great bird, mercury grey, was already fidgety. Abruptly it made its move, leaping clumsily along the beach like someone running for a bus with a bag of shopping in each hand; then, with a thrashing of its mighty wings, it was suddenly in the air, a metre or so above the surface of the river, flying past them then climbing in a steep arc high above the tree line.

Penny was kneeling on the seat at the back of the boat,

legs apart for balance, filming the whole episode. The heron had disappeared for a moment, only to swoop back into view overhead, circling the river, gliding from one side to the other. Columbine craned her neck to follow its path as the canoe drifted lazily past the little stretch of sand.

"Here it comes again!"

And with what was unmistakably a sense of purpose, the bird was now heading upstream towards them, wings pumping, picking up speed, razor beak piercing the air. As it passed over their heads they could hear its beat, feel its draught, see the glint of amber in its eyes, then it climbed again, working to gain height for an angled dive, wings tucked, rapid and direct into the water, shattering the surface with an explosive splash. Within a second it had launched itself again, something shiny and indistinct in its beak, to soar above the river, water dripping from its feet, up and away to hide in the dense canopy of the trees.

"Fuck!"

Neither Penny nor Columbine had witnessed the kill. As they turned to follow its flight the boat had edged into the bank with a bump that had made her twist around and caused him to lose his balance. Instinctively pulling out an arm to grab the edge of the rocking canoe to steady himself, the frigid fingers of his other hand had lost their grip on his phone and it fell over the side and sank to the bottom of the murky water before he could react.

"Fuck!"

"What happened?"

"You've gone and made me drop my fucking phone!"

"Say what?"

"You should have watched where we were drifting, for Christ's sake!"

"I was watching the bird. Like you were."

He was looking over the side of the boat helplessly. The water wasn't deep but it was dark and it was cold and it was opaque. Beyond the surface he could see nothing.

"Hey, I'm sorry."

"I had about a full minute of video," he was muttering to himself. "Fuck – and I've lost my phone." He was splashing about in the water with his paddle like a blind man looking for a key buried deep in a sand dune. "All my contacts, my messages…"

"It was an accident, John. Hey, relax, I'll get you a new phone."

He tossed the paddle into the boat and gave her no answer. After a moment he grabbed it again and pushed the back of the canoe away from the bank where it had been snagged in a mess of roots. He didn't want to talk to her. For several minutes he didn't even want to acknowledge her.

The journey back to base was solemn and, as Penny had foreseen, lasted too long. Barely a word was spoken. Each paddled at their own pace, switching from right to left, from left to right at will, the harmony of the first hour lost forever. The canoe wavered from one side of the river to the other, making a zigzag of slow progress, each becoming more tired and colder and more miserable. She got angry at his inability or unwillingness to follow her strokes. He ignored her, thinking about his phone, looking up at the darkening sky which threatened rain. They reached Port d'Enveaux just as the dampness arrived on a thin wet mist in the air. The little wooden office was closed and there was no-one to meet them so they heaved the boat up on to the shingle as far as they could and left it there with the paddles and the life jackets for the owner to find them in his own time. The café was shut: a windblown notice told them it would reopen the following Easter.

They drove back to Frettignac with the heater on full blast.

"If you need to make a call you can borrow my cell," said Columbine. "I *am* sorry."

He nodded, peering through the wipers, and concentrated on the road, glistening in the half-light. She switched on the stereo for the radio but Penny's own music boomed out. He reached to turn down the volume; he knew she had no taste for his choices. Covering his hand with hers, soft and already warm, she twisted the dial back to high. *You listen to your music*, she was saying. *I don't mind.* She placed her hand on his knee and gave it a gentle squeeze. He looked across at her and they shared a shallow smile. He could never be angry with her for too long.

13

Within a day Columbine Snow had presented Penny with an expensive new phone, selected from the enormous range at the new tech store in the centre of Périgueux. It was a different brand to his old one and not the one he would have chosen for himself but he was not so churlish as to refuse it on those spurious grounds. And although his familiar old number was lost forever, she had helped him set up a new account, had retrieved as many of his contacts as they could find, and she had even snapped herself with a smile and an ice cream and put it on his home screen. She had been as good as her word and by that had admitted the accident, and the loss of the glorious footage of the heron in flight, was her fault.

The very first text message he received was from Stephanie Chimes; she had tried to ring but couldn't get hold of him. For obvious reasons. *"Just to say, all paperwork in order. Contracts signed at both ends. Overthrow delighted to proceed. Green light for all concerned. No doubt your solicitor will confirm. More details to follow. Regards, SC."*

It was almost December. He wondered if next summer

was a feasible start date. He felt sure it was. So, around six months to lift-off.

It was still early days but money for the project was not flowing in. Nor were there signs of even a trickle. Invitations for sponsorship had been largely ignored or rejected or would be dealt with in due course. The *municpalité* had promised to consider a modest grant in the new year. Representatives of the regional government, mindful of previous broken promises, had replied that a sum could be forthcoming but they needed more detail of the proposal. National bodies were unimpressed. The only contact from the EU was of polite interest and confirmation that the application for aid would be channelled to the appropriate people. It seemed that the British Council were batting the ball from one desk to another. And for organisers of national lotteries, *le Musée des Frères Steeples* was at the back of a very long queue.

Neither Penny nor members of his support team were duly concerned at this stage. They had to be patient, he reminded them: assistance would come when there was a visible, tangible project to promote, once the building was presentable, once the media had latched on to the story, once the world woke up to the fact that five unseen Impressionist treasures from the 1880s were to be exhibited in the heart of the region where they had been created.

Joyce Sweetacre was in touch. She had seen an article about the Steeples paintings in a British Sunday review weeks ago and it had taken that long for her to put two and two together.

"I don't think I actually registered the name, John. It didn't cross my mind at the time, you know, the artist being the brother of *your* Steeples, *our* Steeples. I can be a bit dim, I know. So, what's the word? Have they made the link?"

She really had no idea that the works had been authorized and Penny relished telling her the full story, with its triumphant ending.

"You'll have them all here? Under one roof? John, that's *so* exciting! Can I do anything to help? I must let Cilla know the moment I put the phone down on you. Listen, I was calling to see if you'd like to come over for a spot of supper with us. Yes, over to Le Bugue. Hughie's back from Toronto at the weekend and I thought we could have a nice evening together, the three of us. Or perhaps more. Cilla and her husband too, perhaps. I'm sure you'd get along. He's retired. Very keen on antiques. Rather an expert on footstools, in fact."

"Do you think I could bring a friend?"

"A friend? Do you mean *a friend*?" He could hear her laughing to herself. "A lady friend?"

"As a matter of fact, yes. Would you mind?"

"Of course you can, my dear. Fetch her with you. Lovely news. You two serious?"

"Fairly."

"Fairly? That sounds like you're hedging your bets."

"No. Yes, okay, serious. I suppose."

"I'd be delighted to meet her. Of course. What's her name?"

"Columbine Snow."

"Sweet. A Brit then, I presume? Not a French girlfriend?"

"She's American, actually."

"Oh."

"That a problem?"

"No. Not at all. She's not a vegetarian, is she?"

"No."

"Or a fundamentalist?"

"A fundamentalist? No. What do you mean, Joyce? Why do you ask?"

"I read an article about them. I don't imagine Hughie would appreciate breaking bread with a creationist."

"She's not. Relax."

"Fine."

"She's very nice."

"I'm sure."

"Well, thank you for the invitation."

"Yes, well, let's say a week Saturday, shall we? Sevenish?"

"Perfect."

"No food allergies? Nuts? Gluten? Shellfish? You? Celandine?"

"Columbine."

"Columbine. I'm sorry."

"No, neither of us."

"Perfect."

"How's Fiona, by the way?"

"Oh, Fi, poor girl. She dropped out of Southampton. Always on the cards, wasn't it? You knew her. Knew what she was like. Did three weeks, said she still hated it. Too many books to read. Lazy mare. She's just started a job, at Lidl's, apparently."

"Lidl's?"

"Mm, I know. Not even Waitrose."

"Well, that won't be forever."

"I damn well hope not, John. For her mother's sake!"

"The *municipalité* will offer you an emergency loan for that amount."

"Well, that's something, at least."

"I think you would be wise to accept, *monsieur*, before they change their minds."

"To cover…"

"To cover the first year's tenancy of the property, that's to say the *temple protestant*, its renovation and the restoration of *électricité*."

"That amount won't pay for everything."

"It's the best they can offer, *monsieur*. It is an expense that no-one budgeted for."

Penny was on the phone to Marie-Françoise Perrier and the call had gone on longer than he had expected. He was pacing around his study with his mobile to his ear. He should have begun a lecture ten minutes ago.

"So, for the rest?"

"So, for the rest, that is for you to find. I am sorry."

"The demolition of the annexe, the levelling of the embankment, the provision of a car park – all these are conditions the council itself has imposed!"

"You are fortunate that the planning office have found time to even consider the scheme, Monsieur Penny."

"Is there an agenda, *madame*, to thwart the project? Tell me."

"Not at all."

"To slow it down?"

"Not at all. This is your imagination, *monsieur*."

"What about Besse?"

"I am not at liberty to speak about individual representatives. You must realise that, surely. And Monsieur Besse can speak perfectly well for himself. All I will say is you are mistaken. Monsieur Besse is very much on your side."

Penny did not believe her; there was something vindictive about Besse. It was hard to tell if she was lying, and harder than ever over the phone.

"Okay, so why is there so much obstruction?"

"You exaggerate, *monsieur*. It is normal. We are trying to help, but the wheels turn slowly. It is the same in England, I think. The only other way to provide funds immediately would be to divert money that the library would receive."

"So, a grant is out of the question?"

"For this year, yes. Your application will remain on file. In the meantime there are many other bodies you could apply to for financial support."

"Yes, I know. I have done."

"Well, good luck with them."

"Thank you."

"I hesitate to pour cold water on things, Monsieur Penny, but have you not considered delaying the project? In a year's time perhaps you could have guarantees of support."

"I need to strike while the iron is hot, *madame*. If I don't exhibit the paintings now then somebody else will. We will be left behind."

"Yes, well, I do understand."

"This is the only chance we will have, I am sure of it."

He thought he could hear the woman shuffling papers on her desk. After a moment she spoke again:

"So, regarding the works, shall I email you a list of contractors?"

"I would appreciate that."

"Businesses the *municipalité* has dealings with. Make a few telephone calls, *monsieur*, select who you need and let me know. I will put in a word, get you a discounted price. *Tous les dons sont les bienvenus, non?* Every little helps."

"Indeed."

14

Major Russell Forrest was speaking to a journalist encamped in what looked like the man's sitting room. His good eye twinkled cheerfully from his ruddy, disfigured face as, in his soft Scottish tones, leaning back on a well-upholstered sofa, he repeated how surprised yet delighted he was to be named in the New Year Honours List. *Sir* Russell, he said aloud and smiled modestly, almost apologetically, Penny thought.

He was watching the BBC News on the satellite television which was attached halfway up the wall of their hotel room like a reproduced work of art in its shiny, black plastic frame. Columbine had gone shopping on the Boulevard Haussmann with her good friend Elise, leaving him with some time to himself. He studied the man again, listened to what he had to say. There was something very impressive about this former soldier, and something he recognised too, for he had seen his broken face before, had heard that rich voice sometime in the recent past. The interviewer posed a question about Syria and Penny's memory was jogged. It had been just like this before, watching a television report in a hotel bedroom: Penny waiting to leave at Bristol airport before his flight back to Bordeaux four months ago, listening to this man talking about the scale of destruction of the ancient monuments in Palmyra by the soldiers of ISIS, or Daesh, as the French called them. Forrest was an expert on this aspect of Ancient History, had retrained as an academic after his retirement from the army and, as Penny had learned at the time, had dramatic experience of rescuing artefacts from looters in time of war. In the man's time as a captain in Basra between 2003 and 2005 he had spent a great part of it protecting and restoring artworks and ancient treasures to war-damaged museums and storehouses, tracking down both Shia insurgents and Saddam loyalists who had tried to destroy or steal them in the smoke-filled confusion of battle in that southern province. The work he did was recognised not only by military men but also by grateful scholars and historians: his reputation was already made before he became victim of a landmine which blew away his left leg and much of his face.

The interview was over, the face of a theatre actor filled the screen instead. Penny muted the sound, fired up his laptop and searched for more background on Forrest.

Following his discharge he enrolled at university and also involved himself in Paralympic sport, going on to work as an athletics coach for the British team in the Beijing and London Paralympics. In his late forties he married a French journalist. In a recent article his political ambitions were mentioned, including the part he was keen to play for the Remain campaign in the forthcoming EU referendum.

Sir Russell. A knighthood well deserved, thought Penny. And he was perfect: well respected and admired, cultured, a man of integrity, a Europhile, an art lover. And yet Scottish. That gentle, comforting Edinburgh accent was not such a problem, nor was his habit of ending his sentences with a fadeaway, nasally drawl. The doubt for Penny was that although he could produce a very passable impression of that type of refined vocal pattern, it was hard to reproduce the tones specific to Forrest himself. Nevertheless, his mind was made up: to give a noble edge to his quest for money, to add a slab of gravitas to his campaign, he would borrow the major's reassuring voice for a burst of telephone lobbying and see how many purses a knight's reputation could open.

The year came to an end in a tiny restaurant in Montmartre. There were parties in Paris they had been invited to but Penny had had enough of Elise. He surprised Columbine by whisking her up to the Sacre Coeur, showing her how different the view looked at night with the twinkling city lights laid out like a starlit tableau before them, and breezing through the crowds and into a charming bistro just off *la Place du Tertre* where the best table in the house had been reserved for them. They toasted the New Year, looked forward with excitement to the future, and once again he spoke of his plans and where he could see him, *them*, in five years' time. She told him to slow down, to take one thing at a time, to keep his feet on the ground. Suddenly she had stopped being quite so frivolous.

It was almost midnight; their meal was long over. They had both drunk a lot of wine. The whole restaurant was lively, people on the very edge of a celebration – customers, waiters, chefs, *plongeurs* and passers-by, waiting to topple into a riot of convivial well-wishing, an explosion of noise and warmth and good will. Almost time to chink glasses again, to embrace, almost time for long, significant kisses.

The thought crossed Penny's mind that she still looked serious, a little uneasy. Columbine smiled, picked up his hands across the table and caught his eyes, his pale blue eyes which were searching for something. In the Oxford blue shirt she had bought him, with his top two buttons undone, she thought he was the handsomest man in the whole of Paris. The room was hot with bodies and the air was filled with chatter and music and, even at this hour, with the rattle of pans and the smells of cooking. The candles on their table were flickering towards their final flourish, their shifting flames tall and buttery yellow. It was almost midnight on New Year's Eve, *la Saint-Sylvestre*, with firecrackers already exploding in the dark streets outside, when she whispered to him, in words that cut through the hubbub like a sword, that she was two months' pregnant with their child.

15

It had been almost three years since John Penny had last spoken to the features editor of *Dordogne Libre*, and he noticed that in that time not only had the man lost most of his remaining hair but he had also put on a considerable amount of weight around his waist. Penny's mind returned to the dinner party at the Château du Beautrottoir and the conversation he had been forced to have with his emaciated wife while across the table the journalist chewed the fat with the baron.

Penny had forgotten his full name and during their meeting in one of the empty conference rooms at AULA he was encouraged to call him simply Bertrand.

"You will remember the article we ran on your *Espace* some time ago, John. The new venture you are proposing will give us the chance to do something similar. A boost of publicity, yes?"

"Which I would certainly welcome."

"But of course. And our readers will want to be informed. I will write a piece in advance of the opening of the new museum – in May, you say?"

"Or June."

"Or June. And nearer the time we can do maybe a double-page feature. Or a longer article in our weekend supplement."

Penny was not ungrateful but he had heard this before; a pattern was emerging. In terms of both publicity and financial assistance, little was on offer in the short term but generous promises were made for some unspecified later date. There had been plenty of interest from the local media and he had been asked to provide a short press release – *400 mots maximum, s'il vous plaît* – that could be distributed nationally. As the new gallery was still in part a building site and the artwork remained in England, however, there was little to illustrate his narrative.

"And how is our friend the baron?" Bertrand suddenly asked as if to draw a line, rather prematurely, under their discussion of Thomas Steeples.

"The baron?" asked Penny a little irritably. "I'm afraid I've rather dropped off his radar. I'm sure you know more about his activities these days than I do."

"I did meet Ludo in the in the autumn, in fact," said the journalist, shutting down his tablet and removing his glasses. "They'd been abroad. Just back from Florida. He was telling me about the house being used as a film set. A television production, in fact, with scenes filmed both inside and in the gardens, starting in the spring. You know anything about that? A new script, apparently, *Les Frères Caramasse*, a kind of updated version of Dostoyevsky. Set in France in the 1930s. Sounded fascinating, I thought: murder, sibling rivalry, intrigue and all. Have you read much Dostoyevsky, John?"

"A couple, but not *The Brothers*."

"It's one of those classics," Bertrand laughed, "that everybody reveres but you find no-one has actually read."

It was at this point that Penny stopped listening and reminded his guest that that he had a seminar to supervise imminently, which was in fact untrue. He did have a busy afternoon, however, and needed some time to catch up with a growing pile of unread students' work. More importantly he had been invited on to a chat show at *France Bleu Périgord*, the local radio station, to talk about the museum project; he was due there at three thirty.

It was his first opportunity to address a radio audience of a few thousand listeners and he was determined to take advantage of it. Unfortunately the slot coincided with Columbine's first ultrasound scan, scheduled for the same afternoon. She had wanted him, urged him, more or less ordered him to go along with her, but the radio date was already arranged.

"Then cancel it!"

"I can't just cancel it!"

"Well, reschedule."

"Listen, Col, they offered me that specific time. I've got to take it. Think of the publicity I can generate. I might not have another chance."

"Of course you will."

"I'm not taking the risk. Anyway, why not rearrange the scan?"

"'Cause that date suits me and it obviously suits them."

"Well, you'll be fine on your own, I'm sure."

"I want you to come with me!"

"I'd just be in the way."

"Don't you want to see our baby, *your* baby, wriggling around inside me?"

"Well, yes, I do. But they'll give you a photo, won't they? And I'll come next time. Definitely. I promise."

She had walked away from him at this point.

"If that's how you feel," she had said, noisily filling the sink with breakfast dishes.

"Listen, I'm sorry. It's just an unlucky clash."

"Fine."

"Fine?"

"*Fine.* I said! Go to your radio show."

"Don't get upset."

"I'm not."

"I said I'm sorry."

"Go to your radio show. It's okay. Go. We can catch up later and tell each other how great it all went."

"Okay. If you don't mind."

"Whatever."

By the time he was getting comfortable in the soundproofed studio at *France Bleu*, a quarter of an hour's walk away across the river on the north side of the city she would be lying on a hospital bed with a sensor on her belly. He felt only a small pang of regret. He thought it suited her to be independent, to be self-contained like he was. She had carried this baby further than her first and had made no fuss about that to him. He had noticed a sense of relief back in January, of course he had, when that date was passed. He had made no comment, but why else was it marked on her kitchen calendar with an asterisk inside the shape of a heart? Meanwhile she was strong, she would continue to be strong, the baby would be healthy and he really needed to be promoting the exhibition. It was simply a matter of priorities.

In spite of a certain nervousness, an undercurrent of anxiety related to her recent medical history, Columbine was overjoyed to be pregnant again; that much was clear as the sparkle in her nut brown eyes. She had been desperate to put her marriage behind her, and a child with a different man on a different continent would help her close the door on that miserable chapter and lock it away for good. And Penny wasn't just a different man; she knew she had loved him once and could love him again if he would let her. She had found him guarded, wary of her, and was a little shocked if not surprised by his caution. She had been patient yet determined, and little by little had won a place in his heart again: a toehold only, perhaps, but he *had* let her in, had allowed her the chance to stake her claim. And with this baby, this new life growing inside her, this shared joy, she knew he would let his love for her spill out in the fullness of time; he would invite her into his life unconditionally, he would welcome her and her child, *their* child, in a family embrace that nothing and nobody could ever break apart.

It had taken Penny two full days to come to terms with the fact that he would be a father. He was happy to see the excitement in her eyes, to hear the thrill in her voice as she told him she was pregnant. He wondered why she had chosen that moment to tell him, in a noisy restaurant, seconds before the carousing of the midnight celebrations. Did she think he would be angry? Was she denying him the option of reacting in that way in the midst of backslapping and hugs and smiles and laughter? Did she really doubt he would be as joyful as she was? Was she so unsure of him?

To be honest the doubts and uncertainties came from within him; he had never given a thought to fatherhood. The idea of having a child with any of the other women he had known was absurd; they were playthings, amusements, happily, *deliberately* ephemeral. He knew she was different – he had known that from the start, three years ago: she was a woman who had come to mean a great deal more to him, a woman he respected, a woman he had loved, properly loved. But could he really turn back the clock? Did he love her now? He had not wanted to let down his guard but here she was, adorable Columbine, and yes, he could love her again after all. But it was all too soon. She had rushed him, harassed him, and was now presenting him with a reality he had never asked for. *Un fait accompli.* Why couldn't she wait? Was she so desperate to have him, or just to have a child by him?

Someone at the back of the bistro had counted down the seconds. *Dix...neuf...huit...sept...* Others joined in, louder and louder. He had stood up, stepped around to her side of the little table and pulled her to him. *I'm so happy*, he had said as the cheers rang out and the firecrackers exploded outside. As they kissed, he had felt the tears on her cheeks wetting his own; her face was hot with life, her arms refused to let him go until a drunken stranger patted them on the back and pulled them out into the street with everyone else, spilling out into the cold night air to join the crowds whose enrapt faces were already lit by the oranges and golds of a thousand bursting fireworks.

It had taken two full days to convince himself that a child was what he might want, that a family could be part of his plans for a future that he had never really foreseen. Two days of fluctuating from dismay to delight, from alienation to humility, from irritation to forgiveness to a confused, unmoored acceptance. He thought of his own father: a kind heart but shrivelled and battered by his circumstances, a man short of time who could offer so little beyond rare, awkward expressions of affection, a rickety role model and one he could barely even remember. He had tried to hide his doubts from Columbine, to offer up a smile, a mirror to her own good spirits, but no-one was more perceptive than she, he knew; she could sense his unease and yet understood it, forgave it.

"You'll be a great daddy, John," she had said, holding him closely to her, tight like a lifebelt.

"Will I? How can you be so sure?"

"I can tell. I can see it. There's just so much good in you."

The radio interview was fun. He was given plenty of time to talk about the *Espace* in Frettignac and how the discovery of the paintings had demanded a larger gallery to combine the fruits of the two brothers. His interrogator was a young, quick-witted journalist with a sparky sense of humour for whom local radio, Penny thought, would be a first step on a successful career path in the media. Moreover he promised to have him back on the show in the summer.

Columbine was waiting for him in her flat. She had arrived an hour before him and a pot of coffee she had made, standing on the table in front of her, was half-empty and almost cold.

"What took you so long?" she said, preferring not to get up off the sofa.

"I called at a bookshop on the way here," said Penny, pulling off his jacket.

"I thought you'd come right back."

"I bought you a cake."

In front of her, beside her empty cup, he placed a small cardboard box tied up with a narrow silver ribbon.

"It's a *religieuse*, your favourite."

She offered a tired smile.

"You're forgiven."

Kicking off his shoes, he collapsed on to the cushions next to her.

"So, how was the scan?"

"Good. It was good. Here, take a look." She shuffled across closer to him and passed him an envelope. "All's well, they said. Heart pumping just fine."

Penny put on his glasses to examine the blurry image.

"There's its tiny head," she pointed.

"Did they ask you about wanting to know, boy or girl?"

"They could tell me, sure, but I didn't want them to. We'll wait and see, yeah? You okay with that?"

"Best way."

"And I've got a date. For the birth."

"Late July, you thought?"

"The nurse said the sixteenth."

"Sixteenth of July. That's the day after my dad's."

"And the day before…" she hesitated, "his."

"His?"

"Patrick's."

"Oh. Right."

"Sorry, John. Didn't plan to spoil the moment. It just came out. You'd like a coffee? I'll make some fresh."

"Okay."

"So, the sixteenth," she said, slowly pulling herself out of the seat. "You realise that means we'll have to put Nice on hold."

"Will we?"

"Well, sure. You wanted to go for Bastille Day, right?"

"I know. I've already spoken to Joyce."

"Joyce?"

"About managing the gallery that week."

"Well, she can still do that. You'll be busy right here looking after me and the baby."

"I suppose I will."

"Well, don't look *so* disappointed! We can go to Nice another time. The three of us."

"Of course we can." For the past minute he hadn't taken his eyes off the grainy image of new life forming, a life he had helped to create. "You're right. We can go any time we like."

*

Less than an hour later Penny was driving back to Frettignac. Columbine had reading to do for an assignment due in three days; he was better out of the way. In any case he had work of his own to do – marking, a backlogged pile of it, easier to contend with it all in his own space. The sky had cleared as dusk fell and there was a chance of a frost. His car, his old 206, had, if nothing else, a very reliable heater. He had planned to buy a newer model months ago but had not got around to it and now his money was stretched to the limit. He accelerated out of a bend and on to a straight road through a forest, his headlights cutting into the shadowy gloom. He switched on his music, listened for less than twenty seconds and decided he preferred to hear the silence after all.

Columbine was a lovely and lovable woman. The thought of her made him smile. He was lucky to have her, he told himself. So why the doubt, echoing in his mind? Some might have said that Penny loved himself too much. He enjoyed his own company, he would admit; couples and partnerships and all that interdependency had never sat well with his disposition. He had always preferred to be self-sufficient, self-energising. Since he was ten years old he had been making decisions by himself and for himself, shaping his own destiny, making his own mistakes, relishing his own successes. Within a matter of weeks this American woman had taken over, or at least it felt like that some days. She had stopped him smoking. She had bought him clothes he didn't need and a phone he would never have picked. She had planned Christmas in Paris for them both, she had involved herself in his project, she had even, without invitation, rearranged his kitchen drawers, for Christ's sake. She had rocked the boat – in the case of the heron on the river, quite literally. And now she had presented him with the prospect of being a father.

The road surface was slick and, as the thought of ice crossed his mind, he gripped the steering wheel to take a sharp corner. The headlights of a car coming towards him flashed into his eyes and then passed by in a blur. His hands were tight, rigidly tight, so tight that they were hurting. He was coming into the pale glow of a village, he braked gently, moved down a gear, then another. He relaxed his hold and took a deep breath. He understood the root of his anxiety: for the first time since he left Oxford, John Penny was losing control.

16

Behind the chapel an agile man in a hard hat and a harness was partway up a sycamore tree, slicing off high limbs with a buzzing chainsaw. It looked as though he had already cleared most of the clump whose removal would lend a good deal more light to the building. On the ground a pair of lads in damp fluorescent jackets were collecting fallen branches and feeding them into a large shredding machine attached to their pick-up. One of them had parked it at an awkward angle in the space that had been created by the demolition of the annexe a week earlier. Not far away, an earthmover was chewing into the embankment, dumping soil and stones into a dumper truck sitting on the edge of the road whose driver was darting in and out of his cab, one minute lending a hand with an oversized shovel, the next lighting a cigarette and sheltering from the squalls.

Penny flicked the switch which caused the wipers to arc hesitantly across the windscreen and clear the glass, momentarily, of the soft mist that was collecting there as droplets of rain. From his vantage point, tucked into a muddy space just off the Route des Eyzies, he could watch the men working across the road, some more industriously than others but all seemingly oblivious to the weather.

Again he cleared the windscreen. A white Renault van had just arrived on the scene, the driver visibly struggling to find somewhere to park. He crept in as close as he could to the doors of the chapel and switched off the engine. It was the electrician visiting the site again – a lean, fidgety man recommended by Marie-Françoise Perrier whom he had met once before. He had been given a key to the building and Penny watched as he pulled up the collar of his coat, waved to the man in the digger, and then headed into the building. A moment or two later he reappeared, spoke to someone in the passenger seat whom Penny hadn't noticed, and then opened the back doors of the van and tugged out several coils of coloured wiring. His young mate followed him inside the chapel carrying two large cardboard boxes.

And so it went on. The wood cutter clambered down and the shredder was switched off, filling the air with something closer to silence. The three of them took a break, sheltering in the cab of their truck with flasks of coffee. The earthmover continued to chunter away, wobbling forwards and back, nibbling at the rocky ground, the electrician re-emerged to pick up a toolbox from the back of his van.

Another juddery swish of the windscreen wipers; it looked like the drizzle had almost stopped. Penny switched on the engine, clipped on his seatbelt and pulled the Peugeot back on to the roadway, heading for Frettignac where he had an appointment at the bank.

Thanks to Sir Russell Forrest, or rather as a result of requests made in his borrowed voice down several influential telephone lines, promises of money had already been given to help pay for the renovation of the old Protestant temple.

Penny had contacted the major's MEP, improvised a way around a few tricky obstacles – he had no idea the two men knew each other quite so well – and convinced him to raise the project with whichever cultural committee he had access to. As a consequence an email arrived offering an immediate, regretfully modest grant of €2,500 with a promise of a larger sum once the gallery was up and running.

He had also telephoned a representative of a large health insurance company to which, he had discovered, Forrest had business links. To his surprise he found himself talking to a director who needed no arm-twisting to agree to sponsor the project to the tune of £4,000 for the first year in exchange for advertising space at the gallery and on its website. A similar positive response for a smaller amount came from a retail group whose profile had become interwoven with Forrest's in their shared commitment to the EU referendum Remain campaign. Wheels began turning within wheels: modest, unsolicited amounts dribbled into the bank account, firstly from a budget airline, then a French producer of brandy, and yesterday a British holiday company which specialised in southern France.

Penny was heartened but knew that funds in the pipeline could not pay his immediate bills. He needed a business loan to keep the ship afloat, probably for at least six months, and this is what he had just been explaining to Monsieur Griotte, the narrow-eyed manager of the local branch of the *Caisse d'Epargne du Périgord*.

The bank had always sat in its splendid position on the corner of the *Place de la Résistance*, occupying a three-storey building of honeyed stone whose upper windows offered a view of the square, the bridge, and beyond the trees even a glimpse of the Vézère. It had been set up over a century ago by a philanthropic society of men as a local savings bank and this homespun image was one it endeavoured to maintain in spite of faceless globalisation on the one hand and, on the other, a fairly recent scandal caused by individual misjudgement. The reassuring, familiar emblem of a pair of chirpy squirrels gathering walnuts had been a feature down the decades but had, since the turn of the century, become a modern logo, stylized to the point where the animals had been transmuted into unrecognisable squiggles. The *Caisse d'Epargne du Périgord* was plucked many years ago by more muscular players and was now but a tiny part of a conglomerate of international banks, an enterprise far too large to be directed by even the most astute society of philanthropists. Wherever the shiny suits made their decisions these days, it was certainly not in the same dusty universe as the archaic branch of a regional savings bank in Frettignac-du-Périgord.

Nevertheless the townsfolk should be grateful for small

mercies. Monsieur Griotte, fastidious, scrupulous, with the wrinkled skin of a wise old turtle, was a local man at least and his was the only bank left in town. *Société Intégrale* had closed their premises a year earlier. *Online banking is the future*, they said. And they were probably right.

"I have listened to you with interest, Monsieur Penny," said Griotte, leaning back in his sturdy leather-backed chair, "but I am not in a position to agree to a loan for that amount."

Penny felt empty, betrayed, having mistaken the man's geniality and creased smile for easy acquiescence.

"As you would admit, *monsieur*, your plan is not a conventional business plan. With respect, I see it more of a vanity project than a business plan. I see no evidence of likely profits within a year, two, even five years. It is a worthy venture, I agree, *monsieur*, one which ought to have more backing from the public sector perhaps, and I wish you luck, but without collateral – and you say you own no property, neither here nor in Great Britain – even a modest business loan is out of the question."

"I see."

"Perhaps another bank would see it differently, but I have doubts. The climate is dictating that banks take fewer risks these days, you understand. Here at the *CEP* we specialise in loans to individuals to buy property, in long-term mortgages and such.

"So a personal loan might be possible."

"Yes, as I said. We could look at a loan of a smaller figure, say €5,000. Your repayments would have to be affordable, of course. You have given me details of your income, so I can see that within those parameters we could arrange something. Here's the relevant leaflet with our current rates. A matter of filling out a form, either with one of our cashiers or online. It would be easier, of course, if you had a long-term contract with your employer."

"It's just a matter of time."

"Well, then there is nothing to stop you applying in the future."

Griotte stood up, flattened his tie over the soft hump of his belly and offered a weathered hand across the tidy desk. The interview was over before Penny had had time to let the rejection sink in.

"I do wish you luck with it, Monsieur Penny. I am a lover of art myself – more in the modern idiom, to be honest – and am eager to see the Steeples work first-hand."

"Thank you for your time, Monsieur Griotte," said Penny, letting the man's hand fall away.

Closing the office door behind him, he took in the look of curiosity on the faces of the knot of customers queuing in the overheated hall and strode past them and outside into the cold, damp air.

"The name is Bagshaw. I'm calling on behalf of the British Council. Yes, it is a bad line, I'm sorry. I'm only up the road in Paris, for goodness sake. That is Mr Penny, isn't it? Mr John Penny?"

"Yes. I'm Penny."

"I'm calling about your application for a BC grant, Mr Penny."

"Oh, really? What can you tell me?"

"Good news, in fact, sir. I unearthed an application you submitted two or three years ago, sadly unsuccessful, and then there's your new application for – what is it? – the gallery in Bergerac?"

"Frettignac."

"Frettignac, yes, sorry. Well, yes, the second one has been viewed favourably, you'll be pleased to hear."

"Excellent."

"Thanks to some forceful lobbying, I understand. It appears you have one or two influential backers this time, Mr Penny."

"Yes, the new gallery has a higher profile."

"So, anyway, it looks like we are prepared to make a donation to the start-up. I've been told £4,500, and on review that figure will be repeated annually."

"That's generous. Thank you."

"Oh, don't thank me, Mr Penny. Thank the British government. In fact thank the British taxpayers."

"Thank them on my behalf, please. I don't meet very many of them these days."

"Indeed. I must say it looks like an interesting project. A fraternal link, as it were, between books and paintings, two artistic representations of France and, I dare say, England too at that *fin de siècle* period."

"Exactly. I was lucky to get access to the paintings, of course. But the combination, I think, will be quite spectacular."

"Do I detect a northern accent there, by any chance, Mr Penny, buried under layers of continental sophistication?"

"I did live in the north of England as a child."

"I thought I caught a flavour. I can always tell. You never lose it really, do you? And absolutely no need to. I'm from Lancashire myself, as you can no doubt tell. A town called Colne, near Burnley. I dare say you'll know it."

"No."

"That surprises me. Anyway, I have to modify it a bit, of course, otherwise nobody in London would understand me. You found the same I suppose?"

"Actually, no. I have always been readily understood. If I went to Manchester now they would probably think I came from Surrey."

"Oh no, that's where you're wrong, Mr Penny. It still shines through, even on this poor phone connection. I've never been one to deny my roots. It's a mistake, if not a crime, in my book. Southerners are secretly envious of our heritage, I reckon."

"I haven't noticed."

"We still have a place up there, in the Dales, in fact. Yorkshire, I know, but still. We get up there as much as the job allows."

"Well, that's very interesting, Mr...?"

"Bagshaw."

"Mr Bagshaw. Sorry, you did say. And so, you are in Paris right now?"

"Just passing through."

"Will you be able to visit here, see how we are doing? File a progress report?"

"No, I don't think so. I'm just the messenger on this

one. If you could email the address on our website just to confirm your account details, Mr Penny, and we'll get the money over as soon as."

"Thank you."

"If you can confirm a date I'll see what I can do to fix up a VIP for your grand opening, shall I?"

"Could you?"

"Well, we *are* attached to the Foreign Office. Maybe someone at the Paris embassy. I'll let you know."

"That's very kind, Mr Bagshaw. It'll be early June, I'm thinking."

"Well, as soon as you know for sure, eh? Maybe I'll try to make it down myself."

"Yes, why not?"

"I'll bring you a box of Eccles cakes."

"If you must."

"Nice chatting, Mr Penny. Good luck with it all."

Even though it was not her first pregnancy, Columbine followed her doctor's advice and enrolled on a short course of antenatal classes, partly to learn the procedures in France but mainly so that she could share the experience with her British birth partner. Penny duly went along to the first session but had excuses not to follow it up, or reasons, as he preferred to call them, bona fide reasons: an early evening tutorial, an important meeting in Frettignac, an unexpected problem with his car. It was not a question of him avoiding involvement with her pregnancy; after all, it was his child too. But when he asked her about how she felt, how a class had gone, she would sometimes shut him down, insist she was behind with her work and needed some quiet time. Fair enough, then, he said to himself: she was the one who was actually pregnant.

From time to time the matter of the baby's name arose. To him, her choices were twee, drippy and/or too American. To her, his suggestions were eccentric, difficult to spell and/or too literary.

"Hey, I don't want to fight over this!" she would say. "This is supposed to be fun."

"So stop coming up with names that would make even the Disney Corporation gag."

"We'll discuss this sometime when you're in a better mood."

"I'm not in a bad mood."

"Whatever we decide tonight we'll hate it in the morning."

"So we'll pick a name the day it's born."

"The day *he* or *she* is born."

"Right, he or she."

"But we need a shortlist."

"So where do we start?"

"We're going around in circles."

"So let's just leave it. I've got a load of essays to mark anyway. Do you want a drink?"

"You've always got essays to mark."

"Yes, and I never seem to get around to marking them."

"No, I don't want a drink."

"You sure?"

"Yeah. I feel bloated. Have done all day."

"Go and have a lie down."

"I don't want to rest."

"Go out for a walk then. Get some fresh air."

"Not a bad idea."

"Try and think of some decent names while you're out."

"You staying here tonight?"

"I will if you want me to."

"Whatever."

"Do you want me to?"

"Make your own mind up."

"Okay, I'll stay. I can stay tonight. Hey, are you crying? You crying, Col?"

"No. Yes. It's nothing. I can't help myself right now. Just the slightest thing…"

"Come here," he said, pulling her towards him. He could feel the swelling of her middle as they held each other. "Listen. I'm sorry. I can be a bit self-absorbed."

"Me too, I guess." She smiled and dried her face with the back of her hand.

"You've got every right to be."

She pulled away from him.

"Fresh air was a good idea."

"I'll come with you."

"No. You stay. Start your work. I'll be fine."

"You sure?"

"I'll be fine. I'll just go around the block for ten minutes. Shall I pick up pizza on the way back?"

"Sounds good."

"Sorry for being a bitch."

"Sorry for being an arse."

"Forgiven?"

"Forgiven."

Having two homes had become a point of contention. Columbine preferred living in her flat in Périgueux, handy for AULA and her doctor's. Ever since the winter had bitten for real she had been reluctant to ride her scooter, and Penny had forbidden her to even sit on it until after the birth. He preferred to live in his house as not only was it more comfortable, the increased number of commitments he had in Frettignac dictated that he spend more time there than he did in the city. He knew, however, that she wanted them to be together all of the time. He knew that she had few friends and got lonely. Nevertheless there were times when he deliberately stayed away from her place for little reason. He needed his own space and he was determined not to bend to her every whim.

"Joyce? Is that you? It's John."

"Hello, stranger! How's everything? Celandine and the bump okay?"

"Columbine."

"Sorry, Columbine. How is she, the darling?"

"She's okay, thanks. Due her twenty-week scan in a few days."

"How exciting for the both of you."

"It is."

"So, is this about the gallery? Any developments?"

"Well, yes and no. Things are moving along. They've

surfaced an area for a small car park, still left a great pile of earth in the corner, mind. The inside of the building's coming on slowly. No, I'm really ringing to speak to Hugh, actually."

"Hughie?"

"Is he there?"

"No, he's been in New York for the past week."

"Oh, okay. It doesn't matter. Some other time. It's just that, well, I was hoping… I just wanted a word about money. It really doesn't matter."

"What do you mean, John? Spit it out."

"Well, this whole venture is costing a small fortune, as we knew it would. We've been given bits and pieces from sponsors, a grant here and there…"

"But…"

"Well, exactly. I've been using my savings to keep it all afloat. All the building costs, then there'll be security to fix up, dehumidifiers…,"

"It sounds like quite an outlay."

"Extras in the contract's small print like air conditioning, things I'd never really thought of, Joyce, and then publicity…"

"You're running out of funds? Really?"

"Not quite, but basically I need a loan. Twenty, maybe even thirty thousand to be safe."

"You've been to the bank?"

"Of course. No joy. Nothing more than a piddling amount."

"I honestly don't think Hughie will be able to help, John."

"I thought, you know, through his bank. Giltmann-whatever it's called."

"Giltmann-Rusard."

"One of the largest banks in Europe."

"In the *world*, John."

"Well, exactly. So, don't they do loans to help start-ups, to give customers a kick-start?"

"I don't know the banking world like Hughie, but my understanding is that banks like his are only interested in operations dealing with billions. They finance construction, mineral exploration, pension schemes. He talks about currency exchange and commodity trades and futures, whatever that means. I've never heard him talking about putting a few thousand pounds into a small business. It's like chalk and cheese. You still there, John?"

"Deep down, I think I knew that."

"But I can ask him."

"Would you, Joyce? Perhaps he could make an exception. Or knows someone who could."

"I'll mention it."

"Is he back soon?"

"He's not sure. Might have to call in in London for a bit. He'll skype though, probably tomorrow. I'll mention you."

"Thanks, Joyce. Plead my case, won't you?"

"I'll do my best. I'll give him your number anyway."

"Thank you. Anyway, how are you? How's the painting? Anything new?"

"I've been trying my hand at portraits as a matter of fact. Not easy, John."

"Difficult to get a likeness?"

"Well, I've been tackling poor Cilla, bless her. She's such a brick. She's getting fed up sitting for me, I can tell: wearing the same blouse and pearls day after day. I keep her sweet by feeding her barley sugars. It's not finished yet but I think I've made her look rather like Margaret Thatcher."

"Christ, she must be devastated."

"No, John, *au contraire*. She's actually cock-a-hoop with it."

It was already March and the weeks were racing by. The year seemed to be speeding up and Penny was struggling to keep up with its momentum and have all his plates spinning at the same time. There were days when he split his life into parallel strands; he told himself it helped to keep a sense of perspective.

As the Easter holidays approached he found himself taking stock again. On a personal level, his life was generally good: he had a girlfriend who loved him and who before very long would produce their precious child. They bickered and sulked, the pair of them, but that was normal, wasn't it? She was awash with hormones and he was doing his best to support her, but, well, she wasn't the only thing in his life right now. On another level, he felt that the project, the gallery, his ticket to a sort of fame, was also on track. Nothing had fallen apart, there had been no calamities, the premises would be finished, the art would arrive – he just needed that financial cushion if the whole venture wasn't to cripple him. The third level, his professional life, his academic life, was less rosy, however. He had not read a new book for six months. He had failed to mark whole classes' assignments, had missed several tutorials, had delivered feebly prepared lectures and had upset some of his students with his ill temper and sarcasm, even the better ones. Especially the better ones.

Much of this litany of unprofessional behaviour had been fed back to him late one afternoon at a swiftly convened session of a wing of the university hierarchy, a panel of concerned and disappointed individuals including his natural defender, the mousy *Chef de Faculté*.

"We have been very satisfied with your contribution, as you know," the white-haired lady had said in what turned out to be summary remarks. He had never met her before and had already forgotten her name but not her steely look; she had the hard eyes of a hanging judge and had been given, or more likely had taken, the responsibility of speaking for the group.

"Very satisfied."

There were five cold sets of eyes staring at him. She went on:

"With the work you have done with our students, and with your endeavours in Frettignac where you have raised the profile not only of the author Steeples but also, by association, of this institution. We have all applauded you, encouraged you and, of course, we have rewarded you."

One member of the panel, a bald man with tiny circular glasses, coughed loudly. Penny wondered if he was having some kind of fit.

"Until now," said the woman, administering the blow of an axe. The man fell silent and wiped his mouth with a handkerchief.

"For some reason, and we have listened to what you have said to us in mitigation, your standards have slipped very markedly this year and most especially this term. As a result the panel has decided that you are hereby served with a warning. It is the first and final warning, Docteur Penny, as these are not negligible failings. It is a warning that without a clear improvement in every aspect of your professional conduct in the coming term, we will have no alternative but to terminate your contract."

I only have a one-year contact, he thought to himself. *Don't the fools know that? They might not want to "renew" my contract but they can't very well "terminate" something that will already be at an end.*

The members of the disciplinary committee had already risen and were filing out of the room. The *Chef de Faculté* came to him and offered a word of consolation and a pat on the shoulder.

"We're all on your side, Docteur Penny," he said softly. "We want you to do better. I believe you will."

Penny was left alone in the large room, floating in the silence and the gloom. Someone had switched off the lights and outside the sky was already darkening. By the clock on the wall he could barely distinguish the hands that were showing ten minutes to six. Suddenly the hall was illuminated by a flash of white light, and there was a crash of thunder which seemed to make the walls shake. Within seconds the storm broke and rain lashed angrily against the tall windows, a barrage of water-bombs bursting on impact. And still he sat, motionless, watching the patterns of water battering the panes of glass, waiting for the next thunderclap, the next blinding flicker of lightning. He had known nothing of this meeting earlier in the day. It was not until after ten that he had discovered an email summoning him in no uncertain terms. When he had left Columbine's apartment after breakfast that morning he was in a cheerful mood; they both were. It was the last day of the term and she had her twenty-week scan at the hospital at five o'clock. He had promised he would join her at the appointment this time, would hold her hand this time while the nurse rubbed her tummy with jelly, while they waited open-mouthed for the little moving image to appear on the screen. He had promised.

17

"It's bad news, Monsieur Penny, but it's a good thing we discovered it now before it was too late."

"What are you talking about?"

"*La toiture.* The roof. It leaks. Not too bad, but bad enough. All the rain over the weekend, now we can see."

Penny was walking around the cold interior of the old Protestant temple with Rodrigues, the building contractor, glum expressions on the faces of the pair of them. He had come to like Rodrigues, a thoughtful man of few words. Those he did utter were succinct and delivered with rapidity: it seemed, as much as with his building materials, he didn't care to waste his breath.

"Look how it has run down the inside of that wall."

The space had been shut up for four days due to the Easter holidays and it looked gloomier than ever.

"So what needs to be done?" asked Penny.

"I had a lad up a ladder earlier," said the builder. "There are loose tiles up there, some broken. Been there for a hundred years. Underneath he found some of the joists are rotten."

"Shit."

"Exactly. Just this one side, *monsieur*. Most of the roof is pretty sound. But here…" and again he touched the wall where the plaster was slick beneath his fingers and then gazed up at the ceiling, "up there we'll need to start to fix it."

"So, what? Tiles? Woodwork?"

"*Oui, certes.* I can get some scaffolding up by the end of the week. But it's a matter of finding a roofer who's free."

"You know people?"

"Of course, *monsieur.*"

"So you can make some calls?"

"I'll get you a roofer, don't worry, Monsieur Penny."

But Penny could not help but worry. In more than fifty years he had never owned a property of his own. He had never had to employ a tradesman to mend even anything as insignificant as a dripping tap. He was as far outside what people might call his comfort zone as he had ever been in his life.

Columbine looked tired, even a little anaemic, and he should have kept his irritation to himself. They were spending a week together in the house in Frettignac before the start of the summer term. It was supposed to be a time of relaxation and rest but inevitably Penny found himself in demand to make all manner of decisions relating to the gallery.

He had received a long email from the company he had chosen to install the security system – CCTV, lights, alarms, 24-hour response. According to his contract with Hatcher Cross the company had to be approved by Overthrow, and they were informing him that the English were satisfied apart from a stipulation that the site be floodlit around the clock. Penny was being asked to authorise the installation of extra lights – *the four corners of the building would be adequate, at a minimum height of 3m* – at an additional cost to what was already, as Madame Perrier would have said, an elevated price. *Our equipment is "technologie de pointe", state of the art*, the company manager had reminded him many times. *You will find no better systems this side of Bordeaux.* A puzzling phrase, Penny thought, as to the other side of that city was primarily five thousand kilometres of open ocean.

Meanwhile he had found Nicolas Duchemin to be enthusiastic, cooperative but hopelessly indecisive. For each sentence of text on the website he was building, for every caption to every photograph, it seemed he was needy for Penny's approval.

"You know I could have set up that site for you," said Columbine from the one armchair where she had been dozing with her feet up on the other.

"I think it would be beyond you, Col."

"No, I know what I'm doing."

"You've only been on the course five minutes."

"I tweaked my daddy's site. I do know the rudiments."

"You never said."

There was no response. She was working through a large bar of milk chocolate.

"And you haven't even finished those information sheets you said you'd do for me."

He half-regretted speaking out but he could already see that he would end up doing them himself. Like everything else.

"The texts are on my computer."

"Are they? All of them? All four of them?"

"Most of them."

"You've sourced images?"

"A few. Enough. More or less."

"So basically you haven't finished. That's exactly what I said."

"I'll do it. I said I would. I will."

"When?"

"I don't know when. Soon."

"Soon? Don't tell me, you've got other things on your mind."

"Excuse me?"

"You keep telling me you're *pregnant*, that you're not *ill*."

"Oh, fuck you, Penny!"

She heard the kitchen door shut and shuffled round to see where he had gone. He was already out of sight, striding past the circular plot of weeds and up through the sprouting green walnut trees, towards the crest of the hill where the fresh, sweet wind was blowing, and where he could catch the soft spring sunshine on his face.

There was no word from Hugh Sweetacre. Joyce would have passed on his message, he was certain of it. So, her husband couldn't even be bothered to pick up the phone and say *Sorry, mate. No can do.*

Not too far from his wits' end, Penny had begun to think unconventionally, in a way Columbine would have described as *outside the box*. The only other banker he knew, and this was a long shot as he had known him only as *the son* of a banker, and that thirty years earlier, was his associate at Oxford, Angus Barrington-Smith. Barrington-Smith *père*, as the twenty-year-old Angus was keen to remind people, was a trustee at Lovatt's, a private bank with offices two minutes' walk from St Paul's Cathedral. It was a fair guess that Angus, whether he had left Oxford with a double first or with nothing more than a souvenir scarf, would be found a desk somewhere in the organisation and that in the intervening years he would have risen painlessly up the polished marble steps of the Lovatt's hierarchy. In any event it was worth a phone call.

It took Penny a dozen clicks of internet research to discover that Mr Angus Jocelyn Barrington-Smith was indeed an employee of the bank, with special responsibility for Commonwealth clients.

"I'm very glad you've finally ridded yourself of that dopey '*ee by 'eck, it's grim up north* accent, Penny."

He smiled to himself. It had taken the man less than five minutes to play the Lord Snooty card.

"I can confirm what I told you back then," he said. "Northern vowels, those open, flat vowels you despair of, Barrington, are ideal when it comes to speaking French. Take it from me, I live here. Those strangulated vowels of the Home Counties make French pronunciation sound as if it is being spoken by a Dalek with a cucumber up its arse."

He heard the man chuckling.

"Daleks don't have arses, Penny."

"You know what I mean."

"It's so good to josh with you, old man. We should have kept in touch really."

"I think we've moved on into quite different worlds, you and I."

"I suppose you're right."

"Anyway, what are your thoughts?"

"Thoughts?"

"On the museum project."

"Your museum project, yes. I'd love to see it, Penny. When it's all up and running and such. I read a piece in the Sunday rag about it. Making a name for yourself, eh? Good for you. Harriet and I have a place down there, you know. We do visit *la belle France* fairly regularly. Avignon. That near you? I can never remember the name of the village."

"Not really. It's probably a five- or six-hour drive."

"Oh, right. Then we'd have to do a detour for you, old man."

"Yes, I suppose you would."

"You ever marry, Penny? Bag yourself a wife?"

"Me? No. Still happy flying solo."

"Thought not. I get the impression any woman of yours would have to play second fiddle to you and your latest punt at fame."

Penny gave the man a moment to indulge in his sarcasm.

"So, anyway, what about the loan, Angus? Do you think it's feasible?"

"Well, as I said, Lovatt's is a private bank. I am sure you are aware that that means our client base is principally HNWIs."

"Sorry?"

"High-net-worth individuals."

"It's not a label I've ever come across."

"Well, it means, frankly, millionaires. Of which there are many more than you'd imagine. A million doesn't go so far these days. Try buying a house in London with anything less."

"No thanks."

"Some of us have to."

"So…"

"So, you're not holding a portfolio which we could manage."

"No, I'm not wanting to invest at all. I'm hoping, actually I'm begging, for a loan. A small loan."

"Yes. I understand."

"So, couldn't you make an exception?"

Barrington-Smith laughed.

"Oh, Penny, you're such a lovely chap! Still wet behind the ears, just like you were in the JCR."

There was a moment's silence. Penny couldn't take much more of the banker's superciliousness.

"Listen, Penny. I can talk to one of our minions downstairs. See what I can do. Special favour, that kind of thing. What are old chums for, eh?"

"That's very kind."

"You were asking for 30K, was it, or 40?"

The higher number was tempting. Ever since Madame

Perrier had informed him that the *municipalité* was not willing to pay for roof repairs to the chapel – she implied that the council were in fact prepared, reluctantly, to let the whole project wither on the vine – numbers in tens of thousands had been spinning around in his head.

"Thirty thousand."

"You're certain?"

"Thirty thousand should cover it."

"And repayments? You looking at a ten-year schedule? Shorter? Longer?"

"I hadn't really thought it through."

"Tell you what. I'll get one of the girls to email you the options."

"Thanks. That would be helpful."

"So, can you let me have your bank details? I'm guessing Jersey, sensible chap like you?"

"It'll be a local government account, actually. A cultural committee, not my private account."

"That's fine. Actually a better bet. Public sector, guarantee of a bail-out if things go tits up."

"I'd not thought of it that way."

"Sure you don't want the 40K?"

"Let's call it thirty-five."

"Whatever you say, old man. Just let me have those numbers nice and slow. And an email when we've wrapped up, just to confirm everything?"

Penny was giving a rather pedestrian lecture on the representation in literature of the industrial revolution when he heard his mobile ringing in the pocket of the jacket he had hung over the back of the chair on the far side of the podium. As the students submissively filed out twenty minutes later he discovered that the missed call was from a number he did not recognise. He pressed it to call back and on the second ring he heard a familiar voice.

"Bagshaw."

"Oh, it's you. I didn't recognise your number. Sorry, I was teaching."

"Very noble."

"Well, it's what I'm paid to do."

"I rang with some news for you, Mr Penny. Good and bad. Mostly good."

"I see."

"I've been in touch with people and there's a very good chance that the cultural attaché at the embassy will be available, and willing, to open your gallery for you."

"The cultural attaché?"

"Yes. At the embassy in Paris."

"That's wonderful!"

"I knew you'd be happy. And he's a lovely chap. You said end of May, last time we spoke. So, still May?"

"Oh. Well. Not necessarily. It could be but we've hit a snag this end."

"It always happens."

"So, I'm thinking it's more likely to be June."

"Early June? Mid-June?"

"I'd say mid-June. I should be able to let you know very soon. I'll need to check everything with my builder and the roofers."

"Roofers? Oh, *that* kind of snag."

"Unfortunately."

"My old man was a roofer, for his sins. Spent most of his working life taking roofs *off* buildings though, not putting them up. Factory demolition, that sort of thing. You'll know what I mean, Mr Penny."

"I'll let you know our date as soon as I can."

"Thank you."

"And the bad news?"

"Oh, yes. Well, I say bad news. It's just a darkish vibe doing the rounds in Whitehall. I assume you've been offered an EU grant?"

"Yes. A modest one with assurances of much more later."

"Assurances? That's the point, Mr Penny. It's all dependent on the referendum. People here are still confident that we'll stay in, but if the vote goes the other way, then any funding for British projects is up in the air."

"But mine is a French project."

"Is it? English writer? English artist? English curator? Don't worry, it might not happen. We'll vote to remain and everything will go on as before. As I say, it's just one of many rumours floating around here at the moment. You're better off out of it, Mr Penny, believe me, down there in the Dordogne."

The chill of spring had already yielded to the mild air of early summer, the tulips on display in the *jardin public* in Frettignac had bloomed and wilted, the blossom on the cherry trees, the apple and the peach had long since drifted away on the breeze, and on the vines fresh green leaves had unfurled while beneath them buds of fruit were forming. It was time for fields of sunflowers, for geraniums and garden roses to bloom, for daisies and poppies and wild orchids to peep out from the meadow grass.

Columbine Snow had noticed little of the season's change. Her swelling burden was tiring her more with every passing day. She was often nauseous, needed long hours of sleep, and regularly woke feeling light-headed or feverish, sticky with perspiration. Her doctor was a kind man who spoke passable English, a font of wisdom and reassurance and good sense, and she always felt better after she had seen him. More and more Columbine was to be found only in Périgueux, in the comfort of her own flat, in the city but rarely at the university; she had all but dropped out of her course. Penny, meanwhile, was as sympathetic as he was predisposed to be.

He was consumed with ticking off tasks from a list he compiled on the memo page of his phone: some were done, others still to do.

Promo materials:
This was theoretically the domain of Duchemin but the young man needed supervision. Nevertheless Penny had given him free reign over social media activity. Leaflets for regional tourist offices had been designed and were due from the printers imminently. Similarly a visitors'

programme of the exhibition, price pitched, upon consultation, at €3.

Price of entry:
Still to be decided. €7 made a round ten with a programme, but was it too high? Under-18s free?

Press/TV:
This is what Penny was enjoying most of all. Journalists tended to flatter him; it might be a game but he was happy to play along. Articles had appeared in *Sud-ouest* and a couple of French arts magazines. Somewhere he had been referred to as a *pioneer*, elsewhere as a *guide to the hidden jewels of an Anglo-French collaboration*, moreover *a guide with a silver tongue and a golden smile*. He had been told to expect a visit in June from writers from both *le Monde* and *the Guardian's Weekend* magazine. Other titles had been in touch, promising to send people down to Frettignac once the museum was up and running. Meanwhile he had appeared on *TV7 Bordeaux* – viewers had found him *tout à fait charmant* – and had an interview on the national *Arte* channel coming up.

Presentations:
He had addressed the *Faculté des Arts* at the Université de Bordeaux and the entire teaching body at the AULA hub in the same city. A talk he had given in the offices of *Tourisme Périgord* had been roundly applauded. He would give the same address with a few minor tweaks to *Bordeaux Tourisme et Congrès* in the second week in June.

Adrenalin would begin to fizz the moment the thought of it crossed his mind.

Display boards:
The exhibition furniture was being supplied by a fitters in Bergerac. The panels on Monet and Cézanne, Zola and Hardy – text and images now complete – were being produced in AULA's own resource.

Security:
Could the security people install their systems while the roof was being repaired? He needed to ask. The tiling was inevitably more extensive than had been foreseen; to complete it on time the roofer had insisted on employing an extra worker, adding to the cost.

Surface of car park:
This had been laid weeks earlier but now there was concern over damage caused by the scaffolding. The displaced earth had largely been removed but there was still an unsightly mound of topsoil in a corner of the parking area.

Volunteers:
He had to speak to Camille Rousseau and Amande Puybonieux about drawing up a list of volunteers to staff the gallery. He had been assured this would not be a problem. He needed to liaise with Joyce on this.

Catering:
They would offer drinks and finger food at the opening of

the gallery. Camille Rousseau was on top of this. He could trust her to keep the costs somewhere short of extravagant.

Date:

Sunday 26th June. The date was already engrained in his memory. Everybody had been told, the contractors several times. The paintings were due to arrive on Thursday 23rd. Bagshaw from the British Council had been in touch with news that the cultural attaché would regrettably not be able to attend so late in the month. The embassy promised to find a replacement, however, which was generous of them.

Invitations:

The first item on the agenda at their next meeting. The great and the good must attend the opening. Camille Rousseau would know whom to suggest and Penny had his own ideas for a guest list. Meanwhile the Musée d'Orsay in Paris had confirmed that a representative would visit Frettignac in early July, date to be arranged.

End of term:

There was plenty to do at AULA, mainly admin at this time of the year, once the exams were done.

Columbine:

He must look after Columbine. Well, obviously.

18

It was Columbine who broke to him the news of the death of Amande Puybonieux's elderly mother. The woman's name was Madeleine, she told Penny, and at the age of ninety-four she had died in her bed in a nursing home in Le Bugue. The death was of only superficial interest to him: he had never met the old woman even though he had lived in her house for almost four years. He listened out of courtesy; it was clear to him that Columbine was touched that the bereaved daughter had delivered the news to her personally. She had driven up to Périgueux to see her, to have a chat over coffee and cake, to ask how she was feeling eight months into her pregnancy. Her mother had been suffering from dementia for years, she said, but physically had withstood many more than anyone had ever expected.

"Amande was quite matter-of-fact about it," Columbine was saying, standing at the kitchen counter waiting for her kettle to boil.

"What are you looking at?"

"Nothing."

"Yes, I know my hair is a mess."

"No, I was just daydreaming," insisted Penny. "Let me do that. Go and sit down. Rest your legs."

"No. Stop fussing. I prefer to stand just now. I'm tired of resting my legs."

Penny took a seat instead, parking himself on one of the wooden stools by the kitchen table.

"It didn't come as a shock," she went on presently.

"So I suppose she and her brother will inherit the house. My house."

"Just Amande," she said with authority. "Seems like the brother isn't in the picture at all these days. We talk about most things but she really doesn't like to talk about him. Something happened, I guess. Something she wants to bury. He must have moved away for a reason. Some real dark reason. I don't push her on it."

"Did she invite you to the funeral?"

"She didn't mention it. I guess they don't even have a date yet. In any case, I don't want to go. Not in this state. I don't think I'd feel strong enough. And I didn't know the woman."

The kettle clicked off as a plume of steam spilled from the spout.

"She told me a story about her, though." Columbine checked to see that Penny was listening. "About her mother."

"What about her?"

"It's a story Amande herself was told a long time ago. One she never really believed was true. But she said in recent times she had thought more and more about it. It was something that was supposed to have happened here during the war, when Madeleine was a young woman, married but not much more than a girl. It seemed she fell for a German soldier and got pregnant. Of course keeping the child was out of the question and it was terminated in some clinic some place on the other side of the country. That's really sad, isn't it?"

"If it's true."

"Amande thinks it might be."

Penny noticed that she was stroking her belly, slowly caressing their own little child as if it were already born.

"Is it kicking again?"

"No, it's gone pretty quiet lately. Saving its strength, I guess."

She reached up to pull down two mugs from a shelf.

"She told me her mother had said stuff," she went on, turning back to face him. "Stuff that made no sense, with the dementia and all. She would ramble on about a whole bunch of weird stuff, she said. But one time, maybe more than one time, she had told her, had told Amande that she was not *the first*. Not the first child. She took it to mean that she had been born minutes after her brother – they were twins, did you know? – and so in that respect, no, she wasn't the first. She knew that already; it was often mentioned as kids, the brother would claim a sort of superiority, a seniority in a playful, points-scoring kind of way, she said. But her mother had insisted: no, she wasn't *the first*. Got real angry."

"I don't expect she'll ever know one way or the other now," said Penny.

"No. Guess not."

Father Matthieu had arrived at the church of St Lucien in

Frettignac-du-Périgord as an energetic priest in his late-thirties and thus had known Madeleine Puybonieux for over thirty years. He had often visited her home, supported her through times of illness, heard her weekly confession, even brought her baskets of apples from his little orchard every September. She had told him everything about her daughter's condition as an adolescent and the time his predecessor had suggested the girl be confined to the *Couvent des Soeurs de Supplication de la Sainte Thérèse* in Périgueux. He had comforted her whenever the memory of her husband's disappearance flared up. When her son had given in to such despair that he felt he had no choice but to take his own life, Father Matthieu had offered her priceless consolation. He had watched her grow old, dressing more and more in clothes of black or shades of grey, as he himself had grown old. He had seen how the disease had gradually robbed her of her spirit, her clarity of thought. He had observed at close quarters the evolution of a sad but living woman into a trembling husk.

Among his aging flock Father Matthieu had known many cases like Madeleine's: souls for whom communication had become little more than a smile prompted by the touch of a cheek, for whom the word of the Lord made as little impression as a shower of rain on desert sands. And no more unique was his experience of seeing a final, brief flicker of light in their fading eyes. He had witnessed this phenomenon before, this moment of clarity just before the fire burns out, this unexplainable pre-death rally, this so-called *terminal lucidity*, and he saw it, heard it, sitting at the bedside of Madeleine less than an hour before she passed on. It was a confession of sorts he had listened to, the words of a wretched woman desperate to shed her secrets in this life before it was too late. He shivered as she revealed secrets too harrowing to be kept beyond her death; too raw even for him to keep, her trusted ear, her friend and confidant, who had promised that the dear Lord, if not earthly justice, would forgive her her trespasses.

As John Penny walked into the offices of the *Dordogne Visiteur* magazine on the Thursday morning before GOD – Gallery Opening Day – he heard the chirrup of a text message landing in his phone. He paused to read it: *There will be police at the house today. Family business. Sorry to disturb you. Amande P.*

Madeleine Puybonieux had mentioned the *cercle magique*, specifically the half that caught the morning sun, the semi-circle of earth on which the first rays of light would fall, the first soil to absorb the new day's warmth.

The *Commissariat* sent up a team of three who took little time to unearth the tiny bones of a human foetus that had collected about a metre and a half below the cracked surface of the ground. The discovery, following the directions of Father Matthieu's reported insights, was quite predictable, but what surprised them more was finding the matching remains of a second foetus buried a hand's width apart from the first. Linking the two was a loose, tarnished necklace with a tiny silver cross.

It was late afternoon as Penny drove up to the house to find a single police car still sitting on the stony driveway. Tape had been set up to ring the circle of earth where a mound of dark soil had been piled up to the side of a deep pit in the ground, open like the jaws of a wolf. Amande Puybonieux was standing in the shade of the leafy branches of a walnut tree in conversation with a female detective. The sunlight was glinting off their polished shoes.

"Madame Puybonieux," he called, walking over towards them.

"Monsieur Penny, *bonsoir*."

"Ça va, madame?"

The woman looked exhausted.

"*Oh, ça va*," she said with a sigh. "*Merci*."

He sensed that the detective had been consoling her in some way but he was unsure. He remembered what Columbine had told him, he put two and two together and was halfway to reading the situation. The woman was harder to read, and stronger than she looked. Her face had more colour than usual and was a florid pink; he guessed she had been outside for most of the day, watching and waiting in the sun.

"It must be distressing," he said.

"It is. But I'm okay."

"Thank you for your text."

She looked up at him through her old frameless glasses and smiled.

"There were two of them, you know," she sighed. "Twins. She carried them home. Tiny little pups. A pair of poor lost souls, like Jean-Yves and me."

19

John Penny could not remember ever being quite so excited about anything in his life. He had always been a books person, a man of letters rather than of art, but then he had never been quite so close to art, so intimately close to real art, as he was now. In fact he could smell the oil on the canvas and the stain of the varnish on the new bevelled frames, he could touch the ribs and blobs of flecked colour, the smooth lines, the rippled shapes and patterns creating light and shade. The five glorious Steeples paintings were right there in front of him, leaning in random order against the bright cream paint of one of the newly plastered walls of the old chapel.

He had made certain that he was there to take delivery of the collection personally, he had eagerly opened up the dark double doors as the silver-grey VW van with its British registration plates swung off the road and on to the new tarmac of the car park. Two burly men had emerged, one talkative and the other less so, they had shaken his hand, exchanged a little small talk and then proceeded to unload the vehicle of its precious, substantially packaged cargo. Along with the five bulky items were two large wooden boxes containing the sketches which required both men together to lift into the hall. They had come from London, the driver said, which was self-evident as Penny had swiftly located their accents. Over on the Shuttle, down as far as Poitiers, overnight in an Ibis, and here today. *Always a pleasure to drive on French roads.* And once the paperwork was signed they were straight back on them, heading north towards Le Mans and on to Calais.

Now Penny couldn't decide which one was his favourite. Broadfoot had considered *Les Gabares de Begerac* to be the finest in terms of artistic excellence and he had a point. It made Joyce Sweetacre's effort sadly redundant. He moved over to the painting of the bridge: the arches emerging from behind the dreamy haze of blues and greys and their filter of sunlight. Next to it was the portrait: Jonathan and Béatrice, their faces dappled in a light that spoke of bliss and innocence, yet he could now see even more clearly how Thomas had used the contours of the fruits, their russets and their purples and their running juices to convey an overt sexuality to the work. *Le Jour du Marché* was the largest of the canvases. It would take two men to hang each of them but especially in the case of this one. It was a riot of colour, of vitality, of movement. He was standing too close to it, of course. It needed distance to be fully appreciated; he would have it hung on the far wall, it would be the first picture you saw as you entered the hall. What a first impression it would make! He stepped over to view the final work: *Le Château de Beynac*, of course, a scene familiar from his canoe. Although the castle, its ramparts and the church were bathed in a coppery sunlight he felt a heaviness, a darkness in the artist's treatment of the cliff, the trees and the earth below. Steeples had captured a sense of menace and of conflict that he had not noticed before.

He had still not decided on a layout for the exhibition and he needed to make up his mind very soon. Columbine had suggested splitting the hall into two with a central board or a series of boards and devoting one half of the room to Thomas and the other to Jonathan. Penny was coming to the conclusion that a stark division would take away the collaborative element, would sever the fraternal link. He was beginning to think that interspersed components of each brother's work would be more effective: a panel with the first verse of *Doctor Tombo* posted beside *Les Gabares de Bergerac*, for example, and *The Fruit Tasters* should not be far from the new flat-screen showing the video of Jonathan and Béatrice.

He meticulously covered the frames, activated the security systems and prepared to leave. He would be back the next morning with a clear head and a team of helpers, and together they would set up the place for real.

By Saturday afternoon everything was in place. They had finished on schedule and could do no more. He had hoped to find time to visit Columbine but the hours had somehow flown by. He had tried to speak to her in the morning but there had been no reply. She didn't mind him being away, she had said a few days ago. She understood, of course. The last time she saw him she had apologised for missing the opening.

"It's your day, John. I really don't think I'd feel up to it right now. The cramps again. I've felt like shit all week. I'll be fine here, don't worry."

"You look a bit brighter today."

"I'll just rest up and eat candy."

"And I'll see you on Sunday night."

"Not before?"

"I'm going to be really tied up, Col."

"I thought you'd make it back here each night at least."

"I could, I suppose. It's just so much more convenient to be based in Frettignac full-time just now."

"Convenient for you."

"Well, yes. I *am* running the show. I need to be there."

"Whatever."

"Don't be like that, Col. Once the gallery is up and running I'll give you all the attention you want."

"And the baby."

"Of course. And the baby."

Penny drove up to the house and parked. The place was awash in sparkling sunlight. He felt physically tired but mentally abuzz. It was such a spectacular evening he decided he would go for a run – he hadn't done his circuit for a while – and it was just what he needed: half an hour, stretch his legs, get his heart beating, push away all the niggles and snags that had cluttered the day.

The climb along the edge of the vineyard was a slog and he found it hard to match his breathing with an uncertain rhythm in his limbs. Beyond the Garrigue estate he entered the forest and in the shade of the high pines and oak trees he recovered a steady momentum along the rough, undulating pathways. The woods held a dampness, a shadowy mustiness which he loved. He passed clumps of mushrooms, caught the smells of leaf mould, of herbs, of wild garlic, he ran in and out of ribbons of sunlight streaming between the trunks. Presently he reached the crest of the long, grassy flank where the telephone mast sat in its locked square of railings like a caged giant. He slowed to a canter, then to a walk, facing the gentle breeze, raising his arms above his head, filling his lungs with the warm, sweet air. Below him stretched the valley, the patterns of shifting greens and greys and browns, a patchwork of sloping woodland and fields studded with tiny buildings, distant farms, a village with its church, the curve of trees that sheltered the hidden river. He was thirsty, his calves were aching, but his overriding feeling was one of contentment. He had read about the so-called *runner's high* – endorphin release, increased body temperature and so on – but this was somehow more intense, a purer joy of simply being where he was, in this moment, both physically and spiritually; he was standing on the edge of a future he had fashioned for himself and, coursing through his veins, fluttering inside his chest, was a thrill of anticipation, and, on a higher plane, somewhere in his soul he felt, just for an instant or two, a most dizzying sense of euphoria.

He lost track of how long he stood on the hill top. Suddenly he felt cold, the sweat evaporating from his face, his shoulders, his limbs. He turned and started to retrace his steps, gradually picking up the pace as he rejoined the forest tracks. Eventually, beyond the leafy lower vines, the corner of the walnut grove came back into view. There was no sign of Noisette, no scurrying of her little dog among the bushes. On he ran, past the bank and down into the field, through the familiar lines of trees. Over his tramping footfall he thought he could hear the murmur of voices, and, sure enough, as soon as he approached the rear of the house he saw figures, several figures, men and women striding about carrying canvas bags, metal poles, rolls of tape. From their uniforms he could see it was a second visit from the police.

Once again the circular garden was being ringed off as the struts of a tent frame were quickly erected on the edge of it. He heard the sound of a small diesel engine starting up around the side of the house.

"*Qu'est-ce qui se passe?* What's going on?" he asked an officer who was standing directly in front of his back door.

"*Vous êtes qui?*" said the man, widening his stance and straightening up to meet his stare.

"*J'habite ici.* I live here," insisted Penny. "What's happening? I thought the police had finished their digging a couple of days ago."

The police officer was still looking at him with suspicion, getting the measure of this panting, sweating man who had just emerged from the hills.

"*Excusez-moi,*" said Penny. "I need to pass. As I said, I live here."

"*Désolé, monsieur, c'est défendu.* You cannot enter. *Entrée interdite.*"

"What do you mean? I live here! I need to get inside, take a shower. Can't you see I've been out running?"

The officer looked across to the activity on his right.

"*Madame?*" he called.

A female officer in plain clothes heard him and walked over. Penny recognised her as the detective who had been talking to Amande Puybonieux at almost the same spot two days earlier.

"*Ah, oui, monsieur,*" she said quietly, turning to face him. "*C'est Monsieur Penny, non?*" So at least she had recognised him too. "Unfortunately the house has become a crime scene."

"Has become? What do you mean? *Même l'intérieur?*"

"*Oui, la propriété entière.* I cannot say very much more to you, *monsieur. C'est un cas historique, vous comprenez.*"

"But I need to go inside," repeated Penny who, standing in the shade of the building, was beginning to shiver.

"You have been away for long?" asked the detective.

"About fifty minutes. Look, I need to have a drink, a shower, get changed."

"*C'est compris.*"

"So I can go inside?"

"You may enter the house, *monsieur.* Do what you need to do. But you cannot stay here. As I said, it is a crime scene, the whole property. We must disturb nothing. I will give you ten minutes, *monsieur.* And I am sorry, but an officer will have to accompany you while you are inside."

With no change of expression on his face the policeman stood aside.

"An absolute minimum of disturbance, *s'il vous plaît, Monsieur Penny. Dix minutes, j'insiste.*"

Suddenly, carried by the breeze from the top end of

the grove, came a wailing like the sound of an injured animal. Everyone looked up but the thick foliage of the trees obscured the view. The howling started up again: faint, broken, then a stronger moan, a female voice in lament. Penny stepped forward into the grove and found a sight line up to the ridge. He recognised the voice and now could see her, a hundred metres away or more, the thin silhouette of a woman, rocking madly from side to side, flailing her arms against her head, pulling wildly at her hair.

"*Sorcière!*" she whined, and now he could make out her words. The wind was tugging at a loose scarf around her neck and billowing her skirts. "*Sorcière!* She's a witch! The Devil has her now! She was always a witch!"

The detective joined him and followed his line of vision.

"It's Noisette," he said. "She lived here once."

The faint, desperate yowling was still reaching their ears.

"Yes, we know all about Madame Garrigue," nodded the woman. "We know all about Noisette."

The rooms at the two-star *Hôtel de la Fontaine* were small but clean and adequately comfortable. From his open window Penny had a view of the stone church of St Lucien and a section of its little cemetery, and he watched as a clamour of rooks rattled across the darkening sky.

Finding accommodation had been easy but he was tired and frustrated. Showering, then rapidly gathering a few items together under the watchful eye of a taciturn police officer had been an unnerving experience. He felt as though they had actually suspected him of some crime simply by his association with the house. He wondered what they were looking for. They had already unearthed the remains of the unborn twins; what other secrets did the place conceal? As he left he had noticed a large pale blue tent-like screen had been erected to cover most of the *cercle magique*. A small earthmover had been driven around the side of the house and was already starting to flex its steely muscles. Two police officers had changed into loose-fitting white overalls. There was neither sound nor sight of Noisette. A third policeman had encouraged him to start up his engine, ushering him away.

The inconvenience would have mattered less were it not for the fact that tomorrow was to be one of the most important days of his life. He had remembered to collect his suit, a clean shirt and tie and, thankfully, a printed version of the speech he had prepared to give at the opening. He had hurriedly packed a bag, picked up his laptop, his glasses – so easy to forget – his wallet, his watch and his car keys. He hadn't realised until he closed the door of this hotel bedroom, this frugal, echoey shelter for the night, that he had left his phone behind in the inside pocket of his other jacket. So, indeed, tired *and* frustrated.

20

The solemn, single bell of the church of St Lucien rang long and clear through the streets of the town, softly into shuttered bedrooms, stridently into open-windowed kitchens. Over a pot of coffee and a selection of bread and pastries, the conversation in the little breakfast room was dominated by the news that had broken overnight and had already found its way on to the local radio bulletins. Thanks to crucial information from an unnamed source, the police had found the remains of a body, believed to be an adult male, buried in the garden of a property in Frettignac-du-Périgord. Forensic reports suggested that the bones could have spent fifty years deep in the soil.

The squat, middle-aged woman who served him breakfast had her own contribution and addressed it to all in the room who cared to listen. A group of Dutch tourists concentrated on their food and pretended not to understand. Her mother had known the family that lived up there, she said, up the road, *chez Puybonieux*, where they'd dug up the fragments of those dead babies.

"Madeleine must have killed him," she declared, a spark of excitement in her eyes. "You know, killed her husband. He was a playboy, *maman* told me once. Had an eye for a pretty lady. She must have wanted to put a stop to all that, I'll bet."

Penny, in spite of his close knowledge of the scene of the crime, had no insight into the motive for a murder committed fifty years ago. He nodded, said something banal and noncommittal and left the room. Alarming though the news was, he had other things on his mind.

Nevertheless, the woman's instincts were not far short of the mark. Two days after his grisly disclosure about the aborted babies, Father Matthieu, burdened with a secret as heavy as a tombstone, had yielded to his conscience and had spoken to the police detectives for a second time. Madeleine was dead, her sin had been absolved in her confession and her punishment was not for this world. Her husband Jean, the victim of her brutal assault with a meat cleaver and the subject of lies and gossip for half a century, deserved a Christian burial at the very least.

A loose scattering of puffy white clouds hung in the limpid blue sky of a warm June afternoon in the Dordogne. There was no threat of rain and the caterers had been able to set up outside in a corner of the car park without concern for the weather. Groups of people were already gathered close by, helping themselves to drinks and canapés offered by a pair of young waitresses, a niece of Camille Rousseau and her best school friend. John Penny picked up a glass of champagne on his way into the hall and noticed how, apart from the string of bunting at its edges, the light blue awning set up by the caterers resembled the tent the police had erected to shield their previous evening's excavations.

There was a hubbub of relaxed conversation, French and English voices, swirling around the old chapel. People patted his shoulder and stopped their private discussions to smile and congratulate him, to chink their glasses with his as he passed amongst the guests. Most he recognised, a few he did not.

He caught sight of the slight frame of Camille Rousseau, who had dressed up for the occasion in a smart lemon jacket and skirt; standing with her husband, who had also made an effort involving a tie, together they looked as though they had dropped into the gallery on the way to a wedding. They were deep in conversation with Marie-Françoise Perrier, her sober-looking husband, the former mayor Frédéric Besse and presumably his wife, who had an undisguisable wig of lustrous golden hair, a voice like a parakeet and a plate of food replete for the six of them.

Rodrigues the builder, for whom Penny had developed a growing respect, stood with a colleague, the electrical engineer and one or two others of the men who had worked on the site throughout the months of winter and spring. Nicolas Duchemin was leaning against the wall on the far side explaining the merits of Steeples' *Le Pont à Frettignac* to a very beautiful young woman around whose smooth-skinned shoulder his free arm was draped. Penny straightened the knot on his tie and made a mental note to introduce himself to her later. Friends from the media had arrived, of course: a couple of editors, photographers, radio presenters, representatives of local tourist offices, people of whom he had known very little only three months earlier.

A shrill burst of laughter caught his attention. In a flamboyant, feathery fascinator that wouldn't have looked out of place at Ascot races, Joyce Sweetacre, flanked by husband Hugh and long-suffering friend Cilla, had most likely made some salacious *double entendre* relating to *The Fruit Tasters*; two or three other people in her orbit were giggling noisily. Griotte, the crinkly-faced bank manager, moved away from them as though their raucous English voices were in some way toxic. In doing so he bumped into a pair of well-dressed, handsomely tanned individuals who were admiring *Les Gabares de Bergerac* and who turned to accept his apologies. It was the Baron du Beautrottoir and his wife Mirabelle, *la baronne*, who looked ten years younger than she had the last time Penny had seen her. The baron was wearing a pair of tassel loafers in mushroom grey suede; he caught Penny's eye, smiled briefly and looked away. He couldn't imagine who had invited them, but it would do no harm to be back in the sphere of the wealthy.

Three or four colleagues from AULA had just arrived, squeezing through the double doors with partners in tow. The *Chef de Faculté*, who had maintained he would be unlikely to come, glanced shyly around the busy room looking for a place to be inconspicuous.

And so it went on, a slow dance of sorts as groups split and re-formed spinning around the room, stopping to observe, to chat, and move on, this way and that as an exhibit, an open book in a glass case, a captivating photograph, an intricate sketch, an antique map might catch an eye. There was little doubt that the five large frames, the Steeples artworks – two on each long wall and *Le Jour du Marché* at the far end – were the most glittering of the treasures, and Penny felt a paternal pride in seeing his guests bathed in their brilliance.

He pulled delicately away from a slurry of compliments pouring from the throat of one of the academics he had addressed weeks ago at the Université de Bordeaux. He had one eye on the door, for the guest of honour was late. He looked at his watch: ten minutes past three.

Somebody was tapping at his elbow.

"Monsieur Penny."

He spun round to find Amande Puybonieux, dressed in a well-cut floral outfit he had never seen before. He wondered moreover if she hadn't applied a trace of lipstick.

"Madame Puybonieux."

"*Désolée, monsieur*. I know you are occupied with your guests. I just wanted to let you know that the police have left. They have finished at the house."

"So I can go back there later?"

"*Oui, monsieur*."

"Well, that's a relief."

"I tried to phone, *monsieur*, but there was no reply."

"No, my phone is at the house. I left it there in all the confusion last night."

"Well, I'll leave you to your guests."

She was on the point of shuffling away when Penny remembered to add:

"I'm sorry to hear about your father, *madame*."

"*Merci, monsieur.* I don't really want to talk about it, if you don't mind."

"No, of course. Of course not. You're staying though? Have a drink with us? A little food?"

"Yes, I will. The gallery is marvellous, by the way. You have done so well."

"We all have, I'd say."

Suddenly he heard the voice of Joyce Sweetacre from across the room:

"John! John, darling! Looks like your VIP has arrived!"

Penny stepped outside into the car park where a space had been reserved for the man from the embassy. A deep red Jaguar saloon pulled into the bay and almost caught the plump backside of one of the waitresses who was crossing the car park with a tray of empty glasses. An elderly chauffeur staggered out and opened the rear doors in turn for a youngish woman from the consulate in Bordeaux and a fellow of about forty with thick chestnut brown hair and the beginnings of a paunch which even his bespoke tailored suit could not disguise. This had to be Geoffrey Flossing, the under-secretary from the economic development desk at the embassy in Luxembourg. *Sorry*, Bagshaw had texted a week ago. *It's the best they could do. Summer holidays.*

"Mr Penny!" he said, stepping on to the pristine tarmac and offering a soft right hand. "A pleasure to meet you. I've heard all about the museum."

"It's very kind of you to come," said Penny. "Perhaps you'd like a glass of champagne and I'll give you both the tour?"

"Splendid! It's Jonathan, isn't it?"

"John. Jonathan is the artist's brother. The famous writer."

The man's tie was a vivid pink. And it was at this early stage that Penny guessed correctly that his luxuriant coiffure was not entirely his own.

"I see. Yes, two brothers, of course, I remember. By the way, a lovely old building, isn't it? A mill of some kind in its day?"

"Actually a chapel. A Protestant temple."

"Very good. Splendid. Yes, a little drink would be nice. Took longer than we thought to get up here from the city."

And with the woman from the consulate two steps behind him, a smile of some insincerity on his lips and a condescending touch to Penny's elbow, Flossing marched across to the caterers' stall where a fresh glass of sparkling wine was already being poured for him.

"I've heard a bit about you, John."

"Really?"

"Indeed I have. You're an Oxford man, am I right?"

"Yes, very much so. Eighty-three to eighty-six."

"Eighty-six," the under-secretary repeated, taking a sip from his flute. "You're a little older than me, but it's my brother that knew you. He was up there about the same time. Ollie. You remember a chap called Oliver Flossing?"

"I can't say I do, actually," said Penny.

"He was a scientist. A rather brilliant one. Pure Chemistry. First-class honours."

"I didn't really mix with the chemists."

"Well, your loss, John. We'd still be in the dark ages without them. Anyway, he does remember you."

"It's such a long time ago."

"And you know Sir Russell."

"Sir Russell?"

"*Sir* Russell Forrest. You'd heard he'd been knighted, surely? He's a pal of yours, isn't he?"

"He's a supporter."

"He must be. I hear he's been lobbying ferociously on your behalf. I've been told to mention him in my speech."

Flossing patted his jacket pocket as Penny coughed and looked to make eye contact with the woman from the consulate.

"Shall we move inside?" he suggested. "There's quite a crowd waiting for us. Under-secretary? Would you like to follow me?"

It took fifteen minutes to guide the visitors around the gallery: it was a superficial tour but Penny had a sense that many of the guests were starting to get impatient.

It was time to address the throng. Duchemin ushered a knot of people away from *Le Jour du Marché* to create a small space, as instructed, for Penny and Flossing to occupy. Penny checked the inside of his jacket for the two folded pages of his speech, printed in large font so that he could read it without resorting to his spectacles. He cleared his throat, chinked together a pair of wine glasses until the hall fell silent and was about to start speaking when a photographer squeezed up through the crowd and insisted on a series of pictures for *Dordogne Libre*. Several other people, inspired by the idea, took out their phones and followed his example. Finally, slightly alarmed by the number of flashes affecting his eyes, Penny raised a hand to calm his audience once again.

"Mr Under-secretary," he began, "*mesdames et messieurs*, ladies and gentlemen!"

It was an occasion when only a mixture of French and English would do. His speech was in French to a large extent, but in deference to several guests he had to include a number of succinct translations.

"*Bienvenue à l'ouverture officielle de notre nouveau musée,*" he continued. "*Le Musée des Frères Steeples à Frettignac-du-Périgord!*"

There was a ripple of applause. He smiled and looked down at his notes, prepared to plough on. As the clapping rose and fell away, he heard a muttering from the back of the assembly. He glanced at his pages once more, heard a shout, an angry shout, and, feeling a sudden dissipation of goodwill, sensing the mood in the room shift from warmth to cold, he quizzically looked over to Flossing for support.

"*Sont truqués!* They're fakes! *Sont tous truqués!*"

There was a commotion as people took their eyes off Penny's unease to turn to the source of the heckling. It was one of the journalists, holding up his phone, and now several other guests had followed suit, exchanging mutterings of disbelief, showing their neighbours images on their mobile screens.

"They're all fakes!" someone else exclaimed. "It's here on YouTube."

The guests were already grouping randomly, pushing

to see what exactly was being shown by the people who were online. There were gasps, here and there a little booing, someone called out *Oh, John, what have you done?* Someone else uttered the word *charlatan*. Meanwhile the woman from Bordeaux had found the posting on her tablet and moved between Penny and Flossing to share it with them.

Penny has already fished out his glasses. He cannot believe what he is seeing, watching a film of some fifty seconds as the blood drains from his face, as his heart flutters and flickers faster and faster, as his knees go weak, as a film of sweat forms on his brow. The heat in the room has suddenly become intense and there is an overpowering smell of stale sweat. All the while, on the screen a man wearing an orange boiler suit and a black balaclava to conceal his face is painting a canvas that rests on an easel in a nondescript warehouse. Zoom in, we see intricate detail of dabs of colour being studiously applied, zoom out to reveal a part-completed painting later to be known as *The Fruit Tasters*. Then similar details of other incomplete works being created: *Le Jour du Marché, Le Pont à Frettignac*. A close-up of a signature being hurriedly applied by left-handed brushwork: *Steeples*, just about legible, painted into the bottom left corner. Then five canvases on their five easels, extravagantly introduced to the audience as in mime by the man in the balaclava. The film cuts to an outdoor scene: the canvases now appear in a row along a path, leaning against a painted stone wall. Zoom out, and part of a farmhouse is revealed: Penny recognises at once the home of Gareth Overthrow. The artist in the orange boiler suit comes into view and skips in front of the paintings from left to right, from one to five, like a child playing hopscotch. And then a page of text appears as the visuals fade out, and all those in the room who understand English can read the words: *The Steeples paintings are all faked. I know, 'cos I did 'em.* At the very end of the message is the bright yellow emoticon of a winking smiley face.

Those guests who are not watching the footage for a third or fourth time, those who are not sharing their dismay, their disappointment, their disgust with those around them, are instead staring hopelessly at John Penny, at the ghost of John Penny, desperate for an explanation, an answer, a denial they know he cannot give. They see him loosening his tie, undoing his top button, noticing that Flossing has done the same.

"Mr Penny!"

The under-secretary, realising that he too is in the hall under false pretences, is pulling at his sleeve.

"Mr Penny, for Heaven's sake! Haven't you anything to say? Did you know any of this? Can it be true?" If only fractionally, the man's hairpiece has moved nonetheless.

Penny tries to speak but his throat will not release the words. He is unsure if there is any oxygen in the room. He sees only faces – bleak, angry faces and defeated eyes, and then the compassionate expressions of those who will always want to believe in him no matter what: Camille, Amande, Joyce.

"I'm sorry," he says finally as the frozen scene in front of him regains its life. "I've no idea what to say. To you, to anyone."

Before Flossing can answer, Penny steps unsteadily into the crowd of guests, which parts like an unrehearsed piece of choreography. He hears voices but the words mean nothing. He glimpses random faces: the red lipstick of Duchemin's girlfriend, the shimmering wig of Madame Besse, and, accentuated by the pastel colours of his clothes, the tanned complexion of the baron, whose lips form a wry, unfathomable smile.

Somebody, a journalist, shouts out:

"Who's the guy in the balaclava, Monsieur Penny?"

"What have you got to say?" asks another, before someone else, a woman, wants to know, "Is he a friend of yours, John?"

By the doors he catches sight of the Sweetacres.

"I can't do this, Joyce," he mumbles, heading outside.

The woman's party face now offers only the sympathetic expression of a mourner.

"John?"

"I'm so sorry," she hears him say. "Lock it all up for me when they've gone, won't you?"

His car, like most of the other guests', was parked along the roadside, tucked into the verge, *à cheval*, fifty metres or so from the chapel. One of the reporters who had followed him out, barking questions, had wandered back inside having been pointedly ignored. Penny's mind was still spinning, he needed a cigarette but had none. He flopped into the 206, threw his jacket on to the passenger seat and turned the key in the ignition, eager to flee the scene. There was no response from the engine. A line of cold sweat was trickling down his back to the top of his trousers. He tried again: nothing, not a flicker of life, not a whisper of sound. He tried again and punched the steering wheel so hard he thought he had cracked it apart or else broken a bone in his hand.

"Fuck! *Fuck!*" he yelled to no-one, to himself, to everyone, and felt no better for it.

Suddenly there was a bang on the roof and a tap at his window. It was Hugh Sweetacre. In spite of himself he wound it down.

"This is a bit *déjà vu*, isn't it, old sport?" said Sweetacre with a wide grin. "As they say in this country."

"Fucking car," said Penny, eyes forward.

"It is the same old *bagnole*, isn't it?" asked the financier, stepping back for a proper view. "Yes, you still have the dear old Peugeot. I do admire your loyalty."

"Can you help?" Penny spat out the words like a wad of old chewing gum.

"I'm afraid not. We're in Cilla's car and, sadly, she's got to leave right away. Don't worry, I call back later to pick up Joyce. Good of you to land her in it."

"She's a friend."

"Pity it's a Sunday, mate. Old Gaston'll be at home with a bottle of lager and the Grand Prix on the telly if I'm not mistaken."

"Don't worry yourself, Hugh. I'll walk."

Sweetacre stepped aside as Penny pushed open the door and narrowly missed his leg.

"Tell Joyce I'll call her tomorrow. Tell her thanks. Tell her she's an angel."

Sweetacre had turned heel and was strolling back to the museum. He started to whistle a tune, stopped halfway and shouted back:

"You're such a loser, Penny. You're a fake, just like your precious paintings."

Penny kept close to the verge, facing the oncoming traffic. It was a busy road even on a Sunday. His hand was throbbing, he was finding it hard to concentrate on his feet, on his breathing, on his immediate plans, on anything at all. He had walked about half a kilometre when a small silver car heading into town on the other side of the road passed him slowly and crawled to a stop. Through the driver's window a voice called his name. He recognised first the voice then the neat, fluffy grey hair of Amande Puybonieux. He crossed the road and lowered his head to see her face.

"*Montez, monsieur*," she said softly, as though she were talking to a child in distress. "Get in. *Je vous en prie*. Let me drive you home."

An hour later and there was still a little life at the old Protestant temple. An observer sitting in the lay-by used several months earlier by John Penny – a spot he had chosen to watch through a rain-spattered windscreen the efforts of the labourers fashioning a home suitable for a collection of fine nineteenth-century art – would have seen just three remaining vehicles. The claret-coloured

Jaguar carrying the under-secretary at the economic development desk of the British embassy in Luxembourg had long since departed. As had the majority of the guests, still in shock, some still gibbering about swindlers and trust, others still lost in silent feelings of sorrow or betrayal or simply of confusion.

What an observer would have seen now was the caterers, a man and his wife, owners of a popular little *charcuterie* in town, packing away the final components of their awning, neatly folding up the bunting until next time, stacking everything they had brought with them into the back of their van.

A second van, white with British registration plates and an unfamiliar name on the sides, was stationed directly in front of the doors of the museum. Two young men, both in white tee-shirts and jeans, had been coming and going for the past forty minutes but the open doors of their vehicle made it difficult to see exactly the nature of their tasks.

Suddenly the doors of the building were shut and the men got into their van as if to drive away. From behind it a tall, stoutish woman of about fifty came into view, putting a set of keys and a mobile phone into a leather handbag. She waved at the men, who were already sitting side by side, deep in conversation. Berthed in the car park was a third white vehicle, this one the whitest of them all, a gleaming open-topped Bentley whose driver, a grey-haired man in an expensive summer suit, had spent the past quarter of an hour wriggling, shuffling, mainly on the phone, lolling in his leather seat without ever wanting to leave it. The woman collapsed into the passenger side and leaned over to kiss her driver, who guided the car out of the car park and, with a screech of its tyres, accelerated away in the direction of Les Eyzies as if it would turn into something worse than a pumpkin were it to spend another second in the shadows of the old chapel.

A moment or two later the white van slowly pulled into the car park to turn around and head out in the opposite direction. And as well as noticing how correctly the driver behaved – signalling right with his indicators even though the road was perfectly clear – an observer would also have had the chance to read the words printed on the van's flank above a foreign telephone number and to the side of a stylized representation of an adjustable spanner: words both strange and unpronounceable to the typical man or woman bred in this corner of Périgord: *David Penny & Son, Plumbing and Heating Services.*

21

The excavator had been left at the front of the house, dried mud on its caterpillar tracks, its mustard yellow cabin sheathed in dust, but there was no sign of life, either in the house or in the garden where the circular patch, the magical vegetable plot, the cursed ground, the burial site, had been roughly flattened with spillages of earth here and there on the surrounding gravel.

John Penny had neither the time nor the inclination to examine it. The moment he got inside he headed straight for the chair over which he had hung his jacket the previous afternoon. He found his phone in the pocket, as he knew he would. The battery was low but strong enough to show ten missed calls and two voicemails. One of each was from the roofer, who had called to remind him that there was an outstanding bill of several thousand euros. There had already been a call from a journalist while he was on his way home. The rest were from Columbine's mobile. He checked the times: a couple from yesterday afternoon around the time he had been out running, a couple an hour later by which time he would have been on his way down to the hotel. Then three others, calls ten and fifteen minutes apart, made around 8pm. The final one was logged at 10.29 that morning; he would have been at the gallery by then. He accessed the voicemail, also recorded the previous evening, and waited to hear her wish him good luck, to tell him she was fine and was looking forward to seeing him very soon. The voice he heard was deeper, however, harsh and angry, not her voice at all; an American voice nevertheless, a woman's, the voice of someone at the very end of her leash: *Penny, for fuck's sake, why don't you answer? Get over to the hospital right now or I swear you'll never see Columbine Snow again!*

From some near-exhausted source, adrenalin bubbled through his body again. Whatever the message meant – it was obviously an emergency – he had to get up to Périgueux and see Columbine straight away. He hadn't drunk enough to stop him driving but he had no car to drive. Amande Puybonieux had dropped him off five minutes ago but then she had gone directly home to Les Saules. He couldn't expect her to come back and drive him into the city; the old woman had endured as much trauma as him and despite a brave face looked utterly worn out. His only option was to walk back into town and find a taxi.

The sprawling, angular complex of the *Centre Hospitalier de Périgueux* is on a raised section of the city and by the time Penny arrived, the lines of lights below were flickering on as the brightness of the long summer's evening began to fade. He had been here only once before and was immediately at a loss as to which direction to follow. Hopelessly he searched a myriad of signs and arrows for the word *Maternité*, and was finally directed by a porter to a reception desk where he had to queue for ten minutes. Finally he was given brusque instructions which involved a walk around to a different wing of the building; he should have come in at the other entrance. How was he to know?

The nurse at the front desk of the maternity department had a friendlier disposition but her face adopted an expression of concern as soon as he explained who he was and the reason for his visit. She advised him to take a seat; a doctor would be with him very soon. Her attempts to calm his nerves had exactly the opposite effect.

A doctor with a harassed look on her face appeared presently, introduced herself and asked Penny to follow her down a shiny corridor and into a small consultation room.

"*Asseyez-vous, monsieur,*" she said, pointing at a plain plastic chair. "Please, take a seat."

Instead of sitting behind the desk, the doctor chose the second seat next to Penny's and pulled it a little closer.

"You are the partner of Mademoiselle Snow, yes?"

She was looking at him with an intensity he found alarming.

"Yes I am. What's happening? Where is she?"

"She is fine, *monsieur*, but extremely tired. She is sleeping. She has a comfortable room. Very private."

"So I can see her?"

"I'm not sure that is a good idea right now, *monsieur*."

"What do you mean?"

"Let me explain. Columbine was brought in to hospital yesterday afternoon. In an ambulance."

"An ambulance?"

"She was suffering from severe abdominal pains. It was clear that her pregnancy had developed difficulties."

"Don't tell me she's lost her baby! Please don't tell me that!"

"Try to stay calm, Monsieur Penny. I know it's a terribly sad time."

"What happened? Just tell me, please!"

The doctor took a deep breath and ran a hand through her hair; this was a conversation she had had before, a conversation that never got any easier.

"The baby had stopped breathing," she said quietly. "There was no heartbeat. We had no choice but to operate, and, well, I'm afraid that the child was stillborn."

Penny had covered his aching eyes with his hands.

"But she was eight months gone," he said, his voice strangled by a throat as dry as dust. "Almost full term."

"It can happen, *monsieur*. Until a baby is born kicking and shouting there are no guarantees, even with a healthy mother."

"Why?" he howled.

"Why?"

"Why did it die?" he asked, looking up at her through unbidden tears.

"The most likely explanation is a problem with the umbilical cord. It was retrieved tangled, almost knotted, which could have cut off blood and nutrients, possibly for several days, maybe longer."

Penny's head fell back into his hands. The doctor placed a hand softly on his trembling shoulder.

"Take your time, Monsieur Penny. I have to leave you but you can stay here a moment. I am truly sorry. We all are."

Sensing nothing in the void around him, he didn't hear her leave. He must have spent five minutes staring at the walls of the room and seeing nothing at all.

He emerged into the corridor and the dazzling lights stung his bloodshot eyes. He decided to head straight for the wards; he needed to see Columbine, to hug her, to kiss her, to tell her that he loved her, that they would get through this together. He found himself in another corridor, lined with doors to individual treatment rooms. A nurse passed him and smiled: he was just another overemotional dad. One by one he peeped in through the windows, and in the room at the very end of the corridor he saw the shape of Columbine, covered in sheets, the back of her head, a smudge of dark brown hair, her name inked in neat handwriting on a whiteboard above her bed. He turned the door handle and crept in.

He had set no more than a single foot in the room before he was pushed back into the corridor by a large woman with spiky bleached hair, a fake US Army tee-shirt and shorts and an aggressive expression on her face.

"Get out and stay out!" she hissed.

With her forefinger poking him in the chest she forced him backwards halfway down the corridor.

"You're Penny, right?"

She had an unrefined American accent and seemed to have walked in out of a gangster movie. He nodded, lost for words.

"You're not welcome here, bud," she went on. "Col won't see you. Not after what you did. Or rather what you *didn't* do."

"I lost my phone," he pleaded. "I got your messages only a couple of hours ago. I came straight here. I need to see her. Let me past. It was my child too."

"Not so you'd notice, is what Col said. You gave no mind to it, she said. Let her get on with it by herself."

"That's not remotely true."

"There's the exit, Penny. She'll call you, if you're lucky."

He made a move to sidestep her but she was quick to block him.

"What are you doing?"

"Ain't it obvious?"

"Who are you anyway? You've got no right to stop me."

"Who am I? Who am I? I'm the person she came to when you let her down. I'm the one friend she can rely on."

"Pamela?"

"Pamela, that's right. So you *were* listening to her some of the time."

"How long have you been here?"

"She called me Toosday. Got a flight the very next day. Been here four days."

"I didn't know she'd asked you."

"Should I be surprised? And she didn't ask me. She didn't have to."

"Please let me in, Pamela."

"Hey, Penny, you're not listening. Beat it. I told you already. We don't want you here."

The woman turned her back on him and headed towards the room where Columbine was sleeping.

391

"What was it?" he begged. "A boy or a girl?"

"A girl," she shouted without looking back. "She called her Beth. It was her mom's name."

Penny thought he would never sleep again but once his brain finally shut down he slept solidly for around seven hours and woke up at half past nine with a raging headache. He had never slept in Columbine's flat before without her being there too. There were signs of her everywhere, of course: in every room, in every cupboard, on every shelf. On the bedroom floor was a large soft leather bag he did not recognise, presumably belonging to Pamela McVie, on top of which he saw an American travel guide to France, bookmarked at the section on the south-west. In the bathroom he found some paracetamol and swallowed three with a glass of water. He would see Columbine this morning – it was a priority. Pamela had been overexcited, she would soften, come to see his point of view.

He forced himself to eat breakfast in a café and rang Gaston to check that he had picked up the message he had sent from the taxi. Yes, they had found the car. Yes, the keys were where he said, under the wheel arch. Yes, they had it there right now. Yes, he'd let him know.

Voicemails from reporters were already stacking up on his phone: *Dordogne Libre*, *France Bleu Périgord*, *Sud-ouest*, they all wanted a comment about the gallery. He ignored them all.

When he arrived at the hospital Penny found Pamela to be no less of an obstruction than before. Engrossed in something on her mobile, she was sitting on a chair that she must have pulled out of Columbine's room and into the corridor by her door. She must have expected him to come back. She was wearing the same grubby tee-shirt but had put on a pair of loose camouflage pants. He wondered if she were sleeping in the hospital somewhere. He wondered too if she had a hunting knife strapped to her calf. She caught sight of him as he approached and stood to intercept.

"Good morning," said Penny, hoping for a fresh start.

"Don't waste your breath," said the woman, gesturing to him to turn and leave.

"How is she?"

"How is she? She lost a baby, for Christ's sake! *How is she?* you ask, like she's had a tooth pulled out or something."

"Just tell me. Is she awake?"

"Yeah, she is. Just about, after all the meds they've given her. But she won't give you the time of day, Penny. You've had a wasted journey."

He made to reach for the door but she put herself between them and scowled.

"Don't think you're getting in there, 'cause you ain't." Little bullets of spittle flew from her lips. "You hear me this time? She ain't forgiven you and I don't reckon she ever will."

"She will. I know she will."

The woman leaned into him, her face barely six inches from his own.

"You don't get it, do you?" More spittle, this time

Penny felt it on his cheek, smelt her coffee breath. "For a college professor you ain't so smart. Leave the building and don't show your face round here no more."

He tried to place a hand on the door but she bumped him away with her chest. He was wasting his time with this self-styled bodyguard.

"Thanks, Pamela," he said with a hollow smile. He turned to leave. "I'll call back tomorrow. You can't keep me away for ever."

"She won't see you!" she shouted back at him as he withdrew.

"Tell her I love her."

"She won't see you, Penny! She never wants to see you again!"

He found an empty table in the hospital canteen and drank a milky coffee from a plastic cup. He had spoken to a nurse about his frustrated attempts to see Columbine but the woman had unhelpfully reminded him that in such times of distress he should respect the patient's wishes. His mind rebounded to the gallery; he needed to call Joyce Sweetacre. Mercifully Hugh did not pick up and it was his wife, just in from a half an hour's deadheading, who gushed her lengthy commiserations before Penny could say his piece.

"Everything was in order as you left, then, Joyce? You didn't have a problem with the alarm or anything?"

"No, it's quite straightforward once you remember which order to push the buttons in."

"It doesn't appear that we've much of value to protect in there any more."

"Sadly not. I still can't believe it."

"I still love those paintings, Joyce, at the end of it all, you know." She heard a weariness in his voice as he went on slowly, "I know I'm clutching at straws. I'll have to read the small print in the contract, see if we can't keep them."

"But they've gone, John, remember? They've already taken them away."

"Taken what away?"

"The paintings. The sketches. Everything."

"Hang on. What do you mean? When?"

"Yesterday. When everybody had left. You told me to let them take them."

"*I* told you?"

"I spoke to you. Don't you remember? One of the chaps handed me his phone and you spoke to me. You told me it was absolutely okay to let them take the paintings away."

"Joyce, I did *not* speak to you on the phone."

There was a moment's silence.

"Joyce?"

"Well, someone did. Someone who sounded exactly like you!"

"Calm down, Joyce. Tell me precisely what happened."

"What happened? Well, just as the last few people were leaving, they turned up with a van. Two young men, North Country accents but quite agreeable, very nice in fact, very polite. One was a black boy, rather handsome. Like a young Obama."

"Joyce, tell me what happened."

"They were looking for the manager. I explained who I was, they said they had come to pick up the paintings, all the Steeples material. I was taken aback, of course, everything so sudden, but the other one, the white one, said he'd ring you to check and then passed the phone to me. That's when you told me it was all above board and they were to be allowed to clear away all the artwork. Which they did. Very efficient, they were. Finished the job in less than an hour. Still, Hughie got a bit stroppy waiting for me in the car, poor man!"

Penny felt cold. The air was warm but the fingers holding his phone were almost numb.

"Joyce, it wasn't me. It was somebody *pretending* to be me. Don't you understand? *Impersonating* me. Did you get a good look at the van?"

"I didn't pay it any attention, John, sorry. White, definitely, perhaps a Ford. I don't honestly remember."

There was another pause. She wondered if he'd cut her off in a fit of anger. Then his voice again, drained of life:

"They'll be back in England by now."

"And I was so pleased with myself," she said. "Oh, John, I really am sorry. Have I been a dreadful fool?"

He rang Stephanie Chimes but her number was no longer recognised.

Gaston called to let him know that his car would be ready to be picked up late afternoon. *No, it will not be as good as new, monsieur. I cannot guarantee it will run on much longer. I can keep an eye open for something similar for you, five years younger, perhaps?*

There was call from Nicolas Duchemin which he ignored.

He walked back to Columbine's flat trying to calculate how many reasons had piled up for him to feel sorry for himself. The sun was high in a cloudless sky and the heat made him light-headed. When he arrived there he found the only chilled drink in her refrigerator was half a bottle of skimmed milk. He hated being in the apartment alone. He came across her iPod and scrolled through her music vainly hoping to find something to cheer him up, to remind him of her, but her music was bland and vacuous and sentimental and he gave up. After five minutes he decided to leave and catch the bus back to Frettignac.

By the time he had walked up the hill from the bus stop Penny was overheated, sweating heavily and exhausted. His mind could take little more. The house was cool and he found a cold beer, hooked off the cap and drank the whole bottle before thinking about doing anything else.

His computer had collected several emails while he had been away, mainly messages of dismay or sympathy from people too nervous to make a proper phone call. Duchemin had written to ask him how he should respond to the barrage of abuse on social media and begging Penny to provide him with a statement which he could issue to the press. There was a single sentence from the roofing contractor telling him again that he needed to be paid for the work on the chapel. The only email he wrote was a terse question to Stephanie Chimes, which bounced back to him within minutes: her address was invalid. He tried to find the Hatcher Cross website but it had disappeared; how could an entire business suddenly no longer exist? He was slowly beginning to measure the extent of the scam he had been a victim of when another email landed in his inbox. This one contained a longer message – a full two paragraphs, in fact – carefully and empathetically framed by a member of the governing body of AULA, *Base de Périgueux*. Penny read it quickly, the short sentences bouncing off him like rubber darts: regretfully, and *for a number of disparate reasons (see below)*, his contract with the university would not be renewed.

Tuesday morning brought a motionless layer of cloud and a sultry breathlessness to the air. Penny had slept fitfully and didn't know which way to turn. He woke up hungry but couldn't face breakfast. He took a long shower and saw how the flesh around his nipples had begun to sag. He drank two cups of strong coffee and watched a squirrel jumping from one walnut tree to the next, all along the row until it was out of sight. The only thing he was sure of was that he had to see Columbine; he needed her to forgive him, to accept him and give him back a sense of direction.

He walked down into town to pick up his car. He paid with a credit card whose flexibility he was beginning to doubt. The old Peugeot sounded as sprightly as a car ten years younger; Gaston was a magician. He checked the gauge – he had half a tank of petrol – and, winding down both windows, steered it on to the road out of town towards Périgueux.

Parking outside the hospital in the middle of the day was difficult and, at any time, expensive. He was beginning to know his way around the corridors of *Maternité*; he smiled emptily to a nurse he recognised and plodded on towards the room where Columbine would be waiting for him, sitting up in bed, a little colour in her cheeks, forgiveness in her heart. And the pitbull Pamela would be banished or, at worst, muzzled and chained to the radiator.

A young black nurse was just coming out of the room with an armful of bedding as Penny approached.

"How is Columbine today?" he asked.

"This room is empty, *monsieur*," said the nurse, pouring the sheets into a laundry trolley. "Mademoiselle Snow left earlier."

"Earlier?"

"First thing this morning."

"Is she well enough to leave?"

"The doctors must think so. She discharged herself in any case. She left with the other lady."

"The American?"

"*Oui, monsieur, l'Américaine.* They left together. As you can see, the room is empty."

He put his head around the door and saw that her name had been erased from the whiteboard, which gleamed like a pristine canvas.

Penny drove as fast as the traffic would allow to Columbine's flat; he was not surprised to find it as empty as the hospital room. Her clothes, her books, all her personal possessions had gone. The kitchen was spotless, the furniture tidy, the bedroom immaculate. It was an apartment awaiting the next occupancy, an apartment whose previous tenants were not coming back. He tried to phone her but her number went directly to voicemail. He left a message: *Columbine, I love you. Please let me speak to you and tell you properly.*

He sat in his car until the sweat on his forehead ran down his nose and dripped on to his lap, creating a little wet patch on his shorts. He decided to drive the short distance to AULA and was held up in traffic outside the theatre whose costumes they had hired for Elise's video such a long time ago. He remembered the day Columbine had squeezed his hand and gazed longingly into his eyes, rehearsing the look of Béatrice for her English lover.

"We gave the costumes back, Col. You don't need to stay in character any longer."

"I'm not," she said. "This is me, John. Just me."

And then the echo, with its trace of reassurance, with its hint of a taunt:

"I'm not," she said. "This is me, John. Just me."

Suddenly the driver in the car behind him was tooting his horn for the third time; the lights had changed.

There were very few people at the university buildings. When he arrived in his study he couldn't face packing everything up, all the books and files and resources and equipment. Most of it was old hat, used and reused, exhausted just like him. He wondered if he would ever use any of it again, if he would ever teach again. He found a small cardboard box and spent ten minutes filling it with the bare necessities: texts he could not part with, favourite collections, a file of his own greatest hits. The rest he left behind like a jumble of dusty ruins abandoned after a hard, protracted battle.

Thankfully he met no-one he knew. Most of the people working were office staff or cleaners, decorators or electricians. He wandered into the musty staffroom for a final time. His pigeonhole was stuffed, as usual, with flyers and junk mail from publishers. As he flung it all in the bin he noticed a postcard which he retrieved: it was a cartoon showing a line of lemmings following each other over the edge of a cliff. To one of the sorry animals a flag had been added, drawn in with a pen: this lemming, part of the long parade to oblivion, was carrying a Union Jack. Penny smiled and turned the card over – it bore a Swedish postage stamp and he recognised the chunky handwriting at once:

Dear John,
I am sorry. I was quite wrong. Good luck – you will need it.
Henrik

It was already five days since the result of the referendum in the UK had been announced. Of course it had caught Penny's attention, but rather as a glancing blow; just as shocked as everyone else seemed to be, he had absorbed the bare bones but hadn't found the energy to quite work out any of the consequences.

22

Penny was surprised to discover that the blue door to his house was unlocked. There was nobody inside, no sign of an intruder, no-one was lingering in the garden. He came to the conclusion that he must have forgotten to lock it when he left that morning.

A warm breeze had picked up and the clouds were slowly dispersing like groups of children in a school-yard drifting sulkily into classrooms at the end of break. He was drifting too, floundering in limbo. He had been driving for forty minutes and could remember nothing at all of the journey. The only thing he could recall was that before leaving AULA he had phoned Columbine's number again but had received no answer.

He felt pangs of hunger but the even the thought of food made him nauseous. He stood in the kitchen and looked out through the window at that familiar view, those familiar ranks of trees. He had always imagined this army of foot soldiers marching away from the house, up towards the top end of the field, but today, as the sun slipped behind a cloud and the sheen of the leaves dulled, they became a manifestation of something quite the opposite: with their branches waving aggressively in the wind, bearing fleshy, green, unpinned grenades, they had turned, they had become a platoon advancing towards him, towards the house; he could hear their boots stamping on the dry earth, raising dust, kicking stones. As he retreated, he caught sight of his reflection in the window: staring back at him was the face of a haunted man, a face he no longer recognised.

His phone rang and the infantry became nothing more intimidating than trees in a walnut grove. The caller was the roofer. He was running out of patience, he said. He knew where Penny lived. He was on a break on a job in town and would be up there in fifteen minutes to have a conversation.

Penny couldn't face him. He couldn't face anyone apart from Columbine. She couldn't avoid him forever. He rang her number once again. Five rings, then voicemail. He wanted to howl like a wounded dog, to let his tears flow like a river.

He had lost control of his breathing. Sweat from under his arms was gathering in patches, soaking his shirt. He picked up his keys, walked out of the house and slumped into his car. He reached for the cigarette packet and remembered that it was empty, crumpled and torn. He steered the car down the hill into Frettignac but did not stop, heading instead south over the bridge. He drove neither fast nor slowly, in a trance, following a line of traffic, a truck, then a bus, trailing it for several kilometres into Les Eyzies until he grew tired of reading the words on the back of it and took a different turning. He was heading vaguely south-east but had no plan, no aim, no target. He switched off the radio; the gibberish was only aggravating his headache.

Presently he joined the road that flanked the Dordogne river and he pointed the car eastwards. His petrol gauge told him he had around thirty more kilometres left in the tank. He realised he had no idea where his wallet was. He was on a road he barely knew, a road running flat through the valley, past fields of dazzling yellow sunflowers and swaying corn, past sloping woodland, wayside buildings of dusty golden stone and cracked plasterwork, dozing in the heat. He drove past blurs of fruit trees, row after row, pears and apples, and peach orchards trapped under expanses of netting like hostages. After a while – how long he couldn't tell – a sign told him that he was arriving in the *commune* of Beynac-et-Cazenac, skirting the very edge of the Dordogne. Some deep instinct had ferried him here, it seemed, something pulling him to this spot. He slowed down, caught sight across the river of the little gravelly beach where they had once stopped to take photos of the castle. There were canoeists there right now, two couples drinking, laughing, looking up to the cliff and shielding their eyes from the glare.

Governed by the same impulse that had brought him here, he left the Peugeot in a car park by the side of the road and headed to the steep cobbled street that wound its way up the hill towards the castle. He needed to be up high, he told himself, to be away from the smell of diesel, to breathe cleaner air, to have an open, clear view of the landscape before him.

The climb is harder now, his legs feel like logs of wood, he has been feeling lightheaded for an hour, punch-drunk like a boxer who has taken too many hits and is still expected to fight on for nine more rounds. He stops and sits on a low wall to catch his breath. One or two tourists nod to him as they pass on their way down the narrow, uneven steps.

On his slow trek to the summit he finds a folded twenty-euro note in the back pocket of his shorts but has no recollection of ever putting it there. There is no queue at the ancient gatehouse where he pays an elderly lady eight euros for a ticket and wanders into the walled enclosure of the château. A few small groups of visitors are ambling around, stopping to take a photograph, to read a detail in a guidebook; most appear to be heading out of the grounds, their visit already over, the afternoon at an end. Penny walks on purposefully and yet with no true plan. Following the line of the wall that runs along a lower courtyard, he reaches a higher plateau from whose outer parapet, built of stone laid centuries ago, stretches the full southern view of the valley. He leans against the wall and takes a series of deep breaths. The air by the river had been still, weighed down. Here the wind is blowing in sudden stiff gusts, reddening his cheeks, chilling the sweat on his brow and the dampness of the shirt that sticks to his back. Close by a woman in a headscarf is talking to a boy of about ten – her son perhaps – pointing out aspects of the view; the tail of her scarf flutters like a little flag. Beyond her, to her right, the wall runs down to a lower space, to the squat rectangular chapel, to the perimeter of a flat area of lawn, to what looks like the corner of a small church garden. To his left the wall traces the edge of the sheer cliff, and rises steadily to join the high grey edifice of the fortress with its great castellated tower and flanking turrets, their tiny windows and conical roofs pointing to the clouds. The sun peeps out for a moment, lending the stone a creamy, yellow hue and casting him in shadow.

He looks out and sees the greens of the hills deepen a shade as the fragmented clouds pass over the sun once more. Way down in the bosom of the valley he spots the shape of a tourist boat steering its languid course around the bend, too far away to pick out the faces of the passengers. He strains his weary eyes but other faces are coming to him instead, visions of people he knows, rising from the valley into the space before his eyes, filling his consciousness with silent smiles, wordless expressions of contempt, of disappointment, of apathy. He sees them in unhurried series, familiar faces, in and out of focus, individuals merging randomly into unrelated groups.

He sees the pale, bony countenance of his father, then the fleshy head of Frédéric Besse, the old mayor, then Jean-Louis Lachêne, Baron du Beautrottoir, the baron who never was a baron. He sees the narrow-eyed banker Griotte, the ruddy complexion of Gareth Overthrow, and Luis the sweet, young, damp-haired Catalan. He sees Hughie Sweetacre smirking, Simon Broadfoot wiping his nose, and Jean-Yves Puybonieux, whom he knows only from a faded wedding photograph. Camille Rousseau appears, in conversation with Stephanie Chimes and his mother, who is looking away, stroking a fat dog. He sees a weeping teenager – his brother David, then his sister Michelle, slyly peeking around his bedroom door as he is getting undressed for bed. He sees Fiona with her golden ponytail, coffee-skinned Florence in her swinging braids, exasperated Elise Correia, Gaston *le garagiste* and then Mr Archer, his old French teacher, mouthing the silent question: *to be or to seem to be*? He sees Rodrigues the builder and Duchemin with his long, shaggy hair, and the grandfather of Jasper Couttes inviting him to cut a pack of cards. Penny shakes his head, clenches his fists, closes his eyes, begs the faces to leave him in peace. Why are they tormenting him? He is better than any of them.

But the procession is endless: he sees the mournful Noisette petting her timid little dog, he sees under-secretary Flossing loosening his pink tie, he sees the angry roofer, the broad, Nordic face of Henrik, dear deflated Joyce looking so sad, Amande Puybonieux staring at him curiously through her old, frameless glasses, a twenty-year-old Angus Barrington-Smith, Zacharie the head gardener and the snarling Pamela McVie. He is waiting for Columbine but she doesn't come, she doesn't join the parade. Instead he sees Marie-Françoise Perrier waving a perfumed handkerchief, he sees the student in Trois Rivières unbuckling his belt, he sees the baron's Uncle Charlot spilling food into his lap, a bleary-eyed Marie-Jo in a sulk, and Sir Russell Forrest, a man on a television screen, a man he's never met. He sees himself as a youth, silently mimicking a schoolteacher and making his friends scream with laughter, he sees himself at Oxford, long hair and embarrassment, himself with the neatest of beards, himself happy and then miserable, himself anxious, at his wits' end, waiting, still waiting for Columbine but she doesn't come.

Suddenly he hears a shriek and the flood of faces stops. The woman in the headscarf is standing a metre away, agitated, gulping breaths of air, doing all she can to stop herself from wailing. Her son covers his eyes, gripped by fright. High above them both, Penny is standing on the wall, a foot and a half's width of rough, grey stone at the cliff edge. He must have climbed up here in some sort of trance to confront the faces, to let them hear his pleas to leave him be. Below him is a dizzying emptiness, an unforgiving drop of hundreds of feet to the rocky outcrops dotted with raggedy bushes precariously rooted in the cracks, then further down to a knot of treetops, the thin strip of road, the narrow curl of the river glinting like an unwound ribbon of metallic tape.

The sun hides its face behind a scudding bank of cloud. He is standing, tottering, feet apart while the wind whistles around his ankles. He sways like the high branches of a buffeted tree, steadies himself, unsure of why he is here and what he will do next. *A lethal lunge…* He hears the woman squeal as he seems about to swoon. His face is burning but his sweat has turned to ice. The river has stopped flowing, frozen in time, as flat as glass. Then to his left he hears a second voice.

"Monsieur?"

He turns his head and almost topples over. Below him stands a stranger, an old man in a flapping raincoat. Beneath his tousled, white hair his waxy face holds a calm expression, his watery eyes fixed and resolute. The man speaks again, his voice as soft as a girl's caress, a steady hand reaching up to Penny, beckoning him down.

"*Descendez, monsieur. S'il vous plaît.* Please come down. *Doucement, hein?* Easy does it."

PART FOUR

Amande

1

According to reports on the local radio station, last night's storm, the first real gales of the spring, caused considerable tree damage and several of the minor roads were blocked this morning by fallen branches and flooding. Fortunately for me I have no need to travel anywhere today and I have plenty of food in the house to last the week. The temperature has dropped, the air today has a wintry chill to it, but there is a stillness now and the walnut trees in the sodden field sit battered but motionless, still dripping with the last of the rain. When I stepped outside this morning, apprehensive, to survey the scene, I was not surprised to find many of the top branches of the older trees twisted or broken or ripped away completely, lying metres away like debris on a battlefield. I am unconcerned: these trees needed pruning anyway, and the storm was nature's own violent way of cutting back decay. In a day or two I will get some men in to finish the job and tidy up. Most of the trees are unscathed; they bend with the wind, they are full of spirit, defiant, almost indestructible.

The house too takes a battering in its stride. One small length of guttering has come loose, but not a single roof tile is out of place. Even the so-called garage space, as flimsy-looking a structure as you could ever see, seems to roll with the punches. I considered re-advertising the place when I lost John Penny as a tenant; his monthly rent was a steady income for near four years, but I decided instead to sell my apartment and move here myself. And so here I am, sitting at the table where Penny took his meals, writing the final pages of his story.

I was lucky that the apartment sold so quickly. I lived there a long time but neighbours came and went, a good friend of mine from two doors down passed away last All Saints, and suddenly here seemed somehow more appealing to me in spite of the memories more bad than good. I want to live here for the rest of my days, I have decided. I want to leave a brightness, a warmth to the house, to a place that has seen more than enough dark times. I have removed the old, rotting board above the doorframe, the one whose flaking letters painted in my grandfather's day were not even recognised by Penny as Puybonieux at all. He would smile to know that I ordered a brand new sign from the man on the market. For the past two months any caller to the house has been welcomed by a varnished strip of oak bearing the name *PUIS BONHEUR*.

I took a rest from writing, prepared a little early supper and have lit a fire in the hearth which is already warming the room. Some weeks ago I restored my brother's wedding photograph to its rightful place on the wall by the fireplace. I found it in a cupboard upstairs, hidden under some bedding, no doubt cast away by Penny. I'm not angry with him for removing it. He couldn't be expected to live with images of my family after all, I realise. I noticed he had taken it down one summer but I felt it small-minded to complain. I see the frame but can barely make out the faces from my seat. It is dark enough now to switch on a table lamp.

I have heard not a word from Columbine Snow since she left Périgueux and I doubt now that I ever will. She left our little town, this time for good, hating it and probably everybody in it. So sad, for she had some friends here, people that truly cared about her. She and her American friend left the hospital in a hurry, I do remember. She telephoned to tell me that she was too upset to see me but she would be fine. Her friend was a nurse. I was not to worry, she insisted. Her voice sounded frail, *monotone*, like I was listening to a ghost. They had arranged to stay in a hotel together in Biarritz, she said, where she would rest until she had regained her strength. I was sworn to secrecy; on no account was I to tell Penny where she was. I gave her my word, which, of course, I kept.

Penny, too, disappeared almost as quickly, and he too had his supporters, his admirers. I do not wish to take sides. Even I, who knows their story as well as they do, have no desire to paint one as an angel and the other as a devil. I have tried to be even-handed and if anyone is to judge them then it is you, clear-sighted reader, from your distance of impartiality.

Meanwhile the old chapel remained closed throughout the autumn. Under the direction of Frédéric Besse it has become a rentable exhibition space shared with a permanent display of all the Jonathan Steeples material. It was renamed the *Musée Steeples et Salle d'Exposition de Frettignac* – a clumsy title which most people here have already turned their back on, preferring to call the place, for want of a snappy acronym, simply *Chez Jonathan.*

It is safe to say, for all her wordlessness, that Columbine is to be found back in the United States, not so very far from her father's home, I am guessing. Her only consolation – and even if she never thought about it, believe me, *I* did – was that she was not in Nice when the Daesh fanatic drove a lorry into the crowds along the *Promenade des Anglais* on the Fourteenth of July. I know they had plans to be there – they might have been there in the thick of it, the *three* of them, watching the fireworks display.

As for Penny, he *has* been in touch, more surprisingly, and not simply through a transfer of funds to cover his last month's rent. Knowing what I do about the parlous state of his finances, I was touched that he made a point of at least seeing me right. Quite unexpectedly a card in his hand arrived here several months ago. I have it in front of me now. The picture is a watercolour representation of Bristol Cathedral and inside are the words in French which I can translate verbatim:

> *Chère Amande,*
>
> *I am truly sorry for leaving you, among others, to clear up my mess. Sadly I will not, indeed I cannot, come back to Frettignac, but I will love the place forever. As a practical person, if you ever need to leave in a hurry, I suggest: drive south as far as you can, in my case to*

Toulouse. Train to Girona, plenty of planes from there to the UK, where I will not stay for long.

I will go to Canada. I think I can live well there. It will be a new start. I will find a project, maybe a wife and some happiness if I deserve it.

Best wishes,

John Penny

In tune with the times he withdrew from Europe.

It makes me smile each time I read it. *I will go to Canada*, he writes, as though he is still believing in his own legend, in his own encounter with destiny. Well, I think, it is better to believe in something than in nothing at all. And I sense a little humility too: *some happiness, if I deserve it.* But which Canada, I wonder. Victoriaville, Québec, less than a five-hour drive to Bangor, Maine? Or Victoria, British Columbia, an endless flight away across three time zones on the very rim of the Pacific Ocean, about as far from Frettignac as you can get without falling off the edge of the map?

In front of me now I have arranged a second piece of correspondence, one which will need a brighter light shone upon it. It arrived here in an envelope, postmarked London, a few days after Penny's card. It is a letter that I moved from table to table, from room to room, juggling it in my thoughts, in my conscience. For it was addressed not to me but to Penny himself. A private letter I have no way of redirecting, and still no right to open. A private

417

letter at a dead end which would never have been opened, would never have been read had I not taken a knife to the envelope myself. It is unforgivable, I know, to pry, to be so curious as to commit what some would consider to be a crime. But had I not given in to such shameful instincts then my story would have been deprived indeed of its proper denouement. In fact, if I hadn't read and re-read the letter I don't believe I would have ever written down this story at all, and for this reason I feel partly, if only partly, justified. For just as my lamp now shines on the pages, the words themselves shine a light on the motivation for the deeds which finally undid my tenant. The address is given simply as London, the handwriting in blue ink: loopy, neat, feminine.

Dear Trevor,

As you see I have stuck with letter etiquette but I cannot think of a less appropriate epithet to describe you. As children, David and I tolerated you, were even nice to you from time to time, but I cannot say that you have ever been dear to us.

When you left home thinking you were so much cleverer, so much better than the rest of us, it was already a relief to see the back of you. When you crawled back to us for the holidays it was like the lights going out in our home. You were already like a stranger to us. Mum had you back, fed you, washed your dirty clothes and you treated her like a skivvy. She didn't deserve that.

We thought you might have changed in these past thirty years. We thought you might have mellowed, regretted the shitty arrogance of your younger days. I even came close to forgiving you for what you did to me and Mark. Do you remember him, Trevor? My fiancé all those years ago? He hasn't forgotten you.

Your reaction to Mum's death proved to us that you still felt that she, and we, were beneath you, even beneath your contempt. David never hated you, Trevor, until then. That was when our mix of emotions, the indifference, the anger, a bit of jealousy even, hardened like concrete into a shared hatred. David and I felt exactly the same. Her funeral took place in spring but it felt like wintertime. It poured down all day, the rain was icy and relentless. Five mourners bade her farewell. Just five. Can you imagine the desolation? We had to turn our bitterness on someone, so we turned it on to you.

It has taken these two years to think of a plan and execute it. You might imagine that over that amount of time the edges of our hatred would soften but they didn't. That tells you something, doesn't it? And we both have busy lives, you know, other things than you to think about.

I was offered a partnership in the agency I've been with for twenty years. I specialise in online marketing these days. I never married. Became married to the job, I suppose, but I don't mind. It's fulfilling and I am probably several times richer than you and David put together. Not that he's hard up, mind. No creditors chasing him, Trevor. He's still up north, of course, never likely to move anywhere, was he, our David? He has his own business, plumbing and so on, happily married with three lovely kids, living in a big house on the edge of the moors. He has his season ticket for the football. He couldn't be any more contented. We see each other every couple of months. You may be interested to know that his daughter, my brilliant niece Katherine – and yours too, as it happens – has applied for Oxford; she's such a clever girl, yet modest and with both feet firmly on the ground.

You were untraceable for a very long time. Though you were happy to be hidden from us, it was your vanity that led us to you: your Google profile told us that you were still in France, still at that college, promoting your pet project, the Steeples museum. Your blog needed some serious help, by the way. We found the library website too, with a clip of that lame video of you dressed up as the Victorian poet! Embarrassing.

More research led me to a place in Somerset where they have a small Steeples museum too. Perhaps you've been. David and I called in. What we found interesting there were the details about the life of Thomas. You know, the brother, the artist. There's so little about him on the web. You've probably seen as much as I have. The lady in the museum put me in touch with an old bloke in the village who had written a book about Thomas, never published commercially: a retired art teacher at some private school, passionate about Steeples the painter. Of course I had to meet him. We had a lovely chat, I bought a copy of his book, a pamphlet really, and read it from cover to cover on the train back to Paddington. It was fascinating to read that Thomas had visited France *at the time that his brother was writing there. There is no proof that he spent any time in the Dordogne but it seems likely that he did. We know for sure that he met some influential people in Paris: artists and writers, and he came back to England inspired by them. His only works on display or in declared collections are early watercolours, a couple of modest landscapes in oils and scores of portraits of dignitaries which became his speciality. You know all this, don't you, Trevor? I apologise if I'm telling you nothing new.*

I do not imagine you know very much about Mark, though, even if you knew him intimately at one time. Mark has built up quite a reputation in the UK in the past ten years. I believe he calls his style "post-industrial fantasy". He shows in all the major galleries, does work for TV and film as a consultant, and he's even done work for our agency. We still see each other from time to time. Mark was interested in one of the Steeples oils, particularly, the one of the sunlit abbey at the Bishop's School. "A heavy hand aiming for the light touch of Monet," he said. "Take a look at Monet's Rouen Cathedral paintings, that's what he was trying to capture." Poor Thomas had ambitions, we supposed, but he hadn't quite the talent. We had to make him a slightly better painter than he actually was.

The plan to invent a catalogue was hatched between Mark and me. I told you he remembered you, didn't I? He was prepared to start painting a mock-Cézanne the very next day but admitted he wasn't up to it and wouldn't get it right. Fortunately he knew people that would. He did those delightful sketches of Durdle Door, though. He was so desperate to contribute. You screwed him once and, well, now he's helped screw you back.

Gary Overthrow is a boyhood friend of my ex-husband Rob, thankfully still on speaking terms with me. He did owe me a favour, in fact, as I managed to get him a few corporate tickets for Twickenham a while ago. He does actually own the farm where the paintings were "discovered". I understand you visited him there. When I asked him about you, he had to admit that you had left no great impression on him. The woman who played the part of Stephanie Chimes is a professional actor. She's been on TV in bits and pieces but works mainly in the theatre so I didn't expect you'd recognise her. We've been friends for ages. In fact we shared a flat in my early days in London and that's how I first got to know her. I knew you'd like her in that role, Trevor. We wrote a script together but I think she preferred to improvise. She's very good, isn't she? I designed the Hatcher Cross website for her cover but I took it down weeks ago. Nobody else was fabricated or planted into the story; Mr Broadfoot of Earles really is Mr Broadfoot of Earles. Once the wheels were set in motion, things took on their own natural momentum.

Mark's contact, a friend of a friend, both to remain anonymous, provided a series of works using old materials that were conceivably authentic for long enough to create interest and, more importantly, to pique your vanity. It was literally a case of knowing a bloke who knows a bloke who works on the shadowy *edges of the art world. They are really great, aren't they? Painted in 2015 in a garage somewhere in Dorset, I think. We calculated that even if there were doubts about them, you would be the last person to succumb to them, so eager would you be to exhibit them as part of your expanded Steeples collection. I was prepared to end the charade once we had your money for the loan but David wanted to let it run – run until you'd built yourself a higher pedestal to fall from. He has a sharper sense of revenge than you might imagine, our brother. Who would have thought?*

I wasn't planning on writing to tell you all this but David insisted. Finally I agreed that you should know the truth, that you should know that the seeds of your undoing were planted so close to home. If it makes you feel any better, be aware that I do feel a bit ashamed of myself, and of the fact that what we did to you tasted so sweet.

But please don't think I've gone soft, Trevor. It will cross your mind to show this letter to the authorities, the police, whoever, as proof of some conspiracy to defraud, defame you, whatever. Put the thought out of your mind would be my advice, for it could lead to a greater wound than any we have inflicted on you so far.

Do you remember the summer of 1986? I had moved to London by then but came home for a week or two to give Mum a hand after her stroke. You were busy writing the outline of a thesis or something, weren't you? Something about French writers through an English prism. As what I guessed was a displacement activity

I remember you designing a nerdy cover page and you asked me how exactly the colours dispersed when white light was shone through a prism. You knew David and I had a copy of that Pink Floyd album somewhere. Remember, we actually used to <u>share</u> a record collection? How weird, even for twins! I had a peek at what you were doing while you were out of the room once. I saw the pages of photocopied French script, the title almost identical to the one you had planned, the imprint of the University of Quebec. And I remembered the author. Lapointe. Easy for me to remember: at college we were sometimes allowed to use Lapointe acrylics, high-quality paints imported from Switzerland.

About the time of Mum's funeral there was a lot of talk about plagiarism in the news, on the radio, in the papers. Students cheating with their A Level coursework, degrees even, lifting essays straight from the internet, that kind of thing. You were in my thoughts at the time, I was more than furious with you. Something made me google the name Lapointe, google the University of Quebec, and like unearthing a hidden treasure I found your dissertation in their digital archive. Well, <u>his</u> dissertation. Apart from you and me, Trevor, I don't imagine anyone else knows this, do you? Nobody else has put two and two together in this particular case. Well, apart from our David, of course. It's a kind of family secret. For now, anyway. For ever, if you want.

So, dear Trevor, this could be the very last time I ever write to you, which is perhaps just as well for everybody. If you receive this in your French village then it will be lucky as I don't imagine you'll be hanging on there for much longer. I hope it reaches you somehow. Someone at the library will know where you are, where you've gone, won't they? You deserve to know the truth and I deserve the chance of wallowing in the satisfaction of telling you.

I would say that I hope you have learned a lesson but I am not a preachy person and I am not so blameless myself. All I can say is life must go on for both of us, and I trust you agree that the greater the distance we are apart the better. I don't expect a reply and nor do I want one. I have omitted my new address as you can see. I sold the place in Clapham, by the way. I bought a flat on the South Bank. View of the river and everything. Paid off the bank loan last year. I told you I was doing well for myself, didn't I? As for my email, I changed it months ago. The phone number you have for me is also out of date.

I wish you luck, Trevor, but believe me, we're done.
Michelle

2

I have lost track of the time but it has already grown quite dark outside. Through the kitchen window the heavy shapes of the walnut trees merge into a blurry, shadowy darkness. The yellow light cast through the window picks out the curving near edge of the *cercle magique* and the outline of the pair of rose bushes I planted there. I switch off the light and return to the main room, now blanketed in shadows dancing in step with the flames flickering in the hearth. I add a couple of split logs to the fire, switch on the other two lamps, draw the curtains and resume my seat at the table, still scattered with papers and pens and open books and creased envelopes.

The bushes are ones I transplanted from my tiny garden in Les Saules. I hard-pruned them and dug them out when I decided to sell up, and dug them in here back in October with a sack of manure and they have taken to the new ground a treat. I am sure that in summer they will bud and flower better than ever, producing blooms of crimson and the most delicate cream. The cursed ground is a myth, I have decided. The circle is no more *maudit* than it is *magique*. It is well known that walnuts give off a toxic chemical that can stunt any growth around them, but my father, God rest his soul, knew how to combat it. I will keep the circle clear of leaves, as he did, treat it with a strong fungicide, dig in plenty of dung, and will mix in a load or two of fresh topsoil. For a start I have my eye on that enormous pile of earth dug out of the bank by the old Protestant temple. It still lies in a heap, untouched since last summer, like the burial mound of a slain mammoth. I will get a friend I know with a truck to load some of it up and dump it up here, and coming from so close to a house of God it'll be the nearest thing to sanctified ground as I am ever likely to get my spade into. Around my circle's border I will plant more roses or a ring of lavender or maybe both. A month ago, and right in the centre, I planted *un amandier*, a beautiful young almond tree which will grow and flourish and still be there in its prime long after I have left this earthly garden far behind.

They can bury me with my family in the churchyard at St Lucien's: father, exhumed then reburied, mother, pardoned by her friend the priest, and the baby twins, sharing their wicker box. But not Jean-Yves: his crime was not forgiven in the same way as Madeleine's, a Christian burial refused for my poor brother the sinner. And whenever that will be, for however long the Lord will spare me, this will be the very end of the Puybonieux line. I pray that if a lawyer finds some distant cousin somewhere who may inherit this house, somebody I have never known, it is someone who will come to love this place, come to love the swelling of the fruit each summer, love the pale pink blossom of my sturdy almond, bursting alive each Eastertide, then falling in the spring breeze in showers of petals to cover the ground like a soft carpet of snow.

Here is a very good place to dot the final full stop and put down my pen. The end. Well, a certain end.

There is another. There is another ending which I hesitate to tell: the truthful ending. An ending I have struggled with for days, for weeks, an ending that won't allow me to bury it. For this has been the story of John Penny and Columbine Snow, of Jean-Yves Puybonieux and his mother Madeleine and his father Jean. There is a missing fragment, however: Amande's story. Indulge me, please. For all my reticence, it seems there is at least a little vanity in all of us.

My life of these past fifty years has not been embellished, be assured. The person I have described, quietly flitting in and out of the story, as unobtrusive as a little sparrow, that person is who I am, who I became.

When I was thirteen I began to hear voices. My mother was reclusive, dogged by her own demons. Now we know why. This house was a miserable, anxious place. I was adrift, depressed, insecure, uncertain of my own sanity. I ended up visiting a psychiatric doctor in Bergerac. You know this already.

He seemed a kind man, patient and sympathetic. He bought me sweets and chocolates and handed them out one at a time with a little smile if he considered that I had answered his questions satisfactorily. Every visit there was a different treat. I now believe that his strategy was to present himself as a father substitute to get closer to me. Closer to understanding me as some kind of surrogate daughter. Closer to curing me of my anxieties. And physically closer. There is little doubt that the man is dead now but I still prefer not to give him his name. He must have been in his early forties. I was fourteen and of men I knew nothing.

And here again, forgive me, I hesitate in the telling.

I can remember the doctor saying one day that he was pioneering a treatment of touch, *un traitement psycho-sensuel*: he believed successful outcomes could be achieved more readily by allying analysis and emotional support with a physical bonding. I can still hear the pride in his voice, and feel on my cheek the soft, sickly spray of his sibilants as he whispers those words in my ear: *c'est psycho-sensuel*, his abracadabra. And I still remember the smell of his damp moustache.

It started with a massage of the temples, then of the neck, then of the shoulders. I don't need to spell it all out. He gave it a pseudo-scientific name. What it might realistically be called is sexual exploitation. Or rape in other terms. I was left feeling shivery, grubby, full of shame and fear. But he quietly convinced me I would recover and it was for the best. Told me I could trust him. He flattered me, praised me, filled my childish head with scientific language and comforting words. One session after another, month after month, the same routine. My mother knew nothing of his behaviour, nor of my naive acquiescence, until it was too late. Suddenly I was pregnant and the doctor vanished into thin air.

I was not the first child this had ever happened to, of course. I quickly discovered that at the convent where I was sent on the advice of our priest. Sainte Thérèse's was full of foolish girls like myself, and once they had given birth, training and schooling became secondary to mothering and skivvying for the sisters. Bearing a child at fourteen was as terrifying as if the devil himself were ripping open my swollen womb but the babe emerged alive and robust and I loved him, instinctively bonded with him, just for those few short weeks before he was snatched out of my arms and taken off by the nuns to be handed on to a childless couple from Paris or beyond, people I never knew, never saw. From a state of anger and confusion I slid into a dark tunnel of depression which ran on for years. The years of my youth, of my prime, were stolen from me. I have taught myself to accept this fact. Meanwhile, somewhere in the world there is, God willing, a boy with a name I did not give him but with a face I did, a son of mine, a healthy, happy man of some fifty years who has the right to inherit this home, this land, his birthright as the last Puybonieux.

Sometime last winter I saw a film on television about an Irish woman a little older than me whose situation was much like mine. She had a daughter, I think, after she left the convent, but already had borne a child, a boy, taken from her as a teenager. With the help of a journalist she traced the family who had raised her son as their own, all the way to America in fact. By the time she found him he had already died in middle age, but in spite of that it was an uplifting ending to the story, and a true one at that. It stayed with me for weeks. I saw the actress again in quite a different role some time afterwards but it was still the Irish convent girl I was watching. I wondered if I could have an ending like that, happy or sad, it didn't matter; I just wanted to know what had happened to my boy, this person I have had to trick myself into believing never really existed.

I have done my research. I know the name of the journalist. I know the name of the film-maker. I have tried to contact them both and I await a reply, hoping one day, with somebody's help and the Lord's blessing, to meet that stolen boy, if he will agree to meet me, of course.

And so my story, the story of Amande, does not yet have its ending. I do know, and can now admit to myself, that the story did not end in heartbreak, in the days and weeks of stinging tears and retching and numbing emptiness. It did not end fifty years ago in a dark, draughty convent, but it is a story for the telling when it has its proper ending, for the telling when I have reason and the strength to tell it, for the telling on another day.

AUTHOR'S NOTE

After writing two novels set principally in Dorset, an adopted "home" county for over twenty-five years, I felt I needed to place my third one in a different setting. I chose to recreate two places I know almost as well, with a retrospective vision of the south-east of Lancashire and an assembly of images of the Dordogne.

Ever since I took part in a town-twinning holiday in the summer of 1971 – my first visit to a foreign country was a week in Alsace with about fifty other teenagers from across Europe – France has spoken to me. Not only through its language but its history, its culture, its landscapes, its food and wine. I have known many people just as *sympathique* as Amande Puybonieux, and it was time I placed my next set of characters within its frame.

Themes were suggested by an interest in books and paintings; the degree of knowledge I had ran out, however, when it came to the valuation and exposition of artefacts. For much help in this field I wish to thank Matthew Denney of Duke's Auctioneers of Dorchester, and from the world of insurance, Nigel Cryer from NFU Mutual, Simon Gilbert of Elmore Brokers and Jade Jones of Hiscox.

I am also grateful to Sabine Brousse who gave a personalised guided tour of her charming château near Bergerac – an inspiration for elements of the novel's Beautrottoir. Thanks too, as before, to Warren Shore for his painstaking scrutiny of the pre-edited draft and his wise suggestions for its improvement. And also to Matador Publishing for their help and services in producing and promoting the book.

As for John Penny, perhaps his own novel will be published one of these days. It might turn up eventually in a bookshop not too far along a shelf of fiction from *Forty Barrels More* or something a little rarer by his hero Steeples.

Brent Shore
October 2017

ABOUT THE AUTHOR

Brent Shore grew up in Hyde, a small town on the eastern edges of Manchester. He studied Modern Languages at the University of Nottingham, where he also trained as a teacher. His career took him firstly to North Yorkshire, then to Bermuda, and finally to the middle of Dorset where he has lived since 1991.

Since retiring from the classroom, he now channels much of his energy into writing fiction. *Shillingstone Station* and *Bailing Out* are his first two novels to be published.

Visit: www.brentshore.co.uk
Contact: stories@brentshore.co.uk

SHILLINGSTONE STATION

Andris Fleet's life has been damned by self doubt and insecurity, ever since he was left lame by a mother who had no inclination to care for him and fatherless by a conspiracy to murder in the interests of national security. As his mother admits: *Little Andris, poor lamb, he was born into a cesspool of deceit.*

Aged thirty-five and having made something of his life in the hospitality industry, he chances to find evidence that throws everything he has been told about his father's death into doubt.

A further twenty-five years later and another clue from the distant past emerges which sets him on a definitive search for the truth.

The link between the years of 1960 at the time of the Cold War, 1990 as the Soviet Union falls apart, and contemporary 2015 is the changing face of a small rural railway station in the village of Shillingstone, North Dorset.

Less of a spy story than one of the *generational consequences* of a spy story, *Shillingstone Station* gives the reader a mystery to solve, the coat-tails of a blighted biography to hang on to, and in the end a very human tale of resilience, warmth and forgiveness.

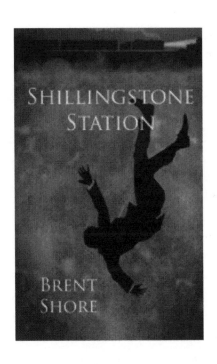

SHILLINGSTONE STATION

BRENT SHORE

BAILING OUT

Follow a kind, lonely heart astray along the most dangerous of paths.

Retirement from the police force and the accidental death of his wife have conspired to turn Don Percey's world upside down and he is fumbling around in the dark. He finds himself at the most isolated, loneliest point in his life and yet, bizarrely, also at his wealthiest.

Resolved to do something exceptionally good, something genuinely noble, he becomes involved in the lives of a poor family from a run-down pocket of social housing – with brutal consequences.

Bailing Out is a far cry from the offices of City banks but ripples from London are seen to radiate to the rural south-west of England. Set among both the affluence and the deprivation of the area, there are elements of a whodunnit, of a fragile romance and of a family tragedy, entangled in a compelling story of generosity and judgement, of compassion and of risk.

When there is so much poverty around, why can't a decent man be allowed to do something significant to help?

BAILING OUT

BRENT SHORE